THE LOST MILLENNIUM

Lieutenant Launa O'Brian.

Captain Jack Walking Bear.

They are the first time travelers, guinea pigs in an experiment that cannot fail. From a future nearly destroyed by plague, they must travel thousands of years into the past to the dawn of civilization. Among tribes of primitive hunters, they will trace a fatal chain of events–and alter history to save humanity from itself.

Book One: First Dawn

Book Two: Second Fire

Book Three: Lost Days

Praise for *First Dawn* . . .

"An excellent debut." —Steve Perry

"The characters are both strong and likeable . . . there's considerable sexual tension between them . . . plenty of adventure." —*Locus*

"A first novel that shows a good deal of promise." —*Analog*

"Nicely developed and tightly focused . . . Moscoe writes cleanly, and his prose is gratifyingly free of the pretensions and clumsiness often marring first novels." —*Salem Statesman Journal*

Praise for *Second Fire* . . .

"Transports the reader back to 4,000 B.C. . . . Moscoe writes clearly and with sensitivity . . . a real page-turner." —*Midwest Book Review*

Ace Books by Mike Moscoe

FIRST DAWN
SECOND FIRE
LOST DAYS

LOST DAYS

BOOK THREE OF THE LOST MILLENNIUM

MIKE MOSCOE

ACE BOOKS, NEW YORK

This book is an Ace original edition.
And has never been previously published.

LOST DAYS

An Ace Book / published by arrangement with
the author

PRINTING HISTORY
Ace edition / February 1998

Cover art by Joseph Danisi.

For information address: The Berkley Publishing Group,
a member of Penguin Putnam Inc.,
200 Madison Avenue, New York, NY 10016.

The Putnam Berkley World Wide Web site address is
http://www.berkley.com

ISBN: 0-441-00510-1

ACE ®
Ace Books are published by The Berkley Publishing Group,
a member of Penguin Putnam Inc.,
200 Madison Avenue, New York, NY 10016.
ACE and the "A" design are trademarks
belonging to Charter Communications, Inc.

PRINTED IN THE UNITED STATES OF AMERICA

10 9 8 7 6 5 4 3 2 1

PROLOGUE

MOHAMMED GAVE THE cab driver his last coins and hoped it was enough. The cabby grumbled and drove off, leaving Mohammed alone in a strange town. He glanced around, hoping he truly was alone.

The low building before him needed paint and repair, but the sign had the traditional phone emblem, familiar anywhere in the world. Mohammed entered.

This late at night, the phone booths lining the walls were empty. Mohammed selected the lone Visa-phone booth this small town rated, hoping there was enough left on his card. He'd have to make the call short.

He punched in numbers he hoped were still good. In a moment Scholar Brent Lynch's friendly face filled the screen. "Mohammed, good to see you."

"Old friend, I need your help."

"If I can do it, it is done," Brent promised without hesitation.

"I found this." Mohammed pulled the source of his trouble from his faded robes.

"What is it?"

Mohammed ruffled the pages. "It is a book."

"I thought you were working with Lady Evans on that dig in Crete. I've been following it live on channel ten-fifty.

Marvelous artifacts. That earthquake six thousand years ago did us a great service."

"Yes," Mohammed agreed.

"Right, I saw you. It was you who spotted the stone altar in the wrong place. Even with her shouting into the mike about it being against the wall and all, I could tell she was only echoing what you said a second earlier. Well done, old man."

Mohammed smiled at the praise . . . and hoped his money held out.

"Just a second." Brent paused. "There were 'technical difficulties' right after you opened the alcove you found behind the altar. After that, I didn't see you."

"You are looking at the 'technical difficulties.' "

"The book!"

"As I hope for paradise, I swear that alcove was sealed until I opened it with my own hands, and this book was the first thing I pulled from it."

"Goddess on a crutch, that would blow Evie away. The old girl does like to write her summer field reports the winter before so she can get them published quickly. Writing on paper six thousand years ago would put a whole new twist on things. What script did they use? Can I see it?"

Mohammed held the title page of the book close to the camera.

"Sweet Goddess and Child, it's in English," Brent whispered.

Numbers appeared on the screen, counting down the few seconds left before Mohammed's money ran out. "Tomorrow I sail back to Egypt. People there will know how to preserve the paper. I found one other oddity."

He held up a small gold bar, then turned it to show the pins on the back.

"Friend, what can I do? Send money? Where are you?"

"I will call from Egypt," Mohammed answered . . . to a blank screen.

Mohammed glanced around as he hid the book again in the folds of his robes. The phone banks were empty. As were the streets he walked, winding his way downhill to the small harbor.

As he turned the last corner, the scent of the sea filled his lungs—and a figure stepped from a doorway.

"Mohammed, I thought you were bringing the book to the Brotherhood so we could scan it and send copies to your learned friend Brent."

"Abdul!" Mohammed stepped away from him even before he saw the gleam of the stiletto in his hands. "I, ah, called Brent from the phones here. There was no need for you to trouble your friends."

Abdul smiled, all teeth, like a Nile crocodile. "My friends are troubled by your lack of trust." Then his voice lost all humor. "We want the book."

"What can the Brotherhood find of value in an ancient artifact such as this?"

Abdul held Mohammed's attention; he did not hear the one who came up behind him. He only felt the knife as it pierced his back.

The last words Mohammed heard were Abdul's, as he yanked the book from his grasp. "We do not know, old fool, but from something so strange, we will discover something."

Scholar Brent Lynch stared at the blank screen, a storm raging inside him. Wave after wave crashed against him, driving him in different directions. His friend was in trouble . . . but he could not help him. His friend had found a book—appropriate to the last five or six hundred years, but impossible six thousand years ago. Brent shivered as his mind struggled to accept the impossible.

He played back the call and froze the screen when the artifact's title page filled it.

"*The Pharmacology of Herbs,* A.D. 1902, Philadelphia," he read aloud. Hearing it did not make it any more believable. His stomach was in free fall. Leaning back in his chair, he glanced at it out of the side of his eye. That didn't change it either.

"Impossible," he breathed . . . and caught himself. It was so easy to interpret the ancients; death had silenced their mouths. A scholar could wrap any viewpoint or hobbyhorse she wanted around the dry bones or potsherds and assume the world of the ancients were just like hers. For sixty years, he had struggled to keep his own mind silent and let the relics speak for themselves.

He hit PRINT SCREEN.

Cycling the call through to the view of the strange metal object, he studied it. A simple bar with pins sticking out of the back at its long ends. Where had he seen something like that?

Brent's eyes widened. Collar emblems the Guardians wore had clutch-pin backs like those. Again, he did a PRINT SCREEN.

"How could a book and a collar emblem end up in a temple closed six thousand years ago?" He muttered to the ceiling. "Terminal, dial up Stewart Milo at the Lady Livermore Labs."

A moment later, a pudgy, beaming face filled the screen. "Brent, long time no hear. What you up to?"

"Enjoying retirement. I may even catch up on my reading."

Stu laughed at the line of required half-truths.

Brent went on. "Tell me, Stu, I have a friend who wants to take up science fiction writing. Something to do with time travel. I told him that's balderdash, but it's not my field. What's the latest?"

"Balderdash and poppycock, old friend. Relativity makes no allowances for time travel or faster than light. Your friend is writing a fantasy."

Brent was ready to give a quick "So I thought," but something wavered around the edges of Stu's last words. Brent shut up.

"Say, Judith Lee is coming by day after tomorrow to see her daughter. You two have always been fond of each other. Why don't you drop by? I can give you a tour of the lab. We've got some rather interesting stuff going on. I could use a reality check from an open mind."

Since when did a physicist need a reality check from a dusty digger in ancient cultures? But it was nice being invited. And if Judith was there . . . "Why not? It's not as if I have to clear my schedule."

"Be at the gate at noon. We can have lunch, and I can show you a test we're running about three o'clock."

Stu hung up, which returned the screen to Mohammed's call. Brent started to archive it, then rethought. Archives were in the public domain, and the Guardians had been known to sift them for their own reasons. Brent popped in a floppy and saved the call to disk, then used a program a free-thinking young friend had provided to erase the system's record.

In the back of his file cabinet, Brent had a collection of things that didn't belong, discoveries that diggers such as Mohammed had passed along to him and which their patrons would never admit existed. He added the disk to his collection. The hard copies went into the trash can, then, on second thought, into his belt pouch. He'd find someplace neutral to ditch them.

It might be nothing, but the crinkle around Stu's eyes had said more than he'd risk to words. In his eighty years, Brent had learned to read a lot that wasn't written, hear a lot that was never said.

The bad thing about retirement was nothing happened. Brent had a hunch that wouldn't be true for the next couple of days.

ONE

LIEUTENANT LAUNA O'BRIAN ran with a gleeful spring to her step. Even her ponytail had an extra bounce to it. Not since she left West Point for—what had the President called it, the Neolithic Military Advisory Group?—had she felt so light. Her heart bubbled enough she could almost fly.

We did it! The President of the United States gave us an impossible mission—and we pulled it off!

Even Professor Judith Lee must have doubted that just two soldiers wandering around the Neolithic could change all history. But when a failed world conqueror's last mad action released a designer plague that promised global death, desperate options were all that was left.

For a year, she and Captain Jack Walking Bear had traveled the Danube River Basin, in four thousand something B.C. Rescuing a handful of captives from the Kurgans' first onslaught had been touch and go. Warning Tall Oaks, the next town in the horsemen's path, and rallying its peaceful farmers to their own defense had turned into a tougher job than even she'd expected. But women and men had stood together in the battle line. Victory meant they'd live to stand guard for another day. Defeat was death or slavery for every one of them. Launa had won her battles.

And what a world she'd come back to! True, there was no President to welcome her. No one had ever heard of the

United States, much less its army. War was a word only anthropologists remembered! Cooperation was the watchword, not control. And no one led, though women did seem to be first among equals.

God, we did it!

Or rather Goddess. Here even the Pope prayed to the Goddess. Launa laughed; Pope Joan the Twenty-fifth.

Launa knew she was drunk on success—and she liked the brew. Every waking moment of every day since Jack recruited her out of her third year at the Point, she'd carried the burden. First she'd been scared they might have to carry out the mission. Then she'd been scared they wouldn't. For a long year the dead hopes of billions of lost souls had hung around her neck.

Well, she'd given them back their hopes. And from the looks of things, the lives they lived here were a damn sight better than the ones folks lived in the twentieth century she'd been born into.

Launa took a deep breath of cool, moist air. The sun had yet to clear the green hills ahead of her. Above her stretched a sky as blue and clear of pollution as any she'd seen over Neolithic farmers.

The road was familiar; she'd been gone a year of lost days only to come back ten days before she ran it the first time. But the hills ahead of her then had been brown with dead grass and dying wind generators. A windmill had given up its mechanical ghost and wound down to rusty death as she and Jack were ordered down to the bunker to watch a world die.

Launa tossed that memory off with a shiver. Today the hills were alive with grass and flowers and covered with a tribe of wind generators. Propellers and eggbeaters of every sort and size thumped away, feeding the energy hunger of this California. The variety of the contraptions testified to the world she'd returned to—and helped create. Six thousand years later, no one could tell another the path for her feet.

Launa had other questions, and this world's Judith would make a beginning at answering them today, but Launa doubted anyone could answer what was foremost on everyone's mind. In another twenty-first century, Drs. Milo and Harrison at the Lawrence Livermore Labs had cobbled together a time transport system more by experiment than comprehension. Judith and Brent had drawn from their anthropology knowledge to prepare Launa and Jack to live in a world that had been murdered six thousand years before they were born.

And a year after they arrived in the Neolithic, a shimmering light appeared at their drop zone. Launa had leaped for it; it had to be a recall. "We've done what we were sent to do. Do you want to risk wrecking it all by staying?" she asked Jack. He hadn't been so sure, but he had come with her.

And at the other end of the line, they'd found Lady Harrison and Scholar Milo of the *Lady* Livermore Labs, huddled over an experiment they'd knocked together to study the unique behavior of energy at this one location on earth.

Judith and Brent stood there, too. Judith held the mongrel puppy that had been the first test passenger of their own Lawrence Livermore time transport. How intertwined these two twenty-first centuries were was a question only the Goddess could answer. Still, quite a few smart people were eager to try. As one of two living people with hands-on experience in the mysteries of quantum mechanics, Launa would happily join them.

A shiver went through her. What coincidence had brought all these players together again? Only she and Jack knew they had lived another past.

Speaking of Jack, she could hardly hear his footsteps. Usually, he set the pace and cadence on their morning runs.

She glanced over her shoulder; the last captain in the United States Army was quite a ways behind her. The bounce was missing from his step as he huffed along. This morning, an oversize sweatsuit flopped around him. This was not the Apache who'd quickly shed his tee shirt even in the cold predawn of a high Wyoming physical training session. *Of course, he's been more of an administrator than a trooper the last three months. How much of a workout does a Speaker for the Bull get?*

Enough to get the Speaker for the Goddess pregnant, Launa answered herself, and bit her lip to stop it from trembling. It had been a breakthrough for the mission for Jack to be named Speaker for the Bull when Kaul could have the title no more. The rational part of Launa knew that. But the agony of having Jack yanked from her side and sent to Lasa's bed still ached.

And the one cloud on her morning was the question she could never answer. Had she really believed the glowing bubble was a recall? Or had she fled her duty so she and Jack could just be themselves, together, makers of history no more?

All her life, Launa had sworn herself to a soldier's duty. Had she blown it the one time it counted? One thing was sure, this twenty-first century belonged to those who were born to it. She and Jack would never be world builders again.

She put on a burst of speed, but knew it for the waste it was. No matter how fast she ran, she could never outrun her doubts.

"Hold up," Jack gasped. Launa glanced back. The captain stumbled to a halt. Bending over, he propped himself up, hands on knees.

Launa wasn't even breathing hard as she trotted back. Rather than stop her workout in mid-session, she marked time while slowly making a circle around him. "You okay?"

She did a quick three-sixty with the practice of one whose life regularly depended on full situational awareness. If Jack needed help, he'd picked a bad place for it. They were a good mile from the gate of the Livermore Labs, and it was another mile to the next cross road.

"Did you see the woman in the car parked by the gate?" Launa could hardly make out the words, but she swallowed the "Say again," before it got out. If Jack was mumbling, he had a reason.

"Yes."

"Don't be obvious, but is she watching us?" The words again were strained through lips hardly open.

Launa quickened the pace of her circling, keeping her eyes level and straight ahead. In a few seconds she was checking out the parked car. A woman had been reading a newspaper as she and Jack jogged by. At a mile, Launa could not make out details. The sun must have poked above the hill behind her at that moment.

"I got a glint off metal," she said through unmoving lips. She didn't know what Jack was up to, but his instincts had kept her alive too many times in the past year. She'd play any game he wanted. "Seemed from the passenger compartment, but it could have been off chrome."

"Hasn't been much eye glitter on the cars I've seen so far." Jack still spoke to the ground.

"Yes," Launa agreed.

"What can you tell me about the person watching from the next road?"

Launa did a half circle. *Damn, there was someone next to a fence post; a small cycle stood behind him or her.* Launa stopped her circling, dropped down on her back and began doing leg stretches. "Can't tell anything about that one," she told a circling hawk, wishing she had that bird's eyes.

Jack straightened up and limped around her, his gaze nowhere in particular. But his squint got real tight when he faced either end of the road. "Wonder what kind of black tech their CIA's got?" Jack buried the question in a cough.

Launa wanted to snap that people who didn't have wars didn't need any of that secret shit they'd grown up with, but she bit back her words.

What's eating Jack? Launa went over the last twelve hours; there had been a few less than wonderful surprises. The Samantha here was just as much a power-game player as the one who had bugged her and Jack in the other twenty-first century. Only this Samantha ignored Jack the way the other one ignored Launa. Still, Jack had made the adjustment to the leadership style of the women who led the farmers down-time. *Hell, he'd ended up consort to the Speaker for the Goddess.*

Icy tendrils shot from Launa's gut to wrap around her heart. Was he missing Lasa and the child he would never hold? He'd wept the night he told her about Sandie and Sam, his first wife and child who died six years before Launa met him. Just because he'd walked away from her bed so readily didn't mean it was easy on him to leave every woman he loved. *What have I gotten us into?*

You don't get paranoid when you're homesick, Launa reminded herself. Homesick she knew well; as an army brat she'd never had a home before the people of Tall Oaks opened their hearts to her. *Maybe Jack's just soldiering better than I am.*

Admit it, girl, this world is as alien as the Neolithic was the first day you dropped in. And you damn near died before sunset because you thought you knew the score. Maybe Jack's listening better to his gut because it isn't tied up with the guilt that's twisting yours into a Gordian knot.

Jack looked down at her, his last question holding in a raised eyebrow. Launa had no idea if these people had a CIA or what surveillance technology it might have. If she'd learned anything in the Neolithic, it was not to fake what she didn't know.

Launa shrugged where she lay and raised an eyebrow to mirror Jack's. She also offered him her hand for a lift, help he knew she didn't need.

As Jack pulled her up, his lips brushed her ear. The thrill of his touch was lost in the chill from his whispered words. "War's only one way to handle conflict, and not the nastiest."

Which left Launa with a lot to stew over as they slowly jogged back. But she kept her head up. The woman in the car was still reading her paper, or, to be more correct, she had it in front of her as they passed. The car was as green as the grass in the field next to it with colorful impressionist splotches standing in for flowers. There was no brightwork to flash back the rising sun. Maybe she and Jack had better hold their private conversations as far from prying eyes and ears as possible.

One thing was sure: Jack's weakness was put on. He'd

been right on her heels as she threw herself into the time bubble. And he had laughed with her, at no loss for breath.

Launa headed for her room, a shower, and a change of clothes before breakfast. But one thing she already knew: Jack was right. They knew painfully little about this world they had helped make. Even if no one was holding a knife to their throats, they better keep their eyes open. They'd spent their first month down-time in a recon. The first month here should be one also.

For the first time, Launa found herself missing Tall Oaks. Oh, she'd never been free of the mission hanging around her neck, and life had been full of twists, many of them terrifying, most painful. But the gentle support and friendship of those people had made it all survivable.

She wondered how Kaul and Lasa, Brege and Merik were doing. Even poor Antia crossed her mind. One thing was sure. They were on their own. No one in this twenty-first century would be sending two total strangers back in time to change anything they'd got wrong the first time.

ANTIA, DAUGHTER OF She who had once Spoken for the Goddess in River Bend, drew an arrow from the quiver at her waist. The flint tip was sharp, curling back to cruel barbs at the edges; the shaft was long and straight. She had fletched this arrow five days ago just for this moment.

In the dark ahead of her, a rider slowly made his rounds of the drowsing horse herd. He was young—and dumb.

His pace was too slow. Antia gained on him though he rode and she stooped low as she glided over the grass, quiet as the gentle night breeze. And when the fool paused, he only had eyes for the horses he guarded. She easily disappeared among the steppe grasses the rare times his glance strayed outward.

Antia shook her head. Launa had taught her of "security" and given a new word to the People's language. Security had kept Antia alive many times since the spring day when the horsemen rode among the People of River Bend. The mounted warriors had left few enough of the unarmed farmers alive.

Antia had lived because her body pleased the raider who put a bloody knife to her throat and made her his consort. She'd waited for the moment when that animal had been distracted by the pleasure he stole from her—and stolen the knife from his belt. The delight that swept Antia as she cut his heart out had been new—and fulfilling. That stone blade still hung from her belt; soon this young rider would feel its caress.

A morning bird called; Antia froze. Twice more the sound came to her, but there were no feathers on this greeter of the dawn. Cleo had closed in on the other guard. Antia glanced to the east; dawn brightened the rim of the world. The others would be at their places, surrounding the camp.

Antia answered with a low *caw*; those who followed after her knew her for the death bird. As she put arrow to bow and pulled the string to her ear, pleasure shot through her flesh. Before the horsemen came and destroyed her world, she had only tasted such delight in the arms of a man. She let fly and watched with cruel ecstasy as the arrow tore into her target's throat.

The youth yanked his mount around, dismay on his face, a croak on his lips. He spotted Antia and lowered his lance. She had a second arrow nocked. This one she buried in his chest, near the heart that no horseman had any need of. The warrior kneed his mount for a charge. It was a weak kick, and the horse responded with only half a will. When Antia's next arrow sank into his belly, he slumped from his mount to sprawl on his back.

Antia swaggered toward her fallen enemy. He lay there, not even clutching for his knife as she stood over him. Reaching for her blade, she brushed aside his breechcloth, and rubbed his face with what she cut from him. As his eyes dimmed, she sliced open his belly and hacked her way toward his heart. She wanted to see the terror in his eyes as her hand closed around it, horror as she ripped his heart from him.

Too soon he fainted. Antia spat in his face and pulled her bloody hand empty from his chest. She had no more time to waste on him.

The smell of blood drove the horses far from her grasp. Antia grabbed her bow and jogged toward the horse people's camp. The day was young; there would be more blood.

The others of her raiding party edged toward the tents of their sleeping enemies. Antia picked a near one and claimed it for herself with a pointed hand. Those near her acknowledged her choice with nods. That settled, Antia signaled the rush.

Without a noise, her followers slipped into tents of their choosing. Inside her own target, the dim glow of embers cast small light. Still, it was all Antia needed to see by.

A woman slept with a babe in her arms. Across from her, a warrior snored. It took only a moment to draw her knife across the mother's throat. Not a sound, only the copper scent of warm blood filled the tent.

Antia took the babe in her free hand, hand over mouth to stifle any cry. *A boy, good!*

Crossing the tent in two steps, Antia dropped her knees hard onto the chest of the sleeping man. He came awake as his breath fled him.

Blinking eyes flew like humming birds, taking in everything at once: the knife at his throat, his son dangling above him, the steaming pool of blood spreading from where his woman lay. Finally, two orbs, wide and white with fear, settled on the grinning, blood-covered demon that was Antia.

"Know, horseman," Antia spat. "You will die, and all your seed with you. Father, brother, son." She tossed the baby in the air, caught its feet, swung it hard at the tent post.

The child was too startled to cry out. Then its skull crumpled as it hit the hard post. Antia threw the body on the glowing coals; it no longer had a face.

"No!" the man screamed, forcing himself up. Rising, he met Antia's knife as she drove it into his throat.

"Yes," she answered as more blood spewed over her.

Antia rose, grinning at how well this day had begun. She strode from the tent, no backward glance, gory knife dripping.

Soren waited outside. "All the others are dead. No alarm was given. I heard a shout from this tent." The words, half report, half rebuke, hung in the cold morning air.

Another time, before the horsemen came, Antia would have listened to the young man's words. But that custom had died with so much else. Antia no longer heard what she did not want to.

"Did one of their old men who speaks for the false male goddess of theirs rise early to greet the sun?" Twice one like that had given the alarm, causing Antia's raiders extra work. Once she even had to explain to Brege and Merik how one of her party had died in the hunt. Lying came easy now that Launa had given a name to it.

Soren stared at the ground, shaking his head. Some did likewise. But others grinned their disappointment that the morning's sport was done. Antia knew the leadings of her bloody heart were shared by enough.

Late, far too late, Cleo galloped up to join them. And she rode from the north, not the west where the herd still milled about. Antia waited for the woman to explain.

"I missed with my first arrow," Cleo snarled as she dismounted. "I think he was getting off his horse to piss," she added by way of explanation. Several laughed. "My second arrow found him, but by then he was running like a rabbit. I tried to catch him, but my shots missed."

Antia nodded. Cleo had been her friend since childhood. She, too, had passed under a horseman's knife, until Antia had cut her free. If anyone tasted Antia's hate for the horsemen and lusted for their death, it was Cleo. The warrior could thank the fates for his life, not any mercy from Cleo.

"That is not good." Alarm was in Soren's voice. "He may bring reinforcements to where we stand. And he is also the first to see and live to sing of it. We will lose surprise."

Antia scowled, but the boy used the words of the soldiers. He had spent too much time at Jack's side. It did not please her that others nodded on the dark portents in his words. But she had learned the power in her own words to drown out the echo of others' words—and even deeds.

Antia studied her company. These women and men hated the horsemen almost as much as she. Few of them understood the wisdom of soldiering in Launa's footsteps. She would tell them what they wanted to hear, and they would follow after her.

"He may well die from Cleo's arrow long before he can sing his song to anyone. Beside, there are none alive here for the horsemen to reinforce, unless they would follow these to death and let the birds of the Goddess feast on them too." That drew a laugh, but many did not join in; Antia knew she must speak on.

"Let us go quickly from this place," she finished.

"What of the horses?" Cleo asked, eyeing the herd grazing in the early morning sun. "This many would leave a trail even a baby could follow back to River Bend."

"Then we will not lead these horses to River Bend. Cleo, take half our people and most of the horses. Run them fast to the north. Let those horses who would stray go their way, but scatter them far and wide."

The woman nodded.

"I will take some horses and the rest of our people with me. We will scatter strays as well."

"Should we not treat the dead as horsemen would, taking heads? And what will Brege and Merik think when we do not return together?" Soren asked two questions.

Antia snorted, and chose which one to answer. "The Speakers have not even remarked on how the herds of River Bend grow. They will not remark if we return separately."

"Maybe," Soren agreed, "or maybe they see and do not ask."

"Either way they are weak," Antia shot back. Brege, Launa, and Lasa saw the horsemen's danger, but did nothing. They were fools, no better than the horsemen she had killed this morning.

Antia was strong. She would show them how to make the horsemen into playthings.

"Hunt well," Antia called when she had mounted. "We must bring much deer meat when we return. Let all see how the Goddess smiles on those who hold their bows in strong arms."

It was that simple to Antia. Show strength, and all would come to her. For that day, she lived.

THREE

LAUNA SOAPED UP with quick, purposeful strokes, the way she had at West Point when there was no time to lose. The decision tree from her threat analysis was as clear in front of her as if it were written on the shower wall.

Option one: They were new here, and Samantha, the Project Administrator, had assigned someone to keep an eye on them and help them out of any trouble they got into. Launa snorted; the problem with that was Samantha had not come across as the motherly type—and there had been two people watching them.

And what type of trouble could they get into in a world that had never known war? Launa's gut tightened; it had been in knots a lot down-time.

The second observer provided the final limbs for Launa's decision tree. Option two: These people had something to hide. Option three: There were two sides here, and she and Jack were the hockey puck in somebody's version of the "Great Game." On that thought, Launa shut off the water.

She toweled quickly and checked out the well-stocked closet. They had everything there, from a miniskirt and halter top that was hardly worth wearing to an ankle-length dress with long sleeves and high collar.

Down-time, Launa had gotten used to wearing next to nothing, but that was a place she'd never go again. Since popping up here around 1500 hours local yesterday, Launa had seen women in some pretty provocative outfits. For herself, she chose a skirt and blouse suitable for her high school that even the Colonel would not have groused about too much.

As she headed for the door, her glance fell on the white leather bag that held Maria's book. That gift from the pleasant Mexican cook at the Wyoming training camp was the one thing that had jumped with Launa both times. She picked it up, feeling the soft texture of the leather, hefting the heavy book inside.

As an army brat, Launa had learned to recognize tanks when most kids were learning their ABC's. It had seemed a good idea if she wanted a career with her dad's old company. But when she volunteered for the Neolithic Military Advisory Group, veggie recognition suddenly got way more important than IDing tanks. That's where Maria came in.

Not only did the woman raise most of the herbs she cooked with and know where to find the others, the old Mexican knew which plants could heal what ailed you. She was a walking pharmacy when they visited a botany reserve.

Launa had tried to learn all she could from Maria, but she would have had better luck drinking the Mississippi dry. Then bombs and automatic weapons fire ended her and Jack's schooling. As they tried to patch together enough gear to go if the President said to, Maria appeared at Launa's elbow with a 1902 book on the pharmacological properties of herbs and a beautiful hand-tooled bag to protect it.

What Launa had done in the Neolithic had been as much for Maria as for the President. Maria's book had come in a hell of a lot more helpful than the pep talk the President gave her and Jack.

Launa had been looking for a quiet place to read when things got confusing and she and Jack ended up making another time jump. The book had been at hand, and she took it. Once again, the book was at hand, and she took it. As the one touchstone to her past—both of them—it felt good in her hand.

Launa had expected Jack to be downstairs already, but he

was just leaving his room as she closed her door. He wore a kilt, much like Brent had worn yesterday. The Apache had foregone the polka dots the old scholar had sported for a plaid that any highlander would have been comfortable with. Launa liked the way it swirled around his knees, but the general impression was spoiled by a bulky sweater that could only be described as frumpy. The color match was off, but not so loud as to draw the eye. Rather, her glance seemed to just slide off him.

Launa bit her tongue before she said anything. She'd dressed for that effect once or twice in her life. She hadn't been very successful as a wallflower, and she doubted Jack would disappear into the background for long no matter what he wore.

Jack groaned as they headed for the elevator. "My stomach is killing me. Must be something about the water." But the corners of his mouth and eyes showed the hint of a smile; Launa discounted his words as intended for a hidden mike.

She didn't like that. Just when she needed to share some good, solid situation analysis, Jack was making it clear he didn't want to talk. Or, worse, anything he said could be a lie.

What Launa really wanted was Jack's arms around her, to feel safe and protected and right—even if those feelings were lies. *Admit it, girl, until you figure this situation out, good or bad, you'll never be safe.*

They rode the elevator down in silence. The cafeteria was located on the ground floor of the high-rise, its windows looking out over parkland. That was something Launa liked about the local architecture. It blended the look and feel of adobe and red brick with towering buildings that left plenty of green for the eye and heart. There was a lot to like about this place.

"Never trust a pretty face," the Colonel reminded her in the voice of the trained soldier. Launa would give a lot to shut that voice up. *I ain't gonna study war no more.*

Jack led the way into the cafeteria, and missed a step. Launa almost stumbled over him. Then she knew why.

Behind the steam tables stood a short, round Mexican woman—Maria!

The woman's glance slid over them the way it must pass over a thousand hungry people every day; there was no recognition there. She turned away to load dough into the oven, the smell of baking bread swirled around her.

Launa took in a deep breath and let it out slowly. She had to stifle a laugh; now Jack really did look like he'd swallowed something bad.

"What the hell is she doing here?"

Launa raised an eyebrow; Jack rarely swore. Since she had no answer, she just led the way to collect a tray and silverware.

Nothing much had changed in the way people ate. Bacon, eggs, pancakes and other greasy fare was first on the list. Launa spotted some cereals, but they looked overprocessed compared to the cooking of the Neolithic. If she didn't want to be sidelined for a week by her stomach, she'd better find something simple. She grabbed a banana, apple, and orange. She hadn't had an orange since Maria last hunted one up for her in Wyoming.

"Do you have any whole grains or nuts?" Jack asked Maria. The woman turned and really looked at them for the first time.

She smiled, a wide welcome that started at her toes and didn't end until several feet above her black hair. Launa wanted to hop the counter between them and see if this Maria hugged as good as the other. It took all her soldier's discipline not to.

"*Sí.* Yes, I have something for you if you like a traditional breakfast."

"Por favor," Jack said.

"De nada," Maria answered.

Launa drew two tall glasses of milk and filled three juice tumblers with one of every flavor offered, before heading for a table with a window view. Jack downed a glass of milk in one pull while he tanked up on juice, refilled the milk and followed her.

"God, it's good to be home," he sighed, settling across

from her. She hoped he meant it, but there was a quiver underlying "home" that sounded more wistful than sure.

For a long moment they watched ducks and geese paddle around the small pond, occasionally raising their tail feathers to the sky as they dunked for their breakfast. These birds were no different from any she'd watched down-time, or in her birth time and place. A hunger rose in Launa for their simple, quiet life, but she knew she'd never have it.

"Here is something for you."

Launa turned from the view; Maria offered wooden bowls and a white leather bag. She started pouring a mixture of grains, nuts, and dried fruit into the bowl closest to Launa with the quiet admonishment "Tell me when you have all you want."

But Launa had no time for the bowl or its contents. The bag out of which poured the mixture was trimmed in a blending of painting and tooling just like those on the book sack beside Launa.

Maria stopped pouring, eyes on the book sack. "That is my family's totem. Where did you get it?"

Launa picked up the heavy bag. She glanced at Jack, offering him a chance to participate in whatever it was she was about to do. His eyes were fixed on the cook, his head slowly nodding. Then he gave her the shrug she'd come to translate as "Go for it. I'll cover your six."

"You gave it to me, Maria, and the book inside it, when you taught me to live off the land at a ranch in Wyoming."

The dark woman frowned. "That cannot be. I could never go to Wyoming. It is outside my people's natural territory."

Launa wanted to know a hell of a lot more about this "natural territory" thing, but before she got a word out, Jack's hand was on hers. The faintest of nods signaled her for silence. It felt good to have Jack cooperating with her in decision-making again, like they'd learned in the Neolithic. As Kaul had taught her, Launa waited to see what came next.

"May I look at your sack?" Maria asked.

Launa slid it over. Maria laid her bag of food down next to it. The patterns that decorated them were not quite the same. They had the minor variations that Launa had come to expect from the craftsmen of Tall Oaks. She smiled to herself; they were just different enough to be the same.

The Mexican traced the fine craft work, one with her right hand, the other with her left. Then she picked up Launa's bag, and the book slid onto the table.

Launa opened it. Across from the title page were two dedications.

To Momma,
Others know your wisdom from of old,
but few know the love you've shown me.
Anna

To Launa,
May these words feed you.
Maria

"That is your handwriting, and your daughter's," Launa whispered. "You told me she sent you the book during her studies back east to be a . . ." Launa made a guess at the proper word in this world's vernacular." . . . Lady or Scholar of plants."

Like a fish floundering in air, Maria's mouth opened and closed again and again before any words came. "My Anna studies the wisdom of plants, but here, on our people's farm plots. We do not read or write. It is not our people's tradition."

The last words came out loud and brittle, formally spoken to please official views and listeners, though Launa strongly suspected Maria had read every word of the two dedications. For Launa, the bleak words opened a void that was quickly buried under one huge question. *What is this "tradition"?*

Jack's fingernails bit painfully into her hand. She yanked

it back, but said nothing for the mikes she was more and more sure waited to record any spoken thoughts.

"Oh, there you are. My, you two are early risers." Those words in the melodic voice of Judith Lee drew Launa's attention to the old anthropologist as she entered the cafeteria, Brent Lynch at her side. "Good, Maria, you're sharing some of your 'Morning Special' with them. May I have some, too?" she said as she pulled up a chair and joined the two soldiers.

"Me too, Maria," Brent added as he settled in his chair.

"Yes, m'lady," Maria said, dismissing herself.

How many times in the Neolithic had Launa prayed for things to slow down just a little bit so she could catch up? That familiar feeling was back. She had too many questions and despaired of answers. And she remembered an intelligence officer's advice: "Never ask a question if you won't trust the answer." She'd better spend as much time figuring out who she could trust with a question as finding the right question to ask.

"I have some unfortunate news for Launa." Judith's green eyes were solemn. "I told you yesterday we could not find your parents in the global database. Last night, we ran a search on your grandparents. On your mother's side, there was no fourth child, only two. We could find nothing of your father's family. The wise women of Ireland are renowned for herbal contraceptives. Families rarely have more than one or two children."

Launa half laughed; so the large Irish families of her own history were unheard of here. But deep inside her, something snapped. The cold bickering of the Colonel and his lady was not a part of this world. The drunken rages and icy silences didn't happen. Launa stared at her two hands as she began to laugh, an empty, hopeless cackle. *And I didn't happen, either.*

Jack reached out, took her hands firmly in his own. Launa rode a whirlwind, every shred of her person wanting to fly away. She held on to Jack's hand, and let the laughter roll out of her.

"I'm sorry," Judith said softly. Her worried glance went to Jack. "What have I done?"

"It's all right," Jack answered, his fingernails biting into Launa's hand, the pain rooting her in the present as her laughter spun her away into nowhere.

"An hour after our drop into the Neolithic, we came across some pretty hard cases. When I asked Launa if we should shoot first and ask questions later, one of several good reasons she gave for waiting was the possibility that she'd be killing her own grandfather, several times removed." Jack captured her cheeks in his strong hands, brought her face around to meet his own dark, steady eyes. A thumb wiped away the tears running down a cheek.

"Well, she's got no mama, no papa, no Uncle Sam, and she hasn't popped like a soap bubble."

Jack's words fought through the hysterical fits that were urging her down a path to nowhere. Did anyone here recognize the plaintive song of the battling bastards of Bataan? They'd survived battle and a death march and hellish prison camps. She would survive whatever ambush today or tomorrow held.

I can, she vowed to herself.

Launa clamped her teeth shut, letting the pain of a bit lip center her. Holding her breath stifled the hysterics. When she surfaced, gasping for breath, she took Jack's hands into her own, gave them a hard squeeze. Her grip must have hurt, but Jack only winked. "Welcome back, soldier."

"Thanks" was all Launa could find air to say.

They let the silence hang there for a moment; then, with a sigh, Jack broke eye contact with Launa and turned to Judith. "What about my family? You know my grandfather."

Judith patted Launa's shoulder like a mother might, and like the Colonel's lady never had, then gave Jack her full attention. "Yes, I studied the Apache ways in my younger days. Juan Walking Bear and his son Samuel were of great help to me."

His breath escaped Jack in a ragged shudder, and Launa knew it was her turn to rest a calming hand on his. Of course, the father who died in Vietnam before Jack was born would be alive in a world that didn't have wars. Still reeling from her own emotional hit, Launa had a pretty good guess at the shock waves now hammering Jack.

A confused parade of emotions quick-marched across Jack's face before it clamped down into the soldier's mask Launa had seen before so many battles in the last year. *Jack's getting ready for anything. Only this time, it's going to be good, partner. This time it will be good.*

"I should have recognized you the moment I set eyes on you," Judith continued. "Sitting here today, you look just like Johnnie, Sam's boy."

One glance told Launa why. The captain showed none of the hard steel that had driven him since the first moment they met. Gone was the drive that had dragged her where she never would have willingly gone. He sat his chair not a coiled spring, but a lump of clay.

What has done this to him? God, don't let it have been me.

"Does Johnnie have a wife?" Jack's words came slow. They sliced into Launa's heart like a dagger. *Down-time, Lasa took him. Is he spoken for up-time, too?*

Judith nodded. "He was married, and they had a child"—Jack shot upright in his chair before Judith hastened to finish—"but both died in an auto accident."

Jack slumped back again. Launa's hand rested on his now, gently stroking his knuckles. The loss was years old, but the tears he shed on their first night in the Neolithic had been just as hot as if it had only been yesterday. His shared grief at the loss of his family had helped her face the loss of an entire world. She searched deep within herself for the words that could reach him now. His eyes blinked rapidly, fighting back tears; his hand seemed to roll over, inviting her touch to the soft palm. She made circles in it, praying the touch was enough.

Jack shrugged. "An old pain." He glanced at Launa, a sad smile twitching the edges of his lips. "But it can still hurt."

Launa swallowed the lump that had grown in her throat. If they had shared a child, would the pain still be as strong? Instead, they'd shared a mission for the last year, and the implants she carried for the sake of that mission had kept her barren. Launa squeezed his hand, a promise of closeness. Jack squeezed back. Promise made and returned.

Judith spoke softly. "I've made arrangements for you to meet Juan and his family on the Santa Carlotta Cultural Diversity Preserve." This Judith cared as much for people as the other one. Suddenly, being somewhere away from all this and alone with Jack was all Launa wanted. Maybe, out there, close to the land, they could find themselves again . . . and each other.

Brent took the moment to filch the book that lay ignored on the table. Launa was too emotionally wrung out to do anything but smile at the perpetual curiosity of the scholar. "That came from our world," she said, turning her attention back to Judith.

"I know you're excited about working with the scholars here at the lab on this crazy temporal effect they've isolated. How strange it must be to run into people like Brent and me, Harrison and Milo, even Samantha, who look just like the people you know, but who have never met you before." Judith laughed, and her eyes sparkled. "However, everyone would understand if you took a few days to yourself before starting," she ended sympathetically.

Brent's nostrils flared as he leafed through the first pages of the book. "Philadelphia? Where's that?"

Maria arrived at that moment. She glanced over Brent's shoulder as she put a bowl in front of him, then stooped to take a closer look. After the briefest of moments, she fled back to the kitchen.

"On the east coast, at the top of Chesapeake Bay. There's a map in there." Launa reached over and with practiced fingers found the right page. "There."

"That's Soradelphia," Judith chuckled.

"Right, city of sisterly love," Launa laughed.

"Maybe you two should help us for the next couple of days." Brent seemed paler than he had a moment ago.

"I don't know what we could do. We just rode the damn machine. We didn't make it. We didn't operate it." Launa glanced at Jack. He nodded. "I think some time close to the earth would be healing for us."

"Good; now that that's settled, let's take a look at the minor details." Judith folded her hands on the table, and her voice took on the brittleness of official words said too often. "Your status is a little confused. I've arranged with the lab for a debit card for your use. You'll only be traveling in the southwest, so Jack won't need a passport. You shouldn't have any trouble." Judith smiled as she pulled a plastic card from her pocket and slid it across to Launa.

There was only one card . . . in her name. Jack would have to stick close. Launa was glad for their short talk with Maria. Without it, she'd be babbling all kinds of questions, trying to make sense of the assumptions that lurked unquestioned behind Judith's words. Launa kept her mouth very shut.

"We've referred your case to the Assembly of Elders for Northwest Columbia. They'll probably refer the matter to the Assembly of Wisdom for Columbia. It could end up before the World's Elders." Judith shrugged.

A detached part of Launa tracked the political landscape, dropping the intelligence into pigeonholes like she had during the recon of the Neolithic. The other part of her put on a warm smile for Judith. "It doesn't sound like much has changed in the last six thousand years. The elders at Tall Oaks had the same problem making up their minds."

"You'll have to tell me all about them when you get back. The written record doesn't go back that far." The green in Judith's eyes was alive; she was a painter with a new canvas to cover. Launa would fill in the colors and textures this woman hungered for—as soon as she figured out where the land mines were.

The four stood. Launa retrieved her book; Brent seemed eager to study it, but he did not ask for its loan, and she wasn't letting it out of her sight. An hour later, Launa and Jack piled into a taxi, headed for the airport. Launa's last glimpse of Livermore was Maria, staring out a window of the cafeteria, her face a wistful puzzle. Launa wondered how much of this world was closed to this Maria, and how high a price both paid for it.

Maria dialed the number she had been given many years ago. Never had she used it.

The phone rang, then clicked several times. Finally a voice came on the line. "Yes" was all it said.

"The two strangers travel to Phoenix. The woman has a book on herbs from Philadelphia. It may be the one. Please, do not hurt them."

The phone went dead. Maria was not sure whether the harsh click came before or after her plea for mercy.

"Dear Goddess, what have I started?"

Senior Guardian Technician Helga bet Turlough liked working days. Junior techs on shift were tied to the consoles. On days, Helga was free to roam the Livermore campus . . . the better to find problem children and weed them out. She reported fifteen minutes early.

Flo swiveled away from the consoles. "Everything normal. Bit of a flap late yesterday. A couple of undocumenteds showed up at Lady Harrison's lab."

Helga glanced up from the logs. "Where'd she get them?"

Flo grinned. "That's the interesting part. Nobody can figure it out. They *claim* to be time travelers or something."

Helga shook her head. "Goddess, what kind of stories will they come up with next?"

"We ran a full background. Woman's clean as a newborn," Flo snorted. "We can't find the European family she claims to have. Guy's got the same fingerprints as a native. Sam says give them the value of the doubt for now."

Helga raised an eyebrow and got a shrug from Flo. One did not question the Project Administrator out loud, even in the Guardian's own inner sanctum. But if Samantha had taken to believing the fairy tales these science types dreamed up, the Guardians better keep their own eyes wide open. "Anything else strange?"

"Nope." Flo swiveled back to her consoles. "The two undocumenteds are into some strange sect that requires them to physically torture themselves at sunrise." She played a scene at triple speed of them doing calisthenics, then running the road.

"Looks pretty ridiculous," Helga said. "Stop the tape," she snapped. "Who's in the car?"

"Cyn. Sam's not so gullible that she doesn't have a tail standing by just in case."

Helga scowled; she wanted that high-profile duty, but Sam picked her favorite again. "Anything else out of the ordinary?"

"Pretty quiet morning. Oh, there was a broken-down cycle on the outer road. I did a maintenance call and got her moving."

"When? It wasn't about the time those two undocumenteds were going through their antics?"

Flo checked her logs. "It was, but don't worry, they never got within a mile of each other."

Helga scowled at Flo, but the watchstander seemed impervious to the judgment. She grinned back. "Mabel's coming back from her knee surgery and Deb's due back from maternity leave. Both of them put in for days. With their seniority, it looks like you'll be back on shift with the rest of us."

"Yes." Helga turned away. "I'll start my rounds. Beep me if anything out of the ordinary happens—anything." Helga would not give Flo the satisfaction of seeing her disappointment. Back to shifts. Blood! But it was only for now. Sooner or later even Sam would have to see that her best senior technician wasn't that flighty Cyn but Helga. Unless, of course, Sam wasn't interested in the best, only the friendliest to her own career.

Well, I can be career-friendly, too. Helga grinned to herself.

FOUR

SHOKIN, MIGHTY MAN of the Stalwart Shield Clan, walked back to the camp of his people. He had risen early to greet the Sun. He had many questions to ask of It.

From his father's time, and his father's before him, this land had been sufficient to grow strong warriors and sturdy horses for the clan. Wars had been frequent enough to give a warrior the honor he needed, and even the occasional head to take for a Mighty Man to show his prowess. This was the way it had been, and should be. It was not that way anymore.

Far beyond where the Sun rose, the rains did not come. Now warriors on hungry ponies came to beg grass to feed their horses. Today they begged, but Shokin saw the long daggers and sharp lances that stood behind the words. He gave before it was taken.

From the rise above the camp, he surveyed the herds of his clan and shook his head. The mares were thin, as was the milk they gave their foals this spring. Many had not lived to graze the rich summer grass. But even the wise men saw no other way for the clan to ride.

One choice Shokin swore he would never take, but someone among the Horse People had. Camps had been found, tents burned, warriors, women, children all slaughtered.

Many heads were taken, though it was clear the camps had died in their sleep. Strange deeds for these strange times.

And stranger still, no one boasted around the campfires. No new heads dangled from horse blankets. Shokin gazed at the Wide Blue Sky. *What do you see that I do not?*

Unbidden, his mind's eye saw again a head that had come to him in a jar—the pastureless Arakk. His blood meant nothing to Shokin, but the one who carried it might mean everything.

The woman who named herself Launa had ridden like a Mighty Man, but wore no more than a farmer's woman. *And behind her rode hands and hands of lances. She could have slaughtered us.*

Shokin knew the farmers. He had ridden among them to the west on his young man's go-about. They were a puzzle; none rode a horse or carried a lance. *In those days of my youth.*

Shokin thought back on the confusing race that greeted his eyes on the day Launa brought him Arakk's head. Then he had thought it was only the farmers, new to horses and unfamiliar with bridles. But maybe Sowon, his oldest son, had been right. "They charge each other, Father," he had said.

The sound of horses at a gallop brought Shokin out of his thoughts. Sowon raced toward him; a string of spare mounts kept pace beside him. He waited too long to rein in his mount; Shokin danced back, away from deadly hoofs.

"What brings you here, reckless as a new buck, my son?"

"Father, one who dies must have you hear his last words."

Shokin mounted as Sowon leaped from his tired horse to a fresh one. There was no time for more words as they raced south.

Merik brought a bowl of soup to his consort, Brege, as she nursed their little one. Morning Mist grew strong. Around them in the Sanctuary of the Goddess, elders smiled to see He who Spoke for the Bull in River Bend nurturing She who Spoke for the Goddess. That was as it had been among the People for as long as any grandmother could remember.

That was the way it should be. Merik wondered if Morning Mist would ever know that path.

"Have our bold hunters returned?" Brege asked her consort, sarcasm thick as the meat in the stew.

Merik shook his head. "You eat of the deer the Goddess gave to me in yesterday's hunt." Brege seemed to take an especially deep gulp from the bowl. She too feared taint on the meat Antia and her followers brought back from their long hunts.

Merik settled down, his back to the east wall of the Sanctuary. The words he next spoke were soft, meant for the ears of only his consort. "I have ridden among the horse herds again this morning. It is difficult to know so many animals, but surely there are two more horses for every one Jack gave over to us after the battle at Tall Oaks."

"That many?"

"Yes."

The tension within Brege exploded in a breath. The child at her breast, drinking in more than her mother's milk, whimpered.

Merik took the baby. "Come, little one." He held her high, bounced her, then rested her against his shoulder and gently rubbed her back. "The Goddess gives much, and the Goddess takes. There is no need to cry, little one, as we wait upon Her."

Brege took another sip. "It is not the path of the Goddess that our child cries for, but the way some hack at the dark forest to make a new path. One does not untimely rip open the womb of the Goddess. We must wait with patience to see what She births in Her own fullness of time."

A loud burp rewarded Merik for his efforts. He cradled the child, letting her suck his little finger as her tiny arms and legs waved. "I could wait on the Goddess easier if Sara returned from Tall Oaks," he said to the little one. His smile brought joy to the babe, who understood nothing of her father's words.

Beside them, her mother did not smile. "The moon is almost as full as when Sara left to sing to Lasa and Jack of what she saw when she hunted with Antia. And to sing our fears of what Antia may hunt within the walls we build around River Bend. Why does Sara not bring back to us their wisdom?"

The couple tasted an apprehension neither had known in their youth. In those days, all walked one path with the Goddess. Now the People walked so many different paths that Merik wondered if some had strayed from any path the Goddess knew. A year ago, that thought would have been impossible. A year ago, the People did not kill, but now everyone in River Bend had blood flowing in their arms because they had let the blood out of more horsemen than a woman could count. Merik glanced at his hands; was blood on them his eyes could not see? Having killed horsemen, could People now kill People?

Merik surveyed the length of the Sanctuary. None of the women or men here had ever ridden forth to hunt with Antia. Yet within River Bend, one in every three, now maybe one in two, had ridden Antia's hunt. True, many did not follow after her again. But they did not look Merik in the eye either.

If his consort brought the People of River Bend into assembly before the Goddess, would they listen to the Words She Spoke? If Antia stopped up some of their ears, would they follow the ancient custom of walking away to their own town? Or would Antia, like the horsemen she hated, put her knife to Brege's throat and put her own words in the Speaker's mouth?

Brege offered her consort the rest of her soup. He shook his head. He was not hungry for food. Truth, yes. Wisdom, yes. Help from the Goddess, or Kaul or Jack, oh yes.

He feared he would have a long wait before that hunger was slaked. He hoped it would not come too late.

She who Spoke for the Goddess in Tall Oaks paused as she reached the edge of town. Behind her, the many homes of the People of Tall Oaks spread out in ordered avenues or meandering paths. As a Speaker should, Lasa had walked the streets, ready to hear any complaint by one person against another. It was the place of a Speaker to settle quickly the differences among the People, lest they festered. Today, no one stopped her.

Often in her morning walks, women and men would call Lasa aside to show her a new art, share a just-spun song or watch a new dance. No one had stopped her for that either today.

Before this spring, never had there been such a day. Lasa doubted any grandmother among them could remember such a day, or had been told by her grandmother of one like it. Not in memory had the People walked the path they walked now.

In the fields beside her, those who worked this day bent over their hoes, nurturing the crops that would in turn nurture them through the winter. That cycle had not changed.

Beyond the field were the women and men who only last year would have been the complainers and artisans, singers and dancers. Today they moved across the pastures in ordered groups, each to the low singing of a girl or boy. Every voice did not join in the song as they moved, nor did they turn their walk into a dance as the People so often did. It was not the art of the dance these women and men practiced; but the skills of the killer.

Soldiers. Lasa corrected herself. Over and over again, Launa had told her there was a difference. "A hand of killers may kill one or two. A hand of soldiers will kill hands and hands."

And Launa had shown with her own body the truth of her words. First she and Jack with five of the People stood against four hands of horsemen in the Battle at the Tree. And when more hands of horsemen than a woman could count lowered their lances and rode across these fields to slaughter the People of Tall Oaks, Launa's battle plan had sung their death song.

Lasa's eyes sought out the long burrow under which the horsemen now slept in death. The crops grew thicker above them and the People whom they had killed. *And above the last child that I and Kaul would ever share. Truly the Goddess sends strange gifts to these strange days.*

The child within her fluttered; Lasa rested a motherly

hand upon her slowly growing belly. *May the People see in this little one the blessing of the Goddess on the strange new way we walk.*

A shout from one cohort drew Lasa. As one, the six double hands of soldiers faced in one direction, grounded their long spears and formed a wall of points no horse could face, no horsemen break. While their captain checked that each soldier was where she belonged, children scampered to position wicker shields in front of the first line of spear carriers. Elders found places in the ranks where they could rest the poles that held more shields above the formation.

Women and men, children and aged stood together to defend Tall Oaks. If they failed, they would die together, or become no better than animals, doing the labor for horsemen that any person should do for themselves. Lasa shivered at the strangeness.

Beside her, Sara rested a protective hand on her shoulder. "Launa and Jack will come soon. Their keen eyes will find us a path away from blood and death. The Goddess is gracious."

Sara was rarely far from Lasa these days or from her waking thoughts. It was after the horrible tale that Sara brought of Antia hunting horsemen that Jack sent the People of Tall Oaks to practicing once again the defense of their lives.

Jack had hardly waited that evening in the assembly for Lasa to invoke the Goddess before he stood and, with quick, cold words, told all that Antia teased a bear that should be left alone. The hunters among them knew the wisdom of his words, but none liked the hard way Jack told each the path for her feet: this one to scout, that one to carry a spear, those to practice with bow or sling. Before the horsemen, it had not been the way of the People for anyone, not even Speakers for the Goddess or the Bull, to tell another the path for her feet.

But the People listened to Jack. With the morning light, they went, determined if joyless, to the task of sharpening the skills of soldiers. And still they did it, even without Jack.

He rode now to the west to find Launa and Kaul, to bring all together that they might go with spear and arrow to the council of River Bend. Lasa wondered what words Launa and Jack would share in that assembly with Brege and Merik, Antia and those who followed after her.

Lasa looked to the hills to the west of Tall Oaks. *Come quickly back to me, Jack. Come quickly to feel our child as it grows in my womb. Bring back Launa, too, and yes, my beloved Kaul, that we may find the words that may yet show the People a peaceful path from the Goddess for all our feet to walk. Dear Goddess, bring them all safely back to us.*

Lasa rested her other hand on Sara's, tried to borrow the simple hope and faith of the young woman. Deep in her heart, Lasa held words she would not share with Sara, or even Kaul. Words swirled in a dark recess she would not name, full of doubt not only that the Goddess would show them such a path, but that the Goddess Herself knew of one.

Shokin dismounted beside a circle of warriors. Within that circle a young man lay. Shokin quickly knelt beside the fallen warrior. His empty eyes stared at the sky. His mouth hung open; no words would come from it again.

"He had no breath for a death song. He told us nothing," one of the Stalwart Shield's young warriors told his Mighty Man.

Shokin studied the corpse with the eyes of experience; a body could tell much without speaking a word. Shokin rolled him over and slowly pulled the death arrow from the wound. The ride and the fall had opened wide the man's back. Death had come quickly for him even as he galloped to bring his story to them.

"He is not of the Stalwart Shield," Sowon observed.

Shokin stood, rolling the death arrow between his fingers. "No, he is one of the wanderers who begged grass from us."

His son drew an arrow from the quiver at his belt and held it next to the one Shokin played with. "The death arrow is almost as long as two arrows. I have never seen such a shaft."

Searching the horizon, Shokin found what he expected; smoke rose to defame the Sky to the south. "Mount, warriors, for war. Carry your lances in strong arms and see with keen eyes."

Warriors were taught from the first time their fathers and uncles placed them on a horse to ride with an eager heart for battle, but there was a quiet about the warriors that mounted up to follow Shokin. He tasted their silence and found it good. Whatever lurked beyond the horizon had killed many warriors without even a death song escaping their lances. Shokin did not want anyone bringing his head in a jar like Arakk's.

Which brought an old vision to his eyes. Some who rode with the woman chief who named herself Launa had carried bows longer than any Shokin had ever seen, longer than anyone would pull while riding a horse. Would such a bow need an arrow like the one that now poked its feathers out of Shokin's quiver?

The farmers had not known war when he rode among them as a boy. And the Horse People had roamed the wide-open steppe, never casting an eye upon the fields that rivers and hills broke into such tiny reflections of the great steppe. Last spring Arakk made war on one of their camps, for plunder and grass. *And I was fool enough to lead my totem beside his.* Not for plunder, but to see how Arakk's warriors fought. Today's ally was often tomorrow's enemy. The farmers had died that day like rabbits. *Have the rabbits now grown strong teeth and long arrows?*

"Father, the dust of a herd." Sowon pointed to the right. Dust as from a large number of horses galloping fast rose in that distance. The rolling land hid whatever lay beneath the brown cloud. If it was Horse People Shokin sought, he should ride for the horses. If it was not Horse People he found, what kind of demons drove those mounts? Had they drunk enough blood today?

Shokin signaled his warriors to follow him toward the smoke, but at a slower, more watchful pace. The sun was halfway up the sky when he trotted across the crest of a ridge. In the shallow depression ahead, tents smoldered and burned. Already the war birds circled low.

Shokin signaled his warriors to a slow trot. They saw

nothing as they covered the final distance to the smoking camp, even though every head swung around in an unending search for any danger the land still held.

In the camp, Shokin posted watchers and sent his son and two others to find where the horses had passed the last night. Then he went among the dead.

The first tent he searched was only half burned; his eyes took in more than his heart could taste. The flames had consumed a woman's body. The warrior had died fighting as a man should, but the knife-stroke that had driven into his throat must have been waiting for him as he awoke. The brains of the warrior's tiny son had been bashed out against the tent pole.

No head had been taken.

"Father, I have found one of the herd guards." The hard simplicity of Sowon's words told Shokin that here was something a Mighty Man must see. Together the two trotted out on the steppe.

The body showed three arrow wounds, one to the back, two to the front. Though surprised, the warrior had fought as befitted a man. Whether the arrows had been of the Horse People or as long as the arrow in Shokin's quiver, they were gone now.

It was the other wounds that shouted strangeness. His manhood had been sliced from him. That often happened when a man died like a woman, but this one had charged his slayer. His belly was slashed open as one might a sacrifice, but the heart was still in him. And his head had not been taken, though he had fought with courage.

Shokin's eyes grew narrow as he scanned the murdered camp. Whoever had done this had been almost of the Horse People, but not. It was as if one made a bow of grass or a lance of brambles. At a distance they might pass for the glory of a warrior, but up close, their dishonorable lie was revealed.

Other of Shokin's warriors had come upon camps burned out like this one long after the wolves and jackals had cleaned the flesh from the bones. The Mighty Man of the Stalwart Shield clan walked back to his mount. Today, he had seen with the eyes of an eagle what others had missed or arrived too late to see. Now he needed the sharpness of a fox to know the meaning of what he saw.

He might say nothing. Whoever did this only killed the weak clans who could not hold tight to their pastures on the high steppe. Shokin shook his head; even if he told no one and ordered silence from those who rode with him, someone would talk. It was the way of young warriors to boast of what they had done and the fear they had tasted and swallowed whole.

And if the Mighty Men of the other clans suspected him of joining his totem with the farmers, they would bring lances. His pastures would feed another, and the totem of the Stalwart Shield would rise no more. No, Shokin would speak of what he saw before the Mighty Men assembled at the autumn gathering.

It took no smoke-drunk shaman to tell Shokin what would come next. All the clans of the low steppe, joining the totems of those newly come from the high steppe, would ride as one to the west. Few farmers would harvest the crop they had planted this spring unless they had strong arms and strong bows.

FIVE

LAUNA GOT HER first look at her new world on the drive to San Francisco—or rather Santa Francesca. It was informative. Few cars were as big as the cab. It stayed in the two right lanes with trucks and other cars its size. Two- or three-wheeled cycles, apparently electrically powered, filled the four narrower lanes to the left. Bikers in bright Nike and Reebok outfits rode the central divider with their own on and off ramps.

The communities they passed were green; trees and shrubs were everywhere. The varied mixture of high-rises and single-family dwellings each had its garden, just like at Tall Oaks.

"Wonder where the water comes from," Jack asked softly.

Launa added that to her list of questions she wasn't likely to get answered soon. She'd had a list of the same sort last year in the Neolithic. This one was fast growing longer.

The airport was smaller than the San Francisco International she remembered, both the terminal and the expanse of concrete runway. There were fewer planes parked on the tarmac.

A flight attendant's "We're holding your plane at gate B-4," ended Launa's rubbernecking. She and Jack dashed for the gate. No boarding ramp, they scampered onto the concrete apron and took the steps up to the plane's door two at a time. Launa was glad she'd taken only the clothes she could cram into a backpack.

Rushed as she was, she still got enough of a look at the plane to run a recognition check. It had the Boeing tail; it could have come off a 777. The engine on the wing was half prop, half jet. Launa had heard of something like that—*ducted* fans? More fuel-efficient, but slower, they hadn't caught on in the world she came from.

Inside, the nearly full plane only had two rows of seats on either side of the aisle. Two seats were waiting for them, well forward of the wing. Launa took the window seat; she'd have a great view. *Wonder what this world looks like from 35,000 feet?*

Traveling for Launa held fond memories. Once the moving van loaded out, she could look forward to a couple of days when all her usual problems were in a box somewhere in transit. With a happy grin, Launa let herself slip into travel mode.

Together, she and Jack stuffed their gear into overhead storage and settled in. Busy as Launa was, she didn't miss the last person through the door. If the woman hadn't been in a car this morning outside Livermore, she had a twin sister who had.

Hiding her face quickly, their "guardian angel" headed down the aisle for the last empty seat, about five rows behind them.

Jack glanced at Launa with pursed lips and a raised eyebrow. Launa shrugged; maybe this trip wouldn't be so happy-go-lucky.

The airplane's climb out showed a Santa Francesca of tall buildings and sprawling neighborhoods, speckled with green parks. Large ships swung at anchor in the bay with others tied up at docks under huge cranes. Ribbons of wide roads cut the city, and even the Golden Gate Bridge was there. From a few thousand feet up, it was hard to tell this wasn't home.

The rest of the trip was a disappointment. There was a dusty haze over the San Joaquin valley, or whatever they were calling it. The mountains hid under a high layer of thin clouds.

Launa gave up, took a quick trip to the rest room, checked her "guardian angel"—reading a newspaper again—and settled into her seat. *If you can't do anything else, soldier, sleep.* Without a word, Jack provided a shoulder to snuggle against.

Launa awoke when her ears started popping on the descent into Phoenix. First thing she did was check the window. She'd never been to Phoenix; she leaned back to give Jack a better view. "Anything look familiar?"

"Yeah," Jack answered slowly. "There's the interstate, and downtown's got its skyscrapers. Suburbs don't seem to sprawl quite as far. Hey, there's the wash where kids used to mess around with dirt bikes. Looks like horses now." Jack shrugged. "Enough to look familiar, and enough to remind you it ain't."

Launa hoped that was good.

They grounded with a bump. Blast-furnace heat invaded the cabin the second the door opened. The aisle quickly filled with people in as big a hurry as any flight Launa had ever been on.

All these people, so close, so strange, triggered the hairs on the back of Launa's neck. Her gut knotted up. Fingers searching for a knife she wasn't carrying, her eyes flitted from face to face, checking each one. All she saw was bored people, rushing to go somewhere and getting nowhere. *Get hold of yourself, girl. There's nothing here.*

Taking a deep breath, she stood and let the crowd move her. Here too, a stair waited for them at the exit. As he climbed down, Jack's eyes swept the field. "Airport was old when I came here in the eighties. They were always talking about changing it, building all-weather docks for the planes."

"Still do." A woman behind them entered the conversation. "But why waste money when we love our weather? Every time they put airport bonds on the ballot, we vote it down. I like lower taxes. Don't you?" As they reached the foot of the ramp, the woman hurried past them, fast walking for the terminal.

Jack grinned. "Some things never change."

With half a smile, Launa agreed. While the others made a beeline for the gate, Jack set a slower pace, giving all of them plenty of room to pass. By the time they reached the terminal, Launa still had not spotted their "trailer."

She suspected Jack was having the same problem readapting to the crush around them. Together the two formed a bubble, keeping their distance from the busy people. Launa wondered if everyone in this world was in such a hurry, or only those who traveled. Lasa and Kaul had been saddened as the People began to branch out, walking the different paths that the times and Launa and Jack had demanded. *What different paths do all these people walk?*

The airport didn't answer any questions. Its walls were hung with Indian blankets and sand paintings, as well as glowing ads for car rentals, real estate and computer networks. How many times had she been in airports no different? The torrent of people soon washed them up among kiosks offering car rentals and buses advertising various destinations.

"Nothing for San Carlos," Jack noted softly.

"Isn't it Santa Carlotta here?" Launa reminded him.

"That's what I meant. What did I say?"

"San Carlos."

"Oops. Better watch myself."

Jack turned abruptly away, heading down the wide lobby, leaving Launa to stare at his back. *What's going on in there? Come on Jack. Talk to me. Please!* When would there be time?

She caught up with him. "There used to be a desk outside," he mumbled, "where they matched up oddball stuff, ranchers, unscheduled haulers, whatnot."

"Sounds like it's worth a try," Launa answered.

Outside, there was a lineup of waiting cabs. "I think I see what we're looking for," Jack grinned.

Launa followed Jack's gaze. A small table with a hand-lettered "Transportation" sign had a large black man sitting behind it. As they approached, the man stood, a broad expanse of smiling white teeth showing through the ebony of his face. "Good afternoon, my lady. You may call me William. What service may I do for you?" Crisp diction and the rolling power of the Queen's Caribbean English were behind his gentle baritone.

Launa returned his smile and got down to business. "We need transport to Santa Carlotta."

The man stroked his chin. "The only coach for points east left in the morning. However, a car came in from one of the guest ranches at Safford. Its owner remained to see if any return fares might be arranged. If you will wait a moment."

He snapped his fingers. A tanned boy ran from where he had been lounging in the shade. They exchanged words in a language that sounded Spanish, and the boy was off.

The man turned back to Launa. "Ignacio may require a few minutes to locate your driver. May I find a chair for the Lady?" He half turned to Jack. His eyes and mouth formed the hint of a question. But it was clearly directed at Launa.

Behind Jack's dark eyes, Launa could see him weighing every word and glance, taking its full measure. His lips were also getting tight around the edges. *I don't care how much you try to play the shrinking violet, Captain, I know you're on a slow boil.* "I require a chair for my consort," she said.

William's eyebrows rose a fraction of an inch, but he turned immediately. Launa didn't know if Jack considered himself her consort, but Jack had not denied it. He'd also taken his own set of rooms at Livermore . . . and stayed in them last night.

As William collected chairs, Launa played over the question and look he'd given her and Jack. William had definitely given Jack's dark skin a slow look, and his nostrils had flared when Launa named him consort. *Have we got a race problem here? Well, Goddess, such does not become You. Then again, Your gospel could be just as bent out of shape as the Christian one.*

Further theology got shunted aside when William returned with two wooden chairs. He seated Launa and left to manage a new wave of travelers. Launa watched and learned. Rather than one or two people climbing into each cab and being spirited away, everyone identified their destination and the black man matched them together. Few cabs left with an empty seat.

Toward the end of this exercise, the boy returned with a fellow in a wilted cotton kilt and sleeveless undershirt. His shapeless hat offered little shade for a face untouched for a week by a razor. Standing to meet him, Launa smelled alcohol.

"The Lady travels to Santa Carlotta," William began.

"I won't be leavin' for another couple o' hours. Maybe I can get a few more payin' passengers."

Launa doubted he'd be safe behind a wheel in another couple of hours. "I wish to leave now."

Her words came out softly, but she put everything into them she'd learned from West Point and Lasa. Calibrated to take hair off any recruit, it should be clear to the guy that if this talk took too long, he wouldn't need to shave.

The black man's eyes widened ever so slightly: Message received. The driver's florid lips fell into a pout. "I'll lose money," he pleaded. "I ought to get a little time away from those stuck-up Mormons. I deserve a little fun," he whined.

Launa kept her eyes locked on the driver as she reached into her purse, removed her credit card and gave it to the concierge. "I'm sure we can arrange it so this man does not lose money and we do not lose time. We have a connection at Santa Carlotta."

"Probably some damn Indian. They've got their own time. Never can tell if they'll show up today or next week." The driver finally wound down. William's eyes grew large as he studied the crest on the card. He tipped it toward the driver, finger pointing to make sure he understood what was important.

The driver's mouth fell open. Then he pulled in his flabby belly and turned to Launa. "When do you want to leave? Where's your bags?" Jack pointed, and the man lunged for the two packs as if afraid they might sprout legs and run away.

Launa turned to William as the driver stumbled across the

parking lot toward whatever vehicle he drove. "I wish to arrange payment now, but keep the account open so that I can determine the Master Driver's tip at a later time."

"I can arrange billing here, Honored Lady."

So Judith's credit card not only gave her a bank account but established social status. Interesting. "Please do."

"I will fill out the purchase and run it through, Wise Lady, and you may close it at the General Store at Santa Carlotta."

Launa smiled warmly, a tool for managing men she'd learned long before the Point. William returned the smile, then spoke quickly to Ignacio, who again sprinted off. Just as the credit check finished the young boy returned, lugging a two-gallon canteen. William presented it to Launa along with a folder containing her paperwork and a pen. As Launa had asked, the cost for transporting two to Santa Carlotta was computed, but tips for the driver and the concierge were left empty. "How much for the canteen?"

"A courtesy, my Lady." The concierge smiled wide as the driver rejoined them.

Launa started to add a twenty-percent tip for William, then added ten more for the canteen. She made sure both William and the driver got a good look at the concierge's tip—and the blank space for the driver's. The black man nodded his pleasure. The driver frowned and started to say something. Launa cut him off.

"I will close this account when we get to Santa Carlotta."

Without a word, she turned to Jack. He slung the canteen over his shoulder and began a quick-march across the broiling parking lot. Launa hadn't noted where their transportation was. Jack set the direction and she guided on him. The driver half ran to keep up.

"Can't ya slow down?" he gasped. They didn't, and he didn't have air for further protest.

Halfway across the lot, they stopped beside a panel truck. An emblem dangling precariously claimed it was an International 4X4. Launa wondered what else was about to fall off. "Grandpa was poor and his pickup old, but he kept it in better shape," Jack whispered sourly, but opened the back door for Launa.

Launa got in; the seat was scalding where the sun had been beating on it. She crawled to the shaded half of the seat, leaving room for Jack. He closed the door and slowly walked around the rig, surveying it with a deepening scowl. Finished, and minimally satisfied, Jack opened her door and stepped across her. He settled in his own patch of shaded seat, but left her the window.

The driver complained loud and long about the hot seat and wheel. Few of his cuss words were new. Launa almost asked him why he didn't keep a towel over them. Nothing he said suggested he had the common sense to recognize her sarcasm—or to shut up.

As the driver threaded his way out of the parking lot, Launa and Jack rolled down the windows. The breeze came in superheated. Sweat poured out of them, quickly soaking their clothes. The wind evaporated the sweat just as quickly and left them cool. Launa was glad for the canteen; they'd need the water.

The driver headed east through a suburban mix of shopping centers and homes. Launa spotted gardens of rock and desert plants. Only the patches that grew food were green. Most of the vehicles on the road were solar-powered cycles or small three-wheeled rigs, but with no special lanes. Like pygmies dodging a rhino, they gave the 4X4 a wide berth. Most trucks and buses had harnesses that pulled electricity from overhead wires. Half an hour later, they picked up speed on a two-lane road cutting due east across flat desert.

Cactus marched across the floor of the desert, heads tall like good soldiers, marching toward the distant mountains. In her mind's eye, Launa again saw warriors heading for an assault . . . and death. She closed her eyes, willed away the memory. *I ain't gonna study war no more. They're just plants, growing where they can. That's what Maria would say. Both of them. You've got a new life to live. Live it.*

For several long minutes, Launa stared out the window, seeing only what was there: the land, the sky, and what grew between them. For Kaul, she lived the moment. Deep within her was a center. Launa reached for it, touched it, settled into it.

Jack brought her back. "Thirsty, hon?" She took the canteen, drinking in the water and the endearment.

Their driver held up a bottle, brown liquid sloshing. "Ya want ah drink?" Launa eyed him; had she missed him nipping?

Beyond the offered bottle, two miles farther up the road, a truck headed into a long climb. A deer bounded from a clump of willows, landing in front of the rig. The trucker swerved, almost missing the deer; the front fender just clipped the deer's hind legs. The animal stumbled a few steps before collapsing on the shoulder. The truck roared on.

Their driver put both hands back on the wheel and slowed. Jack took the canteen from Launa, following her gaze to the tragedy. She checked behind them; nothing visible to the heat-wavering horizon. She turned back to the deer as they neared it.

Her forelegs were drawn up beneath her as if she rested in peace. Her hind legs were splayed out behind her, the black road splattered with her blood. As they passed the poor creature, it followed them, eyes wide, more startled than shocked. Launa saw other eyes, Sisu's, Tomas's, horsemen, townspeople. The deer laid its head down as the driver accelerated away.

"Stop." Jack and Launa spoke at the same moment.

"What da ya mean, stop? It's just a dead animal."

"It is not," Launa snapped. "It's in pain. Stop."

"Ya some sort ah bleeding heart, ya think you're gonna heal the damn thing?" But the driver pulled over.

Jack opened the door and offered her a hand out. Launa waved him off, until she tried to stand and found her legs rubber. She took a tight hold on Jack's hand; he returned the squeeze. His face was wiped of emotion, but he swallowed hard. They walked hand in hand to the battered animal.

The deer started at their steps and tried to stand. Jack spoke soothingly. Launa stared into eyes no different from the many she had hunted in the last year. No, this poor wild thing was a victim of indifference. The deer she hunted were food, and praised for the gift of life they gave.

Jack produced a bronze knife from under his kilt, pitted

from service six thousand years ago. Speaking softly the words of blessing Kaul spoke after his hunts, Jack's hand wandered lightly around the silky fur at the deer's throat; she gentled. He found the place he wanted. With one swift cut, he laid open her jugular. Hot blood jetted out as Jack leaped back. Sighing, the deer lay down her head as if to go to sleep.

"Kaul would be proud of us."

Jack nodded. They stood by until the deer's blood pumped no more. "What should we do with her?" Launa asked.

Jack glanced at the clump of trees beside the road. "Carry her in there. Some coyotes would appreciate the meat."

"We impressed Taelon and Kaul when we brought meat to supper. Think your grandfather would appreciate a meal or two?"

Jack grimaced. "Doesn't show much hunting prowess."

"But it shows we care."

Jack glanced back at the truck. "There's rope in the back."

"I'll get it," Launa said. The driver was none too happy about the idea, but a reminder about his tip settled the matter.

By the time she returned with the rope, Jack had dragged the carcass to the foot of a pine tree. They quickly dressed it out.

Done, they started to lug the carcass up to the truck. The driver let the truck drift downhill. Jack grinned. "He do like the tip you gave the other guy."

Launa wiped sweat from her brow. "If he keeps it up, he'll deserve the same."

The driver spread newspapers over the back deck, but didn't help Launa or Jack when they heaved the deer in. Finished, Jack offered Launa the canteen for a drink. She quenched her thirst, and used as little as possible to rinse the blood from her hands and arms. Jack swapped her a dirty rag for the canteen. He drank, then cleaned himself before they hit the road again.

Launa let Jack have the window this time. Despite the heat, she settled in close beside him. He put his arm around her, but his face was turned away, watching the passing land. *How much of it is familiar? What memories are coming back? Has anyone ever gone to a stranger home?*

They still hadn't talked, but Jack was close. Slowly, they were building a place for themselves. That was enough for now.

An hour later, they turned left off the main road to follow a rutted gravel road beside a shallow stream shaded by willows. In only a few minutes they stopped beside a dilapidated wooden building with two gas pumps. One had a handwritten sign saying it was out of order. The sign was old and weatherbeaten.

Launa got out, stretched, and made ready for whatever came next.

Cyn bet Mythany stretched out beside the pool at the downtown Hilton. She'd better call in. She dialed direct for voice mail to avoid the complications of turning the call into a two-way exchange.

"I followed the two undocumenteds," she said into her cellular. "They arranged transport at the airport for Santa Carlotta and I trailed them until they left Phoenix headed east. Since it would be impossible to maintain an inconspicuous coverage during their time among the natives, I will pick them up when they return to catch their flight back."

There, that ought to do it. How much trouble could someone get into hunting deer with the natives? Cyn folded up the phone and turned it off.

Across the pool, she eyed several unattached men. They returned the attention, their skimpy suits leaving no question about their own appreciation of the bit of string she wore. The next few days would be very pleasant.

SIX

WINTER DAWN LISTENED to the sound of tires on gravel without getting up from her stool behind the counter. She folded her hands in her lap, waiting, as she had throughout her fifty years. A woman of the Dead Ones waited while the white women did what they pleased. But if the next white woman through the door was the one expected—Changeable World would truly change.

Winter Dawn glanced around the store. She knew it for what it was: shabby, shelves stocked more with despair than goods. Except those for the tourists. Those held the echo of a world Winter Dawn could only glimpse.

The door opened, letting more flies into the relative cool of the store. Billy Whitestone slavishly led a couple in. The white woman's deep tan highlighted her honey blond hair. Of medium height, she wore jeans, a plaid shirt, and boots—wise dress for travel in these parts. Few white women were so wise. The man walking behind her had the dark skin, eyes, and hair of the Dead Ones. His kilt and sweater did not change that opinion. Though taller than the woman by a few inches, his bent shoulders and unassuming station made him seem smaller. Then Winter Dawn noticed his eyes. They took in her store with quick, measuring glances. This one's Power was hidden . . . but not very well.

Were these the two she had been told of? Would they, like

First Man and First Woman, lead the Dead Ones from the lower worlds into a whole new Changeable World—or rather, would their book? Winter Dawn did not let her body show even the hint of the tension rising inside her. Still, her spirit danced.

The white woman presented the paperwork for her travel. "May I borrow a pen?"

Winter Dawn offered a broken wooden stylus that held a ballpoint. The woman eyed the driver. Billy grinned broken-toothed encouragement. The woman wrote a tip equal to the first.

Billy beamed and quickly pointed out, "She'll need your card ta close the bill."

The woman produced a card from her belt pouch and placed it on the counter. As Winter Dawn took it, her spirit leaped—the card bore the crest of the Council of Elders. These *were* the two. Struggling to keep her eyes from searching for the pouch that held *the* book, Winter Dawn ran the verification, then slowly punched in the value of the charge, making the required check as if she didn't know this card was backed by limitless wealth . . . and power. Billy drummed his fingers on the counter, impatiently waiting for the machine to acknowledge the financial transaction.

The white woman ignored the formality as she wandered the store. She wasted no time on the flour, beans and canned goods that were the mainstays of the shelves. She spent a minute eyeing the silver and turquoise native jewelry hung from the wall, as well as colorful woven blankets. A pause beside a shelf holding "authentic" native items was brief. She lifted a small clay pot and frowned at the worn sticker announcing "Made in Korea."

The man studied a collection of knives. As the woman came by him, he whispered, "Notice what's missing, Launa?"

Yes, she was the woman, and the Native would be Jack.

Launa shook her head.

"No guns or ammunition." The man's glance quickly took in the entire stock of the store; then he pointed. "Powder and lead for reloading, but no guns. Interesting."

Launa shrugged. "No NRA, or at least not one in Indian country." She seemed to make a mental note. Winter Dawn did too, though she was none too sure what had just been said.

The machine's beep brought everyone's attention back to the counter. Winter Dawn gave the driver one copy of the contract, put another in her till, and left the last copy on the counter for Launa. Billy bolted for the door.

Jack stepped in front of him. "Why don't we get the deer out of the truck?" His smile for the driver showed teeth.

Billy shrugged and slipped past Jack. The screen door slammed behind them. Launa continued her slow browse. She seemed neither surprised nor pleased by the tiny selection.

Jack returned. "Grandmother, where may I dispose of these bloody papers?" Winter Dawn accepted the respect he paid her. What on another day would have raised her opinion of these two, today, made her more cautious. She pointed to a bin and Jack dumped them in, then turned again to her. "We will need hats."

"Yes." Winter Dawn kept her words few; let them ignore her. What she brought these two would be all the bigger surprise. She nodded toward a shelf in the back.

Launa picked up a Stetson and whistled through her teeth. "These cost triple our ride from Phoenix."

"They get tourists from the lake south of here," Jack said, reaching for a hat on the top shelf. "This straw hat's weave is open for the wind to blow through, and it doesn't cost an arm and a leg." He put it on. "Just what we want." He pulled one down for Launa; it fell over her ears. A third fit fine.

"We'll take these two," Launa announced.

"Yes," Winter Dawn said and pointed at a display of feather and leather hat bands beside her.

Launa shook her head. "We'll make our own."

"Yes," Winter Dawn answered softly. If what she had heard of these two was true, they probably could, and would want to.

"We'll need something better than a bronze knife," Jack

told Launa. They returned to a case with a broken glass cover not far from Winter Dawn's watchful eyes.

Launa withdrew a foot-long Bowie knife from its scabbard. "Now this would make a horseman envious. Would have been handy in a couple of the brawls we were in." She checked its balance. "Doesn't weigh any more than my bronze one."

The Native stared at the case, hands clasped behind him, but his eyes sparkled like those of a kid on his first trip to the big city.

"Go on, Jack, pick one," Launa encouraged.

"I shouldn't." His voice didn't match his eyes.

"Go ahead." Exasperation edged the white woman's words.

Biting his lower lip, like some tenderfoot afraid to touch a horse, Jack ran his fingers along the sharp edge of a blade half as long as Launa's. Slowly he picked it up, then hefted it several times. "Good steel," he noted. "Well balanced."

In one motion he flipped the blade and threw. In a blink, the knife sliced into a windowsill at the other end of the room.

"Throws well, too." His grin was a kid's. "I shouldn't have done that," he whispered, "but damn, it felt good."

Launa gave his cheek a quick kiss. "I have no problem with you feeling good."

He laughed as he pulled her close and swung her around. "But I've blown my cover around that grandmother."

"Why worry? She's not likely to aim a gun at you. Speaking of which, we'll need a rifle in the back country."

"Yes," Jack agreed. He retrieved the thrown knife, collected its sister and Launa's Bowie and set them on the counter before Winter Dawn. "Grandmother, do you sell rifles?"

Winter Dawn expected the question; she was prepared. She fixed him with a hawk's gaze. "*You* are one of the Dead Ones."

"Dead Ones?" Launa echoed.

"The name the Apache give themselves." Jack answered

Launa before answering Winter Dawn. "My mother was white."

"But your father was not." She did not make it a question.

"No, he was not white."

"You should make your own bow. You do not need a rifle." She made her words smooth, sure, leaving no handle for argument.

"I am not Apache. I require a rifle." The white woman spoke words full of power and just as closed to dissent. Winter Dawn wondered how a woman so young became so sure of herself. Most young white women were still clay in their mothers' hands.

For a long moment, Winter Dawn met Launa's challenge. Eye to eye, the elder woman tried to see what lay behind the hard gaze of the younger. There was darkness there, and hard steel . . . and maybe death. *We will see whose death,* Winter Dawn told herself as her gaze dropped from Launa's to search for a key. "I will rent you a gun."

Winter Dawn turned to a locked door. Behind it was a small closet with two gun racks. She stood aside to let Launa examine the guns; Jack spoke from the counter. "Most of 'em have scopes. They should have good range."

Winter Dawn nodded. The guns were a mixed collection of bolt, lever, and swinging block action. Launa picked one of the last off the rack and frowned at it. "I've never seen a weapon like this. How does it work?"

Winter Dawn showed her how the trigger guard swung out, releasing the barrel.

"It loads like a shotgun," Launa marveled.

"Ladies find it easier that way," Winter Dawn answered.

The two nodded, accepting without comment that a gun should be easy for a woman to operate. Winter Dawn waited, praying that everything she said would be just as easily accepted.

"I'd like something with a magazine," Launa said, then grinned as she spotted a rifle in the far corner, bolt action open, magazine gaping. "How about that one?"

Winter Dawn put the first rifle back as Launa reached for the other and worked the bolt. "Good, an Enfield action, cocks on the pull back. Easy for a woman, and the British Tommies were so fast with it the Jerries thought they were automatics."

Jack nodded agreement.

Winter Dawn suppressed a grin, though she followed nothing of what they said. This gun was the only one with a magazine; she expected them to choose it. She had prepared it for them.

Launa glanced at Jack; he gave her a wink. "I'll take it." As she carried the gun around the counter, Launa looked it over. "Scope dials from 1x to 9x power. Iron sights are still on it." She glanced at the Native. "I like keeping my options open."

"I need ammunition," Launa said, setting the gun down.

Winter Dawn reached under the counter for the top box. She put a carton with twenty-five bullets on the counter.

"I'll need three," Launa said.

"You will only need one."

"I'll use half that box just registering the sights. I want three." Launa produced her card again.

Things were not going as Winter Dawn wanted. Maybe it would be best if this white woman did not take any rifle from the store. Winter Dawn produced a form. "You must fill this out." She rested her finger below one particular section of the paper, drawing the white woman's eye to it.

Launa blanched.

The questionnaire was long. The print was small, and the entire page cascaded questions. As Winter Dawn hoped, Launa's eyes locked on FATHER'S FAMILY NAME: If what Winter Dawn had been told was true, this woman could not fill out the rental form.

For a long minute, Launa stared at the form. Winter Dawn smelled victory; the book was as good as hers. These two would ride out with nothing more dangerous than the knifes they had chosen.

Then Jack pointed out the fine print at the bottom. "It says here you don't have to mess with all these idiot questions if you provide a bond equal to the value of the gun."

"Do you wish to add such a bond to your charge?" Winter Dawn kept her voice smooth as warm oil. No hint of defeat, helpful as any of an inferior culture must be to a white woman.

"Yes," Launa snapped, leaning into the man's supportive hug.

"Will that be all?"

"Yes," Launa snarled.

"No," Jack added softly. "I'd like a portable radio and batteries. Does my lady object to the extra cost?"

The white woman let her exasperation out in a rough sigh. "Go ahead. But make it fast."

The Native was back in seconds. "This boom box ought to bring in the next star system," he chuckled as he plopped it and batteries on the counter.

Winter Dawn once more had to suppress a frown. *This man cannot know what they carry.* She added up their purchases, the computer peeped and Launa was served with another bill. She scowled as she signed. "God, things are expensive."

Grabbing her new hat, knife and rented gun, Launa headed for the door. Jack quickly loaded up and was on her heels as the door banged shut behind them.

Winter Dawn slumped on her stool. The tension that had gnawed at her spirit from the moment the two entered the store fled her in a long sigh. Never had she met the likes of these.

Just as surely, never had she stood so close to the key that could take Changeable World away from the white woman and return it to the Dead Ones. Winter Dawn would meet those two again. Then they would give her the key. If they would not give it to her willingly, she would take their life blood and their book.

That book would belong to the Dead Ones.

SEVEN

JACK HELD BACK, letting Launa set the pace and direction. God knows, she'd faced enough to test the patience of a saint, and Launa's fuse had never been very long. He snagged their packs as he went by, and managed to balance everything. In the cool shade of some willows, next to a bubbling stream, Launa finally plopped down on a flat rock.

"Can we talk, Jack?" Her plea held a hint of desperation, and the only answer he wanted to give her was a big yes. "Isn't it lovely here under the trees?" was what he said as he pumped batteries into the radio receiver and turned the volume up high.

"Yeah, I guess so, if you go in for hot and buggy," Launa continued, her eyes locked on the receiver. "At least around Fort Sill, you didn't have to put up with so many mosquitoes."

Jack slowly turned the knobs, searching the lowest wavelengths for the echo of her word, or any other sign of a transmitter nearby. He picked up some single sideband chatter, an airplane or two, and what sounded for a second like a modulated beep, but it was gone when he turned back to it. He ran the radio up and down Launa and himself, front and back. He checked their new stuff and packs. No radio activity.

"Think we're clear?" Launa finally asked.

"As best as I can do with what we've got, yes."

"Now can we talk?"

"Yes."

Suddenly, Launa didn't look like she had anything to say.

"Mind if I get into jeans? I'm not riding a leather saddle in this kilt."

Launa laughed softly and nodded.

Quickly, Jack peeled off his cotton sweater and kilt.

"So that's where you had your knife."

Jack turned; it felt good to be comfortable naked with Launa again. He patted the leather sheath strapped to his upper thigh. "Easy to reach. Damn, that was a hot outfit. Mind if I rinse off before I get dressed?"

"Why would I ever mind?"

Laying his knives on the bank, Jack gingerly felt his way across the rocky bottom to the deepest part of the stream, maybe six inches at best. Squatting, he scooped water over his chest and back. "Not nearly as nice as your pond."

Her face relaxed into the first happy smile he remembered for more time than he cared to admit. "That was a nice place. Too bad Frieda had to interrupt us."

"She's not around to growl today." Jack splashed some water her way. "It's nice and cool."

Launa looked undecided for a moment, then loaded the rifle and laid it in easy reach on the bank. In a moment, she shucked her jeans and shirt, and a second later, bra and panties settled on top of the rest. With the gentle breeze caressing her bare skin, she luxuriated through a stretch that brought the proper male reaction from Jack and a sly smile from her. Launa settled down in a few inches of water within easy reach of the rifle.

For a moment longer, they stared at each other across the shady distance. They could have been anywhere: that survival hike in Wyoming, their early days wandering the Neolithic, their last day there. They could be anywhere, but they were here, wherever that was, and not likely to go anywhere else. Whatever they hoped to have here, they must build with their own four hands. Giving himself one last cooling splash, Jack dove in.

"Launa, something's bothering you. Is it me?"

"Dear Goddess, no." Launa's gaze had been wandering their surroundings, focused anywhere but on him. He had her attention now. "I thought you might be mad at me for bringing you here." She shrugged. "I couldn't have been more wrong about a recall."

"Are you sure? Folks up-time get the technology to drop us a line. Any reasonable person could read it as a 'come home' signal. Who knows, maybe it was. They just don't know it yet." He gave her one of the lopsided grins he reserved for when she expected the world to be rational and he knew it wasn't.

"But I thought . . ." Launa stopped, blinked several times and started over again. "Your paranoid act. What's it about?"

"I'm a soldier, and I ain't got my discharge papers yet. Have you? Until we do, I'll stay on active duty."

"What's your assessment of the situation?" the C.O. in Launa asked. Jack answered as her executive officer.

"A lot of what I see looks good. There's a few things that worry me. So far, there's not enough to draw any general conclusions. What's your assessment?"

"The same," the C.O. answered. There was a pause; Jack heard the woman when Launa continued. "I'm sorry about taking you away from Lasa now that she's carrying your child. I'm sorry that Sandie and Sam aren't here for you."

Jack let Launa's words trail off. Waited until any echo of them had passed. "And you're afraid I love them more than I love you."

Launa swallowed hard, and nodded.

Jack searched through the language of the People; maybe they had the words he needed. He was damn sure English didn't. He took a deep breath. "I think Kaul loves you, almost as much as he loves Lasa. I know Lasa loves me, but I'll never replace Kaul in her heart. What about that young fellow from Clifftown, Dob wasn't it? Would you have loved him more than me?"

Launa's blush was down to her belly button. She shivered. "I could claim injured innocence, but there were nights

Kaul loved me as best as he could. And yes, I think I would have made Dob a very loving consort. But I'd never quit loving you."

Jack let himself drift with the current until he was even with Launa. He reached out for her; she took his hand.

"Launa, I love you. I've loved you since the first day I saw you. I will love you with my last breath. The love I had for Sandie and Lasa is not subtracted from the love I have for you. I don't understand how it works any more than I know how the time travel gizmo does. Will you just believe that I do?"

"Yes, Jack." She opened her arms to him.

This world was strange, but Launa's body was familiar. His lips found her as hungry for him as he was for her. His fingers roved to caress breasts, pinch nipples already hardened by the cool air. Legs, alive with their own desire, intertwined. Urgency took them. And the damn rocks hurt like hell.

They broke from the kiss at the same moment, laughing.

Jack stood. "How we going to do this?" He looked down into eyes dancing with mirth. "Your first pond had a lot less rocks."

Launa rose from the water breathless with passion, beautiful as any Venus. "Oh, we'll figure out some way." Then she giggled. "'Course, I half expect a Girl Scout troop to tromp through here any minute. Wonder how they'll take to us?"

Jack kissed her as he perched her on a low tree trunk. Her legs surrounded him, drawing him to her. "If it happens, we'll find out."

"That'll tell us something about this world we made," Launa mumbled. Then their bodies came together. It was a long time before either of them thought about anything but the other.

EIGHT

LAUNA RINSED THE sweat of their lovemaking off Jack, as he did the same to her. It felt good to touch and be touched. It was good to know Jack didn't hold anything against her. Now if they could just relax and enjoy. They dressed and, with the cool efficiency of intimate practice, helped each other conceal sharp edges. Jack did another radio check, got a negative result, then lugged their gear to where the deer carcass attracted flies.

"Wonder when they'll get here?" Jack asked.

"I think they just did." Launa pointed behind Jack. He pulled his hat down low as he switched around to behind her.

Three riders rode slowly into the clearing. A black dog loped ahead of them. Launa pushed her hat back to give them a plain look at her face and raised her right hand to greet them.

The lead rider turned toward her. He was middle-aged, just starting to gray at the temples. Behind him rode an older man, his hair snow white. Trailing them and leading two horses was a younger man about Jack's age. Launa studied that one. Even though she knew what to expect, it was still a shock. He was Jack.

The first rider halted ten feet from Launa, studying her through hard, questioning eyes while he awaited his elder.

The old man stopped beside the first, doffed his hat, and waited until the third joined them before speaking. "If you are the Lady Launa O'Brian, I have come for you."

"I am her."

"The scholar, Lady Judith, named you as one who had a heart open to the many colors of our paths. If that is true, I offer you two weeks of my life. If that is not so, you may well find the next half moon difficult and maybe dangerous."

Launa let the People of Tall Oaks talk through her. "With an open heart, I will follow after you."

"Maybe she will," the middle-aged rider snorted, "but some great white hunter could not wait a few hours to kill one of our deer? Was it you or your man?"

So much for a present. "A truck struck this deer, and left it bleeding and in pain. We freed her from that pain and brought her to you so that she might serve us as food rather than give her spirit over to waste." She faced Grandfather's gray eyes. "Did I do wrong?"

"You honor us and the spirit of the deer. We will praise the deer tonight. And who is this man you bring to us?"

"He is my consort," Launa said as Jack stepped forward and brushed his hat back.

"Hello, Grandfather," Jack said.

The men froze. For almost a minute, three pairs of eyes locked on Jack. Jack's glance darted from one face to another. It was the dog that stirred the men from stone. Wagging its tail, it trotted up to Jack, sniffed, and looked up expectantly. Jack scratched it behind the ear, apparently in just the right place, because it whined with pleasure.

"Well, at least you know me, General Hook."

Grandfather brought his right leg across the back of his horse and slipped from his mount without once taking his eyes off Jack. In a moment he stood beside man and dog.

"Dark-of-the-Moon has never gone to a stranger. How is it that it knows you?"

Jack took a deep breath and faced the old man square in the eye. "I am John Walking Bear who is called Jack. My father died a warrior's death before I was born. He was called

Sam. His father died drunk when I was thirteen. You are my grandfather."

Wordless, the old man touched Jack's chin. Gently he moved Jack's head from side to side, marking every crag, every scar. With his free hand, Grandfather motioned his son and grandson to join him, standing beside him, the four sides of a circle. Launa held her breath, afraid even that faint sound might break the spell that held this strange family.

"How can this be?" Grandfather wove the spell tighter.

"I am of this land, but not of this world."

"Tell us more."

"In the world of my birth, the knife was a path every man must walk. The knife, the arrow and the rifle were not enough. The very clouds rained death until a man stumbled on a poison so terrible I will not name it. Every man, woman and child stood doomed before it. Two people of the knife, this brave woman and I . . ." Jack motioned to Launa. She entered the circle, to stand between Jack and his brother of this time. ". . . rode a machine we do not understand to a time in our past. It was our honor to teach the knife and arrow to a people who did not know that path. We stood with them when the People of the Knife came to enslave. Together, we killed every one of the People of the Knife."

The old man shook his head, as if to clear it; Jack hardly breathed. Finally, Grandfather let out a long breath. "I hear your words, but they are very hard to take into my heart."

Samuel snorted. "How is it you stand here now?"

Jack faced the man, tears in his eyes. "Father, whose face I have never seen, wise people of this world built a machine like we rode into the past. It beckoned us and we rode it back to California yesterday. How and what was done, I do not know. I know that I am here, looking upon my father for the first time and upon a grandfather I have long mourned."

Samuel reached out to touch Jack's forehead, tracing a small scar with his finger. "How did you come by this?"

"I walked the knife's path. Digging a hole in a desert land far from here, I did something foolish, and my shovel bit me."

For the first time, the father smiled, and pointed to his son. "Where did you get that?"

The young man of this time grinned, pulling his long hair away from his forehead to reveal a similar scar. "You know very well, Dad. I was digging post holes with you when I goofed off and my shovel got me." The young man reached for Jack with both arms. "Brother, I'm known around here as Johnnie."

Jack was home.

Johnnie introduced Launa and Jack to their mounts. Both Johnnie and Samuel seemed eager to leave the shadow of the white woman's world, but Grandfather pointed Launa back to the store. "We must pay taxes for this animal and any we hunt."

Launa ordered three deer tags. The bill drew a whistle. "Triple the cost of the ride out. Can Dead Ones pay so much for meat?" Launa asked as she signed the charge slip.

"Indians do not hunt," Sam snapped.

Interesting, Launa mused. After one day in this world, she had a few hard facts and a lot of supposition. *I'm still no closer to figuring out this world me and Jack forged.* Then she shrugged. *Does it really matter? Knowing is hardly a matter of life and death like it was in the Neolithic.*

NINE

WINTER DAWN WAITED in the shade of a willow. Flies busied themselves with the blood left from the deer the two strangers had brought. The Old One had been wise to purchase a tag for the deer. Without it, she would have held them in custody when they tried to leave. Tagged, the white woman was in her rights.

Winter Dawn waited, but this waiting was strange. All her life she waited because Dead Ones had nothing better to do with their time than wait until the white woman chose. As the sun sank lower, Winter Dawn tasted the coming darkness. It was pregnant with possibilities, possibilities she would chose.

She saw the dust rising from the road before she heard the noise of their coming. Two small four-wheel-drive jeeps entered the clearing in front of the store. The first held three men; the second one was full . . . four men. Brakes squealed as both halted. She recognized only William—the tall black man was easy to know and get to know.

Winter Dawn stood. "They are gone. They left an hour ago."

"Did you see the book?" William asked.

"No."

"Are you sure it was them?"

"Walking Bear was sure enough to take them with him."

William gnawed on his lower lip, digesting the situation. Then he nodded. "We need a place to show these young bucks how to use the toys Grandmother Frost blessed us with." He grinned as he used the white woman's own fairy tale to spite them.

"You will not need the guns from the store?"

"Look at what we have." He reached in the jeep; his hand came out grasping black metal, no stock, short barrel, magazine as long as the gun. Though it was totally different from the hunting rifles in the store, Winter Dawn was only too familiar with it.

"You have the Guardians' own guns."

The youngster in the jeep's back seat laughed. "Guardians are so proud of their inventory system, but it is all on the computer, and it is easy to make electrons disappear. Sneaking the guns out was the hard part."

"Bullets?" Winter Dawn knew guns were only metal without bullets. It was bullets that silenced angry shouts, shredded protestors. Bullets would kill white women as dead as natives.

The youth rested his arm on five metal boxes. Five hundred rounds, it said; five more were on the floor. "And as many in the other jeep. We have enough bullets," William growled.

"Let me show you where you can learn to use your guns with no one the wiser." Winter Dawn settled herself in the back seat of William's jeep. Quickly, she guided them back to the main road. A mile back to the left was a dirt trail; they followed it for a half hour before turning onto a path that was hardly more than a hint. She called for a halt fifteen minutes later.

The jeeps rattled to a stop as the trail opened on a green valley. A hundred meters into the field were stacks of hay bales. She pointed. "There are your targets."

William surveyed the cliffs of the box canyon and smiled. "Yes, sound will go straight up. There is no one for miles."

She nodded, proud that he did not make it a question.

"Fellows, set up the targets." The youths howled and took off for the bales, eager as young men are to put their backs into something. Winter Dawn watched them go, waiting to see how William would fill the first private moment they had.

"How easy will it be to find Walking Bear?" William asked.

"You placed the beacon in the canteen, but we need not track him. I know where we can meet him tomorrow."

"You are sure?"

Winter Dawn faced him. "Many times Walking Bear has led great white hunters into our lands. Always he follows the same trail the first day so he can tell the ancient stories. Yes, I know where we will meet him when the sun is high. And he will be only a stone's throw from you when first he knows you are there."

William grinned. "Facing Guardian guns, they will give us the book."

Winter Dawn nodded. "Then the white women will have to listen to our words, listen and change, or we will burn the book and send us all into darkness. Let the Giver of Life draw us back from the darkness of First World to the light of Changeable World. Then we will see who has Power and who does not."

William shrugged. "I trust my own strong arm first and any gods later. Let us show these bucks how to use their guns, and we will be the ones who change the world."

Winter Dawn thought of the two this afternoon. Arrogant white women often passed through her store, leaving a bitter taste behind. Launa had left behind something else. Winter Dawn tried to put her finger on it. She was not weak; if she were, the white woman would not have left with a rifle. No, the woman carried herself with a different Power, a Power Winter Dawn could not name. She wondered how this Launa had come by such Power, and what she would do when she faced seven Guardian guns.

The bucks returned, covered with hay and eager to make the acquaintance of the angry death in the black metal. One pointed his gun at the hay and pulled the trigger. Nothing happened.

He started to stare into the barrel. William knocked it away from his face.

"Ojah, you fool. Have you not read the paper I gave you on these guns? Do you not know what a safety is?"

Several of the youths held their guns up and conspicuously flipped the safety switch off. They grinned at their foolish comrade. He flicked the safety off. The gun went off, fortunately with nothing between it and the other end of the canyon. He almost dropped the gun.

William threw his hands up. "Everyone." They all looked at him. "Stop." They continued looking at him, but hands moved away from the guns that hung from web slings around their necks. "Put your safeties on." They did. "Always keep your gun pointed at the bales." They did.

"Now, let us see what we can learn." William stalked over to a position on their left. Everyone could see him . . . and keep their guns pointed away from everyone.

"Hold the gun at your hip, arms straight, one at the barrel handle, the other around the trigger just as you have seen the Guardians do." They followed his words and example. "Keep your elbows locked. Take the safety off and fire a short burst."

They did. The noise was enough to take Winter Dawn's breath away. The targets were untouched.

William waited for the echoes to die down. "Now, use long bursts and walk your bullets into your target."

The young bucks let out whoops and opened fire. Bullets flew. Grass and dirt flew. The targets took a few hits. William held up his hand. Firing ceased.

"What is wrong with you?"

Ojah scowled. "I don't know which bullets are mine!" He glanced at the others. They nodded, wide eyed.

"Yes," William frowned. "Yes. Ojah, you fire."

The young man stepped forward, grasped the gun like life itself and squeezed the trigger. Gouts of dust and grass sprouted in front of one target. He corrected his aim. As the burst of fire lengthened, a bale of hay disintegrated. Fire ceased when the magazine ran out. The others cheered as Ojah raised his gun to the sky. "Yes!" he shouted.

William nodded. "Each of you, one at a time, do the same."

Practice proceeded in order until only Mani, the computer wizard, was left. He'd been fiddling with his gun while the others shot. "William, look." He swung out a metal bar. "It makes a stock, just like the hunting rifles have." He put the gun to his shoulder and aimed it at the hay. "And there are sights, not as good as a hunting rifle, but they're there."

William held his gun out in front of him, without the

stock, and fired at the bales. His first shots hit close, but the bullets rapidly went high, raining down far past the target. "There is a reason why the Guardians always fire from the hip and why you will do the same. The recoil from the guns must be controlled. Now, put the gun back on your hip and do what everyone else does . . . and put that metal bar back."

Mani didn't look convinced, but he limited his disagreement to a scowl and did as he was told.

Each gunman fired off several more practice magazines, then retreated to the jeeps to reload.

Winter Dawn watched the sun sink below the lip of the box canyon. The sky turned blood red. She prayed to the Great Spirit that such an omen for tomorrow was for others.

William came up behind her. "This place where we will meet Walking Bear and the others. Is it easy to drive to?"

"Tomorrow morning, we will be there long before he is," she answered. "We will wait for him to come to us. They will be so close even your brave shooters cannot miss. May the Great Spirit smile and give Walking Bear the wisdom to give us what we demand rather than face the power that has scattered hay so freely."

She turned to watch the young men, noisy as they made ready for the next day. "And may your young braves do what they must before they discover the difference between making hay fly and shattering flesh and bone."

William grunted agreement, but said nothing.

Winter Dawn shivered. They were the choosers now. They would choose who lived and who died. Once the book from another world was in their hands, this world would change as they chose . . . or they would throw it into chaos.

Winter Dawn wrapped her arms around herself, trying to ward off the cool evening air, knowing the cold she felt was deep within her. Would that change mean freedom for all—or death? Did anyone really know what would happen if they burned the book? Still, it didn't matter. Death would take little from the likes of Winter Dawn. Death would take much from the white women.

With William at her side, Winter Dawn walked into the gathering darkness.

TEN

LAUNA TOOK IN a deep breath, rich with the scent of mesquite and sage, baked earth and wood smoke. To the west, a red sun set behind distant, pine-covered hills. Sky and high clouds cascaded through every shade of crimson, silver, and gold. The gentle breeze to her back brought the promise of a cool evening and dinner. Behind her, Johnnie cooked beans, made coffee, and roasted venison steaks. Scattered around her, Jack, Father, and Grandfather stood, facing west, lost in their own separate meditations. Launa did not need to read minds to know that they, like her, were trying to make sense of the day's gifts.

Johnnie broke the silence. "Oh, Lady, how would you like your steak cooked?"

She turned, smiling at the innocent, eager-to-please look on his face. She'd never seen its likes on Jack's. "Medium rare would be fine," she answered, "and please don't call me Lady. I don't know what a Lady is here, but I doubt I meet the specs."

She grinned at Sam and Grandfather. "If you were to call me by my warrior's station, I would be honored, but I suspect Lieutenant means nothing here. Just call me Launa, okay?"

Johnnie seemed delighted. Sam frowned less, and there was something relaxed around Grandfather's eyes when next he glanced her way. Jack gave her a wink.

After supper, Launa stared into the glowing embers. No

Dante's *Inferno* here. But what did she see? She had so many pieces to this jigsaw puzzle, but none of them fit together.

"Tell me how I died." Jack's father broke the night quiet.

"I was six before I met Grandfather," Jack began.

"That sounds like Cecilia," his father growled.

"And eighteen before I met a man who fought with you on that day." Jack began to weave the story Sergeant Rodrigo had shared with him in a high school cafeteria. Launa compared this telling with the first time Jack had told of a recon platoon probing outside An Loc in the days before the Easter Offensive of 1972. Jack was no longer the emotionless, rear-echelon briefer. He told the story as Taelon would . . . high epic. It had to be that way, how do you translate "calling the world down on your position" to people who never heard of a battlefield radio net? Launa wondered how Jack would describe the chances of a 105 round landing smack on a foxhole.

"You and your men dug deep into mother earth,
letting her shelter you
from those who cried for your blood,
who would kill the song of warning
you would spread far and wide.
From the great engines of your distant friends,
came shells, heavy as a woman, full of exploding death.
Fragments of metal flew through the air,
slashing life from trees and men alike.
Your men huddled in the bottom of their holes,
while hundreds around them died."

Jack looked into his father's eyes; the fire danced in them.

"The battle was won.
The others could stand the slaughter no more.
They turned to flee.
And in that moment, a shell landed,
not on the ground around you,
but in the hole that held you."

Jack paused, giving the man who listened to his death a moment to reflect.

His father nodded. "That would be a man's death, like the warriors from of old." Sam grinned as he turned to Grandfather.

"Yes," the old man nodded, his thoughts lost in ancient lands. "Yet, Jack, you were eighteen before you were told of that."

Jack's eyes swung around to Launa's. She nodded. How to explain the twentieth century they had been born into? Jack faced back to his father. "You walked the warrior's path, but I did not grow up that way. My mother married again, and raised me to know nothing of you. But tell me, how did it come to happen in this world that you met Johnnie's mother?"

Launa drew in a breath. Jack probed, like his father before him, scouting the shadows that haunted this land.

Sam sat back on his haunches; Grandfather filled the breach. "The white woman builds her dams. The great rivers do as they are told, not as the Great Spirit would have them. Just so, other things around the white woman rise and fall. In my youth, they allowed no books on the reserve. In Samuel's youth, they decided it would be well if some of our people learned what was in their books. Sam had much skill with words and numbers. The elders sent him as an eagle, to see what lay beyond our sight."

"I studied in their schools." Sam, now ready, took up the story. "Like the Dead Ones, they also had their young men and women together, learning many of the same things. It was hard work, to catch up with people who learned to read while I learned to set my first rabbit trap. They knew nothing of riding a horse or hunting, and did not care that I did. Except one: Cecilia." Even now, the name brought a smile to Samuel's lips.

"She seemed fascinated by what I told her of our ways. She helped me learn. And when she took me to her bed, I thought I had found a white woman who was different from the rest. Maybe she was, then. She came with me to my father's camp, lived a summer among us, was accepted by the women of the Dead Ones. She sang our songs, danced our dances. When she told me she carried our child, I was proud as any man." Sam grew silent. With a stick, he stirred the glowing embers. Launa wondered what images he saw, created, and destroyed. They meant nothing to her—yet.

"She published a paper on the ways of the Apache. It won her praise. It did not feel good in my belly, this telling of our stories for anyone to read, but I had grown comfortable in the college. I was prepared to live with this woman. I believed we could journey back and forth between the ways of the Dead Ones and the ways of the college. But that was not how she saw it." Sam snapped the stick and tossed it in the fire.

Launa remembered Jack breaking sticks, the son mirroring the father he had never met. Launa tried to keep detached. Here was data, more pieces for her puzzle. Where did they fit?

"Her mother announced that we must go into business with her. Now it is that way with us, the man lives with his woman's people. Is it thus in your world?"

Jack nodded. Sam shook his head.

"I knew that a white man lived much as his consort's people would have him, but I thought the college was that way. I was wrong. What had been my and Cecilia's life before was but a passage. Her true life was with her mother in the great city of Las Ciela. I tried, but there were people and houses everywhere. At least the college had land around it. This great city had nothing but people from the salt water to the mountains. I tried, but I could not stay in L.C. There were angry words between us, and I think they grew worse when Johnnie was born. She had wanted a girl. I was proud of my son." The father smiled across the fire where Johnnie sat listening.

"She sent me back to the preserve before Johnnie was weaned. She paid the tax so I could take bottles and formula to Father's camp. She was very nice." Sam's voice gave the lie to his words.

"And she married a man of business before another year had passed." Jack spoke with surety in his voice.

"Yes."

"I can tell you his name. I bet I'd recognize him."

"If he lived, you might, but he is dead."

"Right," Jack agreed. "He is dead. In my world men

fought with knife and rifle, money and property, and died early. What laid Cecilia's second husband in the grave?"

"The same," Samuel snorted. "The woman owns the property, but it is the man who plies the trade. To please his mistress he works long. White men are more driven than the women. First they must please a mother, then they must please a consort." Sam shook his head. "Never do they know themselves. Never do they know the joy of roaming the hills, tracking a deer, sneaking up until you can almost touch it, dropping it with a single arrow through the heart." Four men smiled at the shared memories.

More pieces for Launa's puzzle. She wet her lips, reluctant to speak, to break the circle of family and men, but one or two more pieces might make everything fit together.

Jack spoke before she did. "At the General Store, you said Natives could not afford the tax to hunt deer?"

"We can't." Sam smiled bitterly. "Not *every* carcass wears a tag. Let whites pay their tax. Pardon, La . . . ah Launa."

"No pardon needed." She glanced at Jack; he'd asked one of her questions. Would he ask the other? He stared into the fire.

"Grandfather, only you carry a rifle. Is that also taxed?" Jack had asked her last question; she gave him a quick nod.

"Yes." The old man spoke slowly. "They say that anything we did not have when the white woman found us is wrong for us. Rifles and cars, books and televisions . . . anything new . . . are taxed. Even the medicines we use must be the old kind."

Jack nodded and turned to Johnnie. His words were brittle as he asked the question. "What can you tell me of Sandie?"

The young man looked away. Once more, Grandfather began the tale. "The waters rise and fall as the white woman will have it. When Johnnie was eighteen, those who speak for them decided that the natives must again try to walk their way. Sam brought many books that the tax assessor did not know of. Johnnie learned to hunt and to read, to ride and to sum. I knew in my heart that it was time to walk a new path, not our path nor the white woman's path, but a new way."

Launa swallowed hard. Here it was again. The struggle to find a different way. But Johnnie was talking.

"I met Sandie at the University of California at Berkeley. She had grown up in Santa Francesca. She was fascinated by my native ways, and I was entranced with her. Dad warned me she'd be just like Mom. I told him Sandie was different, and she was." He fell silent. No one hurried him. Launa lay back on her saddle blanket, resting her head in her hands. The stars hardly twinkled in the dry air. The night sky was black, black as the sky over Tall Oaks. She almost felt at home, but knew she wasn't. The more she heard, the more she knew this was not home . . . might never be however long they lived here.

Johnnie continued. "Sandie defied her parents. They cut her off. Her grandmother was not so harsh. Maybe something you said to her, Grandfather, the one time she visited here, or maybe she was just older and wiser, I don't know. When our daughter was born, we named her Samantha, after her grandmother, and my father. We were driving Sandie's car north. We both had job offers in Portland. We didn't have money for a motel, so we were driving straight through. A big pickup truck came down the wrong side of the road." Johnnie choked, pleading. "I tried to dodge, but that big truck just took off their side of the car."

"The wielder was a woman, and she was drunk." Jack's words were sharp, quick to get the pain over with.

"How did you know?"

Launa sat up. Across the fire, Johnnie's eyes ran with fire, his tears ignited by the glowing embers.

Jack quickly stepped around the fire. Sliding down on Johnnie's blanket, the two embraced. The silence of the night took the sound of their mourning. Two men, sharing one pain. There was no need for words. The two older men and Launa removed themselves from the brothers, spreading their blankets at opposite ends away from the fire.

Much later, Jack spread his blanket beside Launa. He lay on his back, staring up at the night. She reached a hand across to him. He took it, held it tight. Launa wondered what it must be like to have the love of three women contending for one man's heart. She was grateful there was only one man in hers.

She assumed all the questions of the day would keep her

long awake, but it seemed only a moment later that the sky was brightening and Jack was whispering in her ear, "I need you."

"God, do I need you." And they took what they needed and gave more than they got. Launa only once wondered what the noise of their passion must sound like across the fire. She didn't care. It didn't matter where she came from.

Under Grandfather's practiced eye, they ate and broke camp quickly. Launa wanted to sight in her rifle, but Jack asked her to wait until they stopped at noon. "The morning quiet is special." Launa suspected he meant sacred. She could wait.

They rode most of the day alone with themselves. It was not a moody silence. Grandfather or Sam often broke the quiet to point in that strange Apache way, with the nose, at something important. Grandfather and Sam shared the stories of the Dead Ones. Who the Spirit Dancers, or Gans, were for that mountain or another. Grandfather even pointed out where First Man and First Woman led the Dead Ones up from the Fourth World into Changeable World and told Launa the Apache creation story.

Launa listened, not with her ears, but with her heart and tongue. More than hearing words, she ate the stories, swallowing whole the affection and love that was in every word Grandfather and Sam spoke. If Launa could have, she would have purred.

And deep beneath all of this, her subconscious put the pieces of the puzzle together, forming a picture. She was comfortable that in the next two weeks she would reach the right conclusions.

She was not surprised when, with the sun high above them, Jack turned his mount out of line from the others and waited for her. "Honey," he smiled as she came up to him, "can we ride along together? I've got some things to chew over with you."

Launa was ready to do some serious chewing. Together, they'd gotten to the bottom of a lot of things last year. She smiled back; it was good to be talking with Jack again.

A puzzled look flitted across his face. He squinted at a rock pile one hundred fifty meters to their left. "What the hell!" He pointed.

Launa shaded her eyes to study the rocks. Men hunkered down around them. Something flashed: sunlight off metal. *No!* Muzzle flashes. She threw herself from her horse even as she shouted, "Incoming! Hit the deck!"

The sound of automatic weapons fire reached her as she felt the wind of bullets flashing through where she and Jack had been a split second ago.

Behind her, two men shouted as one.

"Grandfather!"

"What are you doing?" Winter Dawn and William shouted as one. More of the young shooters joined Ojah. She could hardly hear his answer over the crackle of their weapons.

"He saw us. He pointed right at me. I had to shoot."

"But they are too far away!" William screamed. "I told you not to fire until I said."

"Walking Bear is shot." Winter Dawn lowered the binoculars that had brought his gore so close she could almost smell blood. She blinked several times but could not get the vision from her eyes. A bullet shattered the rock beside her and William. They ducked, as did the other shooters when another bullet flashed past them.

"You said you fixed her sights to shoot high," William snapped.

"I did, but she is not aiming, just shooting."

"No one should shoot that good," William muttered, huddling behind a boulder, but reaching around it with his gun to fire off an unaimed spray.

Winter Dawn cringed at the noise. Certainly none of William's shooters could do what the white woman Launa had done. Now Winter Dawn wished she had talked more yesterday, learned just what those two knew about guns. As she recalled what they'd said to each other, it dawned on her that they had told her much. She had not known enough to know what she heard.

For the first time, Winter Dawn knew fear. What else did these two know that she knew nothing of? Was it enough to take the life from her and her dream?

ELEVEN

THE BULLETS BLITZING past Launa's head were fast, but not as fast as the changes racing through her. In a heartbeat, she was again Lieutenant O'Brian, United States Army, Commander of the Legions of Tall Oaks—and the one person here with firepower.

Even as she shouted her warning, Launa took in the combat situation. The number of shooters was unknown. She'd dismounted on the unengaged side. One hand grabbed for the rifle, the other went for her saddlebags and the boxes of ammunition they held. The rifle butt snagged her canteen. A yank got both free.

Her horse reared. Its head disappeared in a red mist. As it crumpled, Launa spotted a gully to her right. She tossed the bags and canteen in that direction and turned to face her enemy.

With no time to aim, she snapped off three rounds as fast as she could work the bolt. That cut down on the weapons chatter.

"Jack, we got to get under cover."

Off beside her, Grandfather lay on his back, his chest pumping blood onto the desert floor despite everything Jack could do to staunch it with his shirt.

"We can't move Father," Samuel cried. "He'll die."

"We're all dead if we don't," Jack snapped as Launa used her rifle scope to get up close and personal with the opposition.

A man's head filled the crosshairs. She squeezed off a round. Missed. But the man flinched down. With only one round left in the magazine, Launa turned to run.

More bullets whizzed over her head. She snagged the canteen and saddlebags on the run and zigzagged the short distance to the gully. Without slowing, she went in feet first, protecting her weapon as she rolled.

The dry wash was four to six feet deep, maybe twice as wide. She chambered her last round, stood just long enough to get a good sight picture on someone's heart and fired. He ducked a moment later. She'd missed again.

"Two misses at this range! Sarge would have my head. Should have sighted this damn thing in." She hadn't expected to be fighting for her life before noon. Of course, she'd been none too gentle getting the rifle out of the scabbard either. That might have something to do with it.

Ripping into her saddlebag, three ammo boxes tumbled out and fell open, scattering bullets in the dirt. Launa hunted for a place to short-sight her weapon. Jack and his family slid into the ravine on her right. Launa looked left.

Fifty meters up, the arroyo made a hard turn. The wall would be a good backdrop. She pulled back on the bolt, ready to reload the magazine. It was stuck solid.

That last shot had felt wrong; the recoil was hard. Come to think of it, one of the quick shots she'd snapped off had felt awful light, as if it only had half a load of powder. She studied the ammo boxes. The top one had an ink blot on it.

The woman at the store insisted Launa only needed one box of ammo. Then she'd made sure that box stayed on top. "Damn!"

"Okay, how do I clear a jam?" She cleared a few, and they'd all involved field stripping the rifle. "I don't have time."

Well, the sarge had made some snide remarks about dumb civies clearing their weapons. "Sorry, Sarge, I'm going to be dumb today . . . and fast."

Incoming was slacking off. They probably expected this. "Well, let's do something unexpected." Pulling her Bowie knife, she slipped the blade between the bolt lever and the stock. Gently, she levered the bolt up. For too long, nothing happened. Then, with a snap, the bolt swung up into the retract position—and stayed locked.

"Shit, shit, shit."

The sarge had nothing but scorn for rubes dumb enough to do what Launa did next. Holding the rifle muzzle too damn close to her head, she kicked at the bolt. Once, twice, three times. It moved a bit. She tried once more. It snapped open.

The cracked brass cartridge, however, still clung to the bolt. The Bowie only took a second to send it flying. Launa had a rifle back—and two of the five rounds she'd fired from the top box had been bad. She glared at the jumble of bullets at her feet. Five rounds were still in the box with the ink blot; she jammed them into the dirt wall of the wash. The two extra boxes she'd demanded had a dozen rounds still in them. She chambered one and distributed the rest around her pockets. Sighting in on a rock at the bottom of the gulch, she squeezed off a shot.

A plume of dirt exploded a foot to the left and three feet up the gully wall. "Damn."

Launa adjusted the scope as she moved left a couple of feet and poked her head up. Little shooting. Several of the hostiles were standing around, probably deciding what to do next. She better put some caution back in them. As she sighted in a bit to the right of someone's feet, the scope wiggled against her eye.

She fired without bothering to sight, then ducked just as bullets shredded the cactus above her head. Ignoring the salad sprinkles falling on her, Launa gave her weapon a good inspection. "God damn!"

The guard screw for the scope was loose. It only took two twists to prove what she'd expected; it was stripped. She gave the scope a good pull—it came off in her hand. "You bastard."

With a reloaded magazine, Launa used the iron sights to target the same rock and squeezed off a shot. "High and to the left, again." She snorted. It was time to move. Launa trotted down the gully. As she passed Jack, she dropped the canteen.

"I'll keep them down, Jack. You take care of Grandfather."

From the quick glance Launa got of Grandfather, she suspected that last rites was the only help for him. Jack said nothing.

Using her credit card as a screwdriver, Launa adjusted her sight. Since most of the fire was falling around her old spot, she took a moment for target analysis before announcing herself.

The rock outcropping shot up in two piles. Eight people, two to each side of each pile, were leisurely shooting the shit out of the dirt where she'd been. No, one of them was unarmed. Launa grabbed her scope to get a solid ID on that one. Yep, it was a woman—the woman who'd rented her the damn rifle.

Launa dearly wanted to put a bullet in that one, but she wasn't shooting. Shooters took priority. Launa swept the scope over the rocks. Yes. There was the big black who'd arranged their ride at the airport. He signaled to the others; from the pantomime, she figured he wanted to start an envelopment.

"That makes you in charge." Launa grinned as she traded scope for rifle. Not sure of her sights, she aimed low on the target. As her weapon recoiled against her shoulder, he went over backward.

"Yes!" Launa exulted. "We got one!" she shouted for her own celebration . . . and to let Jack know this was not a one-sided shoot anymore.

"Good going," Jack mumbled without looking up.

"This is a bloody mess." Mani's voice was high with shock. He struggled to staunch the bleeding from William's stomach with a handkerchief.

Winter Dawn glanced around for a first aid kit. There was none. She ripped at the hem of her dress.

Behind her, Ojah emptied his magazine in one long shriek. At the other rock, two alternated firing a few shots, then ducking back behind the rock. Winter Dawn suspected Ojah would die soon if he did not learn from them. The other youths gathered around her, staring blankly at William.

Folding the cloth from her dress, she knelt. Mani took her compress and tossed aside his sopping handkerchief. In only a moment, red bled through the brown cloth. "Someone check the jeeps for a medical kit," she snapped at the men standing around.

"It's not so bad," William laughed, and coughed up blood.

Winter Dawn knew he lied. She also knew that the weight of making their shared dream come true now fell to her. She stood.

"You," she pointed at one of the youths who had not moved, "get a first aid kit. The rest of you, back to the rock. You have guns. Use them. Do like the woman does. Shoot and duck. Always shoot from a new place. Be careful, but shoot."

"You told us her gun would break," Ojah whined, replacing his empty magazine with another.

"It will," Winter Dawn snapped. "Be careful until it does."

The others returned to the rocks. One of those from the other rock sprayed the area where they had last seen the woman fire. Bullets tore the brush and trees apart. Nothing could survive such a hail of death.

No shots answered. Maybe the bullet that was killing William was the last from the rifle. Winter Dawn prayed it was.

Return fire came to a screaming silence for a while, then started up again. But the scrub and cactus that got shredded were around her old position. Launa risked poking her head up.

"Yep, they're all looking in the wrong place," she whispered with glee as she picked out the guy to her left who'd moved out to flank her. The idiot stood as he sprayed her old position.

"Didn't you guys get any tactical training?" she asked no one in particular as she settled him in her sights. His weapon went one way, he another, as her bullet took him.

The firefight came to a roaring halt again as potential targets disappeared behind rocks. Launa glanced down the gully for a target to do a final check on. A rock twenty-five meters away looked good. She settled into a comfortable prone position, set the sights solidly on the middle of the rock, and squeezed.

The rock bounced into the air. "A bit low." Launa made the adjustment.

The second round shattered the rock.

"Right on." Jack congratulated her as he settled beside her.
Launa sat up. "How's Grandfather?"
"Bad. We need a med kit and a hospital, or we lose him."
Launa studied Jack, but the mask that was his face told her nothing. "You okay?"
"I cried for him fifteen years ago. I'll keep him alive if I can. If I don't, he got fifteen more years here than he did there." Jack waved his thumb in the direction of fire. "What we got?"
Launa moved a few paces down the gully, then risked a glance. "Eight hostiles about a hundred fifty meters out. Two of them may be wounded. Weapons are some kind of Uzi lookalike. I don't know what the caliber is."
"Seven or eight millimeter from the hole they make." Jack almost managed to strip the judgment of any emotion, but he choked on the last word.
"They shoot from the hip, spray their targets." Launa continued the evaluation, keeping her voice coldly professional. "They also spend too much time standing up. Or at least they did. I think they've learned their lesson."
"Too bad."
Launa agreed with that. Still no movement; she kept her head up. Jack joined her. "By the way, something's wrong with my ammo. Probably just the first box that nice grandmother insisted we take. Had two bad rounds out of the first five. Discarded five more. I'm using a dozen I think I can trust, but somewhere in the last fifty rounds are fifteen bad ones."
Jack scowled as he glanced over the rim. "Grandfather's horse is down. He had an old 5-mm rifle and a bow. I want them."
"No cover." Launa checked for paths to the down horse as well as keeping an eye on the rock pile.
"Enough concealment." Jack trotted down the gully to where a tall juniper shielded him from view of the outcropping. "Mind going back up the gully to cover me?"
Launa minded. She'd drawn their fire up that way and figured she'd have a few more safe shots down here before they spotted her. Going back into that hornets' nest of lead was the last thing she wanted to do. "No problem. I'll keep them focused up that way," she said as she turned away.

"Thanks," Jack whispered.

As he slipped over the lip of the gully and low crawled toward the tree, Launa hastened past Grandfather and his family to where tumbleweed gave her concealment. She steadied her rifle. The next round would go exactly where she wanted it.

Jack was halfway to his goal before anyone stuck his head up. Launa gave Jack a whistle; he froze behind thin cover.

Whoever the rubbernecker was, for half a minute he didn't give Launa more than part of his face for a target. Launa drifted farther to her right. She was just settling in when three more heads poked up and her target got more confident. He dashed from one rock outcropping to the other. Launa led him perfectly. Her bullet sent him down like a rag doll.

Three shooters sprayed her position, kicking up dirt and rocks, throwing splinters everywhere.

Launa wasn't there; she'd trotted fifty meters up the gulch. Her new position was the farthest out she'd taken and would keep their attention away from Jack. Her opposition was getting more careful; now they kept at least half their bodies behind rocks.

Launa spared only a second to get a sight picture on the gunman closest to her before snapping off a round. "That ought to get their attention."

It did. But she was already moving when they started shooting. Her target had gone down, probably not hit.

Twenty meters farther up the draw, Launa took a careful look-see. Jack first. He'd wiggled his way almost up to the trail. He eyed the horse carcass, glanced back her way, then went back to measuring the open ground between him and what he wanted.

Launa snapped off two rounds, then ducked just before her position swarmed with fire. She trotted twenty meters farther up the gully as she replaced the two spent rounds in her magazine, popped up again, and fired twice. Again she ducked down a moment before she would have died.

Knowing she was getting predictable, Launa ran another

twenty meters and popped up. She got off one unaimed shot before she was down and moving.

Good thing. One of the hostiles had predicted her; his first shot came damn close to putting a new part in her hair.

This time Launa raced thirty meters. She hardly had her head up before someone was walking fire from where she would have been if she'd only run twenty meters. She dropped without firing.

"Jack, you better hurry," she growled as she started trotting at a stoop toward where she'd left her ammunition. When the incoming fire started to slack, she popped up just long enough to fire once, then kept moving.

"I've about had enough of this game, Jack. I could use some help here." As if he were obeying orders, a single report came from down the gully. Incoming fire immediately swept in that direction.

Jack trotted around a bend in the dry wash, a rifle in one hand, bow and quiver in the other, saddlebags over his shoulder and a grin on his face.

"Yes," Launa whispered, hands checking her pockets for more ammunition. None—she'd used up the twelve good rounds.

"Now what do we do?" Launa growled as she and Jack knelt to plan their next move.

"Now what do we do?" Ojah whined as Mani dragged the last wounded youth to Winter Dawn. An obscene smear of red grew longer behind him. Winter Dawn could not tell where the blood came from. She knelt beside him and searched. A tiny hole above the ear showed where the bullet had entered; she rolled him over to see the other side of his head. There was no other side.

Shocked, Winter Dawn let the body roll back over. Trembling uncontrollably, she returned to William. "We will do what we must," she answered Ojah as she replaced the soaked bandage with another. This one did not redden so quickly. Maybe the aid was working. Or maybe William had nothing left to bleed.

"We must leave here!" Ojah pleaded, his eyes locked on the insects attracted by the moisture from the dead youth.

"No!" William started to pull himself up.

Mani rushed to his side and forced him back down. "You must stay down, or you'll bleed more."

"We must not leave, and I'll bleed until I die." William's voice was a rasping whisper.

Winter Dawn shuddered as breath left her slowly. William's belly wound bled again. The shoulder of the other youth was shattered—he would never use that arm again. And the third had a gaping hole where his head should have been.

This was not what she had come for.

She stood, let her gaze sweep over the rock piles. Only two boys still crouched among the stones. They would pop up at random intervals to fire a few shots, then duck down and crawl to another spot before risking their next shots. That was what the woman with the rifle did. The boys had learned from her. Three had paid a high price for those lessons.

What more did those two strangers know that they did not? What lesson would they teach Winter Dawn and the boys if she tried something else? Who would pay for it in blood?

"Enough," she said. "We will stay here through the day. In the darkness, we will slip away."

William opened his mouth—to argue with her, she suspected. Only a moan escaped him. He fainted.

"We will stay here," she repeated. The boys nodded.

"We got to get out of here." Jack snapped the barrel of his gun closed, a new round in it. Grandfather's gun was one of those crazy ones that loaded a single shot like a shotgun.

"You want to kill someone." Launa measured Jack carefully. She'd been around that bend. If Jack's blood lust was up, she'd have to cool him somehow. Unprofessionalism was a luxury they could not afford today.

A curt shake of Jack's head was her answer. "I told you, Grandfather needs help—and we need answers." Jack's glance blessed the strange family tableau, linked by shock and fear. "Uselessness and whiskey killed my other grandfather. Someone's trying to kill this one. We're damn sure not doing any good hunkered down here."

Launa risked a peek. A hand appeared just long enough to send some bullets in their general direction. She ducked; a stray round would kill her just as dead as an aimed one. She sat back against the wall of the wash, and noticed for the first time in a long time how cool it was in the shade.

"Okay, Jack, how do we do this?"

He stood just long enough to snap off an unaimed round, then settled to reload. Done, he wiped at the sweat running in riverlets down his face. She loaned him her neckerchief.

"Thanks." He used it, then offered it back.

"Keep it. Any suggestions?"

"Somehow we need to interest those folks in something other than shooting at us."

Despite herself, Launa grinned. Thus spoke the man she'd fought her way through hell with . . . and for. "Right. Any suggestions beside sending them an engraved invitation? They strike me as too preoccupied at the moment to read anything."

"Yeah." Jack stood—and flinched down at a short burst of fire. Just as quickly, his head was up again, studying the general lay of the land.

Launa joined him, offering the scope if he wanted more detail. They ducked as more unaimed bullets passed overhead. "They're just trying to keep our heads down," she concluded.

"And not being very creative about it. Guess it's time to teach them Ambush 101," Jack drawled.

Launa started going through her pile of ammunition. She tossed aside one round with a dented casing; another felt a tad light; a third was maybe heavier than the rest. She scowled. "No real way to tell what's bad."

"Yeah," Jack agreed as he strung the bow. Johnnie joined them. Beside Grandfather, Samuel keened a lament.

"What are you going to do?" Johnnie asked.

"Grandfather needs a hospital," Launa snapped. "First we got to convince those folks up there to quit shooting."

Johnnie flinched. "Hunting rifles against Guardian guns. It will not happen."

Launa grinned. "They're up against soldiers, Johnnie.

Hasn't anyone ever told you, guns don't kill people, soldiers kill people?"

The joke was lost on him.

Jack handed him Grandfather's rifle. "Can you handle this?"

Johnnie took a peek over the gully wall. "We usually get very close to the deer. I can shoot, but I won't hit anything."

"I don't want you to, Brother. Your soul's too gentle to have blood on it."

Johnnie glanced back at his father and grandfather. "I don't know."

Launa put a hand on his shoulder. "Trust us. We've been there. You *don't* want to go. Today has seen enough blood. Just keep their heads down and we'll take care of the rest."

Jack passed Johnnie a bandoleer with a half dozen rounds in it. "Shoot just enough to keep them down. I'll take the bow."

Launa stood just long enough to send a single reply to the latest burst. Back down, she leaned for a moment against the dirt wall, returning Jack's and Johnnie's determined stares. "I'll drop a ways down the line before I cross over. If they're not looking too closely, the sagebrush ought to hide me enough."

Time hung between them for a moment, Launa realizing with cold certainty that this strange borrowed world could kill Jack—or her—in the next few minutes. Jack opened his arms, and she charged into them. She wanted to hold him tight forever. She knew she risked cracking ribs. His return hug was just as tight. "Take care, friend," she heard whispered in her ear.

"You too, trooper," she answered, and broke from him.

He gave her a wink. She turned and did not look back—and stopped in her tracks. "Jack," she called to his back, "there may be a weapon lying around on your side of the rock pile. I took out its shooter when they tried to envelop us."

"I'll keep my eyes peeled," he called over his shoulder. He didn't miss a step.

TWELVE

WILLIAM DIED IN Winter Dawn's arms; he never regained consciousness. He had come to seize a book and remake the Changeable World. Instead, he had lost his life. Winter Dawn wondered what to do next.

Two were dead, one crippled, and they had nothing to show for the day. How could she kill the two strangers? She shook her head; every time they tried, they died. Should they run? Could they? She doubted it. Launa had shown what she could do with that long rifle. The noise of the jeep engines would draw her all-too-accurate bullets.

Why hasn't that Spirit-forgotten gun jammed! How often did the great white hunters return with their guns broken, bawling about missed trophies and careless Natives? Now she had made bad bullets and nothing happened. *How could the Spirit fail us?*

Winter Dawn choked down the phlegm that clogged her throat, blinked back the moisture welling in her eyes. The time for tears would come later. Now was the time to seize a world.

Gently she settled William's body in the dirt. Standing, she listened. Ojah still squatted, his eyes fixed on William. Mani and the other two boys moved among the rocks, occasionally firing bursts. A single rifle shot would answer them, but not always. It was as if they too were waiting for the dark to slip away, leave this place, and maybe, tomorrow, think of it no more. Leave the dead to the land.

Winter Dawn frowned. Something was different. What was it that evaded her, like a mouse dodging a hawk? In her mind, she twisted and turned, chasing after something. What?

Mani fired a long burst without looking. A lone bullet whistled over their heads in response. Is the woman getting tired? Usually she hit close enough to send rocks flying.

"That is not the rifle I rented her," Winter Dawn realized.

Mani stopped in his tracks, halfway to a new position. "What do you mean?"

"That gun is lighter. It shoots a smaller bullet. Walking Bear has a 5-mm rifle. That is the one that shoots at us!"

"Then where is the huntress?" Mani breathed the question.

"She comes for us!" Ojah screamed. In a moment, he was on his feet, running toward the jeeps.

"No, stay with us!" Winter Dawn shouted. "If they come for us, we can see them as they saw us. Now is our chance." Hope soared within her.

"I will bring him back." Mani slung his gun and trotted after Ojah.

Winter Dawn stooped to pick up Ojah's abandoned gun. With resolve and a grin, she pulled back the arming bolt. It gave a satisfying click as it chambered a bullet. "Let them come. Now we will be the ones waiting. Keep a sharp eye. They are out there for the killing," she shouted to the others.

"Come on Ojah, don't run," Mani called.

The whirling of a starter and the gunning of the engine as it caught was his answer. Tires squealed as Ojah popped the clutch and tore out.

Winter Dawn scowled. They could take their dreams in their own hands even without Ojah. They would do it, themselves, as the bold pair came to them.

A shot cracked out, then another. Metal squealed as the jeep smashed itself against unyielding earth and rock. Winter Dawn whirled to face where they'd left the jeeps, then dropped to make a smaller target. What was happening?

At the foot of the trail to the jeeps, Mani was frozen. "Holy Mother's Tit," he breathed. Then he snapped the stock of his gun into place, raised it, sighted and fired.

"God damn them all to hell!" Launa spat. She'd done such a great job. She'd gone over the top behind a juniper bush. She'd circled wide around the rock pile, never breaking cover. She was perfectly placed to make a smashing frontal attack on their rear.

And then this maniac comes charging down the trail to the jeeps, jumps in one, does a wheelie like it's the last day of school and takes out over the desert—straight at her.

Her first shot was aimed at a tire. It missed. The driver spotted her. They locked eyes. He accelerated at her.

Launa worked the bolt, then aimed between his eyes. Gently she squeezed off the round. His head exploded. The jeep hit a rock, flipped, and tore itself apart as it rolled over and over. The maniac was not belted in. His body flew out on the first roll. Steel and flesh followed the same trajectory, colliding again and again. Flesh went past recognition to tenderized meat.

"Damn," Launa breathed, her gut twisting. How high was the body count now, and still it didn't get any easier.

Movement drew her eye away from the settling wreck. A shooter stood at the foot of the trail to the other jeep. This one put up the shoulder stock. "Shit, now I get a smart one."

Launa pulled back on the bolt. It didn't move.

"No damn luck left at all."

She brought her rifle up to her shoulder, aimed at the guy. Maybe she could bluff him.

He aimed at her, and his finger twitched on the trigger. *No damn luck at all.* Launa tossed the dice one last time and prayed it wouldn't be snake eyes.

Mani stood in shock. He had watched William die. He had dragged Laslo in, knowing something was terribly wrong, too afraid to see why the joker was so quiet, what the bullet had done to silence him.

Now Mani stood frozen as the woman's bullet and the jeep tore Ojah apart, like a hawk rending an unlucky rabbit.

Mani wanted to run, to hide. What he did was lock eyes with the woman. They had come to take what they could not ask her to give. She had taken what no man should have to give—life.

Mani's magazine was almost empty; there was no way he could scatter bullets all over and have enough left to kill this woman. He snapped the shoulder stock in place and took aim. The woman worked the action of her rifle.

She aimed.

He fired three shots.

Her gun flew one way. Her body crumpled.

Crossing the fifty paces to where her body lay, he kept his gun at his shoulder, his sights dead on her. She didn't twitch.

Up close, he could see no blood. That was the way it had been with Laslo . . . until he moved him. Mani rolled her over.

There was a smile on the dead woman's face. Then her eyes opened. "I figured you'd do that."

Her legs kicked his own out from underneath him. The last six rounds in his gun arched into the sky, harming no one.

Launa grinned. Jack had warned the scouts after the first attack at the tree. She had warned her legions before the defense of Tall Oaks. "The dead aren't dead until you make them dead. Never turn your back on a body until its throat is cut."

She'd prayed these poor bastards were dumb enough to be trusting. This fellow was.

She took him down quickly, and just as quickly was atop him, Bowie knife at his throat. He went limp beneath her.

If he'd been a horseman, she'd have slit his throat right then and there to keep him out of mischief. Maybe the last guy's death had mellowed her. With her knife ready to change him from problem to meat, she felt around him until she found a full magazine. If these people were the amateurs she took them for, this dude might do more for her alive than dead.

She rolled off him without warning. The Bowie went to her teeth, her knife hand went for the gun, and her other hand popped out the empty magazine and slammed in the full. She was ready death before he'd blinked.

"Now, let's walk back to your friends with you in the lead. Anything I don't like happens, you die." She might have put more threat into her words if she hadn't been talking past a very big knife. Then again, the Bowie added its own emphasis.

He got up, very slowly, his eyes wide and on her. Launa moved around to get him between her and the rock pile. He walked, his body twisted around, his eyes still locked on hers.

"Look where you're going," she snapped, not so much out of concern for him . . . though if he fell she would hate to lose the cover he afforded. Mainly she wanted him looking away from her so she could risk some eyeball time on the rock pile.

Two shooters were in the rocks. These had been the fellows sending lead in her general direction for the last few years. The lack of shadows told her it probably had been a half hour. Standing beside two bodies and a groaning wounded was the woman from the store. Tiny as she had been, the gun in her hands added several feet to her stature. Launa figured her for the one in charge from the way the others threw furtive glances her way.

Launa's shield slowed. She nudged him. "Keep walking."

He did.

At the foot of the trail up the rock pile, Launa stopped. "Put down your guns," she ordered. "This is over."

The two youths in the rocks started to obey.

The old woman did not. "So long as this gun is in my hands, nothing is over."

Damn, Launa cursed. This little Apache lady and the horsemen outside Tall Oaks had few things in common. Not knowing when to call it quits *would* have to be one of them.

"You will die," Launa answered.

"Today is a good day to die. And if I do, I will lose little. But what will you lose, young woman who has traveled the years like an eagle glides the wind?"

Launa didn't let her gun waver—much. Just what did this woman know? "Unlike you, Grandmother, I have seen many die."

"I have seen many years, but little life. I will not miss it. But you have the power to mold worlds like a potter molds clay. No day is a good day for you to breathe your last."

Launa frowned. The old woman used the present tense when she spoke of changing worlds. Was this just a twist of language, or did it mean something? Before Launa could ask, movement on the far side of the rock pile drew her eyes.

Jack edged around the farthest rock—he had a gun. The shooter closest to him spotted Jack. He held his gun out at arms' length and settled it on the ground. At least one was smart.

"My consort, Jack, now has your back in his sights."

"I know, I heard him come. My finger is on the trigger. I may die first, but we will journey together to the spirit world."

Launa had had enough of killing for no reason. "If I must die, can you at least tell me why? What wrong have I done you? What will my death bring you?" *Maybe we can negotiate our way out of here, if we can figure out where* "here" *is. Kaul would be proud.*

The old woman seemed puzzled, but her gun never moved. Finally, she took a deep breath. "You carry a book on plants, printed in the mythical city of Philadelphia."

Now it was Launa's turn to be puzzled. "I do not have it with me but, yes, I treasure the book for the gift that it was."

"The book was found last week on the island of Crete. Few know of it, and those who do could make no sense of it. Until you appeared."

Now Launa's gun did waver. "My book is already here? You're sure it's not a copy?"

"How would a copy of your book find its way to a temple sealed six thousand years ago by an earthquake?"

Launa's world tumbled—again. *You'd think with all the*

experience I've had changing worlds, I'd be getting used to it by now. "Damn!" The muzzle of her gun sank toward the sand.

"I have a hard copy from the net," her shield offered.

Launa brought her gun back on guard. From his place, Jack shot her a thumbs-up. *What's that supposed to mean?* "Show me."

He drew a piece of paper from his pocket and unfolded it. Holding it between two fingers, delicately as if it were a bomb, he handed it to Launa. It took only a glance. "Yes, that's the title page." *The Pharmacology of Herbs,* 1902 A.D. stared from the page. "You've got it," she asked the grandmother.

"Yes," she hissed.

Launa knew time was critical for Grandfather, but her world was upside down and her knees were barely holding her up. "You—what's your name?" she asked her shield.

"Mani?" The young man pointed at himself.

"Mani, take three steps over that way and sit down. Keep your hands where I can see them." He did. "Now, I'm going to sit down too." Folding her legs underneath her, she collapsed.

Jack stepped out from the cover his rock afforded him. "If you two fellows put your guns down, you can move over to any shade you can find." The sun was passing from the zenith; the rock piles were beginning to cast narrow shadows.

With Mani out of the line of fire, the two young men seemed willing to make their separate peace. Guns were left behind as they sought shade. Fire lanes were down to three; Launa and Jack at the old woman, the woman at Launa.

Launa got back to business. "You seek my book, Grandmother, because something like it is here already. What would you do?"

"Burn it."

"Burn it? Why?"

"Do not treat me like a child," the old woman snapped. "I may not read books, but there are those among us who do. Your book is a 'paradox.'" She stumbled over the word. "If we destroy the one that you carry, this world cannot hold on to the one that is here. If we destroy the book, we destroy this world."

"You want to destroy the book and hurl everyone back into the darkness of First World." Launa hoped she remembered what Grandfather had told her of the Apache creation story. "You hope someone like First Man and Woman will lead you back to Changeable World, but a Changeable World where you make the changes."

"Yes," hissed the old woman with a grin.

"It may not be that simple, Grandmother." Jack joined the conversation. For a fleeting moment, the old woman glanced over her shoulder at him, but her gun stayed aimed at Launa. Launa did nothing; hope was beginning to bud in her that this confrontation could be settled with no more bloodshed.

The woman glared at Launa. "Do not toy with me. If I kill my grandmother as a child, my mother will never be born."

Launa started to nod agreement . . . she'd read the same story. Then her gut went cold with a remembered moment. "I don't have a mother or a grandmother in this world."

The woman's eyes went wide, her mouth dropped open, as if she saw a bird flying without wings.

"Right," Jack drawled, "everybody says, 'No grandma, no me.' Seems logical, but I spent some time with the mathematicians in my world before I got sent to God only knows where. They didn't see it that way. The number dreamers saw causality as something the philosophers dreamed up. When the math guys found numbers that allowed time travel, they saw nothing requiring causality. Philosophers got mad but the mathematicians just laughed."

"This cannot be so. Do not mock me," the old woman snapped, fingers tightening on the gun.

"What do your own eyes see?" Jack pleaded. "Two generations ago, Launa's family died out. Yet she walks this land, no mother behind her. I am the only son of Samuel Walking Bear. Yet I have hugged a brother, he the only son of the same father."

Confusion, anger, and a dozen other emotions fled across

Winter Dawn's face. Her gun went limp in her hands. She blinked hard, as if to squeeze away what she saw but could not believe. When she spoke, her words came slowly. "You have your roots in another world. It is dead. How could those roots sustain you?"

"I do not know," Jack said.

"But you have stepped through time. You would know."

"I ride time the way you ride a bus or airplane. You get on. You go where it takes you. You get off. I could not fly an airplane or tell you what the time transfer does. I just go. But tell me, Grandmother, why is it that you would kill and risk death just to bring this world down? What is so bad with it?"

And they were there. If it wouldn't have distracted the woman, Launa would have flashed Jack a thumbs-up.

Now the woman did whirl to face Jack. In the fraction of a second when her gun was pointing nowhere, Launa could—maybe—have put her down. She didn't. Launa wanted the answer to that question as much as she wanted her next breath. And while the woman answered Jack, her gun never aimed at him.

"You have eyes. You can see what they do to us!"

"We just got here. We haven't seen a lot," Jack led her on.

"My daughter would have lived if she had given birth in a hospital. She bled to death while the midwife could do nothing. My husband, kicked by a horse, lived on with a child's mind. A white woman's surgeons could have healed him. Instead he grew sick and died." The woman raised her empty hand to the sky. "For the white woman, we live our days as our mothers and grandmothers before us. We make clay pots the same as we did when they first came among us. They do not store food in them but decorate their houses. Are they as they were? Do they ride in boats of wood and cloth? No, now they fly through the air. They grow up, and keep us children."

THIRTEEN

JACK KNEW HE walked a bloody edge. This angry woman had found an evil to blame for her pain. Throwing her bitter words into the blistering desert air might heal her. Then again, she might start shooting.

Jack wouldn't have minded taking the risk if it was just himself. He was a soldier, and risk was part of the job. But not today. As much as he had been glad his world-remaking days were past, he was getting the itch to do it again . . . and Grandfather was bleeding to death.

It was time to throw the dice if he was going to change things. Launa had the old woman locked in her sights, but neither one of them wanted more blood today. Jack bet on human need. Putting his gun aside, he stood. "I imagine you're thirsty, Grandmother. I am. If you'll tell me where a canteen is, I'll get it for both of us."

The woman blinked several times in surprise, then pointed at the remaining jeep. Jack trotted downhill to find what he sought lying next to a first aid kit. Gritting his teeth, he picked up the canteen and brought it to the woman. He unstopped the canteen and offered it to her. Still clutching her gun like life itself, she took the gift of water. She drank, then handed it back. He drank, put the cork back in, and squatted down.

"Among the People we have come from, they have a way

of finding a path that all can walk. They bring everyone into their assembly and share what is in their hearts. Is that not done here?" How much of Lasa had survived six thousand years?

The woman snorted. "Yes, there are assemblies—for white women. My son, and many others, went to the assembly in Phoenix. The doors were locked. They shouted their words; the white women sent their Guardians. Guardians with guns like these." Now the weapon was raised to the sky, a shaken, angry fist at any god or goddess who would notice. Like an unheard prayer, the woman's gun fell to the ground . . . to be joined by tears.

"They answered his words with bullets. They killed him and dumped his body with all the others so no one would ever find them. He wanders, uncared for, hunting for the spirit world."

Jack had wondered where the automatic weapons came from. They didn't fit into a warless world. More pieces came together—Jack didn't much like the picture it showed.

But the woman was sobbing now. His upbringing urged Jack to console her; his experience of the last year gave off warnings. Would touching give comfort, or insult, or injury?

He risked words. "The grief you feel has run damp down my face. But, Grandmother, you cannot kill like those who put the ones you loved in their graves. Give me the gun. I promise you, I will change this world."

Jack spoke the words without thought. They came from his heart and were off his tongue before he knew it.

The woman looked up at him, the sun glistening in her tears. "How will you do this?"

Suddenly, Launa was beside them, gun slung. "I'm not sure, Grandmother, but we made this one and we can remake it."

Jack rose to his feet, hands out to accept the gun. "I swear, Grandmother, this world you live in is not the one that bore me. By the Spirit, Goddess or God who listens, I promise your grandchildren will not be born into this world."

The woman held out the gun. "I do not know how you can do what you say, but by the blood of those I love, I will hold you to your promise. If you break it, I will hunt you through any spirit world that I must."

As Jack took the gun, the tension left him in a long, slow sigh. "That's one less problem," he said, turning to Launa.

"Here comes the next one," she sighed under her breath.

Jack turned to follow her gaze. Over the saddle between the two rock piles raced Samuel. "Hurry, son, Father is dying." Then he came to a halt as he took in what he saw.

"You! Winter Dawn! You did this!"

"I and William." Her whisper echoed over the desert floor as her hand swept over the bodies at her feet.

"No!" Samuel drew his knife and dashed for the old woman. "Die! All of you, die!"

The woman stood her ground, waiting death. The two shooters flinched toward their guns, but Sam moved faster.

Jack stepped in front of Winter Dawn. "Halt," he said with the deadly cold the U.S. Army expected of its officers.

The shooters froze. Samuel's eyes grew wide as Jack pulled his knife. Samuel tried to stop. On weathered rock and pebbles, that was not easy. He went down on his butt, knife in hand.

He scowled at Jack. "What do you mean, stranger who calls me father? Do you care nothing for the one you call grandfather? These murderers deserve to die."

Jack shook his head. "Too many have died already today."

"No!" Samuel yelled, bolting for the nearest gun. A shooter leaped too, and would get there first. But what would he do?

Jack shouted, "Throw me the gun."

Beside Jack, the old woman shouted, "Yes, throw it." Obedient, the young man tossed the gun underhanded, arching it high into the air. Jack ran the few paces it took to catch it. He popped the magazine out and slammed the gun against a boulder. The barrel bent nicely.

Samuel collided with the unarmed shooter. The force of their collision kept them both up when otherwise they would have gone down on their own. Their eyes had grown wide as they watched Jack destroy the gun.

With a satisfied grin, Jack turned to Samuel. "Father, you never walked the warrior's path. Guns do not make a warrior. Today you saw what happened when these"—Jack bit back "fools" and settled for—"people made that mistake. With training, wisdom, and a single shot, Lieutenant O'Brian did what their rain of bullets could not. Please, Father, do not make the same mistake."

Samuel stared blankly back. At this distance, under the glaring sun, Jack could only guess at what went on behind the man's eyes. Finally, he sighed. "I am alive because of what you and the woman did. What would you have me do?"

Jack glanced around. He saw the wreckage of a rabbit snare that could not hold the cougar it caught. "Winter Dawn, is that med kit in the jeep full?"

"Yes, and I have more here."

"Can you drive the jeep?"

"Yes."

"Launa, can you police up this situation?"

"No problem, Captain."

"Do it. Samuel, come with me and Winter Dawn. And leave your knife where you sit."

The father obeyed the son.

Winter Dawn grabbed her medical supplies, gave a shoulder wound one last glance and rushed for the jeep. Launa tossed Jack her gun, then began collecting weapons. Samuel followed Winter Dawn. Jack trailed them, thumb on the safety, finger on the trigger.

"Could you kill your father?" Launa asked in the tongue of Tall Oaks.

"May my heart never taste that supper," he answered in the same language.

Jack took the back seat of the jeep, where he could keep an eye on both the folks in the front and make an inventory of the contents of the medical kit.

He quickly forgot the inventory.

Winter Dawn slammed the rig in gear and took off with the wild abandon of a teenager who thought himself immortal. Or of an old one who did not care to live any longer.

Samuel grabbed a handhold and shouted, "Go faster!"

Jack held on with both hands. The wild ride took a very long two minutes and left Jack wondering how he could so quickly forget some of the more dangerous aspects of modern life. Samuel pointed the way, and Winter Dawn drove where he pointed. They screeched to a stop only inches from the drop into the dry wash.

Jack grabbed the med kit and scrambled into the gully, shouting, "Hold on, Grandfather, we are here."

The old man opened his eyes. A tiny smile crossed his lips as he took in Samuel and Jack; then his eyes grew wide.

"It was you, Sister," he whispered as Winter Dawn settled beside him.

"Yes, wise one."

"Why?"

"The angry ones I walk with wanted what these two strangers hold. But I did not want anyone's blood to pay for its taking."

Grandfather's eyes closed. Jack searched for a pulse. It was weak and uneven. "We've got to get him to a hospital. Where's the nearest one?"

"The white women have a clinic in Safford," Samuel said.

"But they do not take Natives," Winter Dawn added.

Samuel nodded bleakly.

"Johnnie, get Launa. If she and that damn official credit card can't open doors, my gun will."

Johnnie was gone like a rabbit.

Grandfather's eyes opened. "And the guns? Why bring guns?"

Winter Dawn shrugged. "The white woman has guns and changes what she chooses. I wanted to do the same."

"But you did not," Grandfather answered.

"No. Maybe with someone else, but not with these two," she scowled.

"Samuel," Grandfather struggled to sit up. Jack grabbed one shoulder, Winter Dawn the other. First they tried to force him back down. He would not go. Then they supported him to face his son. "There is no wisdom in the mouth of a gun, my son. Do not search for it there. Promise me."

"Yes, Father. Though they wronged us, I will not wrong them in your name."

The old man smiled, and a sigh escaped him as he relaxed. Together, Jack and Winter Dawn let him down gently. The sigh did not stop, but went on. Jack breathed out with him, then held his breath, willing the old man to breathe again.

He did not.

Jack looked away, awash in helplessness, rage, and every emotion in between. He had mourned this man fifteen years ago. All through the fight, a rational fragment of him had assured him that losing him again would not be so bad. Still, somehow he hoped that he and Launa could keep breath in him.

They hadn't.

A killing rage swept Jack. He wanted to choke life from a throat, smash a skull to a pulp, hack a body to big pieces, then little pieces, then nothing. No horseman had raised this rage in him. The small, old woman beside him did.

"Go, old woman. Go while my promise echoes in my ears." Samuel's whisper was harsh.

"I go." Winter Dawn fled them. Launa appeared at the lip of the gulch; she helped the woman out.

"Give her your credit card." Jack bit the words out one at a time. "It may get her wounded into a white woman's clinic."

Launa sloughed off a half dozen weapons and quickly produced the card. "Tell them a white woman had an accident with a rented rifle she did not know how to use."

Winter Dawn gave a dry snort. "If you had not known how to use that rifle, there would have been no accident," but she took the card. A moment later the jeep roared away.

Johnnie tumbled into the draw, took in the scene, and began to weep softly. Jack wished tears would come for him, to wash away the feelings that tore at his gut, at his soul. He knelt, as dry-eyed as his father, and asked yet another question.

"Last night you spoke by the fire angry words for the way of the white woman. Today, from Winter Dawn, came the same anger."

"Yes." Samuel nodded. "And I might have been one of those among the rocks if I had been asked and you were not my son."

Jack shivered at how deep the hatred ran. "Father, I must know. If you could turn this world upside down, would you do it even if you did not know where the path would lead?"

Samuel found a stick and began drawing in the dirt. Mountains, rivers, Gan figures appeared. "A wise man once told me how it all came to be. I have heard no story of how it will end. That is not for my eyes to see. But maybe," he squinted at Jack, "maybe your eyes can see beyond my sight."

Jack sighed. The ways of the white woman were wrong; that everyone agreed on. They also were bent on his fixing it. Nobody seemed to have any good ideas on how.

Samuel turned to Johnnie. "There is a cleft in the rocks that will make a good grave. Let us go there." Jack and Johnnie picked Grandfather up by his shoulders; Samuel carried his feet. Together they began the long walk back to the rocks.

Carrying a slung weapon and his share of the funeral burden, Jack quickly regretted not dumping the gun. Launa followed, six guns once more on her shoulders. An idea began to form.

Samuel pointed his sons to a wide crack in the rocks, and they went. Jack remembered that snakes were taboo to the Apache. "Launa, would you clean out that hole? Watch out for rattlers."

"Right." She flashed him a smiling scowl. There might have been snakes there a few hours ago. The noise and shooting had sent them elsewhere. Smart snakes. Launa scraped dirt and rocks out, then stepped aside.

Samuel began a chant; Johnnie joined in. Jack stood, mouth closed. He could not understand a word they said. He did know what he wanted to bring to this grave. Jack stripped his gun, pocketed the firing pin, and slammed the barrel against the rock. Then he laid it in the tomb. Launa did likewise, but offered the barrel to Samuel to smash. He took it, and pounded it against the rocks again and again. It was twisted and bent when he put in the grave. Johnnie did the same to another gun. Jack put all his pent-up feelings into the next barrel. It was a long time before he laid it next to his grandfather. His hands hurt, but he felt better. In time, seven very nonserviceable weapons surrounded Grandfather.

Somewhere in the hammering, tears had come. While they flowed, father and two sons covered the body with rocks, stones, and dirt. Done, Samuel turned to Launa. "We will keep watch here for four days, to see that nothing disturbs the body while the soul finds its way to the spirit world. You may stay with us or go as you are led."

Jack was glad Launa's alien stature gave Samuel the chance to tell both of them what was expected. He also appreciated his father's giving them leave to stay or go. Jack wanted time to ask more about this world, to think, to talk things over with Launa.

"I would stay, and keep vigil with you," Launa said. Her eyes focused on something far past Samuel. "But I think our ride just came."

Jack followed her gaze. A bright red and yellow blimp was making its way toward them. Five hundred feet up, and quite a ways off, still, Jack could make out the large SAR on its nose.

"Search and Rescue," Jack muttered.

"I suspect the secret about my book is leaking big time."

Jack stole a moment as they waited for the blimp for a reality check with Launa. "I made a promise that's going to be a bitch to keep. You have any reservations?"

"I hate to condemn a world based on a two-day recon, but I would have made it if you hadn't. Any idea what we do next?"

"Persuade folks here to send us back down-time. You mind?"

"Thanks for asking," she sighed. "Running away from my troubles there sure seemed like a good idea a few days ago. Not anymore. Somehow we'll make a place for ourselves there. We have to."

"Right. By the way, forget what I said about causality."

"Isn't it true?"

"Maybe. I don't know. Do I look like a mathematician?" Jack shrugged. "From the looks of things, I'd say the powers that be have read that story about killing grandma. I sure as hell ain't going to argue causality with folks in such a hurry to get us back that they turned out the SAR."

They grinned, and began to wave.

FOURTEEN

JACK HUDDLED AGAINST the wall of the blimp's gondola, trying to make himself invisible. Or at least trying to look like that was what he wanted to be. He watched, studied, learned.

Launa was talking. She'd been talking nonstop since they'd been reeled aboard in a basket. As long as she talked, Judith couldn't ask questions. Jack approved of the strategy.

"You use these things for SAR rather than helicopters?"

"Helicopters?" Judith turned the question into a question.

"You know, airplanes, but no wings, just big propellers that whirl around on top of them."

"Yeah," the fellow who'd reeled them in grinned. No older than the kids who'd shot at them this morning, his black uniform had "Guardian" on the left shoulder patch, "SAR" on the right. Jack wondered what patches the Guardians who shot the old woman's kid had worn. Ignoring the distraction, Jack listened.

"We experimented with something like that a few years back. They were gas guzzlers. Blimps do the same job cheaper."

"You use hydrogen or helium?" Launa asked.

The kid's grin widened. It was fun talking shop with someone who understood the shop. "Both. Hydrogen core inside. Helium wrap to keep fire away. Haven't lost one in almost a century. These are good birds. Not fast like an airliner, but let's see you put a Boeing down there where you were."

Judith edged over to where Jack huddled. "How did your grandfather take it when you met him?"

"He's a special man." Jack kept the present tense. No bodies had been in evidence at the pickup site. "Like Kaul, down-time, he has a gift for accepting what he finds."

"He wasn't there when we picked you up."

"No, he'd gone on ahead of us. We were going to catch up later." Everyone dies.

"Did I see a dead horse?"

"Yeah. Would you believe, one of the packhorses got snakebit. While we were shuffling supplies, the others got loose. Sam and Johnnie'll chase them down. They don't want any help; too embarrassing." Jack grinned sheepishly. "Why'd you come?"

"Oh, a few interesting questions came up at Livermore." Judith avoided his eyes. "We thought you two might have some answers. I hope you don't mind us interrupting your vacation. We can bring you back in a few days. By the way, does Launa still have that book I saw when you were eating breakfast?"

"Yeah." Jack kept his face unchanged; it took an effort. "It's in her saddlebags." Launa had dashed back to get their gear. They'd left nothing behind.

Launa finished grilling the Guardian and turned to Judith. "I heard something I didn't understand last night. Samuel wanted to know how he died in our world before Jack was born. When Jack told him, Sam said it was like the 'Warriors from of old.' The Apache had warriors?"

Judith's discomfort was palpable. She fidgeted in her seat, glanced around the cabin. After securing the side hatch, the crewman had gone forward to the flight deck, leaving them alone. Judith put her head close to theirs. "Yes, before the Europeans came, many native tribes warred among themselves."

"I imagine you put a quick stop to that." Jack fed Judith a line to see if she'd take the bait.

She did. "Not at first. You see, the voyage was long and hazardous. Most Europeans were young daughters looking for a place of their own. The native Columbians had not touched the mineral wealth of the continent. Many mines were opened."

Jack hadn't noticed that Judith was given to passive voice. What was she covering up? "Who worked the mines?" he asked.

"Native dependents mostly. You have to understand," she rushed on, "many of the native customs were abhorrent to us: warfare, cannibalism, other things. Over here, Europeans were on their own with little central government." She ran out of steam. "Some things happened that we're not too proud of today."

"Native dependents?" Launa echoed the word into a question.

"Yes, the old dependency system had almost died out in Europe, but this new world seemed to need help adjusting to civilization. The natives were declared dependents of the government and anyone who agreed to care for them."

"Dependency system?" Again Launa echoed. "You say it was dying out. When did it start?"

"With Alexandra the Great. No." Judith stared out the window for a long minute, then grinned. "Right, of course. You two are from the Danube River basin. Now it all makes sense."

"I'm glad something does," Launa quipped. "This conversation doesn't."

"Oh, but it does. Where to start? Everyone knows that six thousand years ago the city-states of the Danube Valley held the Kurgans at bay long enough to force the raiders to look south and east for expansion. Now, we know why. But what was good luck for Europe was bad for Asia Minor. It ended up divided into warring kingdoms, with fresh waves of raiders sweeping in every five hundred years to add to the misery. About 800 B.C. they finally got united, and three hundred years later the Persian Empire was ready to hurl Asia's combined power against Europe. That was when Alexandra, Speaker for the Assemblies of Macedonia, persuaded the city-states from the Danube to Greece to unite and march against Persia. Ah, Alexandra the Great, the greatest Speaker ever to live."

Launa gave Jack a wink. This Judith, just like theirs in Wyoming, did love to lecture. Now, with her in full sail, they were finally getting information.

"Anyway, Alexandra defeated Darius III. There was little love lost between the people and their ruler, as you'd expect when they cannot share their wisdom in assembly. But adding that many assemblies to the People presented a problem, especially when they spoke for people who had never learned to speak for themselves. Alexandra died young, after the fighting was done but before the problems of ruling all those people were faced. Her successors were just not up to the task, I fear."

"Yeah, it's easier to win a war than figure out what to do with your victory," Launa said dryly before Jack could.

"You're probably right. We haven't had a lot of experience. In Asia, wise Europeans were invited to set up assemblies to govern the land. Those held as slaves by the Persians were given their freedom; some even came to Europe. They became tenant farmers, working the land, but growing no interest in speaking for themselves in assembly. Aristota said some people were just meant to be slaves. I disagree, but I can see how she made the mistake. It took two thousand years to absorb those poor souls. And as soon as we finished with them, Columbia came along."

Judith had given them a lot to chew on, most of which Jack didn't like. From the set of Launa's jaw, she didn't much either. "I imagine the Apache warriors didn't take kindly to being declared dependents of a mine owner," she said casually.

Judith sighed. "Yes, they resisted, which only made matters worse. What little oversight there was from Europe mainly saw the locals' point of view. The young women had a free hand, and many other tribes were only too willing to fight the Apache and take their land. It was long and painful."

The three fell silent for the rest of the flight. The blimp

settled down far from the main terminal near a waiting jet. Its interior could have held fifteen; they had it to themselves. In five minutes they were airborne, headed into the low sun.

Once the FASTEN SEAT BELT sign went off, Judith excused herself for the rest room. After listening to Judith, Jack was even more sure of his promise to Winter Dawn. He leaned close to Launa to verify she'd heard what he thought he had.

"I don't know what help these folks want, but I'm glad we can be of service," he said enthusiastically.

"They've built such a nice world. I hope we can give them a hand." Launa's grin had a downward twist along the edges.

Launa settled her head on his shoulder. He closed his eyes. It would be easier if they appeared asleep when Judith returned. His thoughts drifted.

Grandfather was dead, pummeled by bullets intended for Jack. Jack felt a survivor's guilt. True, on the Santa Carlotta Preserve grandfather had lived fifteen years longer than he had on the San Carlos Reservation. Still, it hurt.

But around that pain, a void was forming. He wanted to make this entire world disappear and feel nothing for it. Already he had cut any emotional strings to here. It was as if it was already gone. Jack knew there was danger in that. Danger that these people might become mere shadows for him to play with. These people were real, with pain and steel that could slash him if he wasn't careful.

And he might be wrong. A decision after a two-day recon might need to be revisited after four days.

He drifted into a sleep full of fire and shadows.

He awoke as they descended; it was dark outside. They didn't land at Santa Francesca, but some place closer to Livermore. Judith said nothing more about the book, but she was careful to make sure Launa kept track of her baggage.

After being gone one night, they were back in the dorm. Jack paused while Launa opened her door and checked to make sure the room was empty. About to leave, she closed the door.

Together they showered off the dust, sweat and blood of the day. There were cuts and abrasions to clean and care for.

Launa was careful to keep a towel wrapped around herself. Jack followed suit, unwilling to give the watchers a show.

Lights out, they lay in bed, Launa curled against his side. Jack could almost hear the thoughts spinning in her head. Their objective was clear—get down-time. They would have to use the local machine. How to get Livermore to send them? Jack wondered what the mathematicians here thought of causality.

An hour went by with no words spoken and sleep no closer. Launa slowly teased the hair on his chest, then the hair lower down. She got the reaction she always got from him.

"How do you want to do this?" he asked, wondering how his modest lover would handle making love on camera.

She threw the covers off and mounted him. His hands went to her breasts, caressing, squeezing, moving in rhythm to the pulse of her hips on his. She leaned forward, slowly drew herself up him, him out of her. He moaned with pleasure. She nibbled at his ear. "This is how we win," she whispered, and plunged herself down on him.

Again she leaned forward. He moaned louder, to cover her whisper . . . and because it felt too good to keep inside. "We do what *we* want."

Another plunge, another painfully pleasurable withdrawal. "We will never let them beat us." She rose above him, taking him deep. Throwing her head back, hair flying, she moaned and arched her back. Pinching one hard nipple, he searched lower with his other hand, making circles, then arrowing straight in. She exploded as he did.

Exhausted and spent, she collapsed on top of him. Sleep came much easier after that.

FIFTEEN

NEXT MORNING, LAUNA awoke with Jack beside her. She snuggled closer. Had she actually put on that show last night? Damn it, in Tall Oaks where she came from, that was a sacrament. If perverts put cameras in bedrooms, they were sick.

Of course, where she came from in Tall Oaks, Jack was Lasa's consort. If they were going back, she'd have to face that too. She rolled over on her back and stared at the ceiling. *How will Jack and I fit in down there?*

"Ready to face the day?" Jack asked.

Launa had no answer for her question and didn't expect one anytime soon. "Let's do it." She tossed the covers off and made a beeline for the bathroom. Today was a minor problem compared to the yesterdays ahead—if she could figure how to get there.

Jack was lolling in bed, reading Maria's book, when she finished her shower. "Good lord, there's a lot of stuff here. But how much of it can you trust, like this guy back in the 1700's who said aspen bark was a contraceptive. Is it?"

"Who knows?" She shrugged, hunting for some hidden meaning in Jack's words. More likely, he was just keeping an eye on the book. "I'll trust my implants. Take your shower; I'm starving."

By 0600 they were in the cafeteria; Launa carried the

book tucked under her elbow. Maria stood behind the steam tables. Her mouth dropped open when she saw them. "I thought you two . . . ah . . . had gone. You are back so soon?"

"Yes." Launa smiled as friendly as any tank commander with her target square in her sights. "Everyone was waiting for us. More than we ever would have expected."

Maria cringed.

"It was so hot," Jack added, "you could die of sunstroke."

"Or something," Launa muttered.

"I did not know. I am sorry." From the stricken look, Launa could almost believe it.

"It was an education." Jack grabbed pears and grapes.

"Yes, we gained a new appreciation for what it's like here." Maybe Maria hadn't known of the welcoming committee someone had laid on for them. Launa would give her the value of the doubt for now. "Could I have another bowl of your grains and nuts? I loved what you prepared for us."

Maria gulped. "You did?"

"Yes, it reminded me of home, and why I enjoyed it." Waiting for the cook to fetch the cereal, Launa tapped her fingers on the book. "Wonder why they brought us back?"

Jack collected milk and juice enough for the two of them and staked claim on the biggest table in the room. In Tall Oaks, the forthcoming meeting would be very well attended.

Launa raised an eyebrow as she joined him. "You think eight chairs will be enough?"

"We can pull tables together if we have to."

As it turned out, they didn't need to. As they finished their breakfast, Samantha led Judith and Lady Harrison into the cafeteria. Brent wandered in a moment later.

"You two are early risers." Samantha's voice was high-pitched enough to shatter glass and nerves. "I couldn't believe it when the night watch told me you were at breakfast. Cook, my usual." The Mexican woman was already busy preparing "the usual." Dry toast and half a melon arrived as the other two women returned with coffee cups. Brent, with milk and cereal, settled down at a table within hearing.

"How was the desert?" Samantha asked Launa.

"Hot and dusty as I remembered," Jack answered. "It was nice to see my family again."

"Oh, yes"—Samantha glanced at Jack—"it was your family. Good." She took a bite of toast. "Now, Launa," she said as she chewed, "you have a book with you. Is that it? May I see it?" Without pausing for an answer, Samantha reached for it.

Launa intercepted her. As she put her right hand on Samantha's, Launa rested her left elbow on the book. "Yes," she smiled innocently, "I have a book. Why?"

Samantha withdrew her hand. Surprise, and maybe rising anger, choked off the flow of Samantha's words.

Judith stepped into the silence. "There seems to be some confusion about it and another volume of the same name. May I glance at the title page?"

As Judith rose from her seat, she unfolded a piece of paper.

Samantha regained her voice. "Do you think it wise?"

Harrison rested a hand on Samantha's arm. "It *is* her book."

Samantha shut up.

Launa opened the book between her and Jack, careful to keep one hand on it at all times. Jack added a hand of his own.

Judith halted behind them and laid her sheet of paper down across from the title page. Like the copy Mani had shown her, this one and the book were a one-for-one match.

"They're the same book," Launa observed casually.

"Even got the same poorly inked 'e.'" Jack sounded amazed.

Judith glanced at the other women. "And the dark spots from impurities in the paper." Launa had intentionally kept silent about the most telling verification.

"We must tell her," Lady Harrison sighed.

"No! There is no need," Samantha shot back.

"The problem we face is big enough without making those who must solve it play blind girl's bluff in the dark." Lady Harrison scowled. "Judith, tell them the story of that copy."

Judith settled into the chair beside Launa. "Last week an archeologist opened a temple on Crete sealed by an earthquake six thousand years ago. In a cyst behind an altar we recovered several statues and other items that verify that date . . . and a book."

"A book," Launa and Jack said in unison.

"That's impossible," Jack finished.

"Can I see it?" Launa added.

"Unfortunately, no." Samantha took over the story. "It was assumed this was some sort of joke. The book is not included in the catalogue, and now no one can put their hands on the thing."

Launa suspected yesterday she'd met a few people who could. It was a good thing she and Jack had let the others go. Launa had no desire to make Samantha's problem any simpler.

"How could a copy of this book end up in Crete?" Jack was playing the complete airhead. "We were never outside the Danube basin."

"Well," Judith said slowly, "there has been significant trade between Europe and Egypt for many thousands of years."

"In our world," Launa said slowly, "Egypt was conquered several times by desert raiders and Asia Minor intruders."

"Not here. Their culture stretches back as far and as unbroken as Europe's."

Jack turned to Launa with a sunny grin. "I guess Kaul sailed down to Egypt and helped. That was nice of him."

"But they won't have this book!" Samantha cut Jack off, her voice rising to make the point if Jack and Launa couldn't.

"It won't do them any good, neither of 'em can read. And besides, they didn't get it all the way to Egypt anyway." Launa wondered how much longer Jack could play dumb.

"But the book has to be in Crete so we can find it!" Samantha shouted.

"Oh! I see," Jack mumbled, light dawning in his eyes. "You think this is the same book and you want it back there so you can find it."

"Right," Samantha and Harrison said in harmony.

"Men," Samantha snorted.

"Then I think you may want to hurry," Jack answered.

"We are," Samantha snapped. "I referred this directly to my friend, the Speaker for the Assembly of North Columbia. She scheduled an emergency meeting for next week. They will have to pass it along for discussion by superior Assemblies, but we should have a conclusion by early next year." Samantha was quite proud of herself.

"Next week could be too late," Jack frowned, apparently in pain as he tried to order his thoughts.

"What?" Launa managed not to join the other women. *Okay, Jack, let's see how you play this one.*

Jack scrubbed at his face with both hands. Samantha was about to come out of her seat. Harrison and Judith stared fixedly at him. Launa hardly breathed.

"When you debriefed us after we got here, didn't you say you caught Muffin a week ago?"

"Yes, Friday." Harrison provided the answer.

"That would be March . . ."

"Eighth," Samantha snapped.

"The day our Livermore sent Muffin as a test. Right, Launa?"

"Right," Launa agreed. She had no idea where he was headed, but whatever backup Jack wanted in this tale, he'd get from her.

"You caught us on Monday the eleventh, today's the fourteenth, and tomorrow is the fifteenth."

"So?" Samantha interrupted.

"So we were sent back at nine P.M. on the fifteenth." Jack had moved their jump up a week, but Launa nodded agreement to the lie.

"So!" Samantha was on a fast burn.

Jack ignored her and concentrated on Harrison. "Didn't you say you were doing high-energy experiments, twenty megawatts?"

"Right. With the extra power the wind generators provide, we can do some of the highest-powered experiments in the world." Harrison seemed hooked but just as in the dark as the rest about what Jack was getting at so terribly slowly.

But Launa did. "For us, that's pretty low stuff. We regularly got up into gigawatts and terawatts."

"That's impossible," Samantha snapped.

Launa shook her head. "Not with nuclear plants and major dams adding to all the coal plants. Don't you have any of them?"

"No," Harrison breathed.

"Didn't you say," Jack asked, "other labs did some of the same experiments, but Livermore's results were unique?"

"Kind of shoots the hell out of the scientific method," Launa chuckled dryly. No one laughed.

Harrison's eyes were closed. She rubbed at her temples. "You're saying your Livermore used massive amounts of energy. It slashed a hole in time. The power we've got is enough to break into that tear." Her eyes snapped open. She stared blankly at Launa. "What would happen if we didn't have that rip?"

"Good question," Launa whispered.

"Dare we find out?" Judith breathed.

"Great Goddess on a crutch, I need to make a phone call." Samantha bolted from the room.

"We've got until tomorrow evening," Jack called helpfully after her. Launa kicked him under the table. *You played dumb real good. Now don't push your luck.*

Harrison was on her feet too. "I better go check out the equipment. It was just an experiment. We never intended it for a critical operation." She hurried out.

Judith leaned back in her chair. "Looks like you two have a trip ahead of you."

"Not again," Jack moaned. "Isn't there anyone else to go?"

Launa kicked him again. Real hard.

SIXTEEN

JACK WONDERED IF Launa had ever heard the story of the tar baby and the briar patch. If they stayed long enough, he'd read it to her. For now, he turned to Judith. "Assuming we do go, is there anything else we should know about history?"

"Now that we know about you, the books will need rewriting. You'd probably get a laugh from some of the guesses about how the farmers stood off the horse raiders. Still, there're a few books you might find interesting. I'll get them." She headed for the door, stopping only long enough to snag Brent, who had finished eating . . . but had stayed to listen.

Jack watched them leave. Launa twisted in her seat. She and Maria stared hard at each other.

"Can I get you anything?" the old cook asked.

"I'd love a steak and baked potato dinner with all the trimmings, but I better watch my weight. I don't want to exceed the lift capacity of their machine."

"Potatoes would be nice," Jack mused. "Haven't had any since before we jumped."

"Potatoes are good for you." Maria's voice was soft. "You should have some." Then she went back to her work.

Jack twisted back to Launa. "How much of that new copper jewelry were you wearing?"

"Probably not enough." Launa paused, then added with a glance around, "I suspect Judith will want it for a museum."

"We'll have to replace the weight somehow. Maybe we can have that steak dinner."

Judith and Brent showed up a few minutes later, their arms full of books and journals. They turned the table into a study hall.

"Writing developed soon after your time," Brent pointed out. "Still, the concept of history didn't come for several thousand years. History got its start in the boastful royal archives of Asia Minor. Nobody will vouch for their accuracy."

"Strange, with so much documented history, you only began digging into the past in the last hundred years," Jack mused.

"Hon, it was like that in our China. Plenty of history and tradition no one saw a need to test," Launa said.

Judith's head popped out of a book she'd been searching. "Speaking of China, have you two been to the Yellow River basin?"

Both of them shook their heads.

"Oh." She sounded mildly disappointed. "A friend dug up an early iron smelter and forge. She's trying to date it. Nobody believed her first calculations. They were quite a ways back."

"It happens," Launa replied. "Before writing, it's easy to lose technology to a plague, famine or war. Inventions are made many times if they're trade secrets, handed down from father to son. It's easy to lose it. Tell me about Egypt."

So they spent the next hour on Egypt and the one after that dissecting ancient boat building and sailing. From the pictures Brent had, Jack swore anyone who sailed from the Danube to the Nile six thousand years ago had to be crazy . . . or damn lucky.

The morning was gone before they knew it. Lady Harrison joined them with a lunch tray. "Where's Samantha?" Judith asked.

"On a plane for New York. They've moved the emergency council meeting up to tonight. The World Assembly will meet tomorrow in Geneva. I just hope they can decide in time."

Judith and Brent winced. "Big decisions usually take quite a while for us," Judith explained for Launa and Jack.

"I think there may be a second problem." Lady Harrison put her soup spoon down. "Samantha told me she sees no reason to send a man back. Why not two women, one from our time?"

"So Samantha wants to make the trip." Launa chuckled.

"Dear Goddess, no." Judith shook her head. "She thinks carrying her own briefcase is roughing it. She'd never go. But that will complicate the decision. Not only do we send someone back, but who? They'll never decide by tomorrow night."

Silence fell over the table. The background of normal lunch-hour conversation filled the vacuum.

"It's worse than that," Brent said softly.

Every head at the table turned to him.

"The book wasn't all they found in the crypt."

They waited as he rummaged in his belt pouch. He produced two pieces of paper. The first he laid on the table was an exact duplicate of the page from Launa's book. The second showed . . .

"My lieutenant's bar. What's it doing in Crete?"

"What is it?" Lady Harrison asked.

"That's my army rank insignia. Sentimental me, I took it when we time-jumped. Those sharp spikes on the back pin it to your collar. I left it in Tall Oaks." She shot Jack a quick glance, and he saw the opening to pin down his ticket home. If he could keep his face straight through another lie.

"It's not in Tall Oaks any more, or it wasn't, or whatever . . ." Jack fumbled with words like any dumb male in this world. "There was a war coming when I left, and I didn't want something like that just lying around. I buried it in the woods."

"Where?" Judith and Lady Harrison snapped.

Jack rubbed his eyes. "I *know* where. I can see it. I could go there, but I couldn't tell you." Innocently Jack turned to Brent. "Ever been in old-growth forest? It's all a jumble."

"Right." Brent agreed. Maybe a tad too quickly.

"How did you come by these?" Lady Harrison demanded, picking up Brent's papers.

Judith laid a supportive hand on Brent's. "I think I know."

If Brent was in trouble, he didn't show it. "The digger called me. These articles were thrown out, and the diggers with them. How did Samantha come by her copy?"

"She said something about thanking the Goddess the underground was so easy to infiltrate," Lady Harrison whispered.

"Well, they didn't infiltrate enough," Jack said, hoping he wouldn't have to paint them a picture.

"The Assembly won't have that information," Judith groaned.

"We should send them the second sheet and tell them Jack buried it," Lady Harrison said, but doubt slowed her words.

"If we give the Assemblies all of this to chew on, they'll be talking until a month after the sun burns out," Brent scowled.

Neither of the women disagreed with him.

There was a long minute of silence before Lady Harrison spoke. Her words came slow, as if her tongue had a hard time forming them. "We may have to go on our own."

"Do you thing they'll let us?" Judith asked.

"I will schedule an experiment for tonight. If the lab is not sealed, be there at eleven."

"And if it is sealed?"

Lady Harrison glanced at Jack first, then Launa as she stood. "Maybe we will see what soldiers are good for."

Swallowing a scowl, Senior Guardian Technician Helga bet Turlough arrived fifteen minutes before the two o'clock shift change. Nan Miller was already standing beside the console, so she slipped into the chair. "Anything interesting?" she asked.

"Usual lunchroom chatter is wiping out any single conversation. The wild ones spent the morning with those history buffs going over stuff that would put you to sleep. Speaking of, if you want a fun break, look at what we picked up in O'Brian's room last night. Glad we had the new night camera in there. Wow. She could make a fortune renting out that stud."

Nan shouldn't think with her ass so often, Helga said to herself. She got down to business. "Who's on days?"

"Nobody."

"Nobody?"

"Mabel took off early for a doctor's appointment. Deb called in with a sick child day care won't take. Cyn's flight from Phoenix won't get in until five. You got the lab. Take good care of it." Nan grinned.

Helga glanced at the duty roster. "Sam's checked out, too?"

"Oh, yeah. Bossy is hotfooting it to New York. Check the red file if you want. There's something in it about a paradox, whatever that is, and stopping the end of the world. You know Sam. Everything she does is earth-shaking."

"I relieve you," Helga snapped to cut off Nan's rambling. There were ten minutes left in Nan's shift, but Helga wanted her gone. If Lady Samantha was involving New York, something career-enhancing was coming down.

First, Helga set station four to searching all of today's conversations for "paradox." To keep herself from boiling at the slow pace of a word search, she dug out the red file and read. The Alert Report was informative.

Helga hadn't wasted time in college reading science fiction, but the required list had several of the classics, including the silly one about shooting your own grandmother.

She sat up, her pulse quickening, and ordered console one to do a more refined search on "Samantha," "book," and "Launa." In a moment she was watching the early-morning meeting that must have sparked Samantha's sudden flurry of activity. Half listening, she searched the fax's background. An underground cell in Beijing yielded that bit of information. A dozen troublemakers were making a very nice offering to the Goddess in her Hag visage. She hoped they danced well at the end of the rope.

Console four finally peeped. It had located only fifteen

uses of "paradox," all by Samantha in a series of phone calls that were sealed to Helga's level of review.

This brought a frown. Certainly the rest of those at the breakfast meeting knew the import of their discussion. Yet neither Lady Harrison nor Lady Lee had used the word "paradox" in any of their conversations. As good citizens, they would leave this matter to those responsible. Still, neither of those two scholars had a reputation for political wisdom.

Helga ordered a replay of the lunch hour. Zooming in both video and audio, she concentrated on Harrison and Lee. She could make out nothing through the babble. She dismissed the idea of bringing in a lip-reader; the picture was too grainy.

She turned console four back to real time, but dedicated it to Lady Lee. Console one she dedicated to Lady Harrison. The others she set on normal scan, with a special halt for "paradox."

Lady Harrison was in her lab with Scholar Milo and several technicians. Nothing unusual there; lab rats were always in the lab. She ordered up Lady Harrison's schedule. As she reviewed it, an experiment appeared for eleven o'clock tonight.

Helga flash-messaged the scheduler. "Lady Harrison added a test tonight. Is that strange?"

The clerk looked up with a start. "No, Guardian. Uh, she canceled all her tests after the strange results three days ago, but this one was on her schedule then. She said she was ready to get back to work. Is there a problem, ma'am?"

"No, none at all." Helga cut the connection. "There might well be no problem at all," she muttered to herself. Then again, this test might be just what her career needed.

SEVENTEEN

JACK YAWNED. THIS stuff was dry as sand. Important, deadly important, but he needed a nap if he was to be ready for anything come eleven tonight. "Launa, why don't you and I take a siesta? These two can organize a lesson plan for the next lecture."

Judith looked a bit taken back, but Brent chuckled. "This must be mighty boring after the exciting life you've led."

"Take our word for it," Launa answered as she got up, "exciting is way overrated." That got a chuckle from everyone.

Launa left Jack at the door to her room; she made no effort to keep him. She knew as well as he that his Neolithic gear was in his room. Once inside, Jack did exactly what he said he would—set the alarm for two hours and lay down.

Helga scowled at the consoles. The wild man slept on his back and snored like a chain saw. The wild woman slept on her side. No snores, but no question she slept.

Back in the cafeteria, Lady Lee and Scholar Lynch argued the impact of the Nile culture on the Danube, or was it the other way around? Helga turned off that view, programmed the monitors on the two wild ones to alert her to motion, and turned to routine matters. Someone was writing graffiti on bathroom walls; Helga was going to get her. "Must not ignore the other children."

• • •

Jack awoke two minutes before the alarm would have gone off at four o'clock. He turned off the alarm, bounced out of bed, and headed for the shower. He set the water a tad hotter than normal and spent longer under it. This might be his last shower . . . either way he looked at it. He enjoyed it.

The bathroom mirror was fogged after he finished but he didn't plan on shaving. He'd left the bathroom door open. The mirror over the dresser was fogged. *Camera's got to be fogged up, too!* The air blower sped up, though he hadn't touched the controls. He slapped a kilt around his waist, pulled on a sweater and started cramming things he didn't want seen into places where they wouldn't be noticed.

Helga was fuming. She'd enjoyed the wild man's prance to the shower; Launa had been worth watching too. Showers weren't under observation—water problems and all that. Helga reset the monitors to motion detection and went about her business.

Helga was starting to wonder if something was wrong when both motion detectors beeped. "Bloody Womb," she cursed; both cameras were steamed up as badly as if they had been in a sauna. Her fingers flew over the keyboard as she went through the simple housekeeping routine. Launa first, then Jack.

Launa's camera cleared to show her pulling on her boots and jewelry. Jack's cleared just as he was going out the door.

Helga switched to a third camera to catch them both as they met in the hall.

Jack grinned as he glanced into Launa's room. "Don't you love long, hot showers?" Her mirrors were as moisture-streaked as his.

"Don't know how we got along without them." Launa gave him a quick inspection, as he did her. She was in a skirt and blouse. Her boots were from Tall Oaks, and he suspected her underwear was as old as his. She wore the new copper jewelry she'd picked up at Clifftown—gifts from Dob, whom she'd be going back to just as sure as Lasa was waiting for him. *We'll work this out someway.*

Launa gave him a nod; none of his sharp edges were visible, and neither were hers. *Good; let's go, girl.*

The first surprise Jack got that afternoon was seeing Maria behind the counter. "I'll get some coffee," Jack said as Launa headed for Judith and Brent.

Maria was refilling the various coffee jugs as Jack poured two cups. "Didn't expect to see you here this late."

"I was already home when they called me. The afternoon cook called in sick. I have tomorrow off so I do not mind working two shifts. And I have some fresh potatoes for you."

"Good." Jack smiled. *And who told the other cook to get sick and made sure you got the call back? Just how far does this underground reach? Has Maria's group learned about my promise to Winter Dawn? Will they trust me? And I thought I had problems down-time. Oh God, take me away.*

He smiled as he put Launa's coffee at her elbow. "Maria's got the afternoon shift and brought some of her homegrown potatoes just for us."

"Lord, I missed potatoes with my steak, but we were weight limited when we jumped and couldn't take everything."

Like hell, Jack thought. It wasn't weight, but the massive impact the potato had on Europe when it arrived that kept the first Judith from even thinking of potatoes in their cargo.

"Maybe Launa can donate her copper jewelry to a museum and take a few potatoes back for dinner," Brent offered casually.

Judith went pale enough for her face to match her hair. For a long minute she said nothing. "I'll think about that," she finally muttered. Then it was back to ancient Egypt. She and Brent had stumbled onto something about problems with camel herders raiding the towns of the upper Nile. The long spears used by the defending formations looked suspiciously like Launa's pikes.

"What happened to the camel raiders?" she asked.

"No one knows," Judith answered. "The climate changed, wiping out pastures. Like the Kurgans, they died attacking towns and fighting among themselves. Certainly, they had no more influence on Egypt than the Kurgans had on Europe."

Jack stroked his chin. "No place for them."

Judith shrugged. "If they'd lived, the villagers would have died. It was us or them. I'm glad we won."

Launa nodded. "In our world, the raiders won. Jack and I will have to make sure they don't. Now we know."

"And leave the book on Crete," Judith finished.

They all nodded for the camera.

Helga smiled. *Such good children.* Of course, she'd observed more than one band of conspirators that would have passed for paragons. She trusted no one.

However, as the hours lengthened, they gave her no reason to doubt the truthfulness of what she saw. They studied the ancient past in detail that made Helga glad she'd managed to get out of college with only the two required history courses. The wild ones got their steak dinners, though they left a lot on their plates. Probably too used to starvation rations.

Everything was so patently normal that Helga was rethinking her planned visit to Lady Harrison's eleven o'clock experiment. She glanced at the clock. Nine. One hour to shift change.

Lights and alarms started flashing as if the Goddess had forgotten them.

She mashed the hot line to maintenance. "We've lost video and audio in and around the cafeteria. What happened?"

"We've got our best man handling it," came a bored response. "When they remodeled the Motherless place, some Motherless idiot put the security gear on the same bus with the ovens. They start baking bread, the Hag gets an itch, and it all goes to the pit."

Helga hated women who couldn't talk without every other word being a curse. "It's never happened on my watch!"

"You must not have done many nights here, dearie. Day's fine; night comes, and the Hag shows us her backside. Been trying to get rewiring in the budget for the last two years. Do we get a dime? No! Got to reduce the deficit."

Helga ignored the rambling. If she had to do shifts, of course she did mornings—where the action was. "Shit," she mumbled, nibbling the cuticle of a manicured finger. "I want it fixed now!" she ordered, cutting the link, but not fast enough to avoid a sarcastic "Right away, my Lady's bloody underwear."

Helga glared at the red lights, and slammed code into the keyboard to cut them off. A quick check of her working cameras showed the lights in the cafeteria burning brightly. She wanted to hoof it over there, keep a personal eye on that bunch. Everything in her screamed that they were up to something. This latest only made her more sure.

However, the manual was definite. If some surveillance failed, observation would be maintained through the remaining cameras. She checked the duty roster; the lone guard at each of the gates could not be pulled off. At this hour, the campus was pretty empty . . . of security and people. "Maintenance isn't the only bloody department with a budget problem," she growled.

Leaning back, she checked the clock. Fifty-five minutes before the end of her shift. Relief *should* show up fifteen minutes early. Tonight's shift change brief would be only what she shouted on her way out the door.

Helga tapped her foot. Fifty-four minutes to go. *Maybe thirty-nine.*

Judith cut herself off in mid-sentence, silenced by the ring of the phone. Maria answered it, said "*Bueno,*" and quickly walked over to take the seat between Brent and Jack. "Does the Lady have a problem?" she asked Judith as she settled in.

"No, of course not." Judith seemed too startled by the turn of events to protest. Launa had the impression of a liberal suddenly compelled to live her talk.

Maria settled a sack gently on the table in front of her. "Here are the potatoes Launa asked for. The Guardians will see and hear nothing in this room for the next two hours. Now, we can speak the words of our hearts without fear."

"Two hours?" Jack echoed.

"It will take two hours to fix the electricity to their cameras. I will get a phone call before that happens."

"Guardian shifts change at ten," Brent added cautiously.

"Thanks," Launa said, wondering how and why Brent

came by that knowledge. "Let's assume some John Wayne type will stick her nose in sooner."

"John Wayne?" Brent and Judith asked together.

"Never mind." With both hands, Launa pushed her chair away from the table, adding distance between herself and them. Beside her, Jack did the same, pulling closer to her and apart from the world they now sat in judgment on. Since leaving West Point fifteen months ago, Launa had done many things she'd never dreamed of, but turning six thousand years of history into lost millennia was daunting even for her. She had no time to waste.

"Judith, why should Jack and I risk our lives to get this book to Crete and keep history moving in your channel?" She turned. "Maria, why should we make sure this book never gets to Crete?" Then she eyed Brent. "Where do you stand?"

"In the middle, like where I'm sitting. But no one should have to put up with what I've done to make it, a man in a woman's world."

"But look at what we've done!" Judith jumped in, urgency raising the pitch of her voice. "You said this world is so much better than your own. No wars, technology in harmony with the ecosystem, growth without war and pillage." She stood and held out a hand to Launa. "Yes, I know we're not perfect. Yes, we need to change. Lots of women are working for change. But it comes slowly. How else could we do it in harmony and peace?"

"It is easy to change slowly, in harmony and peace—when you do not pay the price," Maria snapped as she came to her feet. "My people pay for your harmony when they die young, or at the barrels of your Guardians' guns."

"But—" Judith interrupted.

"Sit down, Ladies." Brent put his hands on their elbows and pulled both down to match his words. They sat.

"Judith," he said without looking at her, "you're a wonderful lady. I've known you woman and girl for fifty years. But you have some bad habits from your upbringing. You won't win this one by doing all the talking. Launa, Jack, you've been here for three days. Are there any questions we can answer?"

Jack leaned forward in his seat. Launa leaned back, content to let the Speaker for the Bull do the hunting. She suspected he would leave the final decision to her.

"When did the Europeans first get involved with the western hemisphere?" Jack asked.

Brent glanced at the two women at his side. They seemed content to imitate Launa's silence. "Hard to say. A navigator here and there would make landfall. A few small colonies were even set up, but they never came to much. The date in the children's schoolbooks is 1492. Does that fit your needs?"

Jack nodded. "How many Natives were alive then? How many now?" The question was simple . . . and sharp as a knife edge.

"Give me a couple of minutes and I could find the exact numbers, but it's generally accepted that the native population is only about ten percent of what it was."

Launa eyed the women. Neither disputed the figure.

Jack whistled through his teeth. "Bad as our world."

"I told you we weren't proud of what happened here," Judith snapped. "Communications were primitive. Don't condemn a world for the blunders of a few five hundred years ago."

Launa waved her hand for silence. "What caused the die-off?"

"Disease, mainly," Brent replied.

"White women shared their plagues with us but would not share the cures for them," Maria snapped.

"We had immunity from, not cures for," Judith corrected.

"Again, the same as our world," Jack concluded. "Launa, mind if I take off in a new direction?"

"No." Launa relaxed into her chair. Part of her was ready to condemn these people. Another part was condemning herself. *Didn't we make any difference?*

"Judith told us Alexandra started a great merging of European and Asian culture. It's been twenty-five hundred years. Can you still see the fault lines?"

A bitter smile from Maria was the first response. Judith's face went blank. Brent rubbed his chin. "Son, in every hundred percent, there's going to be a top and a bottom ten percent."

"Yes, Brent, but is the game rigged?" Jack countered.

The old man sighed. "If I was an economist, I'd tell you community property is held in common. If I was a sociologist, I'd have to admit that most of those who got their hands on it early have held on tight and passed it down to their kids. No question, some girls get a head start."

"And if you are Turkish or Armenian or Bantu?" Maria's teeth clicked as she snapped them shut, biting off what might be a much longer list.

"Yes," Judith admitted, "there are two or three hundred cultural preserves scattered across Asia and Africa. But you can't condemn us for not holding everything perfectly in common. Every economy that tried that has failed. People make things grow when they can keep the fruits of their work."

"How many factory owners ever put in a day's work on the plant floor?" Brent snapped. "Oh yes, I know, woman's intellectual work produces more than a man's sweat." He ended in a tone of dripping sarcasm.

"Enough." Launa raised her hand. They were getting plenty of facts . . . and bickering over the significance of them. What she needed was a system. "Jack, you know any standards we can apply to an entire world?"

He shook his head slowly.

"You're not going to do what they want!" Now Maria was on her feet. "We are nothing to them, dirt under their feet. Unnoticed nothings. You can not let that go on."

"We can't," Jack agreed.

Brent rubbed his chin. "Some things are better than this world you've told us about. Some things aren't. How much do you gamble the good that you've got to get the better you want? You've got a tough call to make."

A door opened. Helga spun her chair. It was ten on the dot—and she'd bit off two nails. Helga didn't know the name of the junior watchstander. She didn't care.

As she bolted for the door she made her report. "Monitors are down in the cafeteria. I'm headed there. Be prepared for armed backup."

The watchstander's eyes were wide as Helga passed her.

Had she never had an alert—or was it the machine pistol slung at Helga's side? Helga wasted no time asking.

A door opened. Scholar Milo huffed into the cafeteria. He was a round man and, from the way he wheezed, not used to running.

"Come quickly. We've got the system up and ready. Lady Harrison wants you now."

"She said eleven. We need more time," Judith pleaded.

"The duty Guardian checked our schedule. She didn't seal the lab, but Lady Harrison doesn't want to take a chance."

Launa stood. Jack was already up.

"What will you do?" Judith and Maria demanded.

Jack raised one of his damn quizzical eyebrows. He *was* leaving the decision to her. *Damn you, man!*

Launa took a deep breath, and let the words tumble out from her heart. Even as she spoke one, she wasn't sure what the next word would be. "We will take the book with us. We will take back everything Maria and Judith have told us. We will lay it all before those who are fighting beside us. We will try to find a path that will be just as good for Maria and Brent's people as it is for you, Judith. Is that enough?"

"You promised us," Maria whispered.

"And we will keep that promise." Jack's words were as solid as a stone wall. Launa nodded.

"From six thousand years back, you think you can do that, son? Sounds kind of arrogant to me." Brent fixed them with sharp, unblinking eyes.

Launa met his stare. "We told you how different this world is from the one that sent us back in time. Don't you think we can change this one for the better now that we've seen it?"

Brent's gaze held steady as a hawk's for a moment longer. Then he blinked. "Yes, I trust you to try. It's an impossible burden, but you've carried it before, and I do believe that you're up to trying it again. Goddess go with you."

Launa turned to Judith. Waited. Breath came from the woman in a deep sigh. "Goddess go with you."

Now it was Maria's turn. The woman sat, hands in her lap, eyes fixed on the table. Launa waited.

Maria fingered the knife hidden in her sleeve. It was sharp. It had cut the toughest meats. It would kill Jack.

The strangers had backed their chairs way, but Maria could reach him in a lunge. Should she kill or wound him? Could she?

Her children laughed when she refused to listen at the dinner table to their talk of revolution. "You can't make an omelette without breaking a few eggs. They've got the power, Mom. They won't give it up without a fight," Thomas chided her.

When she'd taken the sharpest knife from the kitchen today, Anna had shaken her head. "Mama, you couldn't kill if the world depended on it."

She could show them.

But would she be right?

"Please come with me. Now!" Scholar Milo urged.

"Maria," Brent whispered.

These two said they had changed the world. Maria eyed the book. Would destroying it bring good or just throw everyone into the darkness? She looked Launa hard in the eyes. "You made a promise. May the Goddess go with you and help you keep it."

"Amen," Jack said.

"We will, Mother," Launa answered and bolted from her chair.

"Go out the back door of the kitchen," Maria said. "It is closer to the lab."

The two were off at a run, Launa with the book, Jack with the sack of potatoes. Brent rested a hand on Maria's shoulder. "You did right," he said, then hastened after Judith. Milo huffed along behind them.

The slamming of the door behind them echoed through the empty cafeteria. Maria took in a deep breath, then let it out slowly. She had not killed, even when her world hung in the balance. Had she judged right—or was she just unable to use the knife? She would never know.

The door opened behind her.

"Where are they?" came a loud, demanding voice.

Maria turned. A Guardian, her gun slung menacingly, swaggered toward her.

Maria stood, arms folded, a smile on her face, just as a good Native should when meeting one who protected her from harm.

"They are not here. Did you know that one of them had a book they said I had written in?" She rambled on, throwing words out that meant nothing even as her lowered eyes measured the rapidly closing distance. The knife rested heavily inside her sleeve.

"Where have they gone?"

"To bed, I think. They have been here all day, talking, talking, talking. How can someone say so many words about things that happened so long ago that not even the oldest grandmother remembers them?"

"They haven't gone to bed, old fool. Their room would show them, or I'd have passed them just now," the Guardian growled.

Just a few feet more. Maria risked taking a step toward her. "They left their books here. Lady Judith told me to look after them and lock up well. They would be back in the morning."

Maria pulled the knife from her left sleeve as she swept that arm to point at the books. Then she lunged with her right.

Rage swept through Helga. The birds had flown, leaving behind this rambling magpie. Wouldn't the woman shut up and let Helga think?

Then she spotted the gleam of light on polished steel.

Those people were so dumb. Did they really think a trained Guardian would be as dumb as them? Helga sidestepped the knife slash with ease, then brought her left hand around to chop the old fool's neck as she went by. The fool was overextended and falling. The blow lost most of its power.

Helga kicked the knife from her hand, rolled her over and dropped, knees hard on the woman's chest. Air rushed out as ribs cracked. Left hand at her throat, right poised for a chop, Helga was ready to ask questions.

"Where are they?"

The woman stared wide-eyed, gasping for breath.

"Tell me where they are, or you die."

The woman spat at Helga, or at least tried to.

Helga chopped at her larynx, just as she'd been taught. She was rewarded with a loud pop. The woman beneath her redoubled her struggle for air, even as her crushed throat would let no more pass. "Point to me where they've gone, and you'll get medical treatment to save your life," Helga lied.

The woman smiled back. With her free right hand she made the Sign of the Star over forehead and breasts, then clasped her hands together in repose and prayer. Her chest still heaved in its involuntary struggle for air. The body beneath Helga convulsed, but the face she snarled at was at peace.

"Blood!" Helga stood and gave the woman a kick. "Where are those Goddess-forgotten pigs?"

The clock in the cafeteria showed 10:10. Harrison's experiment wouldn't be ready until eleven. *So she says.*

Helga took off for the lab at a run—and slid to a halt just outside the cafeteria's front doors. Light streamed from the windows of the lab. Security lights on poles made the park between the cafeteria and the lab bright as day. A blind woman could spot her even in her black uniform.

And buried in the Alert Reports was one from Phoenix. An underground cell may have tangled with those two and was now missing its leader and two others.

Helga grinned hungrily; this was no duck shoot like the old woman back there. What fame would be hers when she caught this bunch! And catch them she would. She'd memorized every nook and cranny of this campus. There were few places she did not know how to get to unseen. All she needed was a little time.

Jack made it to the research building a step ahead of Launa. He opened the door for her. Judith, Brent and Milo were trailing badly. Apparently, jogging hadn't caught on here; Jack shrugged and followed after Launa. The corridors of the research center rang with their footsteps. They headed down the hall for the one lab with an open door and light streaming from it.

"Where's Milo? I need his help," was Lady Harrison's greeting for them.

"He'll be along in a minute. Where do you want us?"

"Just a moment. I'm shortening the checklist as I go. I'm almost done. Stay out of the way."

Jack headed for the row of windows. A quick check of the park showed Milo just getting to the center's door.

"See anything?" Launa asked.

Jack took a moment to scan more thoroughly, then shook his head. "But there've got to be other approaches. Think we should lock down the doors?"

"Would that stop a Guardian?" Launa snorted as the other three hastened through the door. Milo headed straight for the console where Harrison was working. Brent closed and locked the door, then he and Judith made for Jack and Launa. The four of them met in the middle of the room.

"You are not taking potatoes with you, are you?" What started as a schoolmarm's rebuke from Judith ended as a plea.

"Why not?" Launa said.

"Because it would start a revolution in agriculture and a population explosion," Judith answered.

"Right," Brent drawled. "Folks wouldn't be wiped out by famine every three or four years. That would be a terrible thing to start fifty-five hundred years too soon, now wouldn't it?"

"But potatoes are indigenous to the western hemisphere. If they suddenly appear with no evolutionary record, what will people think?" Now Judith was grasping for straws.

"In our world, tobacco showed up as a temple incense in ancient India, two thousand years before it was imported from the Americas." Launa grinned. "Do you have that problem here?"

"Yep," Brent deadpanned. "Amazing how people manage to avoid answering questions they can't."

"But the potato hadn't even evolved in South Columbia six thousand years ago!" Judith shrieked.

"Sorry, Judith." Launa spoke to settle the matter. "This sack is going. You can have my jewelry. You can have my boots. You can even have my knife, but I want the options this gives me." Launa opened the sack. "Dear God, do I. Look!"

The four of them squeezed together over the mouth of the bag. There were a couple of dozen varieties of potatoes—red, green, brown, white. There were also several small envelopes.

"Corn, beans, squash, and handwritten instructions on how and when to plant them," Jack breathed reverently. "Maria doesn't do anything halfway."

"The green revolution in a sack." Brent grinned. "Old girl, you must not stand in the way of this."

"Don't you see the disaster this will be?" Judith pleaded.

"Yes, I do." Launa looked at Jack. He nodded. "This is more dangerous than an atom bomb, but it's got a lot more good in it. How soon can we go?" she called to the scientists.

"Almost there," Harrison answered. "You two get ready. I know exactly what weight the machine transported last time. There's a scale. Weigh in."

Launa handed Judith a copper bracelet. Jack had his sweater half over his head when the door was kicked in.

"Don't anybody move!"

EIGHTEEN

REAL FAST, JACK reran the rules on being a hostage. Rule One was get gone while the situation was new. Unfortunately, getting out of this room wouldn't accomplish anything—he needed out of this century.

Very slowly, he pulled the sweater back over his head and turned around, keeping his hands well away from his body. *Don't look dangerous, Bearman.*

Beside him, Launa did the same.

The opposition was one woman with a very familiar-looking machine pistol. He and Launa had beat seven of them yesterday, but not at this range.

"All of you, over to the windows," the Guardian ordered.

A glance was all the communication Jack needed from Launa. Cringing, he backed toward the windows. In the retrograde, he succeeded in putting Launa's body between himself and the gun barrel. The Guardian sneered at him, but her attention quickly went elsewhere.

Three of the four lab techs joined Launa and Jack, backing toward the windows. Tanya, Judith's daughter, hesitated for a moment until Launa took her by the elbow.

The two Ladies did not obey but drew themselves up to their full official height and descended on the Guardian. Milo and Brent, apparently caught either in some latent chivalry or a bad case of testosterone poisoning, followed the women.

Unsmart, bros, Jack thought, but he kept his mouth shut, like a good hostage who wants to live to tell his counselor how he came by this post-traumatic stress syndrome.

"What are you doing?" Harrison blew at full force. "This is my laboratory. I have a carefully timed experiment that must go forward so we can report tomorrow to the World Assembly of Elders on just what is happening here." She shook her finger at the Guardian. "You are endangering things you know nothing about."

"You might have a point." The Guardian swung her weapon, casually taking in the four. The Ladies' advance on her stopped. "That is, if only your lab rats were here. But why have this pair of dirt-sifters and the wild ones? What would an honest scientist need with these types so late at night, I ask myself."

That shut Harrison up. Judith tried next. "That wild woman has a book that must be returned to the past. You know how long it takes the Assembly to come to a unanimous vote. We have a very limited time to correct this problem. Why do you think Samantha flew out of here so suddenly?"

"Yes," Harrison added.

"So you were sending these two off?" the Guardian asked. She sounded fairly reasonable to Jack.

"Yes," the two Ladies answered.

"A wild man and woman with loyalties the People know nothing about. You fools! With a million loyal and sworn Guardians, you would let these two stampede you."

"What's the matter," Brent tossed out, "you want to go?"

The Guardian looked taken aback by that one. It took her a moment to answer. "I serve the People. I would do as I am told, unlike some overeducated fools."

"It's a dangerous world back then," Brent observed. "People died real soon and real easy."

She patted her gun. "I know how to stay alive."

Brent didn't quit. "And when your ammunition runs out?"

"You will bring me back before then."

Milo was shaking like a leaf, but he piped in on that one. "It's a one-way trip."

"You brought them back."

"That was an accident," Lady Harrison responded.

"Enough of this prattle. Up against the wall. The Elders will decide this tomorrow."

Not if I can help it, Jack decided now.

The Guardian waved her gun for emphasis. The group of four backed toward the other end of the wall, the women protesting, the men grumbling. The Guardian kept her eyes—and gun—on them.

Jack rested his left hand on Launa's back. She nodded. With his right hand he edged his hem up; the throwing knives were waiting. He timed the sweep of the Guardian's eyes and gun from one side of the four to the other. As she swung away from him, he tapped Launa's back: one, two, THREE.

Launa dropped and rolled. Jack got a quick knife off to distract the Guardian. He aimed for her throat—and missed.

"Damn!" Spinning away from the wall, he grabbed his second knife. Next time he faced his problem, she was turning toward him, gun coming back. He aimed for her chest.

Launa charged, shoulders down, Bowie knife coming out of her skirt. It was going to be close.

Brent lurched forward, slapping at the gun barrel.

The Guardian opened fire. Brent shook as bullets slammed into him. Judith screamed as one hit her.

Then Jack's knife took the Guardian full in the chest. She was still trying to bring the gun around, but the recoil drove the fire high.

Finally, Launa was there. Her left arm batted the gun up. Bullets shredded the ceiling. Her right hand drove the Bowie up under the Guardian's jaw. Jack heard a distinct *thunk* as knife met skull. If he looked real close, he might have been able to spot a bloody point sticking out of the hair of her head. He didn't.

Launa supported the Guardian as her arms and legs began to convulse; then she tossed knife and body aside. Her quick glance took in Harrison, Milo, and the rest of the team. "Okay. We've paid for this damn ticket, let's move."

They did.

Lady Harrison and Milo hastened to the console. The techs slowly busied themselves around the room. Tanya tried to stop the bleeding from her mother's shattered arm even as Judith cradled Brent's head. "Why did you do that, you wonderful old fool?"

"Because I was the only one who could." He grinned, then coughed up blood. "All my life I've dearly wanted to slug a Guardian."

For a moment Jack stood, looking down on the old scholar. The Army-trained lifesaver in him told him it was hopeless.

Brent looked up at Jack and Launa. "Don't waste time on me. Go. Make it different."

"We will," Jack promised. In one quick motion, he ditched his sweater and kilt. The boots may have been from Tall Oaks, but they were weight he didn't need. They came off.

"Catch," Launa called.

Jack caught the machine pistol and trotted to the door. He checked the hall while she shed clothes. She was down to the string bikini, winter solstice gift, before she quit. Clutching the sack of seeds, she stepped onto the scales. "Come on, Jack."

One last check. He fired a burst at the sound of leather on polished floors. Someone hit the floor. *Probably just smart.*

Safetying the weapon, he dashed to the scales, putting it down just as he joined Launa.

"You're a little over." Fear turned Milo's voice to a croak, but his hands flew over the keys. "Shed two ounces."

"A potato?" Jack asked.

"Your pants," she snapped as she stripped naked.

"You're ten grams under." Milo glanced up. "Oh." He took in Launa, turned beet red, and went back to his controls.

"Ready," Harrison said.

One of the technicians was gone—to the Guardians? Jack

grabbed the gun and sprinted to the door. Something moved down the hall. He fired an unaimed burst. Shots answered him.

"Where do I stand?" Launa asked behind him.

"You better crouch," Harrison advised.

Jack fired off bursts in both directions. Someone screamed.

"We're ready," Launa called.

Jack put the gun down and raced to where Launa knelt.

"We'll probably be hung for this tomorrow," Harrison said as she threw the switch.

"We'll make tomorrow different—better," Launa promised.

Jack put his arms around her. Then a pastel bubble surrounded them both. "I hope some idiot doesn't cut the power," he heard Launa mutter. After that, all he heard was a hum.

NINETEEN

AS LASA AND Sara watched the People of Tall Oaks drill, Taelon, who led the Badger People in the deep woods, approached.

"Wise Speaker for the Goddess," he began.

"Who wonders as much as you what tomorrow's sun will bring," she cut him off with a smile. The old hunter grinned back; in his years he too had come to know the silence of the Goddess. Beside her, Sara fidgeted, too young and full of the stories to be comfortable with the thought that those who Spoke to her for the infinite might be just as in the dark as she.

Taelon nodded. "One of our hunters met one of Glengish's hunters who now hunt the woods around River Bend. He spoke of a People becoming strange to each other. He did not know why."

Lasa knew why. "Did he speak of how the horsemen ride?"

"No, they hunt the woods between River Bend and Tall Oaks and leave the lands to the north and east to the horsemen, and those who hunt like horseman." He raised a questioning eyebrow.

Sara cringed beside Lasa. The Speaker sighed. "Jack told you that Antia hunted the horsemen and we must stand ready at our bows and spears for the horsemen to hunt us?"

"Yes, oh Lady, but when you hunt the wolf, it is wise to track it, learn where it hunts. I think my son Das and I should find a few of Glengish's hunters and track the horsemen for a while. As a young man, I rode among them. As an old man, I should be wise enough to ride close to them, but not too close."

Lasa raised her eyes to the sky. There was no light to guide her. She looked to the woods and the stream below Tall Oaks; no vision of the Goddess strode from the trees to point to the east, or to shake her head no. Lasa shivered at losing her old friend Taelon. Kaul and Launa had ridden to the west and not returned. Jack had ridden after them and not returned either. Others lay in the earth, dead beneath the horsemen's lances when they rode against Tall Oaks. Could she bear to lose Taelon?

A year ago she would have said no. But now she had heard Launa's wisdom. A soldier needs the eyes of an eagle to range far ahead of her, to see what comes and set the trap that would mean life for her People and death for the others. "Go with the Goddess, wise hunter, that we may find a path for our feet."

"Yes, wise Speaker." Taelon took off at a trot.

"Take many horses," she called after him, "that you may look like a horseman and come swiftly back to me."

"Thank you, oh Lady," he called over his shoulder.

Sara watched Taelon go. "I must return to River Bend."

"Ride fast but with wisdom. Antia has hunted the horsemen to their death. She may be ready to hunt one of the People."

Sara shrugged. "My eyes will be open, but I must bring Brege and Merik the song that Jack will want us all to dance."

Lasa watched them go, the old man and the young woman. "Oh, Kaul, hurry back to me, and bring Launa and Jack with you."

Kaul reined in his mount at the crest of the hill. The sun was not yet up, but the morning light was clear, the air crisp and good. Dob brought his horse to a halt beside him.

"Somewhere out there is a path to our tomorrow?" The young man who led the mounted archers of Clifftown struggled with words as he searched the plain before them.

"So Launa told me. Last year it brought them to us. Last evening a strange light where their horses now graze took them."

The young man shook his head. This from the man who saw so quickly the need for soldiers to stand against the horsemen and turned copper bracelets into knives even before he met Launa.

"What is so strange?" Kaul asked. "You and I ride horses. Our mothers never did. We cross rivers holding on to logs. Why does a log float and you or I sink?"

"I can swim."

"After your father or uncle taught you how. Is it strange that Launa knows a log that lets them swim the seasons?"

"That woman was strange enough."

Kaul chuckled. *That she was, but then these are strange times.* In the valley behind them, the aroma of food wafted toward them. Kaul did not glance back; he knew what he would see. The volunteers Dob had rallied from Clifftown mingled freely with the scouts from Tall Oaks. All were armed now with the red metal weapons Dob had led them in fashioning. Kaul did not know what had the strongest impact on Dob, the copper blade or the words Launa shared of how a soldier must look on land and enemies and use the one to destroy the other.

The handsome young man had impressed Launa with how quickly he learned, and maybe in other ways. When Kaul and Launa had turned toward Tall Oaks, Dob had followed, bringing many brave hunters on this journey to stand beside the People of Tall Oaks and River Bend. Launa called it a "concentration of forces." Kaul wondered if this was how a soldier chose her consort.

Kaul was glad for Launa, and should have been as glad for the help, but he felt none of the lightness in his heart as when hunters gathered to seek a troublesome pack of wolves or a dangerous bear. *We travel to kill horse people.*

All summer, Kaul had listened with Dob to Launa, learning in the songs of her wisdom how the People might hunt the horsemen who hunted them. But he had listened most intently when the soldier spoke of how you might bring fear to an enemy so they fled from the fight. That appealed to a hunter who had frightened away more wolves than he had ever killed.

Once a hunger had come upon him for words with the horsemen, words clear and full as those shared in the Council of the People that showed them the way of the Goddess. Somewhere there must be words, he told himself, that would open the horsemen's hearts to walk in peace with the People. He had tried.

The void between his legs itched and he scratched gently at his empty groin. His manhood had been the price for the words he shared in the council of the horsemen—and his place before the People and at Lasa's side. No one could Speak for the Bull who could not play with the Goddess and bring Her fruitfulness to She who Spoke Her Words.

Kaul kicked his mount to a trot. Into every life came rain. Some brought rich crops, other deadly floods. One accepted the gift the Goddess gave and walked whatever path spread out before you, as one accepted that Launa and Jack were gone. Their horses were too good to be left for wolves. They had kept their loyal vigil through the night. He and Dob would bring them back now.

Star and Windrider came when Kaul whistled them in. The big stallions danced nervously at the end of the halters as he turned them around and headed back.

"The air smells wrong," Dob said, and Kaul agreed. The softness of morning was gone. Each breath was sharp, as on the high plains before a dry lightning storm.

Kaul searched the sky. It was clear, not a single cloud. Now his own mount had caught the nervousness; it sidled sideways, then kicked. Kaul slid off before he was thrown off. Beside him, Dob was having the same problem. The young man was less experienced with horses. Kaul let go of his own horse and the two others and grabbed for Dob's, trying to soothe it. Dob tumbled off, and all four horses took off as a clap of thunder sent Kaul and Dob sprawling.

A moment later, the sun seemed to settle at their feet. Kaul felt heat. Dob started crawling away. Kaul followed. A noise like every bee in the forest followed them.

It was gone as quickly as it had started.

Kaul rolled over, as Dob did. Toward him strode Launa, naked as the Goddess. She held a sack in her hands. Jack followed her, naked too.

"You *are* the Goddess," Dob breathed.

TWENTY

LAUNA HAD EXPECTED problems. Livermore could blow them to atoms or drop them in the wrong place or time. Landing within a stone's throw of Kaul and Dob was too good to be true. *Maybe there is a Goddess watching over us.*

Then Dob decided *she* was the Goddess. *Oh shit.* "I am just a pilgrim, like you, walking the path of the Goddess."

"Who's come home for good," Jack added.

"Why are you on the ground?" she asked, handing Jack the seed sack and offering the two men a hand up.

"The lightning." Dob's voice shook. He backed off more.

"The log you swam in on," Kaul answered, taking her hand.

"Log?"

"The log you ride to swim across the seasons as if they were a river," he added.

"Oh, right, Jack and I have never been around when we arrive. Must have been quite a show, ah, dance?"

Kaul nodded. "It sent the horses running."

Launa turned back to Dob. "I am one of the People, like you." She had never liked the way some women demanded their husbands put them on pedestals. With Jack spoken for, Dob was her second choice . . . if he'd treat her like one of the girls.

"My ears hear your words, but my eyes saw the lightning."

"Your eyes saw nothing but the path that Jack and I

walked through the seasons, and will never walk again. Right, Jack?"

"Trust me, Dob, she's as much a woman as any woman, and can be more of a pain sometimes than all of them put together."

"Oh, Jack." She swatted him. He grinned as he took his licking. Kaul laughed, and even Dob got out a chuckle. Launa laughed too, and ended up in Jack's arms.

"I'll get our horses," Kaul said. "Dob, help me. They've misplaced their boots." Kaul sounded like he was willing to take as much time as she and Jack needed. And bless him, so did Dob.

"Wait until you see what we traded them for," Jack called after them.

"Enough, Jack. First things first. What about us?"

Jack kept smiling, but his hug softened. The poor combat veteran actually looked a tad scared. "We went from the frying pan into the fire and managed to hop back to the pan."

"No Jack, we went from where you and I could be together to this crazy, wonderful bunch of people. And this time, damn it, I'm going to enjoy it. Kaul told me he and Lasa expected us to make a few memories the last time we rode out together. All we did was fuss. Well, we've got a load of problems waiting for us at the end of this trip, and a whole lot of tough choices. In the meantime, I intend to make some very fine memories."

Jack smiled. "What you got in mind?"

Launa found there were advantages to negotiating with a naked man. She could feel his interest against her, and it was growing. She turned. "Good, Kaul's got his horse and ours are coming in." She crossed her arms and waited.

When Kaul brought Star to her, she leaped on, gave a good kick and took off. Jack wasn't far behind. Kaul ended up in charge of the potatoes and the book. At a comfortable trot, he and Dob quickly fell behind.

Launa kicked Star for more speed. He took off at a gallop with Windrider not far behind. Launa relished the wind whipping her hair, caressing her bare body. The horse throbbed beneath her. Jack chased. Good stuff of memories.

She reined Star in at the top of the hill. "God, that felt good. I've got to do it more often."

Jack pounded up, one hand on the reins, the other between his legs. "Now I know why horsemen wear britches," he snorted.

Launa let the sun warm her and the wind dry her sweat. She'd come through fire, blood and time to this moment. She had no idea what tomorrow held. She would settle for right now and grab what she could.

Kaul and Dob arrived. She turned Star and led them into camp. A year ago, she'd cringed at the nakedness of the hunters in their summer camp. Today, she rather enjoyed playing Lady Godiva. The effect was lost on most of the women and men in camp; they'd bathed together often enough. She and Jack were the center of attention only because the whispered word last night had been that they were gone. Now they were back.

Launa slid off Star. "Dob, I want us out of camp before the sun clears those trees." That should give her about a hour, though she suspected Dob could have broken camp in half the time. "Jack, you and I need a bath."

She headed for her pond knowing her orders would be obeyed. Without a pause, she waded straight in. Jack didn't miss a step. When the water was well above her knees, she dove. Jack was right behind her. She swam out to the waterfall and back. When she stood up, Jack was standing right beside her.

"You are going to wash me down with sand and then make mad passionate love to me as if your heart would break if you didn't," she ordered.

"Yes, ma'am, your Goddessship, sir," he said . . . giving her a palm-out British salute . . . with his left hand.

Then he splashed her.

She splashed back, but he could put more water in the air. She leaped on his head and forced him under. He grabbed her legs, launched himself off the bottom and sent her flying through the air in a somersault.

She landed on her back, dove and made an underwater

attack. Prying his legs out from under him, she sent him sprawling into the water on his back.

She leaped on him. He tried to push her away. She held on.

Somewhere in the next minute or so, she went from holding on to embracing Jack, and he went from pushing her away to caressing. Body and soul, they returned to the land and time where women and men played together. Once more, they were the Goddess and the Bull, laughing as one.

They were home.

TWENTY-ONE

FOR HOWEVER LONG they played, Jack forgot everything but her. When Launa stood up, wrung the water from her hair and said, "I guess it's time to soldier," he did not argue.

"Good memories." He smiled.

"Very good."

The sun wasn't over the trees when they rejoined the troops. Dob had them ready to ride. Kaul had scrounged up a breechcloth for Jack. Launa pulled on the leather skirt the hunters had given her a year ago. They were ready to ride.

Dob formed up his troop. What had Launa called it—here it was only yesterday—right: the First Cav of the Clifftown National Guard. They rode out in pairs, seventy strong.

Jack turned to Dob. "May I give you command of the ten who rode with me?"

"I would be proud to have riders from Tall Oaks among us." Dob was taken aback. Jack was glad to make him proud. As Speaker for the Bull, he had a right to a guard. As a man with a major campaign to plan, he wanted rid of administrative details. With that settled, he, Launa, Kaul, and Dob took station ahead of the troop.

"Where do we ride?" Dob asked.

Jack waited for Launa to answer. When she didn't, he did. "With Antia putting hatred in the heart of every horseman the sun shines on, we need all the help we can get. With

Hanna taking fight from the heart of every one of the People she can talk to, we have a problem. Let us ride to the nearest town that Launa visited and see what fear we can return to their hearts."

Launa shook her head. "After they listened to Kaul's songs, their hearts were afire with anger and fear of the horseman's lance. What words must Hanna speak?"

"We will see what is in their hearts when horsemen ride across their fields."

Launa glanced over her shoulder at the troopers that followed them. "Yes. We do look like a horseman raiding party."

"Enough to put fear in my heart when I saw you," Jack said.

"We ride to Laughing Waters." Dob pointed to the east.

They rode in silence for several minutes. Jack rolled over in his mind what they needed to talk about, searching for a place to start. The last three days tumbled through his mind like a ball of angry snakes, busy eating each other, but ready to bite him if he tried to grab a handhold.

Launa began. She chose the simple approach, telling their story from their arrival through to their jump back. It wasn't easy, putting their experience into the words of the People. Launa tried. A few times Kaul interrupted, asking questions to clarify. Poor Dob rode along shaking his head and muttering occasionally to himself, "Such a path, such a path only the Goddess could walk."

"So, Kaul," she finished, "we return to you with a promise made, but not the wisdom to know how to keep it."

Kaul rode on for a long moment. "This world was not the one that sent you. It was different. Better in some ways, and no better in others. Was it worse?"

"We were only there three days. I do not know what it would be like every day, but living under the Guardians is not a life I would choose," Jack answered.

Launa nodded.

"The women Winter Dawn and Maria wanted you to change their world by burning your 'book.'" Kaul stumbled over the English.

The sack of potatoes and seed was slung now across her saddle blanket, with the leather bag holding the book counterbalancing it. Launa handed the sack to Jack and opened the bag. "This is a book. It is full of words spoken by someone long ago and far away, but I can hear them, because they are 'written.' " She opened it to a page at random and began reading about a cure for coughs. "And this is the plant that does it." She held the book up so Kaul and Dob could see the picture.

"Lace of the valley," Dob breathed.

"We call it the Goddess's skirt, but yes, it does help those in the coughing time. That 'book' is full of such wisdom?"

Launa thumbed the pages; pictures and text flew by.

"Those decorations"—Kaul used the word for decorating pots—"speak to you and share all that wisdom." He shook his head. "We cannot burn it."

"Launa, I've got an idea," Jack said, slipping back to English. "We only saw the title page. If we burn it, that might be all we need to do."

Launa frowned. "You're the one who raised the question of causality. Even if we burned it, would that really do anything?"

"Do I look like the world's greatest living mathematician?"

"As a matter of fact, you probably are." Launa laughed.

Jack snorted. "This just gets more and more complicated."

"Not really." Launa closed the book; Kaul and Dob had waited patiently through their private conversation. "We have no wisdom of what to do with this book. We have seen the way the People walk from now until the seasons have changed more times than a woman can count. Let us walk each day with our eyes and hearts open to find a path with open hands, not hands that grasp for what is not ours."

"In the name of the Goddess, yes," Kaul said.

"Amen," Jack prayed. *So we're back in the dark and hunting for a way to light for ourselves and the next four hundred generations. What a job. Face it, Bearman, there three days and on the wrong end of a Guardian's gun twice. Sooner or later it would have caught up with you.* Here life was easy; all there was to worry about was the Horsemen . . . and Antia . . . and Hanna . . . and how Launa and Lasa and Dob and he were going to get along. Damn!

They rode in silence, each mulling her or his thoughts for the rest of the morning. The break for lunch was also quiet.

When they were mounted and riding again, Launa broke the silence. "Kaul, you once told me that Jack and I should make good memories to hold for when we are not together. He is consort to Lasa, yet this morning, we made memories. Have you made such memories?"

Jack gulped; that put it bluntly. Then again, they weren't in their twenty-first century, where you never talked about sex except to snicker. What were the rules here? They sure weren't going anywhere, and if Kaul wouldn't explain the rules, who would? *But did Launa have to do it in front of Dob?*

Kaul smiled. "At Lasa's side, I found little need for such memories, and now," he glanced down at his breechcloth, "all I have are memories. Oh, at festival time, the Bull played as he should, but festivals are only for a time. She who Speaks for the Goddess was always there," Kaul mused with contentment.

"Dob, your father Speaks for the Bull." Now Jack understood his inclusion. He waited for the young man to answer.

"And he plays most merrily during festival time, as does my mother." He grinned. "Many play with the Goddess and the Bull at festival time." He sobered. "But it seems to me that many who play the best are playing with one they know very well. Mother and father never play better than when they are with each other." With a sigh, he finished. "I hope that someday my heart will know how to play as powerfully and well as they do."

Ten, twelve years ago, as a teenage boy, Jack would have found this whole conversation deliciously exciting. But he wasn't a panting kid. He'd loved Sandie, Launa and Lasa with all his being—and, damn it, two of them were with him in a very confusing world. The idea that the only times he and Launa would have together might be at some festival when he'd be little more than a slab of beef, expected to perform for any and all takers, was not his idea of a great time. Strange how the perceived joy of being a sex object paled when you found it unavoidable.

Kaul interrupted his thoughts. "I think I know the question Launa does not know how to ask."

Jack certainly hoped so. He sure didn't.

"Lasa was only a slip of a woman when Bellda stepped aside and placed the heavy weight of Speaking the Words of the Goddess on her young shoulders. I think I loved Lasa from the first moment I realized there was a difference between boys and girls and why." The old man paused to smile at his memories.

"I was so sure she would call me to be her consort. Then she was called to Speak. Bellda Spoke for the Goddess with old Masin at her side to Speak for the Bull. He remained at Lasa's side, as it should be; a new Speaker needs an old Speaker to show her how the Goddess Speaks in the Assembly. But where did that leave me?" Kaul looked at them, his eyes wide in question.

"My heart was angry. I sought the darkest woods. I screamed at the Goddess to get Herself with child, that Lasa wanted me, not some old goat. I shouted many things I would not want anyone to hear. What I did not know was that my father feared for me and had followed. He heard every word, and when I was reduced to wordless tears he came and sat beside me. Oh, was I ashamed." Kaul shivered. "Even now I redden at the memory."

Jack had made a fool of himself a time or two. In his anger when Grandfather died, he'd screamed several things to the silent moon that he was glad he did not have to answer for.

"My father held me as I cried out my sorrow. He told me my pain was in his belly, and, looking into his eyes, I could see it was. Then he told me that Speakers for the Bull also stepped aside. In time, Lasa would choose one to stand at her side and Speak for the Bull. 'Do not play the fool. You are young and life is long. The seasons turn. What is seed today blooms with the next moon and feeds us at season's end. Wait, and see.' "

"Wise man, he," Dob agreed.

"Yes," Kaul said. "I returned to Tall Oaks, and the seasons turned, and Masin stepped aside, and Lasa called me." That ended the story, but Kaul wore an impish grin. No one spoke.

"You three I will tell, and only you three. The seasons between Lasa's calling and mine were not as empty as they might have seemed. The Speaker for the Goddess often gathers herbs in the forest, and a proud young hunter might come across her by chance. We had our quiet play. Masin says that Bomel has his eyes, but I know he wears my nose." Kaul grinned.

Bomel had been introduced to Launa and Jack as Lasa's firstborn, "gift of the Goddess when Masin Spoke for the Bull." But, come to think of it, Bomel did share the same proud Roman nose Kaul sported.

Launa was excited. "Then in time Lasa can step aside. Jack can chose his own Speaker for the Goddess, and you and Lasa can have a home with just the two of you."

That would be a good life for Lasa and Kaul; they deserved it. And it might settle things down a bit for Jack, too.

Kaul shook his head slowly. "These are strange times, and the People have called one Speaker from among the strangers. I do not know what they will do when the time is upon them, but I do not think they will agree that the Goddess would call two strangers to Speak for Her. I feel your sorrow, but I cannot tell you as my father told me that life is long enough to bring to you the desire of your heart."

He turned to look first at Launa, then at Jack. "Hold fast to memories, and make them when you can. I have Spoken for the Bull for many years, and I had the Sight that showed me what other men could not see, but I can see no way for you two to stand at each other's sides as consorts."

Stunned by Kaul's bluntness, Jack could find nothing to say. He glanced at Launa. Her face was blank, neutral of any emotion, nothing to hint at what went on behind the eyes that would not meet Jack's.

The four of them rode in silence the rest of the day. They halted the troop when the sun was low. Roving scouts had a pair of deer to add to the evening's stew.

Launa pitched her and Jack's bedrolls away from the others in the lee of a downed tree. The day's ride had left Jack's muscles aching almost as bad as his heart. Silently, Launa began a slow massage of his legs, butt and arms.

Relaxed almost to the point of sleep, Jack rolled over and gently forced Launa down on her stomach. Then he returned the favor, starting at her feet and slowly working his way up.

As his fingers worked her back, he glanced at Launa's face. Tears traced a path across her cheeks to fall onto the blanket beneath her. Jack gently kissed them away.

"It's not fair," Launa breathed. "It's just not fair."

"Yes," Jack agreed, not sure what he was agreeing with. He worked the muscles of her neck and collarbone.

"To have you and lose you, and then get you back every once in a while. What do they think you are, a library book?"

Jack swallowed a smile at Launa's analogy. He worked his way back down her spine. "I don't think I'll ever understand these people. The passion Lasa and Kaul have for each other. God, I saw how much it hurt Lasa to lose Kaul."

Launa rolled over. "But she's pregnant now."

Jack was glad Launa skipped who got her pregnant. "She did what was expected of her. For a thousand years these people have expected that from their Speakers. Lasa can't fail them."

Launa stroked Jack's face. "And I don't know what to expect. I know what I want. I want you coming home to me every night, to kiss away my tears and put me to bed like you did tonight." She fled into Jack's arms. He held her, not knowing what to do next.

"Well, I've got tonight," she said, wrapping her legs around him, "and I'll be damned if I'll waste it."

Their lovemaking was slow, as if Launa wanted it to go on forever. Jack followed her pace and ended up doing the multiplication tables to keep himself from ending ahead of her.

Satisfied, Launa wrapped Jack's arms around her and pulled him close to her back. After a long while, he felt her shiver.

"I don't know how we'll do it," she muttered, "but we'll make it all come together."

Jack didn't know either, but he prayed they'd find a way. He didn't want to admit it, and certainly he'd never want to hurt Lasa, but the idea of coming home every night to Launa, year after year, left a warm glow in his heart.

TWENTY-TWO

SHOKIN GREETED THE rising sun already at the gallop. As from of old, each Strong Arm made its summer camp a half day's easy ride from any other. If the herds ranged slowly around it, the grass would last until it was time to move south to winter camp. Thus it had been as long as anyone could remember. It could not be that way today.

The death bringer with the strange demon ways struck camps at night or just as the sun rose. So far the demon had not walked among the Stalwart Shields, but Shokin would not wait to see if his magic was too strong, or luck had just been with him.

He rode to gather all the Strong Arms into one camp. There a few warriors could watch through each night. The demons had swallowed small camps. The camp of a Clan might be too much for the demon to stomach.

Of course, they would have to move the camp often before the horses ate the ground around it bare of grass. And, other clans would wonder why the Stalwart Shield gathered as if to war.

A hand of days would be Shokin's. Then he must ride to the Mighty Man of the Clans' camp. Shokin would tell him why they all need make war on the farmers, before the Mighty Man called the Clans together and rode against the Stalwart Shield.

The farmers Shokin had rode among as a young man had

been generous to him. He had even shared blood with one hunter who rode among the horsemen for a season. Shokin wished them well. He wished his own Clan better.

Jack was awake before dawn the next morning. Launa was awake earlier, rousing the camp. Jack grabbed his spear and bow and started looking for trouble. What he got was P.T.

"We're getting soft riding horses. I saw you last night, hobbling around like sick old ladies. Out of your sacks, girls and boys. We've got a fight ahead of us and I'm not going to have horsemen laughing at you."

What followed was an hour-long workout that left Jack out of breath and sweating. At least it did the same for Launa. While the cooks warmed mush, the rest practiced hand-to-hand. They gulped down breakfast as they broke camp.

"Launa, if you're serious about getting ready for a fight, let's pick up the pace. I've got a bad case of get-home-itis."

She raised an eyebrow. "You thinking Antia, or Lasa?"

Oops. "I'm thinking about everyone in Tall Oaks and River Bend that I don't want to see dead."

Launa lifted her hand. "Cavalry, forward at the trot. Ho." They were back to trot, gallop, lead your horse, walk, then do it again. It ate up the ground. Hours later, Jack's backside probably wasn't the only one glad when they rounded a bend in the stream they were following and Launa called a halt.

Dob pointed. "Laughing Waters."

Jack scanned the ground. No hill here; tree-lined streams and open ground in between. The town nestled in a bend in the river that must have given it its name. Crops stretched away from the town, then open pastures with goats grazing and youths watching them. At the moment, both stared at the troop. In the fields, workers also stopped to gawk.

"Let's deploy the troop in a line, one deep," Launa ordered.

Dob stared blankly back at her. "A line?"

"Hon, did you forget to include horse drills in the training manual?" Jack asked innocently.

"Guess I did. I always thought of them more as dragoons than cavalry. Live and learn. Jack, you take the right side of the column out to the right. I'll take the left. Good thing we've got a couple of towns to practice on before Wood Village."

"Yes, ma'am." Jack saluted and trotted over to his half of the regiment. *We need sergeants,* he thought as he led them out. *We'd better correct that oversight tonight.*

The fields began to empty; kids tried to get the goats headed toward the trees. Goats, being goats, headed anywhere but where they were wanted. Jack warned his troops to avoid the small stuff, and keep their intervals open. This was not going to be a knee-to-knee Hollywood charge.

When he and Launa rejoined the command section, he offered some free advice. "I don't think we better let things get too unwound. Goats, kids, and horses won't mix well, and I don't think we'll win any allies by trampling their crops."

"Agreed, Jack. Dob and Kaul, will you go about halfway down to the end and be prepared to repeat my orders? And yes, Jack, tonight we appoint sergeants and squadron leaders."

"I didn't say anything."

"But you thought it loud enough."

Once Dob and Kaul were on station, Launa ordered the walk. The herders, their goats forgotten, scrambled to get off the troop's front. Riders passed most of the goats, and had avoided any major upsets before Launa ordered the trot. The last few farmers decided to get gone, trampling crops on their way.

They were five hundred meters away from town when Launa called a halt. Streets were deserted now. Movement on the right caught Jack's eye. A dozen or so folks with spears and bows had formed a rudimentary defense formation, a log house to their back.

Jack whistled at Dob and pointed. "See that bunch?"

"Yes?"

"Offer them horses if they will ride out with us today."

"Yes!"

Launa formed the troop back into a double column to fit them down the small road that led into town. As they rode among houses, Dob peeled off for recruit duty with several troopers leading remounts. Launa led the rest to the central plaza. As they reached the sanctuary, a pair of very shaken

Speakers for the Bull and Goddess tramped in from the other direction.

"I am Kaul of Tall Oaks, and I walked among you not two moons ago. Yet you fled from me today."

"We fled from all the horse riders," the Speaker for the Goddess snapped. "We did not know you were of the People."

"It is good you have learned to fear the horseman's lance, but no one runs faster then a horse. Horsemen would have galloped, putting their lances in your backs. Why have you not learned to stand like we did at Tall Oaks and put the horsemen in their graves?"

There was a lot of muttering in the crowd, but no answer until the Speaker for the Bull raised his hand for quiet. "Some of our people did walk after you toward Tall Oaks, but on the way they stayed a night at Woodtown and came back to us with more words to talk on, words different from the ones you shared."

"And now that you have faced hands and hands of horsemen who, by the blessing of the Goddess, were friends?"

"I do not see now as I did before," the man replied. "We will talk again."

"It is good to seek the wisdom of the Goddess in the Assembly," Launa said, "but horsemen come to Tall Oaks. We need six hands of women and men to come with us. Will any of you follow after us today?"

The Speaker for the Bull was nonplussed. "First you bring horsemen to show us what we need to stand against, and now you ask us to send people away who could stand with us?"

Jack tried to swallow a grin as he turned to Launa. "Guy's got a point."

"Damn," Launa breathed.

Kaul edged his mount closer to Launa's. "Trade him. Trade him wisdom for pike carriers."

"Right." Launa turned back to the Speaker. "Where to stand can be more important when the horsemen hunt you than how many stand. Rowa has traveled beside me for the summer. She has listened to my words and can sing them to you. I will leave Rowa with you if you will lend me the people I need."

Launa got her thirty volunteers. Jack detailed one of his escort with orders to quick-march them to Tall Oaks. "No visit to Wood Village. No talking to pilgrims from Hanna. You hear?"

He heard.

Dob showed up with ten newly mounted troopers. "There were more, but two were heavy with child. They and their consorts will stay behind. The words they have for the Assembly will set a fire under any cold heart."

That night they organized a cavalry regiment. Launa had departed Tall Oaks with extra remounts, a hundred horses all told. Ten had gone as gifts to towns she'd visited—gifts that hadn't bought much. Ten more were left at Clifftown. The rest now had riders. Quite a return.

Jack had brought out fifty remounts for his escort. He only had thirty spares now. By the time they hit Wood Village, he planned to have a soldier matched with every horse: twelve squads of ten in three squadrons of forty with a command squad of the four of them with six messengers.

"We'll show the horsemen how to use cavalry," Launa grinned, and drilled them as mounted cavalry until near sunset. Then horses had to be cared for and set to graze, and meals grabbed. Jack didn't care who his bedroll was next to, only that it was under him when he tumbled into it.

Shokin watched the sunset, but his eyes were on the dust cloud turned golden by the setting sun. He had ridden into this last camp when the sun was high. It took him only moments to speak the words that sent everyone scrambling to break camp and move the herd to where he had called the Clan together. One young warrior had held back.

"I have hunted with a warrior from one of the new Clans. I would take your words of warning to him."

"Would he ride under our totem?"

"I cannot speak for him. Can I bring him to you?"

"We will ride out tomorrow."

"I can ride for him now."

Shokin had nodded, and the boy had raced out with three spare horses. Before he was out of sight, he had already leaped from the first to another.

Whoever was riding toward Shokin now rode just as hard.

As the twilight deepened, Shokin waited. He could just make out the two riders that raced toward him. Their mounts and spares were flecked with sweat; they did not rein them in until the last moment. Yet stop they did, only two arm's lengths from Shokin.

"I am Mozyr, Strong Arm of the Sharp Claw band of the Swift Eagle Clan. I greet you, Mighty Man of the Stalwart Shield."

"I greet you too, and invite you to meat beside the fires of my Clan. Boys, come quickly and care for these proud horses." Shokin hardly raised his voice, but four lads were there to take the mounts from their riders.

"Care for them well," Mozyr said. "They galloped without complaint. Any Clan will be proud of the ponies these get."

Shokin studied the man as he walked toward the fire and food. The Strong Arm of the Sharp Claw band was little older than the youth who had ridden off to bring him. The wandering Clans had suffered hard times. Many an old or wounded one must have gone aside so that the band could flee quick before its enemies. The fire highlighted scars on the man's arms and shoulders. Although young, he was well tested in battle. Was he old enough to have the wisdom to know how to avoid it needlessly?

"Your warrior tells me tales of demons who stalk the night. I had thought them old wives' tales. I have ridden at night to escape those who would slaughter us. I saw no demon."

"Old wives' tales they might have been. They are not now." As they ate, Shokin told him what he had seen.

"You say farmers and wood runners could do such things to warriors?" Mozyr's voice was half disbelief, but only half.

"I have the jar with Arakk's head. If you had seen this Launa who named herself war leader, you would not doubt."

Mozyr wiped his hands on his arms. "I will bring these words to the Mighty Man of the Swift Eagle."

"Where does he camp?"

"To the west, on the other side of the river."

"Eeh, I promised this Launa that my clan would stay to the east of the river."

"There was only enough grass for one camp here. The

others had to go farther to the west or they might have grazed their horses on your pastures."

Shokin liked the delicate way Mozyr said that. He suspected that grass of the Stalwart Shield lands had helped make the horses strong who had carried this Strong Arm today. If the young man did not boast, he would look the other way. "You and the Swift Eagle Clan may ride with us, if you will follow our totem and let no blood feuds stand between us."

"Tomorrow, I will return to my band and send them to join your totem. I will also ride to our Mighty Man. If he follows my words, he will join you."

Shokin clasped the man's arms as a brother would. "Let us sleep on that."

Brege paced the sanctuary of the Goddess. Had Lasa, her mother, who had Spoken for the Goddess in Tall Oaks for many, many years, ever found the Goddess so silent?

Merik appeared at the doorway. "Antia rode forth this morning before dawn."

"Did many go with her?"

"Less than last time, and no one new went with her. I think that the whispers have reached everyone. Those who would ride with her, do. Others will not. And fewer follow after her."

"With fewer, maybe she will cause less trouble." Brege could hope.

"With fewer, she may not be able to get out of the trouble she causes." Merik was a good man to Speak for the Bull, but Brege would have liked him better if he was not so quick to point out what she would turn her back on for at least a while.

The sound of hoofbeats coming fast grew in the air. "Who would ride so fast into the middle of town? Children may be trampled," Brege snapped, preparing a stronger rebuke for whichever one of Antia's followers was so thoughtless of the People's harmony and safety.

"Sara returns." Merik disappeared from the doorway.

Brege slumped. Did her spirit, taut as a bowstring, now look for any to snap at? *No, just at Antia.* That was not the way of a Speaker for the Goddess.

Brege wished she could talk with her mother or father.

They saw deep into the Goddess and Spoke with Her power. Now she knew why one Speaker was always older. But the horsemen had killed both Speakers at River Bend. There was no one to stand beside her but Merik. "Dearest Goddess, turn your face to me."

Merik and Sara strode into the sanctuary. In a glance, Sara took in the women spinning, weaving, and caring for children. Her stare fixed for a moment on the corner where Soren worked leather; then she walked with Merik and Brege . . . in the opposite direction.

"The legions of Tall Oaks drill. Hanna has stopped up the ears of some who would come to fight beside us, but Jack has ridden to the west to find Launa and Kaul. When the legions are ready to march, they will come here."

"To do what?" Merik asked. And Brege realized that, though she wanted them here with her, she did not know what they could do. It was for the Speaker of each town to Speak the Words of the Goddess for each town.

"Jack will talk sense with Antia, with words or the stone tip of a spear—whichever she will listen to. He says Antia plays with the horsemen. That the horsemen are like a wolf that foams at the mouth. If we do not want to take sick and die, we should leave them alone."

"We do not know what the horsemen are doing. Our hunters refuse to hunt to the north and east." Merik's jaw trembled.

"Lasa will know. Old Taelon and his son Das now ride to see for themselves."

"It would be good to know what happens before us," Merik observed. Brege nodded slowly. Would it be so good to face what Antia did on the steppe when she rode away from River Bend? A shiver went down her . . . and her baby cried its hunger.

"I come, Little Mist." Here, at least, was one thing she knew how to do. She gave a breast for her babe to suckle.

Sara left Brege to mother, and made a beeline for Soren. "Where is Antia?" she demanded in a whisper.

"She rode out this morning, before dawn. To where and

what you know as much as I," he answered, but avoided her eyes.

"You did not ride with her today."

"Nor any day. She has no ears for the words I share among those who walk after her. She gallops for a mud hole full of poison snakes, and listens to no one." Soren shook his head as he finally met her eyes.

"And you have talked to no one of this."

"As many as you have talked to," he shot back.

"I have talked to Lasa and Jack. I will wait a day or two to see if Taelon brings a song of what the horsemen do. Then I ride back to Tall Oaks. Will you ride beside me?"

"Why not? We have plenty of horses. How can Merik ride among them, see the herds grow, and not know what Antia does?"

"And if he did, what would the Speakers do? I do not know. Can you tell them?" The young man was silent as they took her horses to be fed and cared for.

That was the rope that threatened to strangle the People, Sara thought. In years gone by, a woman or a man might be sent forth from the town, to live or die alone because they would not be called back from the strange path they walked. Never had so many searched for the Way of the Goddess and found so many paths—and been so confused as to which one to follow.

Taelon had ridden with the horsemen as a youth. This spring, he had guided his old friend Kaul for many days until they reached the horsemen's winter camp. And he had brought the poor man home . . . what was left of him.

Taelon knew how to ride the steppe as a horseman, and why it was foolish to do so. He also knew he had to. He and his son rode in captured horsemen helmets and leathers. In place of his spear, he carried a long, thin lance. His longbow he left behind . . . for appearance, and for what Launa called "security." The horsemen did not know the secret of the longbow and he would not let them have it, even at the cost of his life.

With two remounts, he and his son could easily pass.

For several days he rode the steppe, between the great

river with many mouths—Jack had called it the "Danube," a plain name for such a great river—and the next one that Launa had forbidden the horsemen to cross. He found several burned camps, its horsemen long since dead, and one camp that he easily avoided.

A second camp he came across as the sun sank low. Das and he made a smokeless camp in a nearby woods. Tomorrow, they would cross Launa's forbidden river into the lake country beyond.

The need to piss woke Taelon as dawn colored the sky. "Goddess," he muttered, "once I could sleep the night through and half the morning." Now he knew why so many old horsemen rose early; it was not to greet the sun. He stepped out of the trees that had hidden them.

As he made water, his eyes rested on the horsemen's camp, proud under the full moon.

Something moved around the camp.

"Das. Das, come quickly."

His son came; one hand rubbed sleep from his eyes, the other carried a bow and quiver. "Yes, Father."

"I see movement around the horsemen's camp. Can your young eyes see what it is?"

The youth squinted for a long moment. "It is too dark, I can make out nothing, but yes, something is moving."

"Get my bow, son."

"Yes, Father. Should I bring the horses?" Das asked as he hurried away.

"No," Taelon whispered after him. "We must not be seen."

Taelon knew what he was seeing. The horsemen had their foolish tale of things with long teeth who walked the night. No horsemen would make war before the sun rose, or after it set. No, this was Antia's doing.

As the sky lightened, he and Das jogged low through the grass, using every dip and roll in the ground as a hunter learned in youth. They were halfway to the camp when shouts and screams shattered the morning air. Taelon stuck his head above a rise and risked a long look.

"What do you see, Father?"

"Stay down. The killing is ending, tents are burning."

Taelon spotted Antia's cruel swagger. "Go back, get the horses. When it looks safe, bring them to me. I will try to get closer."

"Go with the Goddess, Father. Be careful," Das added.

"And you too, son."

Taelon used a shallow gully to get closer . . . and to hide when four riders galloped up with mounts for the rest. He risked another long look as they swung up on their horses. Yes, Antia was the first mounted. She shouted and others raced to do her bidding. While tents burned, the horses of the dead were sent racing to the south.

Taelon waited until the riders were gone before he trotted into the camp. Everyone was dead, hacked, slashed, stabbed—women, children and men. And what had been done to the men? Taelon had been enraged at what the horsemen cut from his friend Kaul. How would the horsemen take such treatment of their dead?

When Taelon heard hoofbeats, he walked from the camp to his son. He got to him well before he entered the camp. Swinging himself up on a horse, he said, "We ride for River Bend."

Das glanced at the camp. "Should I . . . ?"

"No son. You see they are all dead, man, woman and child."

"Yes, Father."

"You can tell River Bend that."

"Yes, Father."

"You do not need to see more. It will be bad enough for one of us to see this camp again in his dreams. Let the Goddess walk your dreams, not this."

Das gulped. "Visions of the battle at Tall Oaks still stalk my nights."

"These are worse."

"Father, a horseman is coming." Das pointed to the north.

"And he will not like what he sees. Let him not see us." They kicked their mounts and raced for River Bend.

Mozyr had brought the word to the Proud Beak band and spent a night with them. In the morning they moved off to join the Stalwart Shield, and he rode in search of his Mighty Man.

The camp had moved; he searched for it and slept a night

beside his horses. In the morning, black smoke rose in the distance. He urged his horse for speed.

He did not slow when he rode in sight of the smoldering camp. Two riders disappeared to the south, but he rode for the still smoking tents.

It was the Mighty Man's camp; the Clan's totem lay trampled in the dust. Everyone—men, sons, women, slaves—lay dead. Mozyr found the Mighty Man. He had died with a blade in his hands. His head was not taken. No! His manhood had been cut from him and stuffed in his mouth.

Mozyr fell to his knees; his scream sent war birds flapping from their feasts. This man had taught him to hunt, and to take the wisdom of the hunt to war, not just anger and fear. He had taught Mozyr when to fight and when to run, and how to run faster and wiser than those who chased them.

This man deserved pastures and grass, and to see the sons of his sons ride home victorious. Instead, he lay dead, attacked in the night, killed before he could pile high the bodies of his enemies around him.

Mozyr took the rest of the day to gather the dead, stacking them with still smoldering tent poles and any dry wood or grass he found. The funeral pyre did not burn well, but well enough to guide the souls it should to the feasting hall of the Sun.

By its light and the fading sun, he searched out where the horses had spent the night before. The demons had herded them to the south and west. Farmers were to the south and west. The next farmer Mozyr found would die. Not quick, but long and slow would be that one's death.

With the totem of the Swift Eagle in his hand, Mozyr kicked his horse to a run. He would join the Stalwart Shields. He would join many Clans and they would pile high the heads to revenge the befouled death of his Mighty Man.

TWENTY-THREE

LAUGHING WATERS SET the pattern. Launa loved the way that facing a cavalry charge changed people's perspective. By the fourth town, the troop could put on quite a ferocious show.

They were ready for Wood Village.

It had been built in a clearing beside a river that offered an easy float for logs to Tall Oaks. The clearing had grown as the woodsmen cut trees. Now farmland and pasture stretched over a kilometer to the trees.

Launa rode twenty meters into the clearing before she raised her arm and gave the order. "Regiment, form battle line."

The troop leader and his first sergeant leading the column held in place as the riders of First Troop formed, knee to knee, to their right and left. As soon as there was space, Second Troop trotted out to the right. The leader picked a spot to halt, then formed the troops to each side.

Launa frowned; he'd gone a bit too far. There was a five-meter gap between First and Second.

Meanwhile, Third Troop had deployed in similar fashion to the left. Their leader didn't go out quite far enough and three troopers couldn't fit in between First and Third. There was an exchange of scowls and words about the stranger habits of the Goddess; then one of them spotted the hole between First and Second. The three raced down the line and filled the gap.

"Good troops," Jack said.

"Very good troops," Launa agreed. Leading horse was nothing like tanks. She was having to reinvent horse drill and maneuver formations. But at least she knew what she needed.

She turned to face front. The deployment had been quick, but not unnoticed. People in the fields fled; no one stayed behind. In the streets, people ran every which way . . . most for the river.

"Listen up, soldiers. This time we charge straight across the pastures and the fields. No stopping until we reach town. If they don't like what we do to their crops, they can complain to Lasa." That brought a laugh from the ranks.

"Dob, these folks know us on sight, so you take the regiment in. I'd recommend a walk, trot and canter. It might be a bit hard stopping if we let the troop get to a gallop."

"Yes, ma'am." Dob saluted like the solid officer he was rapidly becoming.

Launa led Jack and Kaul through the line to the rear.

"Where'd Dob learn that?" Jack asked with a smirk.

"Not from those sloppy things you've been throwing my way," Launa growled, "but it felt good." And it had. The poised respect behind Dob's military honor made Launa feel like the commander she had to be. They got their horses turned around as Dob ordered the regiment forward at a walk. They followed.

From her station, riders blocked Launa's view of the town. As they broke into a canter, thing loosened up. Launa got her first good look of Wood Village. It was better organized than other towns she'd seen; the houses were all situated along a few main roads. Where the main avenue led into town, six people stood.

Launa aimed for them.

Fifty meters from the houses, Dob raised his right hand. Along the scattered line, troop leaders and sergeants did the same.

"Regiment," Dob called.

"Squadron," the leaders echoed.

"Halt," started with Dob and ended with the sergeants.

Most of the troops did. A few of the horses took it in their heads to bolt in several directions, dance sideways, or throw their riders.

"How *does* Hollywood do it?" Jack muttered beside her.

Launa would handle that later. Who were these people in front of her? Six women and men stood in the middle of the avenue, Hanna ahead of the rest. In her hands, she held out a shallow basket, full of fruit and vegetables. Her eyes were closed. Her lips moved in prayer. She waited for death.

"Ah, Hanna," Kaul spoke. "How are the crops, old girl?"

The woman opened her eyes. They grew wide. The basket tumbled from her hands as she fainted.

"Damn, that woman has guts." Launa shook her head. "It would be so much easier if she had run. But she do have the courage of her convictions."

"That she does, hon. Now what do we do?" Jack asked.

"You would have died," a new voice entered the discussion and got Launa's full attention. Masin stepped from the shadows of a log house and rested on his spear. Beside him, several others with bows and spears came forward, "if I had not decided that you did not look like horsemen, and if she," he pointed at Hanna, "had not threatened to talk to me day and night, unceasing for the rest of my life if I drew first blood. Several of you would now have arrows in you."

Kaul laughed. "Talk forever, old friend?" Then he sobered. "The horsemen come to Tall Oaks. We need every bow and spear."

"You killed them all last time."

"This time there will be more."

"And a bear needs a bear trap, as we both know." Masin tossed his spear to one of the others and stooped to pick up Hanna. "Pasture your horses, then come to our Assembly and supper tonight. Since you will ride out of here tomorrow, the People can only talk so long."

Beside Launa, Jack groaned. "Oh, no, not another Assembly with Hanna. And here, she Speaks for the Goddess."

"Well, Jack, it was our idea to come charging in here uninvited, and she did stand up to a cavalry charge."

"And fainted after it."

"Doesn't matter, Jack, she showed she would not run. Whatever her reason not to fight, we've got to respect her now."

The regiment quickly went through the administrative details. Less than a half hour later, Launa led Kaul, Jack, and Dob into town. A messenger came along to take their horses back.

The sanctuary was smaller. Launa dismounted and entered, preparing herself for a long-winded harangue from Hanna . . . and she'd have to take it. Hanna had not run like the other towns' Speakers. She'd stood as solid as any battle line. Here was one person whose refusal to fight did not come from any lack of guts.

On the east side of the sanctuary Hanna sat a simple stool on a raised platform. Beside her stood Masin. Around the room, women and men mingled in groups.

Startled, Launa turned to Kaul. "This is not like Tall Oaks. The women are not on one side of the Assembly, the men on the other."

Kaul shrugged. "A new town may chose a new path. I see Masin's heart in this."

Hanna stood, and conversation died. "You came here with lances and bows. You trampled our crops. You sent women and men fleeing in haste. Why did you do such a thing?"

Kaul stepped forward, but Masin was already speaking. "In your heart, Hanna, you can see the answer to your own question. I could not see what I would do when the horsemen came. You, none of us, could see what we would do. Now we have seen horsemen riding at us with lances leveled at our hearts. Now we have stood, or grabbed a spear and bow, or run. I thank Kaul."

"You would thank those who walk with blood on their hands! You would . . ."

Masin interrupted. "Hanna, these fine people have heard you speak these words in their Assembly. There is no need to repeat them today. Horsemen, real horsemen, ride at them with lances lowered. What will we do?"

Kaul nodded.

Hanna sat, a thoughtful look on her face. Launa eyed the woman. Hanna had always been so sure of herself, a quick, absolute answer for anything tumbling from her lips. Now, as the general babble rose in the Assembly, the woman stared into the middle distance and let the People talk among themselves.

As Launa remembered it, the population of Wood Village had a heavy concentration of the older folks from Tall Oaks who, like Hanna, would not kill another. Launa's first thought had been good riddance when they left. Now she wondered what she had helped to create. She stifled a laugh. She and Jack were creating lots of things they didn't much intend or understand.

"What do they do?" she asked Kaul.

He eyed the assembly. Several women and men circulated around the room, listening, talking, then moving on. "Many wise grandmothers and grandfathers came to Wood Village. I wondered how they would take to Hanna's ways. It seems they have woven their own and now fit Hanna into their basket. Let us see."

Time wore on. Launa stood silent as these people decided their own fate. After today's demonstration, any words would be weak. They waited.

The circulating elders now met in the center of the room to talk among themselves. Several others joined them, put their two cents in and stayed or left as they pleased. Finally, one woman stepped forward to face Hanna.

"We have shared our hearts, oh Speaker for the Goddess. Many of us ran today, and would tomorrow if the horsemen came. We will make shelters in the woods and put jars of grain there for the time horsemen come. Those of us who stood with you today will not stand with you tomorrow. We have seen death galloping toward us. Our hearts have changed."

Hanna used the pause to ask, "Your heart tells you the horsemen would not pause to speak in our Assembly?"

The grandmother turned to Launa's group. "The horsemen did not pause to speak to you at Tall Oaks."

Kaul nodded.

"The horsemen did not speak to anyone at River Bend."

Launa nodded.

The woman shook her head sadly as she turned back to Hanna. "They will not speak to us if they come to Woodtown."

Hanna nodded this time . . . and stood. "No one may tell another the path for her footsteps, but you, wise Tarnio, show the path that we will walk. Let us prepare hiding places in the woods for when the horsemen come. And I will search in my heart to see if I will go there with you, or stay. For," she turned to Launa, "you have shown my heart what it had not seen before. The anger is gone. But I do not know what I will grow in it. I will not choose death, but I do not know how to choose life."

Launa stepped forward. "My heart rejoices at the wisdom in your words. Tomorrow, the horsemen come for us, and we will fight them as we have. But when this battle is done, we would call all the Speakers and elders from many towns together. Somehow, with so many hearts together to light the land before us, we may find the way to choose life for all of us."

"You would call me there?" Hanna's eyes widened.

"We do not walk the same path today, and we may not tomorrow, but every path must be spoken for," Launa finished.

"Maybe that is how the People will walk tomorrow, not one path, but many paths, weaving a cloth that will cover all," Kaul muttered, half to himself.

Launa thought of the Assembly of North Columbia, protected by its Guardians' guns from the likes of Maria and Winter Dawn. Maybe Hanna or the grandmothers of Woodtown had stumbled onto something. *I'll be damned if I'll be so closed-minded as to ignore them.* "Anything is worth a try," she answered Kaul.

"Even listening to Hanna ad nauseam?" Jack seemed only half convinced.

"If we survive the coming fight, we'll have all winter. Why not? And if it changes Samantha and gives Maria and Winter Dawn a chance, I'd listen to Hanna forever." Launa glanced at the Speaker for Woodtown. "I think she's changed. We can too."

Jack rubbed his chin. "Yeah."

Masin cleared his throat. "Some of us did not run or take a sack of grain for the horsemen. These fine people need spears and bows to stand beside them. I will walk after them." Several women and men nodded, including quite a few who had run.

Hanna turned to Masin. Launa got ready to see how far the change had gone in the woman. "Jack gave us fine horses that have helped us lay in more crops than we will need this winter, even after what they trampled. Masin, I will miss your wise words, but walk as you must, and any who go with you may ride a horse of their choosing."

"Thank you, wise Lady. When do we leave, Kaul?"

"With the dawn," he answered.

Brege sat on the veranda of the sanctuary, letting the early autumn sun warm her as she suckled Little Mist. She tried to let the comfort of the moment wash through her. It did not.

Launa had spoken to Brege of the walls she wanted built. The wall going up facing the hills and fields was almost done. A second wall, inside River Bend, was also far along. Posts and planks between the houses along the two broad avenues would stop any horseman from galloping among them. *Yes, the walls are well built in River Bend. What of the walls in our hearts?*

River Bend was not one town, but four compounds, each within its own wall, joined only by the sanctuary and its plaza. And each compound was finding its own people. Antia and those who rode with her claimed the houses on the west side of town, close to the fields where their ever-growing herd of horses grazed.

Antia had ridden in when the sun was high. When she went forth, she led but one spare horse. Today, she rode brazenly through the center of town so all saw the hand of horses trailing her. Had the silent looks of the people said anything to Antia's heart? What did the swift glances her way tell Brege to do?

She knew it was time and past time to do something. She still did not know what that should be. As Antia swaggered back into town from caring for her horses, Cleo and others at her heels, the Speaker for the Goddess in River Bend handed her baby off to another mother and rose to meet them.

Merik came to stand beside her, a shepherd's crook in his hand. The Bull and the Goddess would speak as one.

The beat of horses' hoofs grew in her ears. Brege turned as Taelon and his son cantered into view.

"Where have you been, bold hunter?" Antia asked as they all met together before the sanctuary.

"Where you have been, sad child?" he answered.

Antia took a step back, studying the hunter through hard, chiseled eyes.

Brege took a deep breath, and took the step she know was off a cliff. "And where might that be, wise hunter?"

"Among the dead."

The square was rapidly filling. Some ran off, but they stopped to speak to others who hastened to the square, or went in search of others. The People gathered, even if they did not know for what. But even as they gathered, Antia's people did not mingle, but collected around her, their backs to their homes.

Antia shrugged. "Horsemen often die. Is it not their play to kill each other?" Her grin showed much teeth.

Taelon still sat his horse; he turned so all could see him. "You know me. I rode with the horsemen as a youth. I have seen horsemen kill horsemen. I have fought beside you to kill the horsemen who rode against Tall Oaks. You know me. Hear me."

Taelon slipped from his mount and tossed his reins to his son. "Animals do not belong where the People gather. Go, my son."

Das guided their mounts out the avenue. The hunter stood beside Brege. It should have felt comforting to have Merik at one side, Taelon at the other. Today she walked a path that had no comfort. Brege waited.

"Hear me," Taelon continued. "I have seen horsemen kill horsemen. The horsemen I found dead under yesterday's sunrise were not killed by horsemen. With these eyes I saw who killed them and followed the horses she stole. I followed you, Antia, from those you killed to where you stand."

People moved aside, opening a space between Antia and Brege. It seemed that some moved away from Antia. Others, those who rode with her, moved closer. As ripples on the surface of a pond, the People moved.

"Yes, I kill horsemen," Antia snarled. "All of you standing here killed horsemen at Tall Oaks. We live because we kill. Maybe I live more because I have killed more. And I will kill even more horsemen."

Brege swallowed. The poisoned plant flowered, and invited all to eat. She must stop this meal. "The People met in Assembly and decided for all of us that we would leave the horsemen alone if they left us alone. Did we not all agree?"

Beside Brege, nods came quickly. Behind Antia, jaws jutted defiantly.

"Ha," Antia spat. "Only a fool turns her back on a bear. I trim its claws." From behind her came laughs.

"You do not trim their claws," Taelon shot back, "you tease them. They will roar."

"The dead say nothing," Antia hissed.

"The People of River Bend chose otherwise." Brege sought for the rock that all of the People should cling to.

"The People of River Bend are dead. Those of us who live do not need a stranger to whimper about how to treat a horseman. A strong arm and a sharp spear are the way to treat a horseman. If you will not grab a spear, step out of the way of those who will." Antia advanced, hand on her knife hilt.

Merik leveled his shepherd's staff and stepped forward. Taelon did likewise. "The People have chosen. She who Speaks for the Goddess has Spoken. The People follow."

"I was born in that sanctuary. It stinks of the blood of my mother and father. It reeks of the sweat of the man who raped me and whose heart I cut out. If you would turn your back on the horsemen, turn your back on that sanctuary and let a woman with a strong arm show the People what the Goddess can do to horsemen."

Like a river in flood, Antia and her people pushed forward, shoving all others aside. Most people moved out of their way. Those who did not move fast enough were pushed. Some stumbled and fell. Several screamed as Antia's followers walked on them.

Brege froze; they wanted the sanctuary. In it were babies like Little Mist. If they shoved their way in there, would they trample the little ones?

"Stand with me!" Brege shouted. "Do not let them grab what you do not choose to give."

Around Brege, people hesitated. Merik and Taelon stepped forward, Merik's staff clasped between them. Brege grabbed it with both hands and pushed forward. Beside her, behind her, others joined. What had been a herd of goats, going their own way, become a wall of people, standing with Brege.

And Brege found herself facing a raging Antia.

"Get out of my way!" the woman screamed.

"Your way is the way of the wolf. We will not walk it."

Antia drew her knife, waved it in front of Brege. "My way is the way of life."

"You would raise a knife to the Speaker for the Goddess. Are you no better than the horsemen who killed your mother?"

For a moment, Brege thought she had struck through all the pain and anger to finally lay open the boil that poisoned Antia's heart. Only for a moment; then the rage swept back and Brege tensed herself for the death blow.

A bow twanged.

"Aah!" two screamed as one.

To her right, two who had been shoving against each other stood, transfixed by a single arrow. Brege glanced around. No one with a bow was in sight.

"Do we now draw each other's blood?" she screamed. "Are we People no better than horsemen?"

Along the dividing line, people drew apart, as if coming awake from a nightmare. Antia drew back. "We are not done. That sanctuary is mine. I will have it."

"Not while we live," Merik shot back.

"We will see." Antia turned. "We will return to our homes. We will walk our streets with bows and spears. Let no one who is not with us pass our walls."

Merik put an arm around Brege . . . and she found she had need of support. Suddenly her legs were like water.

"It is done," Merik said. "The wall between us is finished. I hope the wall between us and the horsemen is also complete."

Taelon scowled. "I and my son will ride out again to see what the horsemen make ready to do. If it is bad for River Bend, we will bring word to you quickly."

"The Goddess go with you." Brege blessed him. "Now we war among ourselves. We must know if the horsemen war upon us too."

Sara had come late to the plaza; she watched the People from a distance, Soren at her side.

"Now what will we do?" the young man asked.

"I do not know what the others will do, but Launa taught me well that knowing what is before you is more important than hands and hands of spears. I ride for Tall Oaks."

Soren shrugged. "I ride with you, if you will let me."

"It will be a hard ride, to wear out horses and butts."

"Mine will last longer than yours."

"We will see." Together, they raced for the horses.

Antia trembled with unspent rage and the bitter taste of failure. *I came so close.*

"What shall I do?" Cleo asked.

Antia splashed her face with water, then dumped the entire bucket over her head. It cooled her skin, but not the rage in her gut. "Post a watch. Let no one come inside our walls who does not ride with us. Watch the sanctuary. Let me know what they are doing. Tonight, we will take staffs and beat them from my home."

"Yes."

"And fill this bucket," she said, tossing it at Cleo. "I am thirsty."

"We will have to walk through their part of River Bend."

"None of those goats will step in your path."

Cleo handed the bucket to a young girl. She scampered off.

"Get me four hands of women with heart. Come dark, we will surround the sanctuary and toss them out on their butts." Antia grinned at the thought.

The little girl returned, downcast.

"Where is the water?" Antia demanded.

"Across the street, they closed the gate. They would not open it. They would not even talk to me when I asked why."

Cleo shook her head at Antia. "So quickly they move, not at all like the People of old. Young one, you will have to go around to where the wall is not yet built and draw water far away from the town. Now run."

The girl rushed off. "And we, Antia, will have to send more people to carry water from farther away."

"Not tomorrow, when *I* sit in the sanctuary."

TWENTY-FOUR

AT DAWN, THE Cavalry Regiment rode out. Masin led forty volunteers from Woodtown. Jack trotted into Tall Oaks before noon . . . right back where he was when he left.

Troops drilled, tended crops, built the wall. Lasa greeted him from the veranda of the sanctuary with a proud smile. She patted her rounding belly . . . and reported. "The crops grow well; the harvest will be good. The wall facing the fields is built. Now we work on the smaller wall along the river. Four cohorts of pike drill and another four of mixed bows and slings practice. Each has a full six double hands in them."

Jack did the arithmetic. Sixty each, plus another forty kids and old folks to carry extra shields and run logistics, call each cohort a hundred. Lasa went on.

"Your dragoons form two complete cohorts now, as do those who carry axes. Four double hands of youths ride as scouts," she who Spoke for the Goddess frowned, "but they are young, and my heart tells me they ride more than they scout."

Jack finished his tally. Almost eleven hundred under arms, not bad for a town of two thousand. But he heard the worry behind Lasa's final words.

"What do we hear of the horsemen and River Bend?"

"Too little. Taelon rode out, a horseman's helmet on his

head and his son at his side. He says any horsemen who sees him will see a horseman, not a hunter."

"So long as a horseman does not talk to him, it may work," Kaul growled. "And he said I was foolish."

Lasa blanched. Jack slipped from his horse to rest a protective arm around her. "He is a wise hunter. He will ride where he wants, see what he wants, and be far away before any horseman asks who he is." Jack gently kissed his consort.

Still mounted, Launa glanced away, but only for a moment. When she looked back, she was smiling. "That sly fox will not fall for any of their traps. It was his eyes that brought us home from the horsemen's camp."

Lasa accepted their gift of comfort with a nod. "Sara rode back to River Bend to take Brege and Merik word of what we do here. If she rides quickly, she may be back soon."

"Then let us check the troops."

That evening, as they ate in the cooling air outside the sanctuary, Kaul told of their journey and how they came to return with many hands of horse riders. "And more walk to us."

"More?" Lasa massaged Jack's back, working the tension from his body even as his mind whirled. Across from them, Dob did the same for Launa. *We're in Tall Oaks. This is as good as it gets.*

Jack leaned back and gave Lasa a grateful kiss. "Enough for two cohorts, though I do not know how many can use the bow."

"What will you do with this 'cavalry regiment'?" Lasa asked.

"We will go where Launa wants us," Dob answered.

"As least the commander will." Lasa laughed.

"Yes," Launa agreed.

Jack reran the conversation through his gut, double meanings and all. It didn't bother him. *I guess I am going native. Looks like Launa is too . . . maybe.* Jack had a few more things to cover before he'd call it a night.

"Launa, tomorrow while I check the wall will you put the

troops through their paces? Lasa, can you excuse all soldiers from farming and wall building so they can form for drill?"

"The cohorts will be excused. The others will walk where they will."

"Good." Launa grinned at Jack. "Captain, when do you want to move on River Bend, and how heavy do we go?"

The words were all in the language, but the frowns around the group told Jack that Launa's new meanings confused many. "The cavalry could leave tomorrow," he said, "but I want so many soldiers at River Bend that the numbers of spears alone make Antia see sense. When the horsemen come, they will ride there. I do not want them to be able to chop us up in small pieces. The lone wolf is easily killed. The pack is another matter."

"How many will you leave to guard Tall Oaks?" Lasa asked the question Jack knew would be foremost on her mind.

"More than we had last time, and now the wall is finished. I will not leave you in danger."

"If the horsemen again leave no one alive at River Bend, no number of cohorts here will be enough." Lasa sighed. "Come back to me, wise Speaker for the Bull. Come back to me and our child."

That night, the Bull played with the Goddess. Gently, softly, Jack came home.

"Yes, those must be prepared for the little one." Lasa moaned as Jack kissed circles around her breasts. She caught her breath and went on. "Kaul told me that you and Launa went back into tomorrow."

Jack kept making circles and waited.

"And you came back because you were not done with your labors here." Lasa pulled Jack's chin up, smiled into his eyes. "I hope our child and I can make you happy you returned."

That night, he was.

Launa awoke the next morning as light crept through the eaves of her home. She rolled over. Dob snored softly beside her.

Well, she'd tried it the People's way last night. Dob had been good. But Dob was . . . not Jack. "You made a hell of a career choice for a one-man woman," she muttered as she slipped out of bed. Pulling on the thin linen shift that had become the uniform of the legion and belting it in place, she wondered how Jack's homecoming had been, then decided she didn't really want to know. The People were so wonderful otherwise; why did they have to stomp all over her and Jack's hearts?

"May not matter much longer," she said with a scowl. "Now we got to stand at the bottom of the hill and let every Indian in the world charge over us, Colonel Custer, sir."

Squaring her shoulders, she gave the day's first order. "It's time to soldier, girl. Let's soldier."

Taelon took ten spare mounts when he and his son rode out from River Bend. He stayed at the gallop until dark and slept by the river Launa had told the horsemen not to cross.

Next day he rode well away from the marshes and lakes, out on the steppe. He saw no horses most of the day. Late in the afternoon it was his son who pointed. "Father, look."

Herds, more than he could count on the fingers of his hands, grazed across the steppe. Warriors trotted around them and, distant on the horizon, many fires sent smoke against the sky.

"If we stick our nose too close to that, we will lose our whiskers. We ride around," he told his son.

For the next two days it was like that, a vast and empty steppe, or more herds than a woman could count on hands and feet. Launa could probably count them, but not an old hunter. Das pointed to their right, tried to show him how to count like Launa. "Over there is a herd for every finger on both my hands. I make a mark in the dirt. Now, over there," he pointed to their left, "are more herds, again, one for every finger on my hands. Make a second mark in the dirt. That is . . . 'twenty.' "

"Son, you may count as you will, but since before you were born that was two double hands of herds."

"Yes, father."

"But whether we do it Launa's way or my way, that is still a lot of horses."

"*Yes,* father!"

Since all the herds were close together, it was easier for Taelon to avoid anyone getting close enough to ask him questions. He also never got a good look at any one of the camps. Not good.

He crossed the next river and two days later approached the river beyond which the horsemen made their winter camp. There were even more herds, but enough room for him to skirt the edges.

He did not like what he saw. "Too many horses and too little grass. They will have to go somewhere, and soon." And he knew where these horses would go for grass.

Next morning, Taelon trotted up to a bluff. Herds grazed as far as he could see. Warriors jealously milled around them. But small groups of warriors, always with a totem, rode to the northeast. Taelon picked a group with two totems and followed.

Shokin galloped, totem behind him. Mozyr, now Mighty Man of what was left of the Swift Eagle Clan, galloped beside him with his totem behind. They rode across the steppe, past more herds than Shokin had ever seen before.

Mozyr scowled. "Has every horse from the high steppe come here? The grass cannot be that bad."

"Yet they come," Shokin muttered. They come and they could not stay. "The Mighty Man of the Clans will tell us what we must do, and it will be done."

Mozyr grunted his approval.

Shokin wondered if they held the certainty they had in times remembered.

It was midday when Shokin rode into the camp of the Mighty Man of the Clans. Tents were everywhere, but a wide swath had been left free. Shokin did not slow his gallop until he came to the four great tents. In the ground before them stood totems, hands and hands of totems. With a curt wave, Shokin sent his son to add another. Mozyr's totem bearer followed.

Shokin dismounted and tossed his reins to one of his warriors. Mozyr followed his lead. "I have never been to the camp of the Mighty Man," the young Mighty Man whispered.

"Walk beside me and we will do no wrong," Shokin said through a grin. "Old Tutzo comes to greet us!" he shouted and opened his arms wide.

For the next few moments there was much pounding of shoulders and checking for gray hairs. Tutzo gave as good as he got and both men ended up laughing.

Shokin introduced Mozyr. "He now is Mighty Man of the Swift Eagle Clan, what is left of them."

"The night demons?" Tutzo frowned.

"Night hunters, but as flesh and blood as you and I. I will show you with my knife when one of them is in my hands."

Tutzo rubbed his beard. "I have heard that Shokin's sharp eye sees the farmers as warriors now."

"A woman, farmer-dressed, brought that fool Arakk's head to me in a farmer's jug. She led many lances to my camp."

Tutzo's eyes narrowed. "And let you ride away to tell us to ride there no more."

"Yes." Shokin hissed the word like an arrow in flight.

Tutzo frowned as his glance swept the camp. "We need more grass. Strong clans war on the high steppe. Many ride this way to avoid the wrath of those strong ones."

"Can no one go back?" Shokin whispered.

"No one dares, and now some of those fierce warriors sit at the side of our Mighty Man. Watch your tongue, old friend. I do not know what game they hunt, but their swagger knows no bounds. They live to pick fights. Their knives are like none I have seen. Made from the Sky, or metal they say has fallen from it. They call themselves the Chosen Ones."

Shokin was glad for the warning as he entered the tent of Galatan, the Mightiest of Men. Galatan sat where he always had, but around him were a new bunch. Their heads were shaved, except for one long lock that hung down their backs like a horse's tail. Their eyes were those of hungry hawks; they fixed Shokin in their unblinking gaze as he strode toward them. He made his face a warrior's mask and stared back. Shokin broke from their stares only to greet the Mighty Man of the Clans.

"Hail, Galatan, two more totems stand beside yours, the Stalwart Shield and the Swift Eagle. We follow where you lead."

"Hail, Shokin." Galatan stood to answer. "I will lead you to victory and skulls. And soon. When the sun rises tomorrow, two of the farmer slaves you took with Arakk will be buried in the dirt they dig. They will be alive when we put the earth over them. In two days, every Clan will ride for the east and put every farmer in the ground with those two." Galatan laughed. "Let us see if they like being that close to the earth."

Shokin nodded. "I have ridden among them. I know where they gather. If you give me the honor, I will lead the Clans to where we may fight many good men and take many honorable heads."

Beside Galatan, the strange warriors scowled and spat. "Farmers. What honor have they?"

"Arakk and the Stormy Mountain Clan fought the farmers and is no more." Shokin threw the warning out and folded his arms.

One of the shaved-head warriors hefted an ax; its head was large and shining. Sky metal, Shokin guessed. "The Stormy Mountain Clan were women. They would pull up their skirts and run from a squalling baby girl. Women could take their heads, and I hear one did." He whirled his ax. "It will be fun to spread her legs."

Shokin remembered the woman Launa. This braggart might find her a hard woman to take. Shokin kept his thought to himself. "I will return to my warriors. Five days from tomorrow, we will meet you by the river where the great hunt was two summers ago. We will lead you straight and true to where we can fight the farmers' warriors."

Galatan clapped Shokin on the shoulders. "But tonight we

feast. The women have fermented much mare's milk, and these mighty warriors brought a new seed to smoke. Ah, the dreams they give."

Shokin did not need dreams. What he needed was to keep his skull on his shoulders. Tonight he would keep his own counsel.

Before Taelon spread a camp that must have every horseman under the sky. Those he had followed rode straight into it. He and Das turned aside.

In the shade of trees along a small stream, Taelon settled their mounts before turning to Das. "Son, I must see more."

"Father . . ."

"Do not tell an old hunter to watch out for the bear's hug," he said, cutting his son off. "If I am not back by sunset tomorrow, ride straight and swiftly to River Bend. Tell them more horsemen than a woman can measure—even Launa—ride toward them. There is not enough grass to feed their horses. They will come quickly. You must do this, son."

The son grasped the father's shoulders. "I will do what a soldier must do, Father. Goddess go with you."

Taelon appreciated the prayer. Of late, the Goddess seemed to have been busy at other hunts. He hoped she would glance his way today.

TWENTY-FIVE

THE SUN SANK low, but for four days, the sun had not gone down on Antia's anger. The days were hot. In the part of River Bend that followed her, water was scarce.

Across the street, the gates were lashed against them. The hole in the wall at the end of town was open, and anyone could go for water or a refreshing bath. But many who went did not came back. Antia had seen them on the walls, calling to their friends still with her to come out, to stop this foolishness. Now only Cleo and ones like her led water parties, and they went armed.

They were shoving at the gates, too. They blamed Antia for them after her late-night foray to take back the sanctuary. Someone must have told them she was coming. Brambles had been scattered on the ground after dark. Thorns had cut her people's feet. Surprised, they cried out in pain. In a heartbeat, people appeared with torches to light their way—back to their compound.

Pushing and shoving and pulling had broken out several times the next day. Arrows had flown. One of Brege's followers was gravely wounded. Her anguished moans floated through the cool evening air.

Antia had drunk no water since yesterday. She waited for the others to see in their hearts that her path was the only one for the People. Instead, the People did nothing. They let the few who hung around the sanctuary with Brege speak for them. *They* had never heard their mother's death shrieks. *They* had never had a horseman's bloody knife at their throats, smelled the horseman's stink as he raped them until they bled, heard the laughter as he tossed them aside and went looking for another.

They did not know the horsemen. Antia did. The only way to meet a horseman was with a knife. And if the sheep wanted to go down into slavery, that did not mean Antia must let them do it to River Bend again.

"Cleo, everyone, quickly, bring your short spears. Let us sweep them from the sanctuary before they know we are coming."

Taelon scowled; he'd gotten deep into the horseman's camp by staying in the trees by the stream. And he knew nothing more than he had when he started. The camp was big . . . very big, and noisy and confusing. Some of the tents were made of poles bent back over to make a small hill. Other poles rose tall to lean against each other, with skins and felt blankets wrapped around them. Still others were wide and low like the ones Taelon had lived in many years ago.

"Many different places to sleep, maybe many different types of horsemen." Taelon remembered horsemen fighting among themselves . . . it almost seemed a game to them . . . a game that killed. Would all these horsemen ride together or fight among themselves? Jack and Launa needed to know.

In the midst of the camp would stand the tent of the mighty ones. There would be the totems of the clans who pledged to fight together. Taelon had to know how many totems stood there.

He trotted to the stream and studied his reflection before he drank. Dark hair, short and with a round face, he was no tall, fair warrior. He could not take his knife and swagger as a warrior, but, if he walked meekly as a slave?

Slipping his knife into his boot, he shed helmet, quiver and bow. A slave might meekly go about his master's bidding without explaining himself. Eyes downcast, Taelon hurried from the wood and lost himself in the flow of people, animals and children.

Around him, horses raced. Men and women laughed and shouted to each other. The smells of roasting meat and stale dung filled the air. Taelon kept to the traveled avenues, but always to the side, away from any clump of swaggering warriors.

Near the center of camp, that became harder. As a hunter, Taelon knew how to lose himself in grass or woods. Now he strove to lose himself in the throng around him. Like a fish, he let the currents of people move him, but always where he chose.

Suddenly, the people quit moving.

He was in the square with the four largest tents. In front of him, several men were yelling, haranguing the crowd. Behind them were the totems he had come to see. He counted; first all the fingers of one hand, then the next, back to the first hand and again to the second—one of Launa's twenty, plus three.

The last totem he recognized—a round shield, painted red, with eagle feathers dangling from it. That was the totem he had ridden with. What did they call it, the strong shield clan? Something like that.

Taelon turned; he'd seen enough. Twenty and three clans had joined together. One totem had been enough to rock Tall Oaks early this summer. Now twenty and three rode against them. Launa and Jack had to know this.

Suddenly, two men grabbed Taelon by the arms. Two more threw lariats over him, lashing his arms to his side. They yanked him by the ropes; he resisted for a moment. Then, rather than be dragged, he went where he was led.

They pulled him to the front. The haranguers seemed happy to have him. His captors strutted proudly. They threw questions at him, none of which he understood. He tried to remember the word for "What" or "Why." For his effort, he got slapped.

A girl who couldn't have been more than ten was carried, kicking and screaming, before the men. They laughed as her captors struggled to tie her up. She gave one a solid kick in the stomach; he doubled over. Another slapped her hard enough to bloody her lips.

Tied and bound, the girl huddled in a sullen lump. They repeated the same question to her several times, then added a kick before she answered them. Then she spoke to Taelon.

"They want to know who is the one who owns you?"

"I do not know. Why?"

"So they can give him a horse."

"Why?"

"Tomorrow morning, we will be alive when they bury us. They want us to be the first to go into the earth, to tell the Goddess that they will soon send all the People into the earth. They must trade your owner a horse for your life."

Taelon nodded dumbly. He opened his mouth to speak—then kicked at one captor, yanked his ropes from the other's grasp. Free, he bowled over two more men and dashed for the space between the great tents, loosening the lariats as he ran.

He was building up speed when someone tackled him. A moment later, a blow to the head sent him into darkness.

"What is that noise?" Brege asked, taking Little Mist from her breast.

"The drum. Either the horsemen have come or Antia is loose," Merik said, dashing for the door. He glanced out. "Yes, it is Antia. She has brought short spears into the plaza." He disappeared through the door shouting, "Everyone, to me!"

The drum pounded louder. It was the signal intended to announce the horsemen. Now it beat for Antia. Brege shuddered, but she had matters to attend to. "Mothers, take the babies." She handed Little Mist over to a grandmother. "We must get them away before Antia's people trample them." She should never have brought the children back into the sanctuary after the first clash . . . but a sanctuary without babies had never been. *I must learn to think of what has never been,* she chided herself.

Two streams of people tried to get through the single door. Women and men charging forth to meet Antia, and mothers taking children to safety. It was slow for everyone. Somehow, Brege found herself being moved ahead of the others.

Once out the door, Brege turned to her right, away from the direction the mothers took—toward Merik and Antia.

The two groups had collided in the middle of the plaza. Antia had gotten no farther than she had the first time. Was the woman's heart so scorched by her hatred of the horsemen that she could not see how much like them she had become? Now she brought spears to the sanctuary, tried to beat people into following her rather than letting each walk the way of the Goddess.

Somehow, I must find words that will open Antia's eyes. Carefully, Brege wound her way through the crowd until she stood beside her consort. Across from him was Antia.

Rage had become a living thing inside Antia. It drove her, and she drove it. She used it, like a horseman's whip, to egg her people on, to hurl them against those who stood between her and the sanctuary.

The spears should have driven through the herd that blocked her way now. Instead of the points slashing and piercing, instead of spear butts knocking aside those who blocked her way, the spears became a line. Held in both hands by her people and the others, the spears divided them. The spears become a wall between them, and like a wall, it did not move.

Antia shoved. Those beside her shoved. Those across from her shoved back. They grunted and groaned. Nobody moved.

"Enough, Antia. Can you not see? Is there nothing of the Goddess left in your heart? This is no path of Hers." For the first time, Antia saw who stood across from her. Brege.

Antia took a step back. "Can you not see? Are you so blind? The horsemen come for you, and you wait for them to come. They are not like wolves or bears, a few wander here, a few wander there. Those we can drive away or kill as we chose. The horsemen are cunning. They gather together. So many will come at once that no one can stand against them." Antia paused for breath—and to draw her knife from her belt.

"And you, Antia, have caused that," Brege whispered. Her words were soft, but no one could have failed to hear her. "Launa set the boundary on the horsemen. They did not cross it. But to kill them, you crossed it. What rides at us, you called."

"No, you do not see. Yes, at first we hunted where we would, but no more. Now the horsemen ignore Launa. Now more and more horsemen ride where Launa forbade them." Antia raised her knife. "These we meet with the blade, the only words they hear. All of you, ride with us. Let us show the horsemen that what is ours is not theirs for the taking."

Brege shook her head. "You started the killing. Now you do not know how to stop it. Like a horseman, you live by the knife." Antia saw sorrow in Brege's eyes. And pity.

"The knife is all I need!" she screamed—and drove it deep into Brege's belly.

"No!" Merik screamed. "No!" Every tongue seemed to shout. Every tongue but Antia's and Brege's.

Again Antia looked into Brege's eyes. Now she saw surprise . . . and pity still. Brege looked down. Antia's gaze followed hers. The knife was buried up to its hilt in Brege's stomach. Blood poured over the blade onto Antia's hand.

"Like a horseman, you chose the knife," Brege whispered, "and like a horseman, you are covered with the blood of a Speaker for the Goddess in River Bend."

"No," Antia whimpered, her anger quenched by the red spreading over her hands. "No."

"Yes," Merik growled. And caught Brege in his arms as she collapsed. "Somebody, get Glengish. Tell her to bring her satchel of healing herbs. Quick!" Merik called as he carried the Speaker for the Goddess into the sanctuary.

"No, no, no," Antia whispered. What had she done? She couldn't have. Oh, if she could move the sun back in the sky. Let it hang there again and give her back that moment.

But daylight was fading beyond recall.

Cleo took her by the arm. "Come. I will get you water to wash with."

Antia held her hands in front of her, crimson going dark as the light faded. People moved away from her. Were they sickened by what they saw, what she had done? She shook her head. "There will never be enough water to wash these hands."

"I know," said Cleo.

"Where is Glengish?" Merik shouted. The moon could have waxed and waned since he called for her. He settled his consort on their bed and reached for the knife that stuck from her belly.

"No," Brege feebly reached out. "It will bleed the more."

"But you cannot live with a knife in you."

"We both know I cannot live with this wound."

"Yes, you will," he wept.

"If you ask it of me, I would do most anything."

Glengish paused a moment at the door to take in the scene, then came to kneel on the other side of Brege. "Does it hurt?"

"It is beginning to. I am thirsty. Could I drink something?"

Glengish felt gently around the knife. Brege's breath came out with a hiss. "You are bleeding into yourself."

"I know."

Merik raised tear-filled eyes. "Grandmother Glengish, you can heal Brege. Your herbs and poultices healed so many who were hurt in the battle at Tall Oaks. You can heal Brege."

"The Goddess heals many, but a lance jab to the belly, an arrow in the lungs . . ." The old woman shook her head.

"But the one who was hurt two days ago—" Merik started.

"Is dead." Glengish cut him off.

For the first time, he saw the blood on her. "We could do no more for her. We gave her to the Goddess. I will do all that I can for Brege." The old woman brushed the younger one's hair from her beading brow. "I will do all that I can."

• • •

Taelon came awake to a trembling question. "Are you all right?" the small voice asked him.

His head felt as though a bear had clamped its jaws on his skull. "I live, little one." He opened his eyes; the girl huddled, knees pulled up to chin, in a corner of the tent. "How are you?"

"Frightened," she answered without flinching.

"The dirt is not over our heads yet. Where are we?"

"In a tent, behind one of the great ones."

"How long have I slept?"

"These men sing and dance. I think they feast. It is growing darker."

Taelon nodded. "And when they have drunk enough that they sleep like a dead log in the forest, we will leave this place."

Even in the dim light, Taelon saw her eyes widen in hope. "Can you do that?"

"Yes, little one," he promised. "Now take a nap. We will need to be wide awake when they are not."

"I cannot sleep."

"Then rest, little one. I must listen." The girl settled her chin on her knees. In time she may have slept.

Taelon measured the day by the deepening dark in the tent . . . and the carousing outside. He had a guard, maybe two. They had friends who made sure they were not left out of the feasting. The more noisy stops made at the tent, the more hope rose in him. Still, he kept his knife in his boot and the ropes binding him tight in case someone wanted to see the offerings for tomorrow.

Long after darkness was total in the tent, the noise of the camp died down. When the guards snored, Taelon rolled to where the girl was. "Little one, wake up." Gently, he nudged her.

She came awake with a start and a shriek. She also kicked him in the knee. "Quiet, little one, it is only me."

"I am sorry. I guess I did sleep."

Taelon said nothing. He leaned against the tent wall and waited for the snoring to resume. Just this side of forever, it did.

"Inside my boot, you will find a knife," he whispered.

In a moment, cold fingers groped his ankle. "I found it!"

"Now hold the knife while I cut my bonds." Her grasp was weak; he said nothing when her wobbly grip on the knife cut into his flesh. She did the best she could.

When he was free, he quickly cut her loose.

"Now, we leave." On the wall opposite the tent flap, his fingers found a seam. His knife opened it. He peeked out into moonless dark. Compared to the darkness of the tent, the stars were as bright as noon. Nothing moved. He widened the hole, slipped through and pulled her out.

She bolted; he yanked her back. "Slowly, little one. We walk like we belong here." Standing tall, like a proud warrior with his young lover, he walked away. "Where is the stream? We can follow it to my son and horses to take us far from here."

She pointed to his left. Arm in arm, they went into the night. Around them came the night sounds of a horsemen's camp. Drunken men sang and shouted. Somewhere a women was beaten; another shrieked in passion. Other couples wandered the night, but none of them wanted anyone close. That suited Taelon just fine.

They were well away from the camp and working their way upstream before dawn brightened the sky.

TWENTY-SIX

JACK RUBBED HIS backside. Just standing close to a horse made it ache. He'd been on a horse most of the last two weeks. After four days off, it was time to mount up again. From the way Launa slapped the loose end of the reins back and forth in her hands, she was planning a fast ride to River Bend. *There's going to be a lot of aching backsides if I can't slow her down.*

With Jack stood most of the command structure of Tall Oaks, taking the salute of First Legion as it rode out. Across from them, Second Legion stood proudly in ranks, pikes or bows at port arms. It would have made a Prussian drill major proud. Except the twenty or so kids scampering around each cohort. Their wicker shields were ever ready to form a protective wall when ordered. Their energy level was too high for them to stand still in ranks, but they had too much enthusiasm to wander too far from their mothers and fathers, sisters and brothers. Slouching behind each cohort were elders, shouldering shields on poles that looked like nothing more than big umbrellas. These would protect against plunging arrows.

The defense of Tall Oaks was the People of Tall Oaks.

Jack had intended to take a chunk of Second Legion to River Bend. Then Lasa explained with one of her gentle smiles how she had juggled the ranks of the two legions to concentrate all the pregnancies in the Second. Many had celebrated the victory over the horsemen by beginning the expansion of their families. Lasa's was only one of many waists beginning to bulge.

"You can take them if you need them, or take the men from the two cohorts and form them into one," Lasa offered.

Launa shook her head firmly. "We are *not* creating a male military caste here. If we deploy them, they deploy as a unit."

"I think First Legion will be enough." Which really said nothing. Jack had no idea what was in front of them. Lasa did offer Jack both the Dragoons. Those cohorts, trained to ride into battle and fight on foot, either as pike or bow, were the most versatile in their little army. Today, First Dragoon had ridden out ahead of the rest. They would be his scouts.

Today, Lasa had mounted up the combat troops of First Legion. Shieldbearers, both young and old, would stay behind. "Hope Brege has that wall built," Launa interrupted Jack's reverie. "If she hasn't, we may wish we had those kids."

"If that wall's not built, we'll need more than shields."

Jack gave Lasa a final hug and kiss. "Go with the Goddess, and come back to us," she whispered.

"I will," Jack promised.

Kaul rode up as Jack mounted.

"I thought you were staying," Jack said.

Lasa looked forlornly up at both the men she loved.

"We seek a path from the Goddess. It is out there. I will not find it waiting here."

With a sigh, Lasa sent both the men of her life forth with "Go with the Goddess."

There was nothing left to say. Jack kicked Windrider into motion. Dob was leading the Cavalry Regiment by. Jack, Launa, and Kaul joined him. It was a three-, maybe four-day ride to River Bend. Jack could only guess what he'd find.

The young girl stumbled over a tree root and sprawled on the ground. Terror and darkness had given way to exhaustion; she plodded forward with only half-seeing eyes. Taelon could not leave her to her fate, or to the sharp questions of horsemen. He pulled her up on his back. Somewhere ahead was Das.

The sun was well up and Taelon's muscles were screaming before he came upon the horses. Das stepped from a bush, arrow nocked and ready. "You were long, Father."

"And I would be dead if the horsemen had their way."

Das eyed the girl as Taelon set her down. "She too, an offering to their foaming-at-the-mouth man goddess."

"Can she ride?" Das asked.

"Yes," she answered.

"We must," Taelon added. "Launa must know twenty and three totems stand before the tent of the horsemen's mighty man. Twenty and three clans will ride against River Bend."

They mounted and rode quickly out onto the plains.

Shokin had intended to ride forth early that morning. A year ago, he had been with Arakk when he sacrificed a farmer woman, spread-eagled to the Sky. She had not accepted the honor like a warrior, but screamed and shrieked. Shokin suspected the two farmers today would be just as noisy. What message could such people carry to the Sky or goddess?

Like a tiny thrush, the news that the two offerings had vanished flitted through the camp. Mozyr made signs against evil. "Again our offering disappears. First the man at the winter camp, now this. It is not good."

Shokin checked the tent where the two spent the night. There was a new slit in the back and the guards were still drunk. If he had his way, they would be the offering.

Shokin remembered the old slave someone had grabbed; there had been a power about him. Shokin had wondered how he kept his poise in slavery. Now, the warrior in Shokin wished him luck.

The delay made it unwise for Shokin to remove his totem from the gathered ones. He stood with the other Mighty Men as two slaves dug a pit, and listened to their pitiful cries become muffled as warriors put the dirt over them. No, those two would have nothing worthwhile for the Sky to hear.

Now, Shokin made his excuses and rode out, Mozyr at his

side. The sun was high when the Mighty Man of the Swift Eagle Clan pointed. "Something is strange about those riders. Two rode away from the bloody camp of my Mighty Man. As we rode into the great camp we now ride away from, two followed us."

Shokin squinted. "But there are three where you point."

"One is small, like the girl that was to have been offered this morning. One wears no helmet, carries no lance. I have watched them long. They ride fast, but they do not change horses. I will talk with them." So saying, Mozyr pulled in one of his spare mounts, leaped to it, and kicked it to a gallop.

Shokin did the same. Even if Mozyr was only seeing what he wanted to see, it was strange for a horseman to lead spare mounts and not trade off before he tired one. With a whoop, the warriors behind him joined in the chase.

"Father, they gallop for us."

"Ride for the marshes!" Taelon shouted at his son and the girl. From the great camp, he had headed for the swamp and lake country that bordered the great bitter water. On the plains there was no place to hide. There, at least they would have a chance to use their hunter's skills. If they could make it.

Taelon's horse carried the greatest weight. It slowed faster than the others. Das slowed with him.

"No, son. Race with the wind. You must tell Jack and Launa twenty and three totems come for River Bend. Now, toss me the rope to your spare mounts."

"Father?"

"Horsemen want horses. Give me your spare horses and ride for the fens. Lose yourself there, then get to River Bend. Go with the Goddess, but go!"

For a long moment, Taelon feared his son would not obey. Then with a jerky nod, Das answered, "Yes, Father," and tossed the rope that led his remounts. Taelon caught it and slowed. With a final backward glance, Das kicked his horse for speed and raced to catch up to the girl. She had not slowed.

Taelon waved, then glanced around, looking for a place to set a trap that would at least trade time for his son's life, if not his own. He checked his quiver. Four arrows. Ten hunted him. He would give them a fight that would make the ones who lived proud to carry his head.

He reined his mount in by the first tree he came to. Quickly, he threw the remounts' ropes over a limb. He wanted the horsemen to come for those horses, but he wanted them to come through him. He strung his bow and took five paces back toward the steppe. Setting an arrow to string, he grinned. The horsemen were not galloping quite so fast now. One raised a hand and the others halted outside bow range.

Taelon saluted them with a raised fist.

Shokin frowned. "He challenges us like a warrior."

"The other two are getting away." Mozyr pointed.

"Let them. As a boy, I hunted in those swamps. You will search long in there and find nothing. No, we have what we hunt. Is that not the slave who went obediently to the offering, until the girl told him what he was? There is the man who fought free not once but twice. Now," Shokin rubbed his chin, "how do *we* capture him again?"

"My warriors will spit him on our lances!" Mozyr shouted.

"And he will put those arrows in four of your warriors who will die of the slow, stinking death. A great battle comes. Now is not a good day to die."

"Are you a coward?"

"Young warrior, I am an old warrior. One does not grow old at the head of the sharp lances of a clan by being a fool . . . or a coward."

Taelon waited, and when no headlong charge came, he waited some more. He knew the men who talked were Mighty Men from the totems behind them. One totem he did not know; it held a dead eagle, dry wings spread wide. The other totem he knew . . . the red shield. Maybe he would not die today.

While the horsemen talked, Taelon backed slowly to his horse. It was no use to run. He pulled out the round shield he had included in his horseman's disguise. Rapping it with his bow, he pricked his thumb with an arrow and smeared his blood on the shield. A thin line of red ran across the tanned hide of its cover.

"What is that animal doing?" Mozyr spat.

"Reminding me who he is." Shokin dismounted and raised his right arm. "When I was a young warrior, a hunter from among the people we now war with rode among the Stalwart Shields. Like young men are, we were eager to show our courage. We hunted the great cattle. I would have died if he had not been there. And he too lived because I was there for him when he needed me. Afterwards, my father allowed this one to become my blood brother, not as one of the Clan, but as a stranger. Let us see if this one has the scar."

Shokin slowly walked forward, right arm up.

The other one stood for a moment, then dropped his bow and shield. He held up his left arm. With open arms, he greeted Shokin, as one should greet a friend of one's youth.

Shokin laughed and went to him. For a moment, he studied him, looking in the lined face and graying hair for the memory of one young and not yet come to his strength. Yes, his blood brother was there, in this one's eyes.

Shokin kicked him in the groin.

As he doubled over, Shokin brought a fist up to smash his jaw. The man collapsed, dazed, his eyes dull and confused. "Bring ropes," Shokin ordered. "Tie him well this time."

"I will kill him now," Mozyr demanded.

"No. I have questions for this one. And he is *my* blood brother. When he dies, it will be with a knife in his hand. If you wish, you may have the honor of trying to kill him when he has that knife. For now, send your riders to harry the edge of the fens. Those he saved may live, but they will not speak whatever words he stayed behind so they could carry."

• • •

The sun was low when a call came down the column: "Riders coming fast."

Jack and the rest of the command staff pulled their horses out of line to let the riders know where to aim. "We got to get some sort of flag or banner system going," Launa noted.

Jack had found the first day on the trail boring. They'd made this trip enough that the terrain was getting familiar. The scouts were out. The troops were trained. Everything was done. Until the unknowns were defined, there was little to do but cover the miles. Boring.

"Looks like Sara, and that boy . . ." Launa's voice trailed off.

"Soren. They've got those horses in a lather."

"Yes," Launa said. Together, they waited.

The youngsters arrived breathless, but Sara shouted. "Antia returned from her hunt . . . This time Taelon followed her. He saw what she did . . . He told all of River Bend . . ."

"Fat's in the fire now," Launa murmured.

"The People are divided," Soren added. "Antia's people have taken to their part of town. The gates to the other parts are closed to them."

"When was this?" Kaul asked.

"Two noons ago. We rode without stopping," Sara answered.

"A lot could have happened in the meantime." Not for the first or the last time did Jack wish for a decent radio net.

"We could dismount a couple of cohorts and push the cavalry ahead with spare mounts," Launa said.

Jack shook his head. "Brege has plenty of spears, and they have not talked sense into Antia. Adding another hundred or two will change nothing. Bringing a full legion with horse support might. Boot her in the ass, don't just piss her off," Jack said, paraphrasing the old German strategy.

"We must tell Brege you are coming." Sara turned her mount.

"Not on those horses you won't." Launa raised her hand. "Messengers, remounts for these two."

The only troops with spare mounts was the communication squad. They swapped them quickly with Sara and Soren.

"Stay with us for a meal," Launa offered.

The girl and boy threw themselves on their new mounts. "No," Sara called. "Brege must know help is coming." The two were gone at the gallop.

"Think we should pick up the pace?" Jack asked.

Launa laughed. "And just this morning you warned me against getting there too tired." Launa brushed stray hair from her face. "Lasa gave us enough dried food so we don't have to cook. The horses carry oats to supplement their grazing. I guess we could push the troops on until dark. Their asses will be sore, but they'll get to skip weapons drill. Isn't army life wonderful? Every cloud has a silver lining." She snickered.

"You take point and get the vanguard moving. I'll take the word down the line," Jack said as he turned Windrider.

Throwing himself into the troop movement simplified one part of his life. Well after dark that night, when he finally collapsed into his bedroll, it didn't matter who was next to him. After the coming battle, if they lived, would be soon enough to untangle the strings of his official and private life.

Merik stayed at Brege's side. Some time during the night the fever came. He wiped her body down with damp cloths to cool her, then covered her when the chill took her. He knew he was losing her, but he could not let go. Not yet. The moments when she was lucid, when she would smile at him, or ask him to sing one of the songs they had made for Little Mist, were worth it.

Glengish came and went. She brought tea that Merik slowly dribbled into Brege's mouth to take some of the pain away. The Wise Woman checked the wound, helped it drain. Each check was followed by a shake of her gray head. No hope did she offer.

Others came for only a moment. Some had played with Brege as a girl. Older ones had mothered her. All now mourned her. None asked Merik what River Bend must do. River Bend must wait on Merik and Brege today.

Merik was not so lost in his rising grief that he did not hear Antia's whispered name spoken behind him. A time would come when she would have to answer for what she had done.

Custom decreed that one who took another's life be banished from the People. That way had been from of old. Never had anyone taken the life of She who Spoke for the Goddess. There was no custom for this. Like so many new paths they walked, Merik needed a new custom. But not today. Today he held Brege's hand, watched each breath, treasured each moment. Today was full of her. The empty tomorrows would come soon enough.

Das swatted at flies. The sun was high; it was hot and muggy in the fens. He paused and dismounted. Clonbe, the girl, dismounted and picked leeches from her horse as he did from his. He studied his mounts' hoofs; the water was not good for them.

"We must travel faster," she said.

"We cannot travel faster in this swamp, and they wait for us on the plains." At sunrise Das had gone to look. Two riders had been in sight. He turned back before they saw him.

"We must travel fast," she said, and her face took on a faraway smile. "Horsemen think little of girls. My mother called butterflies to her with a bit of honey. Maybe I could call a horseman to me."

"They would kill you."

"Not if we killed them first."

A year ago, Das would never have talked of killing a man. Now a child helped him plan how. Something must be wrong with him to do such a thing. Maybe, but if it helped him live, the People would hear what his father died for them to hear.

The sun was high when they knocked Taelon from his horse. He managed to land well, roll over, and stand up. He was shoved toward a tent. Bowing low, he entered. Behind him came the blood brother who had kicked him.

They stared at each other across a dead fire. Neither spoke. A woman entered the tent, knelt between them, and bowed to the ground. His blood brother spoke; then she did.

"You are in the presence of Shokin, Mighty Man of the Stalwart Shield Clan. I am Teckla, once a woman of the Gray Fox People, now a slave among the Stalwart Shield. Who are you?"

So the friend of his youth had lived well. Taelon looked him square in the eye and answered. "I am Taelon, who leads the People of the Badger and fights beside Launa, war leader of the People of Tall Oaks."

Shokin nodded as he listened to the woman's translation. Then he stood and used his knife to cut Taelon's bonds. "Do not flee. Many are eager to put an arrow in you if you do."

Taelon would not leave; the Goddess had brought him where he wanted to be. "Thank you," he said to Shokin—and the Goddess.

Shokin sat again. "We are strange birds. Our people make war to the death. Yet we shared a warm summer in our youth. I will not let them torture you. When you die, it will be quick."

"Is death all we have left to us?"

"Hear me well, friend of my youth. You killed Arakk and his pastureless Clan. With him, you killed many young sons of other Clans. Now all the Clans ride against you. Farmers who have never carried a lance or ridden a horse cannot stand against the cloud of lances the Clans will bring."

Taelon listened . . . and smiled within himself. Shokin's words wound down. The man was not as confident as he appeared. Fear lurked around the edges of those words, or sad resignation.

"My friend Kaul took words to the winter camp that would have stopped this blood. You would have killed him, but you could not. Arakk brought hands and hands of lances to Tall Oaks. All are dead, and the sky sings no song of how they died. You would have buried me, but I live, talking with you and not the Goddess. Your sky has no power where the Great Goddess walks."

"The Great Sky is everywhere and has power over everyone!"

"The sky is not over Arakk, only the dirt we put over his grave. Look into your heart. You and I rode together. Why let these wanderers lead you to destruction with them? Your people and mine have lived peacefully together. We can again. Do not ride blindly to your death with them."

"Friend of my youth, if I do not ride beside them, they will ride over me," Shokin said sadly.

"Then my friends will put all of you in the ground." Taelon spoke as if it were already done.

Shokin swallowed hard. "In a few days, we will know who is right." He squared his shoulders. "You are safe in this tent. Do not leave it until I come for you. My sons will guard you, and they drink only water. You *will* be here in the morning."

"By the blood we share, I will not leave this tent until you come for me. The Goddess brought us together in our youth, and now in our wisdom. Who is to say what our wise eyes can see?"

Shokin shrugged. Or maybe he was just stooping to get through the tent flap. Taelon could wait to find out.

"Help me. Help me. Won't somebody help me?" Clonbe called plaintively, first in the People's tongue, then in the horse people's. She heard a horse approach, and twisted around to see.

A horseman grinned at her from a stone's throw away. "What is wrong, little girl?"

"A lion attacked my horse and ate it. I ran away, but I hurt my foot. I cannot run anymore. Will you please help me?"

"I will help you, little girl," the man said and dismounted. He did not come quickly to her, but eyed the glen where she lay. The grass was not high enough to hide a man. The tree that shaded her was thick with leaves. He watched it long and hard.

"Please help me," Clonbe pleaded. Then, too exhausted to sit up, she collapsed onto her side.

The horseman came forward, lance in hand, and jabbed the tree above her several times. Content, he reached a hand down for her. "Come, little girl. You missed a feast, but the Mighty Man of the Swift Eagle Clan will have another just for you."

"Oh, good." Clonbe smiled back, and reached for him with her left hand. He took it and lifted her up.

Her right hand came free, and with it, the arrow she hid in the folds of her dress. She threw all of her strength behind it, driving the arrow into his stomach. As it entered, she twisted.

"Aah!" the horseman screamed, letting go of her and grabbing for the arrow. "What have you done?"

Clonbe danced away before he could recapture her. "A little girl has killed you, mighty warrior," she laughed.

He swung the lance at her, but she was too close to stab. She ducked, holding his attention as Das rushed from his hiding place not five paces from where the horseman had dismounted.

In a heartbeat, Das was on the horseman, his knife slashing his throat. Hot blood splattered Clonbe. She grinned as she wiped it from her face. "What will you tell the sun, weak horseman, when he asks how you died?" she taunted as he died.

Das stripped the body of quiver and knife and dumped it among the reeds. Returning with their two horses, he frowned. "The horseman had two horses. Their hoofs will be sound. We can ride them until our horses' dry."

Clonbe shook her head. "If a warrior rides alone with four horses, no one will question. If you and I share four horses, someone will want to know why a little girl gallops the steppe. You take the four horses and ride." She hefted the dead man's bow and quiver. "My people have hunted the swamps since the first rains fell on the earth. I will follow you on foot."

For a moment, Das seemed ready to argue with her. Then he nodded. "Walk quickly, wise one. One of us must tell

River Bend that four hands of totems and three ride together."

Clonbe laughed. "Both of us will. Look for me when you ride into town."

"I will," Das promised, and mounted.

The sun was low; the sanctuary in River Bend grew dark. Brege's fever rose. She moaned in pain, begged for water, and would have scratched at her wound if Merik did not hold fast to her hand. Not since early morning had her eyes been her own.

Merik looked up as Glengish entered. He waited as she felt Brege's forehead, removed the bandage and studied the wound. She shook her head. "She is leaving us."

"I cannot let her go."

"You must."

The sound of hoofbeats interrupted them. A bedraggled and dusty Sara dashed in. "I have talked with Launa. She brings the First Legion of Tall Oaks," Sara shouted. Then she saw Brege.

"Oh, dear Goddess!"

Merik was on his feet. "Ride to Launa. A soldier must know soldiers' wounds. Antia stabbed Brege in the stomach. Bring her here quickly. Surely she can save her."

"I have ridden all night and all day for four sunrises. I will ride until I find Launa again." She turned on her heel. In a moment the pounding of hoofs began again.

Das rode until dark, pausing only long enough to switch from one horse to another. Even the great river Jack called the Dniester he took at the gallop. He saw no horsemen. That was good for him, but bad for River Bend. Father had told him that meant they gathered in their war camps.

The night was dark. He slowed his pace, allowed the horses to graze as they walked. When the moon rose, he changed horses and kicked his new one to a trot.

TWENTY-SEVEN

SUN STREAMED INTO the tent when Shokin brought rope to bind Taelon's hands. A warrior with squinting eyes came with him.

"I am Berok," he said, announcing himself. "I speak your words. Shokin says you will ride with me as we go to war on your people. And I may not be able to hit a horse with a rock until it tramples me, but the warriors who ride with my father will rejoice to put many arrows in your back if you run."

"Tell Shokin that my friend Kaul rode long to the winter camp to find a way the horse people and the People could walk together. I will not run away from a path with him."

Berok spoke with Shokin. The Mighty Man shook his head. "No path lies between the Sky and your goddess. You are a fool."

"I will be a fool for both of us so long as blood is in us."

Shokin left, shaking his head. Berok nudged Taelon with more gentleness than he would have expected. "Come with me. We have a horse for you even my mother could ride."

Sara greeted the sunrise by kicking her horse to a gallop. Her legs ached; her hands were raw from the reins. Her thighs bled from where the horse blanket had not been as soft as it looked four, five days ago when she first mounted up.

Through the night, Soren and she had talked until their

voices were little more than a croak, trying to stay awake, trying to keep from falling off their mounts. Sara would have been asleep before she hit the ground.

Now she paused to let the horses drink and to drink herself. The dried fish she had taken from River Bend the first time was a memory. The ache of her empty belly was a small pain among many.

She changed her blanket to a new horse while it browsed. It took three tries to haul herself onto a horse. Soren had trouble mounting, too. "You do not need to do this," she told him. "Only one of us must find Launa. You are tired. Wait here."

Soren snorted. "You were asleep when the horses stopped for water. We rode this far together. We will ride on together." He kicked his mount twice before it would abandon the grass it grazed. Reluctantly, their horses trotted from the stream.

The sun was high. Launa spread the column along a stream to water the horses and gulp a quick meal. Moving five hundred mounted troops was turning into a learning experience. You didn't gas horses, they needed fodder. That took time . . . time she didn't have. With no convoy radio net, orders were passed up and down the line by shouts or messengers. Launa was reinventing obsolete technology . . . and gaining a better understanding of why the old-timers lost battles. It was time to end this break and get the column moving. *Sure could use a drummer.*

"Scouts coming in," Kaul noted.

"Mount up!" she hollered as she turned to where Kaul pointed.

Around her, cohort commanders and file sergeants echoed her orders, leaving her free to hold her breath. With the scouts rode Sara and Soren. They came to a ragged halt in front of Launa. The two clung to their horses' necks.

"Brege is dying . . . Antia stabbed her," Sara blurted out.

"No!" Kaul bolted forward to catch Sara as she fell off her mount. "Not my daughter. No one would hurt She who Speaks for the Goddess."

"Antia did," Soren said—and fell off his horse. Sprawled on the ground, he finished. "Merik asks you to come quickly. He says Launa sings the songs of soldiers. She must know the healing of soldiers' wounds."

Launa listened to the hope in the young man's voice, and knew it was misplaced. It was easy to shatter a human body, so hard to heal it. "Where did Antia stab Brege?"

Sara put a hand to her own stomach. "Here."

Launa shivered. Upper left abdomen. Impossible to miss intestines. Antia used a horseman's knife, six-inch blade. The wound would be deep. A piece of cake for a MASH with surgeons and anesthetic. Chest and abdominal wounds were a death warrant as late as World War I.

Kaul snatched two horses away from messengers and threw himself on one. "We must ride for my daughter."

Launa wanted to scream *I can do nothing*. Biting her lips, she grabbed a spare mount and threw herself on Star. There was no way she could deny the command in Kaul's voice. She obeyed.

A cohort commander trotted up. "The soldiers are ready to ride. We await your orders."

"Move out," Launa said without thought. Orders she could give without reflection. It was life she could not figure out what to do with. "Messenger!" she shouted.

One was at her side in a moment. "Tell Jack that Kaul and I ride for River Bend. Ask Jack to bring the cav and dragoons quickly. We may need 'peacekeepers' to stop a 'civil war.' "

The messenger repeated the orders, working to get his mouth around the English words. Then he was off for the rear.

"We will go with you." Sara tried to stand, but failed.

"You will come with the soldiers. You have ridden hard and long enough for this moon. Join Jack. He will push the soldiers along. Tonight, we will all be in River Bend."

Kaul kicked his mount to a gallop. Launa followed, changing in that instant from the commander of a fighting force to a lifesaver with no hope of saving a life. She had come six thousand years to help them learn to kill. About binding up wounds, she knew no more than they. In the end, all her knowledge and command authority ended helpless before the face of death.

Star caught up with Kaul; the stallion would let no one

pass him. They rode, pushing their mounts and themselves for every bit of extra speed they could get. Launa concentrated on the ride, tried to keep her eyes on the land they galloped over . . . still, memories flooded her mind.

Again she saw Brege, the daughter, bravely interceding with her mother to give the soldiers' dogs a chance to hunt for a lost child. There stood the witness, white from the shock of the slaughterhouse the horsemen had made of River Bend, asking Launa to make her a soldier. And the scared kid going into battle not an hour later rather than let the Kurgans butcher twenty more.

Brege had guts, and smarts, searching with Launa for just the words to mobilize Tall Oaks and holding her half of the line defending Tall Oaks . . . even as she went into labor.

Brege had been smart enough to know that someone battle-savvy and people-smart would be needed at the resettled River Bend, and she had finagled herself into the job of Speaking for the Goddess there. And that job had killed her. Was killing her, unless Launa could come up with some miracle.

Star leaped a small stream in a single stride. Branches whipped past Launa. She concentrated on the ride. Even if saving Brege was beyond her reach, she still might save River Bend from a civil bloodbath.

Kaul's horse was slowing, spent. He signaled a halt to change horses. They were off one and on another in a flash. Behind them, the sun sank lower. So did Launa's spirits.

The day was hot, but Jack felt a chill as he trotted up the line and spotted Sara and Soren. Any news from River Bend that brought them racing back had to be bad.

It was.

The first order of business was pushing the legion forward—fast. That was the easy part. Lasa haunted Jack as he gave the necessary orders. *Her oldest daughter is hurt. Maybe dying. Do I tell her?* Jack punted the question. Grabbing two messengers, he got them remounts. "Tell Lasa of Sara's message."

"What do we tell her to do?"

"Whatever the Goddess leads her to do," Jack sighed.

• • •

Merik washed Brege's sweat-bathed face with a cool cloth. She tossed and moaned. Occasionally, she would cry out. The stench from her wound filled the sanctuary.

Glengish sat across from him. She kept her fist closed, but he had seen what she hid . . . a freshly chipped piece of flint. Its edge would be sharp. Brege would hardly feel the cut . . . and it would free her from the agony her life had become.

"Launa will be here soon," Merik pleaded through tears.

"The Goddess Herself could not heal her now, Merik."

Merik dipped the cloth in cool water, wrung it out and once again dabbed at Brege's face. Gently, he wiped her throat, her breasts. So often he had covered them with kisses. The vision of this body, so alive, so passionate, going to dead clay filled him. His stomach revolted. He collapsed beside Brege and wept.

"Love. Love, are you there?"

There was light in Brege's eyes. She smiled weakly at him. "I did not mean to leave you so soon. I am sorry."

"Mist and I will be well," he promised. And meant it. "Go to the Goddess."

Brege moaned. Her body shivered. The spark was gone from her gaze. She shrieked in agony.

Glengish reached across, the flint in her hand.

Merik placed a hand on Glengish's. "She is my consort. I will send her to the Goddess." He drew the copper knife Jack had given him. Even in the dim evening light, its sharp edge gleamed. He traced the lines of Brege's throat with the knife point, remembered kisses, and found the place where life throbbed.

Before he could stop himself, he pressed.

Blood splattered his arms and face. It spurted over her breasts, and ran in rivers down her throat. Her body tensed, as if in cruel passion, then went limp.

The ache that had lived in Merik's chest for three days and nights exploded like lightning. Before his eyes he held the knife, running red with his consort's blood. The rage that had lurked in his gut engulfed him. Now it had a name. Antia. Antia had done this.

Glengish began to keen a death song. Merik would hear none of it. Jumping to his feet, he bolted from the sanctuary. At the door he paused only a moment to remember where Antia's house was. He ran for it. Behind him, he heard Glengish call his name. Heard her footsteps following him.

He raced from the plaza. "Where is Antia?" he bellowed. "Where is the death woman?"

Riders approached. Merik paid them no heed. "Where is the woman? Will no one show me the face of the death bringer?"

"I am here," came a soft voice behind him.

He whirled. Antia stood at the corner of a house. Haggard, with the dried blood of her assault dark on her, she stood straight, unflinching. "I am the one that you seek."

"Do not do this thing," Merik heard Launa say behind him. Again he turned. She and Kaul reined in exhausted mounts a stone's toss from him. "Blood of the People cannot wash away blood from the People."

"She killed Brege. She killed the One who Spoke for the Goddess!" he screamed.

"And to the Goddess she will answer," Launa whispered.

"How can she breathe, when Brege does not?" Merik wept.

"I do not know, son," Kaul said. "I do not know. But in Antia's blood is no answer. There is bad blood between the horsemen and us. They come. Let the bad blood between the People end here. If it does not end with you, when will it?"

"I want Antia dead!" Merik screamed. "I want her as dead as Brege." He whirled and charged Antia. The woman did not move. She waited for the knife blow.

Raising his arm, he slashed down—and buried the knife halfway to its hilt in the post beside her.

Face in her face, he spoke with trembling words. "Leave the knife. Leave the blood on it. When the horsemen have come and died, I will face you, that knife in hand. One of us will die."

"Yes," Antia whispered.

Merik ran. He ran from the ache in his heart. He ran to gasp out the agony in his chest. He ran past the sanctuary and down the avenue. He ran out the gate at the end of River Bend and through the trees. He splashed without slowing across the river and ran on. He ran until he could run no more, and where he dropped, he wept.

Launa watched Merik race away. She knew he could not outrun the anger and the agony. Launa had galloped here knowing she could not save one life. At least the Goddess had given her the chance to save another. Not that she wanted to save Antia. Still, the horsemen were coming. If Antia died under Merik's knife, would her followers stand in the line to save River Bend?

On second thought, Launa was none too sure she wanted to share a battle line with Antia's crowd. She'd better segregate her forces. And keep Antia alive.

"Cleo," Launa said, spotting Antia's deputy. "Take Antia to her house. She is not to leave there. You will watch her."

"Yes." The woman nodded and took Antia by the arm. The empty warrior let herself be led. *Would you feel better if Merik had buried his knife in you?* Launa knew she should post a suicide watch, but did not. *If she wants to solve the problem that way, let her.*

Launa glanced around. Kaul headed for the sanctuary. With a shiver, Launa followed. The longhouse stank of gangrene. Without a fully equipped surgery, death was inevitable and would have been greeted when it came. A glance showed Launa it had been hastened. Now she understood the blood on Merik's knife. *Sweet Jesus, the poor man had to kill his own wife.* No wonder he wanted Antia dead, himself and personally.

Funerals were not high on Launa's list of ways to spend her time. She had five hundred troops coming who needed food and a place to sleep. With Brege dead, Merik wiped out by grief, Antia under house arrest and Glengish tied up with funeral details, the command structure for River Bend was a shambles.

Launa spotted the carpenter Samath. Until Hanna threw him out for taking up arms, he'd been a good deputy. Launa had a hunch River Bend had made use of his talents. She took him aside and explained her problems. Samath nodded. "I will tell the cooks there are more to feed. The People will open their homes."

Launa left with Samath to see to details.

There was about an hour of sunlight left when the scouts filtered through the valley of River Bend. They did not pause, but kept riding, scouting out the far side of the river and over into the next valley. Launa approved. Bomel, first child of Lasa who shared Masin's eyes and Kaul's nose, was turning into a wise scout commander. She'd have to compliment him in front of Lasa and Kaul when this was over.

A half hour later, Jack and Dob led First Cav and Second Dragoon in at a trot. Launa reported the situation. Jack took the news of Brege's death with a terse "I expected that." The way breath left him told Launa he'd still hoped for better. Launa finished her report with "Things have stabilized, but we'll have to do something about unit cohesion."

"Another funeral," Jack groaned. Together they went to pay their respects at the sanctuary.

Glengish greeted them. "Even in death, we are divided. Some would bury Brege beneath the floor of the sanctuary. Others would place her in a soldier's grave outside the wall, the first of many we will lay there in the days to come. What say you?"

"What say Kaul and Merik?" Launa returned question for question.

"Kaul we have not asked. Merik has not returned."

"We will follow after them," Jack said.

At sunset, the first of the cohorts rode in. As the dusk deepened, others straggled up. Volunteers took their horses. Samath saw that all were fed and bedded down. Late that night, he offered Launa and Jack his home.

"There is a woman I think will share her roof with me while you stay here," he finished his offer with a hint of a grin.

Launa was glad to have a place to lay her head. Her butt hurt from the long ride. Her ego bled for the medical help she could not give, and she suddenly felt none too sure about the command challenge that lay ahead. She shivered, the vision of Brege, pale and bled out, would not leave her. Jack came to her, held her, said nothing. They swayed together, from exhaustion as much as the pleasure of each other's closeness.

"Would you do it for me?" Launa asked.

"Do what?"

"Give me peace if the wound is mortal?"

Jack was quiet for a long time. "I don't know."

"We may have to, Jack. An arrow in the lungs or belly isn't going to heal. Herbs and poultices won't work."

"I know," Jack growled. "But the human body's a strange thing. Sometimes it can heal . . ."

Launa pushed Jack away. "Reality, Jack, not wishful thinking. If one of us takes a body wound, it's over. If you can't make the call, let Glengish or some local. Brege suffered horribly the last few days. Don't make me. I won't make you."

"I'd rather invent body armor," Jack drawled.

Launa pulled him back to her and hugged him. That was the way to go. Don't worry about what you couldn't do. Concentrate on what you could. In Jack's arms, she could almost believe that there was nothing they couldn't handle.

That night, she slept in Jack's arms.

Launa came awake quickly the next morning, but was slow to get out of bed. She stared at the ceiling. Beside her, Jack woke. He started the morning off by staring at the ceiling too.

"I hate funerals," Jack muttered.

Launa grunted agreement, but knew that today's funeral would either bind these people together or tear them apart. With the horsemen due any moment, the people of River Bend had better find a way to stand together. Launa had a strong suspicion that the burden of pulling these folks together rested firmly on her shoulders. And all she wanted to do was stay in bed.

She threw the covers aside. Wordlessly, the two dressed and went to meet the day. The sanctuary was their first stop, for breakfast, and to check on their friends. Kaul had slept beside the body of his daughter. Some time in the night Merik had returned. Eyes red, he sat, back against the wall of the sanctuary, staring blankly at the body of his beloved.

Outside, Launa and Jack shared porridge with Samath and

Glengish. Those two took the moment to introduce them to the ones who led the legion of River Bend. Brege and Merik had organized them as Launa and Jack had taught.

"The crops are heavy," Glengish said. "Some are already harvested, but others now must be. Still others will ripen later. Can we use your people to help us in the fields?"

"Is there a way to call all the people together if the horsemen come?" Launa asked.

"A drum beside the sanctuary," Samath pointed.

"Then let everyone work this morning in the fields," Launa told Glengish. She turned to Samath. "Will you show Jack and me the wall you built?"

Samath and the construction crew that gathered around him were a reflection of the entire population: proud of what they had accomplished, saddened and shocked by what the last few days had brought them. Jack paused in their walk to check one of the fences built between houses along the main avenues. It rattled in his hands, but the lashings held solid. Branches and saplings six to eight feet high would discourage any jumpers.

But no fixed defense was impregnable. Given enough time, the horsemen could tear down the fence and free themselves to gallop among the townspeople. Launa took a step back.

Samath grinned and pointed. Most of the houses abutting the main streets now sported nests beside their chimneys. A weave of sticks and split logs would protect one or two archers. "Brege told us we must have a fence to protect us from the horsemen, and places for archers to protect the fence that protected us."

So Brege had listened well to all Launa had shared during the futile effort to build a wall around Tall Oaks last winter. A shudder went through Launa; the woman was so good. Had listened so well. Why hadn't Launa spent more time telling her about the dangers of being an agent of change?

Because it wasn't part of what they taught you at the Point. And there wasn't enough time last winter to cover everything. What she left unsaid had killed Brege. *What will I leave out in the next few days that will kill all of us?* Launa did not like the taste of her own fallibility.

They came to the wall that had taken so much of River Bend's time, and now blood. The inside slope was steep; they'd planted it with grasses. To keep people off it, split logs formed steps up it at intervals. Launa took the steps two at a time.

The top of the wall was dirt six feet across protected by a wooden palisade with ports for archers. Outside, the ditch was five or six feet deep and twice as far across at its lip. Where necessary, retaining logs reinforced both the ditch and the wall that sloped evenly above it. A dozen watchtowers of wood and wicker were spaced along the wall.

Launa turned. Jack was taking the measure of a similar tower over the sanctuary. "Quite a command post," he concluded.

Launa wasn't so sure. "Bit isolated. The sanctuary will be surrounded by horsemen."

"For a time, yes, but we'll be scattered all over, everyone fighting their battle. Horsemen can gallop around, putting pressure on first one place, then another. We're giving them interior lines. Someone's got to keep your defense coordinated." Jack made perfect sense. Still, Launa didn't like the idea of him on an island awash in very angry horsemen.

The two walked the wall until it petered out at the west edge of town, leaving a gaping hole about thirty meters across.

Samath was embarrassed. "We have worked hard. Brege had us start from the side where the horsemen first came. She wanted us to make what we built very strong. We have not finished."

"And you will not finish." Launa smiled grimly. "You have prepared a battlefield. Now we fight the battle."

A youth of maybe twelve ran up. "Grandmother Glengish asks for you to come to the sanctuary." With a sigh, Launa turned to face the enemy within.

Before the sanctuary stood Kaul and Merik, dirt-covered, antlers and bags in hand. They had dug a grave; Launa waited to be told where. Kaul spoke only when they stopped in front of him. "My daughter asked to be made a soldier. She fought with you at the Battle at the Tree and before Tall Oaks. We will bury her in a soldier's grave outside the wall she built."

"And she will be carried as a soldier should be," Launa said as she stepped to the drum and began beating it slowly, in a soldier's dirge.

People came, some unsure, others grim-faced and armed. Jack strode forth and issued one order. "Form the legions. River Bend to right. First Tall Oaks to left."

Two cohort commanders took their stations. Arriving commanders guided on them. Troops came, walking somberly, and fell into place behind their officers, forming ranks and files. The cohorts grew as people came, bows or pikes at order arms, checking who was to their right, their front, then falling silently into place. The stream slowed to a trickle as the last holes in the ranks were filled. The proud defenders of River Bend stood, rank on rank at attention.

Jack did a smart about-face and saluted Launa; ten, maybe fifteen minutes had passed. "The legions are formed."

Launa ceased her dirge beat. While she had done it, her mind had found its center. She had not thought of why she did it, of her friend . . . almost sister. She nodded to Kaul and Merik; then she and Jack followed them inside.

The women had cleaned the body; it was wrapped in a linen sheet and lying on a bench. Taking two spears from the wall, Launa and Jack ran them under the head and foot of the bench and invited the elders of River Bend to lift. Glengish and others quickly joined in. Launa led the way from the sanctuary with Jack at her side. Kaul and Merik trailed the body out.

In the sunlight, they halted. "Legion of River Bend," Launa ordered, "lead the way to the grave of your Speaker for the Goddess."

Samath stepped forward. "Follow me," he ordered. Turning, he headed down the avenue to the south gate. The youth who had summoned Launa and Jack came forward, removed the drum, and took up the slow dirge Launa had stopped.

On command, troops faced right, then stepped off, each unit marching to the same pivot point to make the right turn to follow Samath. The drill moved the troops in a synchronized ballet to their commander's will. Paired cohorts of pikes and archers marched slowly by, intermixed with bands of ax or club wielders.

When the last of River Bend's troops had passed, Jack stepped forward. "First Legion of Tall Oaks will honor the Speaker of River Bend by following her."

He and Launa stepped off, left foot first. The pallbearers followed. Kaul and Merik trailed them as First Legion faced left to march up the rear.

Samath had not failed Launa. He brought River Bend's legion to a halt to one side of the simple grave. There was plenty of room for First Legion to form to their right. Launa led the party of mourners to the graveside.

During the time First Legion took to march to its place, and for those not in ranks to arrange themselves along the wall, Launa studied her troops. They had stayed in step, turned corners smartly, kept their ranks and files aligned. People watched, and not just the onlookers. Heads in ranks had craned to get a look at the other legion. Facing a charge, everyone's life depend on the solidness of the next trooper. Would they hold or run, leaving you to die?

This would be the moment they held close to their hearts when they faced the onrushing horsemen. Would the memory hold them together, or send them running? Launa was willing to bet her life these soldiers would hold. Her life, their lives, and six thousand years of history.

People waited now. Launa glanced around, looking for who would lead Brege's funeral. Others glanced around. Nobody spoke. For a thousand years, these people had lived together, united by the memories of grandmothers. There was no memory for a moment like this. There was no liturgy, no ceremony. If they survived the coming days, what they did here would be remembered. If they died, they would be forgotten.

Launa stepped forward and turned to face her troops. Mind a blank, she opened her mouth, and prayed the words would come.

"People of River Bend, People of the First Legion,
we mourn the death of Brege, who Spoke for the Goddess.

We mourn her death, but we celebrate her life.
She lived that we might walk together with the Goddess.
She lived that we might find a way through the darkness
of these days to a new path with the Goddess.
She is gone from us,
but while we live and breathe,
what she lived for is with us.
While we live and breathe,
we walk together.
While we live and breathe,
our feet search for a path to take us into tomorrow.
The horsemen come to River Bend.
We, here, will stop them.
But let us not do this at River Bend.
Let it be remembered,
Let it pass from old to young, and from mouth to ear,
That we, standing together, stopped the horsemen here,
at Brege Town.

Launa paused. Murmurs spread through the ranks. What started as a nod of the head ended as a word: "Yes!"

The legions before her began the chant. "Brege Town, Brege Town, Brege Town." Those on the walls behind her took it up just as quickly. Launa waited for it to quiet. That took a while.

"Will you fight together for Brege?"

"Yes!" shouted the legions.

"Will you fight together with me?"

The answering roar was louder.

"Will we fill this grave with horsemen?"

"Yes!" the legions screamed. Pikes pounded the earth. Feet stomped. Launa had never felt so alive. With these people she could do anything.

Behind her, Jack cleared his throat. "We got riders coming in fast." As the pandemonium flowed around her, Launa turned. Two riders had crossed the ford below the town and galloped for her. One wore horseman leathers, the other a linen smock. Word passed through the ranks; the roar mellowed into silence. All stood quietly in ranks as the scouts came to a halt before Launa.

She recognized the one in leather. "Das, where is Taelon?"

"Dead," the young man cried. "He died to slow the horsemen that I might escape. He says you must know twenty and three totems gather. Arakk brought one to Tall Oaks. Twenty and three come to River Bend."

Launa did the arithmetic. One to two hundred warriors per totem. Call it three to four thousand warriors. She'd brought four hundred and eighty. Brege Town had paraded maybe six hundred—including some pretty small kids with slings. "Three or four to one." She whistled.

"Twenty-three totems, two legions," Jack drawled behind her. "I like the odds."

Launa whirled to scowl at Jack's humor . . . and saw Brege laid out for burial. *That is why we're here. It never slows down so we can do just one thing.* Launa looked at the other mourners. No one seemed to know what to do next.

Gritting her teeth, Launa paced off the distance to the grave. *I don't want to do this.* She dropped into it.

"Hand her down to me."

Kaul and Merik gently did. Brege seemed so light in her arms. Gone was the vibrant young woman, dreaming of the world they would make together. Cold clay now filled Launa's arms.

Now the tears began to flow. Tears for the woman she had known and would never know again. Tears flowed down Launa's cheeks, softening the soldier's armor she had wrapped around her heart. Gently, she laid the body out, adjusted the shroud, and stood. Just as gently, Kaul helped her from his daughter's grave. Launa stooped to pick up a handful of dirt. Letting it sift through her fingers, she whispered, "Until we meet again."

Others did the same, speaking their final farewell to child, wife, friend, Speaker.

Launa faced the troops with dust on her hands, tears on her cheeks. "The legions are dismissed."

Cohort commanders took up the order. River Bend's cohorts dissolved. First Legion did an about face in unison, stomped off two steps to the shout of "One, two," and then went their way.

The troops of Brege Town paused to watch, then started talking among themselves. "I don't think they liked being outfancied at drill," Jack muttered. "What have we started?"

"What matters is what we finish," Launa growled. "I don't want to put any more friends into graves if I can help it. Let's go plan to finish the horsemen."

Berok kept Taelon at his side, which usually meant he rode neither at the head or the tail of the Stalwart Shield's herd of warriors. Taelon made a habit of nodding whenever he saw Shokin looking his way. Shokin seemed to be looking his way regularly.

They arrived at a river crossing when the sun was high. Shokin spread his warriors out in a single line, facing east. Mounted, they waited.

There was dust in the sky; from one end of the horizon to the other it turned from blue to brown. It took a lot of horses to do that. The brown cloud moved toward them across the plain. It flowed around groves of trees and over and down the roll of the land. Slowly, Taelon began to make out the men who made the cloud.

A small band galloped at the head. Behind them, other small bands spread out across the steppe. Behind them, the plain was covered with riders and horses. They came at Taelon like an army of ants. Only these ants galloped and grew larger as they came closer. Taelon swallowed. "Oh, Goddess!"

"Did your heart see Arakk as all the horsemen under the Wide Sky?" Berok chided him. "Look upon the Clans, and see the death of your weak mother god."

Taelon kept his silence after that. Jack and Launa had showed him they could make a killing trap on the open steppe and in farmers' fields. They would weave a trap to snare this wild pack—if Das had warned them what was coming.

Then Taelon shivered, and knew fear. Could even the two soldiers find a path to death for so many men?

TWENTY-EIGHT

LAUNA WAS IN trouble. With maybe a thousand troops at her side, she was about to face every pissed-off horseman this side of China. That was bad. Worse, her chain of command was a tattered wreck: Brege dead, Merik sitting morosely by her grave, and Antia under house arrest. Launa needed commanders and she needed them quick. She also needed a plan for the coming battle. Launa did what any peaceful farmer following the Goddess would do. She called a meeting.

Of course, Launa's meeting was a war council. She issued a commanders' call to all her cohort leaders. Local attitude being what it was—no one could tell another the path for her feet—she got a lot of extras. For once, Launa didn't mind. Today, she was on the prowl for links to add to her chain of command. Any warm body that showed up was in danger of being drafted into leading something.

Launa focused the meeting by drawing a map of Brege Town on the clay floor of the sanctuary. The two main avenues cut the rebuilt town into roughly equal quarters and led to the wall that protected the east and south gates. The north gate faced the river. The trees and water restricted cavalry movement there; it would not be a major threat axis. The west gate was a gaping hole.

Brege had built the fortress Launa had described to the commanding general at West Point that afternoon when he'd asked how she would defend a Neolithic town against horse raiders. Then, Launa had been confident she could beat all comers. Now, she recognized her confidence for what it was—ignorance.

She studied her map, imposed force vectors over it in her mind, studying where things could come unhinged. Swallowing the sigh she felt, Launa faced her troops with the determined scowl the U.S. Army expected of a commander.

"I will command the west gate and the west street leading to it. To seal the hole, I need two pike cohorts. One to keep the horsemen we catch in, the other to keep any who want to rescue them out. At each of the other gates, we will hide one pike cohort. On command, pikes will advance up the avenues, taking away the horsemen's room to ride, and killing those who do not or can not get out of their way."

Cleo snickered. "A walking wall of points the horsemen can not run away from. Good."

"Kaul," Launa continued, "are you up to commanding the east gate's pikes and defending the east wall? The horsemen will try that wall to draw our attention and people there before they attack the west hole. Are you ready to lead?"

"I am ready," he growled, the old power back in his face as he nodded. "I will keep them off the wall of my Brege's town, and be ready to drive the horsemen back down the east avenue."

Launa nodded and went on. "Cleo, the pikes that follow after you will hold the north wall. It is possible a few may try to force the river side. The wall is lowest there."

"I hope they do." A hungry, tiger smile was on Cleo's lips.

Launa looked around, taking the measure of the Tall Oaks people who had marched in with her yesterday, and the Brege Town people whom she hadn't seen since spring. "I need someone to command the south gate."

"I will." Samath stepped forward. "I have spent enough time in my wood shop. It is a good time to fight."

Launa glanced at the Brege Town cohort commanders who would defend the south wall. They nodded approval. "It is yours."

The man grinned. "After this meeting, come to my shop.

We woodsmen have made some new shields that may keep the horsemen's arrows away, even when they pull the bow in your face."

"Good." Launa did not appreciate the interruption, but with these people, ideas sprouted like weeds; she'd have to take a look. She continued. "The archers that accompany each cohort will cover the outer wall. Then, when the horsemen are in the trap, they will move to the rooftops along the inner wall so they can shoot down the horsemen in the streets."

"Like shooting fish in a pot," an archer commander observed. Everyone laughed.

"These fish will be shooting back," Launa reminded them. The chuckles died.

Launa studied her map. The four streets divided Brege Town into four compounds. A map at the Point would dub them "A," "B," "C," and "D," or one, two, three, four. The alphabet hadn't been invented, and numbers were still a vague concept.

"Dob, your cavalry will cover the inside wall between the east and north gates. This will be the Dob compound. Bomel will command the next compound. Your Dragoons will stand between the east and south gates. The ax and extra archers of Brege Town will hold the walls on the west side of town." Launa looked up, waiting for someone to come forward.

Glengish smiled. "I will be mother to the soldiers who stand between the north gate and your west hole. Killalla, you followed after Antia and know the town between the south and west gates. Will you lead there?"

The young woman who had helped Jack out of the winter camp, half dragging, half carrying Kaul, stepped forward. "Yes, with a joyful heart, I will show the horsemen my thanks for the hospitality they gave me last year." No one laughed. They were all in line for such hospitality if this trap failed.

"Then it is done." Launa pointed to each of the four quarters of Brege Town and named the compound. "Dob, Bomel, Killalla, Glengish." Launa slowed and looked thoughtfully at her map. "Now, what do we need the horsemen to do?"

"Come in quick and dumb," Jack answered. "If they watch us too long, they'll smell your trap."

"We can't afford a long siege, but we can't let them bypass us and head straight for Tall Oaks," Launa mused, and Jack shivered. Kaul's eyes went wide. The thought of Tall Oaks' leftovers defending against twenty-three totems chilled them.

Jack shook his head. "They cannot ride past us. They got no dependents. Antia showed them what happens to a camp within our reach. Like a snake, we eat the egg. They ride here first. They will fight here first."

Launa would bet her life on that, and the life of everyone in Tall Oaks. "We need them to come in fast and dumb. How?"

"Burn the grass." Killalla snarled. "Their horses are their hearts. If their horses cannot eat, they will not stay long. Gather what crops we can and burn the rest."

Glengish shook her head. "You have a hard heart," she frowned, "but where the grass burns, there *are* few deer to hunt. Maybe your hard heart will help us see the light of many days."

Launa glanced at Jack. "Scorched earth. This is where it was invented. We start burning the fields to the north tomorrow." Launa looked around, found Sara standing in the back of the room. "Ready to go back on a horse?"

Each step looked like agony, but the girl came forward to receive her orders. "Move the herds away from here. Not to Tall Oaks. They would leave a path every horseman would follow. Burn the steppe as you ride south, to discourage the horsemen from following you, and to hide your trail."

Sara shrugged. "I will take good care of them."

"Send us a rider in a hand of days."

"You will send all the horses away?" Dob asked.

"Maybe we should keep enough for the cavalry regiment," Jack put in. "We need some type of mobile reserve to exploit any advantage that comes our way."

"Glengish, could we feed a double hand of double hand of horses?" Launa asked.

"We can try, and if there is not enough, we can always eat them." The old woman grinned at Dob.

"May your stomach cramp, Grandmother, if you ever feast on one of my horses," Dob growled.

The room laughed; it sounded good to Launa. They'd

kept their sense of humor. With luck, they'd keep their lives. "Tomorrow morning, we drill in the streets of Brege Town. Pikes first; everyone else, harvest anything that is ripe or the horses can eat. Good night." Launa ended the council.

Quickly, the room emptied. Launa walked away, wanting to find a quiet place to go over the meeting, looking for what she'd forgot, gnawing each word, each expression for any hidden meaning. Samath stayed close—not so close that she couldn't ignore him if she chose, but not so far back as to be missed. "Yes, Samath?"

"The wicker shields you showed us to weave last winter," Samath began immediately, "hide us from a horseman seeing where we stand behind it, but it is too weak to stop an arrow." The man was kind enough not to mention Sisu; the little fellow had died saving Launa. And he had been only one of several pierced through their shields. If Launa had had time, she would have worked on a better shield. *There was never enough time.*

They walked together to Samath's shop. "Look at this," he said, handing Launa and Jack a shield. It looked like the rectangular shield they'd used in the spring, except for a hide cover. Launa almost dropped her end. It was heavy.

Jack flipped it over. "Good Lord, look." Slipped into the wicker weave were strips of wood, one to two inches wide, maybe a quarter of an inch thick. One layer ran across the face of the shield. Beneath it another ran up and down. "He's laminated the shield," Jack said, marveling at the work.

"And wrapped it in rawhide," Launa finished.

"The deer hide is wet when we wrap it. It dries tough."

"You have made a very tough shield." Launa gave him the praise he deserved.

"Not enough of them. Teasing the strips from the dry, hard wood is not easy, even with the fine tools you gave us. We have shields like these only for the first line of pikes. We have added deerskin to many of the shields in the second and third line." He shrugged. "There are only so many deer."

"You have done well with what you have," Jack assured him.

"We have made a shield for the ax men." Samath handed

over another one. About a foot square and split from a single piece of wood, it was faced with very thick rawhide. "Our hunters brought down several giant cattle. I used their thick hides for these shields. An arrow may shatter it, but if you fight with it this way on your arm," Samath put it on, "any hits will go against the grain. It will stop a knife or ax."

"You have done well to protect the soldiers of Brege Town," Launa praised he. "Troops will live who would have died."

Samath sighed as he took the shield off. "If Brege had worn this, Antia might have had an eye blink to reflect before she struck a second time. We walk as the Goddess calls us."

Jack stared at the shield, slowly rubbing his chin. "Have you dipped the rawhide in hot beeswax?"

"We have many empty honeycombs. There is no strength in them." Launa would have said incredulity underpinned Samath's tone, but the carpenter had learned that when Jack made no sense, he often gave away the greatest gifts.

"Beeswax alone is weak. Rawhide is strong, but can be stronger. Heat the wax as hot as you can, then dip the hide in it and stretch it on a shield to dry. Tell me what you find."

"For a small shield, I could do that." Samath nodded. "Yes, I will, and you, wise Speaker for the Bull in Tall Oaks, will carry the first shield I make."

"Give me the second shield," Jack grinned. "You always grow wiser as you play with my words and see what I never did."

The two men laughed.

"Jack, let us leave this man to his work. You and I have a trap to set." They returned to the sanctuary and climbed the ladder to the watchtower above it. Woven mats that next winter would insulate against drafts now were lashed to the uprights. They hid a climber, but would not stop an arrow. The lookout post itself was protected by split logs and branches lashed to its frame. Jack shook it. "It'll stop an arrow."

Launa tested it; she wasn't so sure. "You didn't volunteer to lead a sector. You want to be a roving backup?"

Jack shook his head. "Your plan requires coordinated actions by units scattered all around the perimeter. From here, I can see what's happening. With a drum, I can communicate. I'll fight the battle from here." Jack glanced around. "Best view in town. And with a few archers up here, we can snipe at officers. Face it Launa, we need command, communications and control to win." Jack put on one of his lopsided grins. "I think I just found us an AWACS."

Launa still didn't like the idea. "You'll need troops to defend the longhouse. Everyone's committed."

"Not Masin and the forty from Woodtown. They didn't fit in with anyone. They'll fit in fine with me here."

Launa went to Jack. He gave her a hug. "Take care," she whispered, "take care."

"I'll be just as careful as you, hon," he whispered back.

That didn't sound nearly careful enough to Launa.

TWENTY-NINE

SHOKIN WAS READY to lead the Clans straight to the place where Arakk first took slaves. Two, maybe three days of swift riding would have taken them there. Instead, the Mighty Man of the Clans rode for half a day, then stopped to hunt. Or maybe it was the shaved heads who rode at his side who encouraged this.

They had been prominent in yesterday's hunt. Waiting insolently for the other Clans to drive the game to them, they had each slain a great buck with their bare hands and knives. Other warriors had tried to imitate them. Two were gored to death, others hurt before Galatan halted such foolishness.

There had been much feasting and boasting around the fires that night. Too long into the night for Shokin. He led the Stalwart Shield Clan out before others were awake. This was no way to ride to war.

And they rode to no war he had ever known. His son had first noticed it. "Father, is that a cloud ahead of us like when the dry lightning burns the steppe?"

Together, they galloped forward. It was still far in the distance when Shokin reined his mount in. "Yes, it is fire."

"But there has been no lightning?"

"Sowon, bring my blood brother to me. Quickly, son. And send another rider to Galatan. The Mighty Man must see this."

The boy was gone, like the wind, leaving Shokin to puzzle what he saw, and what it meant. Where the grass burned, horses did not graze. Where the grass burned, there were no deer to hunt. It happened sometimes that the Great Sky sent down the lightning to bring the smoke of the grass up to It. That was why the horsemen held the grass sacred. The grass was life.

What was grass to these farmers? What was grass to the woman Launa?

That puzzle was unfinished when Sowon and Berok led the hunter to him. They galloped, and so did the hunter. He sat his horse poorly. Still, he stayed on it at the gallop. How well had the farmers and hunters taken to Arakk's horses? To the lance and bow? More questions. No answers. Shokin scowled.

Shokin wasted no time taking their salutes. "The steppe burns, yet we have seen no lightning to call it to the Great Sky. What do you know of this?"

The hunter shook his head. "No more than you. I rode forth many days ago to see what I could see of you. I know nothing of what my people have done in all those many days."

"What would this Launa know of grass?"

"What you and I both know, my brother. That horses eat grass and horsemen eat the deer that eat the grass. After a fire, there is little to eat."

"Is nothing sacred?" Sowon glowered at the old hunter.

"Life, boy. Life is sacred to them."

Shokin's scowl deepened. Always in the face of death, his blood brother spoke of life. Did he not know that death was more powerful? In the distance, Shokin spotted the band of the Mighty Man. "Berok, take this one away before Galatan sees him. Brother, we will talk again."

Galatan and his shaved heads had the same questions . . . and no answers. Shokin was getting weary of questions. He wanted answers. His blood brother had been wise enough to go to the camp of the Horse People to look for answers. "Tomorrow, I will take a band of my warriors and ride straight to the camp of these farmers. It is time we see what there is to see."

Galatan nodded. "That is wise. I will ride with you."

That night, they feasted well on deer caught fleeing from

the fire. Shokin ordered some of the meat slaughtered by the Stalwart Shields set aside for the next day and the one after that. He heard of no such order around the other totems. Some warriors would be hungry soon . . . very soon.

Launa came awake with a stuffed-up nose and a headache. "Damn, who'd have thought I'd be allergic to grass smoke?"

Beside her, Jack sat up in bed and coughed up phlegm. "There's a lot of smoke out there."

Launa quickly tied on her smock. "That's one more thing that didn't make it into the history books. Scorching mother earth makes her a real bitch."

Yesterday, they'd fired the steppe to the northeast. Today they'd get in as much of the crop as possible and burn the fields before sunset. Sara had left with the horses yesterday. You could follow her progress by the smoke to the south and west.

"Don't you love it when a plan comes together?" Jack said, then coughed. They laughed; strange as it seemed, the plan was coming together. Yesterday they'd walked the pikes through a dress rehearsal of their battle, taking each cohort through its deployment and march up its assigned avenue to the sanctuary. Maneuvering around the plaza would be tough, but the horsemen should be blown enough by that time to allow the pikes to risk hanging their flanks for a few minutes. *No plan's perfect.*

Still ideas kept popping up to make the plan better. When Jack told the first cohort he would use drums to signal them, the kid who'd played the dirge at the funeral stepped forward.

"At Tall Oaks, the horsemen had drums."

"Yes." Jack nodded.

"If we use drums, can they not play drums over us?"

Again Jack nodded.

The boy's face split into a broad grin as he produced a large ram's horn and blew a long note, followed by a short one. The deep bass call reverberated through the town. "Have you heard the horsemen use anything like this?"

"No, fellow, and you have yourself a job at my right hand." Jack grinned. "We got music," he chortled to Launa.

After breakfast today, the pikes headed out for farm duty. The cavalry, dragoons, and other skirmishers would do their dress rehearsal. Their job was easier and tougher; they didn't have to stand in ranks and face the horsemen like the pikes. They could hide behind cover and shoot horsemen off their horses as they rode by. They also had to protect the inner wall. If the horsemen made a hole, they'd fill it until the pikes came up.

Flexibility had to be their strong suit.

"Commanders have to stay loose," Launa warned. "Your job is to send people to fight, not fight yourselves. Remember that."

All morning, they walked the compounds, checking fire lanes, strong points, weak points, weighing who could be pulled off to cover one problem, who was best for another. Launa had planned the defense of Tall Oaks around a hammer and anvil that she just knew would work. It had . . . barely.

The defense of Brege Town would be a rolling series of option plays. The players were fully briefed and ready, even eager. Jack would call the plays when the time came.

Around noon came the first surprise. Half of First Dragoon was still on scout and fire duty. One galloped in shouting, "Twenty horsemen with three totems ride fast for Brege Town."

Jack raised an eyebrow. "What's that all about?"

Launa rubbed her eyes, feeling grit in them. Once again she tried to clear her blocked sinuses. "Sounds like someone's got smart enough to take a gander at the opposition."

"Should I mount the cavalry?" Dob asked. "If they are wise enough to know the wisdom of this, should we kill them before they can sing their song, like you did the horsemen at the Tree?"

Launa shook her head. "The battle will be here. Let them see what they hunt. But we will not let them see too much." She turned to the rider. "Tell Bomel to keep the horsemen in sight. Before they come to Brege Town, we must know so that we can make sure they see nothing of pike and bow."

The scout leaped back on his horse.

"Jack, have I forgotten anything?" Launa asked.

"Sounds like everything's covered."

They returned to their walk around.

Shokin was covered with soot. Others around him hacked and coughed. The steppe was burned black. Even some of the trees beside the streams that were so many here had taken fire. The water was thick and muddy. The Mighty Man rode in silence. Even the shaved-headed ones had fallen quiet. In the distance, Shokin could see riders. Some set fires, others watched them and followed. Most were left behind. Few kept pace with Mighty Men when they rode with many spare horses. Still, some did.

"Who are these rabbits who watch us?" Mozyr asked. "Should I send some of my Swift Eagles to bring one before us?"

Shokin shook his head. "It will be a long chase. We can not be sure how it will end. One of your warriors did not return from his search along the fens for the hunter's boy and girl."

Mozyr grimaced at the reminder.

"Learn, young Mighty Man. When you hunt the wolf in its own den, it may bite you. We must fight the battle we choose, where we choose. Watch today, and Galatan will show you how it is done."

Mozyr grunted and said nothing.

The sun was starting down the sky when they splashed across the river below the strange place and guided their horses up a hill to a single tree.

Shokin eyed the valley. "This is the camp where I, Arakk, and Orshi of the Broad Sky Clan took many slaves. But it has changed much."

"Um" was all Galatan said as he eyed the valley. The shaved heads glowered at Shokin as if somehow it was his fault, but said nothing. Their arrival was noticed. Sacks on their backs, farmers scurried for the holes in the cage that now stood around the camp. Those still in the field started fires.

"Even their own grass they burn." Mozyr shook his head.

"How did it go, the last time you came to this camp?" Galatan asked Shokin. Shokin closed his eyes. It was easier to remember that day if he did not look upon this one.

"Each totem crossed at a different ford downstream. We came to rest before the town there." He pointed to a place well away from the wall. "The place was bigger, spread out more. Many came out to meet us. None carried bows or lances. With a whoop, Arakk's Clan began to take heads. Only then did the people run. We chased them down like rabbits."

"They are not rabbits today." Galatan rubbed his beard.

"No."

"But they have caged themselves like rabbit," one shaved head laughed derisively.

Shokin snorted. "A cage that keeps us out. See them carry food into that cage. We will sit outside, bellies growling, as they feast within."

"Their cage has a hole in it." Galatan pointed to the west. "Even now they struggle to set more wood in the ground."

"There is still room to lead four hands of totems at a gallop there." One of the shaved heads fondled his sky metal ax.

"It is inviting. Like the gaping jaws of a bear," Shokin observed dryly.

"Then let your totem not ride there," Galatan snapped. "Arakk said you had no stomach for the fight. Let the Swift Eagle and the Broad Sky Clans ride where you did on that day last spring. When you have drawn all of them to you, I will lead the other totems from the woods to the west. We will gallop through the camp. If the cage has held you out, we will open it for you." Galatan's grin showed much teeth.

Shokin knew when he was being named a weak woman. *When have I wronged you?* Still, he held his tongue. This stank of the shaved heads trying to divide the Horse People who had long ridden the low steppe. Besides, Shokin did not like the smell of this valley. Why should he let insult drive him to fight for what he would not do otherwise?

Mozyr was not so easily put off. "Let me ride with you, Mighty Man. I have blood to settle with those rabbits."

Galatan dismissed him without even a glance. "You have tied your totem to the Stalwart Shield. You will ride with them."

Mozyr's glare was for Shokin. Shokin shrugged. "Wise Galatan, you may want some of my warriors to ride with you. There are three crossings shallow enough for horses to the west of the camp. We found them the day after we burned this place."

"Good. Send a warrior to show us those places. We will send him back that you may know to start your attack on this place."

Shokin trembled with anger, but he held it on a tight rein. The Mighty Man had turned his face from him. Shokin had done nothing to deserve this; still, it was done, and he could do nothing to stop it.

Shokin could challenge the Mighty Man. Galatan might fight him. More likely, one of the shaved heads would use his sky metal knife to put a quick end to Shokin. The Mighty Man of the Stalwart Shield Clan had long ago learned to bide his time. The sun that rose today would set tonight.

Shokin kicked his horse and rode away.

Behind him, he heard laughter. Then Galatan and his new friends began to plan the second burning of this place.

Jack and Launa watched the horsemen's recon unit from the tower above the sanctuary. When one totem galloped away while the others stayed to point and plan, they both raised questioning eyebrows. "Wonder what that's all about," Launa muttered.

"Maybe leading twenty-three totems isn't all that easy."

Launa concentrated on those who remained. "What I'd give for binoculars. They seem interested in the hole in our wall."

Half an hour later, the rest of the horsemen rode back the way they'd come and the two soldiers took the ladder down the tower. Over supper that night, they were still planning.

"I don't want to disrupt the western assault, but I'd like to know when they're coming," Launa mused. "Any ideas, Jack?"

"Putting skirmishers in the trees would be a dead giveaway, and probably mean dead skirmishers."

"We need all the people we can here in town."

"How about putting pigs in the trees? We've got some pretty big boars, and they haven't been domesticated long enough to improve their disposition. If we put several of them in the trees, they would give the horsemen a warm welcome."

Around them, talk stopped. Launa and Jack got several very strange looks. Finally one of the young serving boys blurted. "How will you get the pigs up in the trees? We have seen you do many strange things, but pushing pigs up into treetops . . ." The boy stammered to a halt. "How?" he squeaked.

Launa reviewed their last few words. *Pigs in the trees.* These folks took her literally.

"No, no." She started to giggle. "Not pigs up *in* the trees, but pigs wandering among the trees. Pigs among the trees."

Beside her, Jack was laughing. Others joined in as they too saw the humor. Or maybe seeing their commands slowly slipping into hysterical laughter was funny enough. The poor boy was the only one not laughing. He was beet red in embarrassment.

"I am sorry. I did not understand."

"But you were right." Launa tried to console him. "What I said did not make sense. What you said did. You were right. I was wrong. It is good to question."

The image of some poor boys striving manfully to carry out the crazy orders of their commanding officer by stuffing porkers that outweighed them into trees sent Launa off into another gale of laughter. It was a while before the staff meeting resumed.

That evening, she and Jack were still chuckling over the pig-in-the-tree idea. "Those troops are good. I think they would have tried and probably pulled it off for us." Jack smiled at the thought.

"But they would have wasted a damn sight more time on the project than we've got time to spend."

"Don't go getting serious, Launa. We've done everything we can. Now all we can do is wait. A good laugh can't help but make the time go faster."

"There's other ways to pass the time." Launa reached out and twirled a bit of Jack's hair around her finger.

"So much death on our minds. It is time to remember life."

That night, they did.

Shokin returned to the horse camp at a gallop. It was not easy to find his Clan. The war party had found a patch of grass, not nearly enough for all the horses. Shokin suspected blood was spilt deciding which totems grazed their mounts tonight.

The Stalwart Shield Clan was away from the rest, making camp among trees beside a swamp. Sowon greeted him. "Without you, Father, I could not risk the warriors in a fight for grass." Then his son smiled. "But in the swamp is browse. Their feet may get a little wet, but their bellies will not be empty."

Shokin slapped Sowon on the back as a wise warrior deserved. "I smell meat cooking, son."

"Because of your wisdom, our warriors have something to put in their bellies. Some Clans fight over rabbits. Others slaughtered old mares. Is this any way to ride to war against strangers?" his son asked.

Shokin answered with a grunt. That night, around his fire, he told the Strong Arms how they would fight. "We ride swift and straight to the place we burned last spring. I will tell you what to do when we are there. We and two totems ride for the east end as we did last time. The others ride for the west end."

Shokin did not say why, and the Strong Arms were wise enough not to ask. Without a question, they went to their own warriors. As Shokin settled into his blankets, Sowon did ask. "Why, Father, do we ride far from the Mighty Man of the Clans?"

"I do not know, son. When this is over, maybe Galatan will have a change of heart. Maybe he will not. The Stalwart Shield will grow strong ponies no matter what."

Sowon did not seem so sure, but he did not ask further.

Which left Shokin to wonder what his blood brother would say of today's happenings. "How would you chose life from this wild herd of death thundering down upon us?" Tomorrow, Shokin would keep Taelon close, but not so close he could be dangerous, or make another break for his freedom. Always, there was such a fine line to walk between wisdom and folly. Always.

THIRTY

LAUNA CAME AWAKE wondering if this would be the day. "Think they'll come?" she asked Jack as he opened his eyes.

"We'll know soon enough."

The pounding of hoofs brought them out of bed fast. They got to their door just as Bomel reined in before them. "The horsemen camped last night a hard half-day's ride from here. Most of their horses had nothing to eat but soot. They will come by noon. The Dragoons are falling back as fast as they can."

"Very good." Launa congratulated him. "You must have ridden all night."

A wan grunt was all the agreement Bomel could get out.

"Get something to eat, a bath, and some sleep. The battle will not start until later. Get the rest you have earned." Launa and Jack shared a breakfast with Bomel before walking the perimeter. Going from station to station, they passed a word with every one of the eleven hundred defenders of Brege Town. Here they did a final weapons check. There they sent someone who'd skipped breakfast off for a meal.

Most of these troops had fought to defend Tall Oaks that spring. They knew what lay ahead. They hunkered down; some even dozed. If they were not enthusiastic, they were all confident. Here and there, mixed in the ranks, were a smattering of rookies, people who'd walked in early in the summer before Hanna cut off reinforcements. They hid their nerves in silence.

The pikes who stood with Cleo were silent, too—dead silent. While others built the wall, these had ridden the steppe, hunting . . . deer officially, horsemen in reality. Now the horsemen were coming to them. They lay by their pikes, combed each other's hair . . . and planned tonight's feast.

There were also the "reserves." Every block had a few grandmothers and grandfathers, girls and boys assigned to it. Officially, they cared for toddlers. Unofficially, they were the street watch and runners. If a breakthrough occurred on any street, the little folks would be sent hustling to take the word to the compound commander.

"Not exactly your electronic battlefield." Launa shrugged. "Best we got. It'll have to do, hon."

Too soon for Launa, they were at the sanctuary. The command post loomed over the longhouse. The sun was edging toward noon.

"It's time, isn't it?"

"Each, to our own station, must go." Jack nodded.

"Take care." Launa hugged her man.

"Do good," he whispered back.

Launa turned and, without a backward glance, marched down the dusty street to the incomplete west gate. *Everything is done. Now we wait.*

Antia presented herself to Cleo. "I want a place in the pike line. The first line." It was hard to beg one who once had followed after her, but today Antia would beg. She stood, still spotted with dried blood and old sweat.

"You are not supposed to leave our house," Cleo whispered.

"It does not matter. I will not live to see tomorrow."

"If you want to die, put the knife in your own belly. I will not risk our sisters to let you find a place to die."

Antia burned at the accusation. "Do you think I will let a horseman have my blood cheap? Please. Let me stand in the front of the line. Let me trade my blood for many of their hearts. Please, sister, I know I have taken a life and deserve to give up my own. Do not let my blood flow on the ground for nothing."

Cleo looked long and hard into Antia's eyes, then nodded. She turned and led Antia through the four rows of pikes to the front rank. "Sassa, will you loan Antia your pike and shield?"

The woman's nod was slow in coming.

"Do not worry," Antia said, taking the woman's arms. "I will not need them long. You may have them back soon."

To Antia's right was Alis, to her left Beth. They had gone with her to get water on that long-ago morning. Antia had cut their rope of slavery with her own knife. They grinned at her, happy again to kill horsemen. *Yesterday, I may have led you wrong, but today we fight together.*

Everything is done. Now we wait.

After Jack entered the sanctuary, others closed and barred the door behind him. For better or worse, here he would fight the battle. Masin grinned. "We missed the battle at Tall Oaks. Now you put us in the middle of the battle. At least these old bones will not have to run from place to place."

Jack clapped the man on the shoulder. "Give me six or seven of your best archers. We will enjoy the view." Jack grabbed his bugler and headed up the ladder.

Masin signaled six others and followed Jack.

In the lookout, Jack slowly turning to take in the vista. To the north, the trees hid everything. To the south, east and west was a clear view of the blackened fields of Brege Town. Off to the south was the hill and observation post he and Launa had used last year when the horsemen sacked River Bend. Yesterday, the horsemen had put it to the same use. Jack would worry if they did so today. He doubted they were smart enough.

Jack assigned archers to each side of the tower. "Let me know what you see. Use your eyes. No arrows until I say so."

His "eyes" nodded acceptance of their orders. Jack, Masin and the boy with the ram's horn stood in the center, slowly doing three-sixties. Then Jack rethought himself. "Son, go get your drum. No need to use your horn to announce the horsemen's arrival. We use the drum for the first call."

The boy disappeared down the ladder.

Jack continued his turns. *Everything is done. Now we wait.*

Shokin halted his warriors in the trees. The Swift Eagles spread out under the branches to the right of his warriors. The Broad Sky Clan was on his left. In the shade, they waited.

Mozyr and Orshi joined him.

"How long do we wait?" the young Mighty Man demanded.

"When Galatan has crossed the river and is ready, he will send my son back. Then we will attack."

Orshi frowned in puzzlement. "How do you attack people on a hill like that?"

"We will ride up to it and jump over it," Mozyr snapped.

"That you will do," Shokin agreed. If any warriors should die in such a foolish waste, let the Swift Eagles bleed. He studied the sight before him. "There is a path into their cage." He stumbled over words, forcing them to fit what no horseman had ever seen before. "They block it with wood." Shokin glanced around. "Gather firewood and brush that they have not burned. Maybe we can burn our way into their camp."

Mozyr greeted that with a snort, pulled his horse around and cantered to his warriors. Orshi shook his head. "That young man has much to learn. May he live long enough to learn it."

Out of the corner of his eye, Shokin carefully took Orshi's measure. "Today may have much to teach those with open eyes." He had made the opening, as ambiguous as an unworked lump of flint. He waited to see what the Mighty Man would make of it.

Orshi grunted. "And I will not lead my tribe off a cliff because those landless ones can see no other place to ride."

Shokin knew the words he spoke next could cost him his head. He threw the bones. "You and I have lived in peace with these farmers for many years. I do not want war to the death with the other Clans, but I will not have my Clan vanish from the steppe like the Stormy Mountain Clan." It was said. He waited for the other Mighty Man to pull his knife, denounce him as a coward.

Orshi flipped the loose reins in his hands. "There is wisdom in your words. How do we keep our heads and ride between this place and the other Clans?"

"I cannot see that trail," Shokin sighed.

"Tell me first if you do," Orshi scowled.

Shokin dismounted and signaled for the others to do the same. There was nothing to do until Sowon returned with the word to attack that which could not be skewered on a lance.

Everything is done. Now we wait.

Launa knew she had bad guys in front of her. The pigs had been singing for the last hour or so. From the sound of it, a few horsemen were hungry enough to tangle with the porkers. The pigs appeared to be ahead on points.

Launa glanced back at her deployment; she'd done all she could. One of the archers on the wall pointed. "Horsemen come."

Launa's head shot around, checking the woods she expected soon to explode with horsemen. Nothing.

Then she spotted four horsemen coming around the bend in the river below the hill. Instead of taking the usual trail along the river, they arrowed straight across the burnt fields.

Launa studied the four. Three carried lances. The one in the lead bounced as he—no, she—rode. "Sweet Jesus, it's Lasa! Archer," Launa ordered, "get out the longbows. Cover them. They are not horsemen, but People."

There was noise from the wall as short bows were traded for long ones. Launa worried her lower lip as she measured the gap between her and Lasa, and between Lasa and the horsemen in the woods. Would they bolt out to cut off these four?

Launa sweated the approach of the Speaker for the Goddess in Tall Oaks. Then she remembered why Lasa had risked a grueling ride in early pregnancy. She really sweated.

The horsemen made no move on the detachment. Launa ordered her archers back to short bows and stepped forward to greet Lasa.

"Where is Brege?" Lasa called as she reined in her mount.

Launa captured the horse's bridle, soothed the animal, then looked up at the woman who had shown her how to be a woman in command. "We could not heal the wound. We buried Brege in a soldier's grave."

Lasa covered her eyes with her right hand, her left gripped the horse's reins. For a long minute, her body shuddered in silence. When finally she wiped her eyes, she looked straight at Launa.

"Take me to my firstborn daughter's grave."

"I cannot," Launa said. "The horsemen have come. I feared they would attack you as you crossed the fields of Brege Town. Many more will go into the grave before the sun sets."

"Brege Town," Lasa echoed.

"The People call this place Brege Town."

"Where is Kaul?"

"He commands the east gate."

"I must go to him."

The twenty-first-century commander in Launa doubted any good would come from the two parents sharing their grief only moments before a battle must begin. But Launa, war leader of the People, would not stand in Lasa's way. "The gate is straight down this street, past the sanctuary. Ride slowly. Every archer is hardened to kill all who ride these streets today."

Lasa slipped from her horse. "I will walk."

Katan-ki of the Chosen Ones smirked as he followed the one who called himself mighty among these low steppe clans. They were like children, playing at war. When his father Zuhan-ki rode among them, then they would know fear. For now, Katan-ki rode as a young son should, learning the lay of the land. Real war would come soon enough.

From off to his left came squeals and grunts.

"What are those fools doing now?" Azik-ki scowled, tapping the flat head of his ax impatiently in his left hand.

"The poor boys are hungry, so they chase a little piggy," Pagear-ki snickered.

"From the sound, that piggy is far from little," Katan-ki snapped. "If they keep up this racket, we will be no surprise."

"If the warriors of four hands of totems need to surprise farmers, they are not warriors at all," Azik-ki snorted.

The others laughed at his joke.

"How long do we wait for Galatan to order the attack?"

As if he had heard Katan-ki, the Mighty Man of the Horse Clans raised his hand. "We are all across. Send the boy to Shokin. We will attack after we hear his drums."

THIRTY-ONE

SOWON SPLASHED ACROSS the ford and galloped for Shokin.

"Warriors, mount!" the Mighty Man ordered even before his son was in earshot. Around him, the woods came alive as men strung bows, leaped to horse, couched lances.

"Galatan says attack!" his son shouted.

"And we do!" Shokin shouted as he trotted out of the shade. Where only trees had been a moment ago, a forest of lances now stood. Here and there spirited horses reared, eager for a run.

"Let the drums sing," Shokin ordered. Mounted drummers began to pound their quick tattoo.

"Follow me," he shouted, "and we will again see how red the blood is of these dirt-diggers."

The warriors cheered. Shokin led off at a walk, his totem high at his side. No warrior of the Stalwart Shield would race ahead while that totem flew high.

To his right, Mozyr waved his knife. "Follow me and we will fly like Swift Eagles into that place. The ground will run red with their blood." The Mighty Man kicked his horse to a gallop. The totem and warriors of his clan raced after him.

Shokin continued to walk his horse. To his left, Orshi did the same. Here and there, a young warrior broke from the line. Just as quickly, a Strong Arm shouted him back into place.

No one advanced past the totem. The totem advanced at a walk.

"Sound the drum," Jack ordered as he examined this development. Clearly, this was a demonstration. Some poor dumb soul had orders to play Reno, attracting all the warriors to the front of the camp while Custer snuck around back where the slaughter of women and children would be easy.

Just as clearly, somebody was not playing Reno balls-to-the-wall. "Someone in that lash-up has a little common sense."

Not everyone had gotten the word. Sixty or so warriors raced for the east gate as if their horses had wings to fly over the ditch and wall.

"They're all yours, Kaul," Jack whispered.

"Short bows only," Kaul shouted from the tower by the east gate. "We want to bloody their noses, not chop them into stew."

Laughter greeted his observation.

"And keep your heads down. These are only cute puppies. The she-wolf will come later."

"They do not look cute," the young archer beside Kaul whispered.

"You skinned your knuckles often enough building this wall, now let it fight for you," Kaul answered her, then raised his voice again. "Wait. Let them get closer. Wait."

The line of charging horsemen swept toward the ditch. Here, as at Tall Oaks, they had planted it in brambles. The racing horsemen could not see the bottom of it.

Warriors came at the ditch in full gallop, kicking their horses to leap it. Their mounts arched over the ditch, but the sloping wall offered poor footing. Horses stumbled, sending horses and riders rolling into the ditch and its waiting spikes. Luckier riders kept their balance and fought their way up the wall.

Other riders slowed to a trot, guiding their mounts down

into the ditch. They pitched forward, finding out too late that the ditch was as deep as a man was tall. Many horsemen lost their seats and fell into the thorns. Several fell on the stakes the greenery hid. Screams of horses and men rang from the ditch.

"Now, archers!" Kaul shouted. "Let the arrows fly."

The lucky ones who had made it across the ditch quickly fell to arrows and slung stones.

Now riders on the slower horses approached the wall. They reined in, looked right and left, hunted for a way around the screaming cauldron in front of them.

The archers took them under fire.

Horsemen traded lances for bows, but it was an uneven fight. They were in the open, shooting uphill, on horses panicked by the smell of blood and screams swirling around them. The women and men on the wall stood on firm ground, shot downhill, and only provided a target for the moment it took to shoot.

Many horsemen felt the sting of arrows.

"I see the one with the totem," the archer next to Kaul said. "I can put him down."

"No, daughter." Kaul shook his head. "That one will call them all back soon. Let him live to do that."

Shokin halted the Stalwart Shield warriors just outside bow range. Orshi trotted over to him as Mozyr galloped back.

"Why do you stop?" the one who led what was left of the Swift Eagle Clan screamed. "Ride with my warriors."

"They are doing enough bleeding for all of us," Orshi said dryly. "They are not doing anything else."

Mozyr snarled and reached for his knife.

"Enough." Shokin raised his hand. "The day has only begun. There are enough farmers hiding up there. We need not fight among ourselves. Tuk, bring forward the wood your warriors gathered. Jassan, put flint and stone to your fire arrow."

Five warriors dashed through the milling Swift Eagles to the place where there was no ditch and only wood separated them from those they would slaughter.

Tuk took an arrow in the chest. As a warrior should, he paid it no heed as he hurled the wood and brush he had bound together. Only then did he slide from his mount to die.

Five bundles of grass, tinder, brush, and wood lay against the wood that blocked their way. Jassan spurred his mount, a flaming arrow nocked. Arrows reached out for him, but he fired his arrow into the bundles and returned out of range unharmed.

The flame danced from arrow to bundles.

"Ha," Shokin laughed. "Now we will show them how Horse People fight."

"Bring water!" Kaul shouted. There were jugs of water for drinking on the wall; none were close.

"I will bring one."

Kaul's head snapped around. "Lasa?"

The Speaker for the Goddess in Tall Oaks grabbed a water jug and hustled up the steps. But there would not be enough water in a hand of jugs to put out the fire.

"The fire spreads too fast," shouted the young archer beside Kaul as she grabbed a spear and dropped down the ladder from the tower, hardly touching the rungs. She vaulted through a firing port and half slid, half fell down the grass-covered mound. In a moment, she was knocking bundles away from the gate, swinging the spear like a club. The fire grew but, scattered, it consumed only itself. The wall was left blackened but unburned.

Dumbfounded, the horsemen recovered. Arrows arched for the one who had spoiled their fire.

"Quick, throw that girl a rope," Kaul ordered.

Several did. The youth grabbed one and half walked, half was dragged back up the wall. In a moment she stood, grinning and unharmed, back among them.

"Well done!" Kaul pounded her on the shoulder.

"Very well done," Lasa said. "Launa and Jack will hear of this when the day is done. I myself will make a song of you. What is your name?"

The young woman beamed, then ducked as more arrows

thudded into the wall around them. She glanced back at what she had done, as if taking it all in for the first time . . . and gulped. "My name is Tearee, and you may do what you will, but someone else will knock away the next fire."

"There will be no next fire," Kaul growled. "Archers, string longbows. The next rider who lights an arrow or rides at us with wooden bundles dies quickly and far from the gate."

Lasa came to Kaul wordlessly, accepted his hug, and gave one in return.

Around them, longbows came out of their scabbards. Grim-faced archers would play with the horsemen no more.

Shokin frowned grimly as the fires gutted out that should have opened a path for him and his warriors. He could honor the courage of the one who spoiled his plan even as he wished she had paid in blood for her boldness.

"Let us get more wood," Mozyr shouted. "More fire arrows. We will be ready for such a one as that next time."

"And they will be ready for us next time," Shokin muttered, but Mozyr ignored him, sending Swift Eagle warriors galloping back to gather more tinder.

They returned to Mozyr's complaint of "What kept you?" They died before they had even ridden up to their Mighty Man.

Orshi whistled as the arrows arched over them to take the fire-bringers down. "What arrow flies that far?"

Shokin shook his head. "None that fit my bow, but maybe my blood brother can speak of such arrows. Sowon, bring Taelon to me. I will be over there," Shokin said, pointing to a place a hundred paces farther back from the wall. His son kicked his horse and rode to obey.

As the totems of the three clans trotted to the place Shokin had chosen, the warriors drifted back. Even the angry young men of the Swift Eagle Clan seemed too taken aback by what they had suffered to think of anything to do next.

Some slipped from their horses to run to the side of those who called out in pain. The archers on the wall did not shoot at them, but let them come, a few at a time, to take away the wounded. No one of the Horse People would have allowed that.

Shokin watched and learned.

Sowon galloped to them, Berok and Taelon behind him. The hunter was remembering more of the Horse People's words. Shokin pointed to the fire-bringers in the dust. "My blood brother, what do you know of arrows that fly so far?"

Taelon glanced at the bodies, then measured the distance from them to the wall. "I know that we are not far enough back."

"Still," Orshi breathed.

"I have shot deer twice as far away as you are from that wall."

Orshi signaled his Clan, and the warriors began to back off farther. "Who is this man who brags to us?"

"Let me make known to you my blood brother," Shokin said. "As a young man, this one rode among us for a summer. Now he leads the hunters who call themselves the people of the badger. He also fought beside Launa when Arakk lost his head."

"Any enemy of Arakk is a friend of mine." Orshi grinned, but he did not clasp the hunter's arm. "Maybe we should have listened to the words that farmer brought to the winter camp."

"My friend Kaul may well lead the archers who shower you with arrows when you ride too close to the wall."

Orshi shook his head ruefully. "Their women fight like men and even their men we make into women fight like night demons. What are we doing here, Shokin?"

"We came here to cleanse the steppe of these dirt-scratchers." Mozyr's voice was a strangled scream.

"We are three totems. Where are the warriors of the other four hands?" Shokin reminded them. "We do not fight alone."

Kaul watched the totems back away from the wall. "Someone is wise." Then three riders joined the totems, and they really distanced themselves. "As if they know how far our arrows fly," he muttered. One of the riders had not ridden as well as the others; his head bounced as badly as a farmer's . . . or a hunter's.

"Does that one look like Taelon?" he asked Lasa.

She squinted long. "Yes! It is the old hunter. He lives!" Lasa rejoiced, then sobered. "At least for now."

Kaul gave her a quick hug, then stepped to the inside of the wall. He spotted a boy. "Fellow, run to Bomel. Tell him to tell Das that I have seen his father. He yet lives."

The youth took off running.

Kaul stared at the tower that held Jack. "I have fought three totems to a standstill. Where are the other twenty?"

Jack grinned. "That's the way to go, Kaul. Launa couldn't have done it better. It will be a while before those SOBs try anything. Now, where are the rest of them?"

"Jack, I think we have found them," Masin said softly.

Jack turned, and whistled. Three columns of horse galloped from the woods, straight as an arrow for where the west gate wasn't. It was a good three thousand meters from where they started to pour out of the forest to the hole. Each column was quickly filling that distance. Two, three thousand horse at least. "Great Goddess," Jack breathed.

"Help us." Masin finished the prayer.

Jack crouched behind the palisade, both for cover and to let him observe without being noticed. "Well, Launa, you got all the bastards where you wanted them. Here's hoping the trap holds."

THIRTY-TWO

LAUNA CHECKED HER little fire team once more. A dozen spear carriers, as many archers and slingers. They were almost lost in the thirty meters of front they tried to cover. But then they didn't have to cover it, just look like they were trying.

"Ah, Lady, behind you," the one closest to her said.

She turned to face every damn horseman on the steppe. No line for these guys; they broke from the woods in three columns and galloped straight for her. It was one thing to calculate numbers in her head, another to see those numbers, lances leveled, charging straight for her. *Me! Personally!*

Launa gulped. Her knees went weak; her legs wanted to run. They didn't care where, just run. What she did was turn to face her troops as she slowly unwound her sling and settled a bullet of jagged flint in it. "Steady, soldiers. Steady. Slingers, hit them when they reach the first marker." She'd paced off two hundred fifty meters yesterday. "Put four or five rocks out there. Archers, I will tell you when to let fly. There will be time for only one short arrow. Then run."

"Good," someone croaked.

"Do not worry, I will not lose any of you. We will all live to fight the horsemen in the town. We will all fight again."

"I pray to the Goddess we do," the archer nearest Launa croaked.

The lead horsemen neared the marker. Launa allotted herself only three stones, each bigger than the next. When the third was in the air, she reverted from soldier to commander and concentrated on getting her small band the hell out of the way. Still, it felt good to see horsemen go down to the hail of stones. Grinning, Launa took a step back. "Archers."

They drew arrows to ears.

"Let fly. Now run!"

The line scattered like quail before a hunting dog. No, not like quail. Those on the right went right; those left went left. Being in the middle, Launa had a choice. She dashed left—and vaulted over a hay pile one step ahead of a lance. Two women from the pike cohort caught her. Behind them crouched half the cohort, heads down, doing nothing to attract the attention of the galloping hordes.

This was critical. The horsemen must not slow down. If they did, Launa's tactical advantage would evaporate and the battle would become a slugfest where only numbers counted.

Launa crouched with the rest, not even risking a peek to see if her plan was coming together or falling apart. *It's up to you, Jack. You and your damn command post. I'm down and dumb. Call it right, you hardheaded, lovable turkey.*

Jack couldn't help cringing as Launa barreled out of the way just a hairsbreath ahead of every horsemen ever born.

Like good cavalry, they did not slow down, but rolled right over the opposition, unaware the opposition was only interested in getting out of their way. The lead horsemen galloped straight down the avenue. A few halted beneath the command post, signaling some to head for the north gate, others the south.

"Here's where you get your first surprise, bastards."

Katan-ki galloped behind the Mighty Man. Finally, Galatan ordered the charge. Long ago they had heard Shokin's drums. Still, the weak man waited, riding up and down the line, making sure everyone was in place. Only when the fool was satisfied that all was ready did Galatan return to the front and order the drums to beat the charge.

The fool Galatan would have to die. Sometime during the confusion of the battle would come that moment. The other Chosen Ones rode close to Katan-ki, awaiting his signal. For now, he galloped behind while Galatan led them where they wanted to go.

There was hardly time for three war cries as they galloped from the trees to the gaping hole in the cage the rabbits had tried to build around their camp. Those who should have died to keep warriors from this place scattered. Six hands of rabbits could not stand against four hands of totems.

Still, the trail they rode once they were in this place was strange—not wide enough. Only four or five horses could gallop side by side. There was wood between the wooden tents. A good horse could leap it, but surely there would be easier ways to get in among the women and children. Katan-ki galloped on.

Down one path a woman and child stared at the horsemen galloping by. Katan-ki yelled his war cry and waved his lance at them. The baby ran crying to its mother. She picked it up and gave it a breast to suck. She did not flee.

Almost, Katan-ki reined in his horse, vaulted the wood, galloped to show that slave the proper fear of a warrior. Almost. Instead, Katan-ki galloped on.

There would be time enough.

The Mighty Man reined in his mount before a long wooden tent. Here was space for warriors to gather, shout at each other, decide what to do next. Galatan signaled two totems, sending them down paths that crossed here in this space. At the end of each trail were ways through the earthen hill. Galatan was opening the hill up to bring Shokin's weak ones in. *Good. Let them see what warriors can do.*

Down each side trail warriors galloped, whooping their joy at the day. From above Katan-ki came a long strange noise. He glanced up. A nest had been made. Eyes peered down at him. *Warriors would have shot arrows,* Katan-ki snorted. *These only make noises to their weak mother god.*

Katan-ki dismissed the bird's nest and returned to watching the warriors charge. In the time he had been distracted, people had walked out to stand from one side of the trail to the other. He glanced over his shoulder. People had done the same at the other end of the trail.

"This is good." Azik-ki grinned. "They run to us to be killed, not away from us. They make it easy."

Katan-ki had heard no song of people who ran to the slaughter. He frowned. The soon-to-be-dead farmers stood, long poles slung over their shoulders, longer than a warrior's lance.

"Stranger and stranger," Pagear-ki muttered.

Arrows began to fly from the hill. A few warriors fell to them. Others, hit, did not sway from the charge. *Good warriors. A truly Mighty Man would take many heads with them.*

Suddenly, in less time than it took to blink, farmers knelt, long poles came up, then down, pointed at the charge. Katan-ki tried to see what happened next. He spotted one or two horses leaping high in the air, but the press of wave upon wave of charging warriors blocked his view. Patting his horse to settle it, Katan-ki waited for the victory cry.

Antia marched out with her sisters, grateful that Cleo had given her the place in the center of the line. "Today we show the horsemen our poles are longer than theirs," she growled, hefting her pike. Others growled beside her.

"Keep the pikes shouldered," Cleo ordered from the rear of the line. "You have seen horses shy away from the pike wall in drill. We want these horses to come to us."

Screaming horsemen raced down the avenue. Beside Antia, the women stood, pikes casually slung over their shoulders, eyes ready. Launa had showed them how long it took a horse to run the avenue—and how quickly they could lower and set their pikes. *Launa is so wise. Why did she not see what I saw? But that time is past. Now is now.*

Antia could make out riders' faces now, faces twisted in hate, expectation, exhilaration.

"Lower pikes. Set them solid, girls!" Cleo shouted.

Antia dug the butt of her pike in hard, dropped to a squat and braced it on her left knee. She picked the horseman headed straight for her and aimed the pike at his mount's chest. The horse's eyes grew wide with fear. It tried to halt;

the rider beat it with the butt of his lance. The steed prepared to leap the wall of pikes. Antia raised the point of her pike.

The horse reared and leaped. Antia's pike took it in the gut. For a moment, the horse hung suspended. Then, with a scream of pain, it crumbled. Unable to take the weight, Antia's pike snapped. A flying splinter slashed into her face, but Antia had no time for pain. She scrambled to get out of the way of the falling horse, shouting, "Someone spear that horseman!"

A pike from the second rank did. The horseman's lance arrowed into the ranks of the pikes. "Oh," came from behind Antia; she glanced back. A man in the third rank stood, eyes wide. The lance had gone through him. Slowly, he collapsed.

"I need another pike," Antia shouted. The fallen man's was passed to her. She turned to face front. To her right and left, her sisters had faced horsemen with more time for reflection. Some horses had danced sideways into pikes and now rolled on the ground. Other mounts had stopped so suddenly they had thrown their riders onto waiting pikes. But if the horse survived the first crash, it was doomed by the second.

The horsemen came like waves on the bitter waters. Antia and her sisters had stopped the first wave. Now the second and third waves smashed into the wreckage of the first.

Lances took stalled riders and horses from behind. With no place to go, horses tried to walk on top of downed horses and men. Antia heard the snap of forelegs and the screams of pain. Pike out, she stabbed—first a horsemen, then a horse. The pile grew before her.

Then arrows hit the horsemen. Like a sudden summer storm, arrows flew from everywhere: the rooftop stockades, the towers beside the gate, archers on the wall. Everywhere Antia heard the zing of arrows, the cries of riders as they were hit, the screams of horses as they took what missed. With the horsemen packed in so tightly in front of the pikes, every arrow hit something.

Antia grinned. "Shoot, sisters. Shoot. Let them feel our points." Beside her, the pikes cheered.

"Antia's Pikes!" Cleo called. "Prepare to advance."

That had been the plan. The pikes were to force the horsemen back by advancing up the avenue, giving riders less and less room for their horses. Antia eyed the withering wall of dead and dying flesh in front of her. It reached up to her waist, maybe higher in some places.

"We cannot cross that," a woman in the first rank cried.

"We must," Antia shouted, "and it is best done while they are busy dodging arrows. You in the second line. Advance to take my place and hold your line steady. The rest of you in the first line, follow after me and keep your shields up."

Antia hefted her pike and took a step up on the horse she'd skewered. To her right, a horsemen moved more than a dead man should. She brought the butt of her pike down on his throat. "Watch that one. He still lives."

A pike from the fourth rank jabbed into his chest.

"It is hard to find a place to step," someone called.

"No harder," Antia laughed, "than crossing river rocks when the water is high, and you want to be alone with your boyfriend or girlfriend on the other side."

That drew laughs.

A lot of riderless horses stood on the other side of the pile. Many of their riders lay on the ground, one or several arrows in them. Antia slit a few throats while she waited for the rest of the first line to come up.

"We must do something with all these horses. I cannot see past them to kill the horsemen," she growled. One of the men from the Cavalry Regiment took an ax to the fence. Soon there was a hole wide enough for horses . . . one at a time . . . and the fourth rank of pikes.

"I brought them the easy way." Cleo grinned. "Form a line," she ordered. The thirty pikes formed a loose line across the avenue. Pikes out to keep any horsemen away. Ranks open enough to let a riderless horse pass.

"Well done," Cleo applauded them. Then an arrow took her in the shoulder. "Shields up, everyone. We are not the only ones with archers," she shouted as she crouched.

Someone from the third line came to Cleo's aid with a shield to protect them and a torn smock to staunch the bleeding. Antia turned from her friend to study the horsemen. There weren't many in front of her. Where had they all gone?

Jack grinned. The pikes at the north and south gates had given the horsemen a bloody nose. He glanced down. "Where did that group with the five totems go?" Jack was willing to bet that was the command staff; one of them had ordered the two charges on the gates. Where were they now?

"I think these are the ones you seek." One of the lookouts pointed. "They ride for the east gate, but not very fast."

Jack quickly joined him. "Yes, and they do ride slowly." The archers around the north and south gates were making those streets hot for horsemen. The archers along the main east-west drag were playing it cool. Jack glanced over his shoulder. Horsemen still galloped in the west hole, putting pressure on those inside to go somewhere. With nowhere else to go, they headed for the east gate, but not at a charge.

"Boy, give Kaul two toots. Masin, watch those five totems. When they try to leave, put them down."

The archers grinned as they strung bows. They had watched long enough. They were ready to kill.

Katan-ki trailed Galatan, who himself trailed the Proud Lance Clan as they trotted down the trail. Well before they got to the hill, a line of men and women with long poles formed up before them. Proud Lances they might be, but still they strung bows and tried to shoot down the long-pole ones. Their targets crouched behind oversize shields and seemed no more bothered by the arrows than a warrior was by summer hail.

The warriors were not so unbothered by the rain of arrows falling on them. Soon, few Proud Lances sat their horses. The rest might have broken and fled, but more totems rode behind them, leaving them no room to turn their horses.

Katan-ki edged his Chosen Ones into the shade of one of the hovels, measured the situation, and shook his head. "Only a fool hunts the bear in its own cave."

But Galatan was not ready to turn and run. He pointed at

the wall of wood that kept them from the houses and their women. A warrior kicked his horse and made for it. At the last moment, he had to swerve to avoid slamming into a riderless mount. His jump was not clean.

The horse's forelegs clipped a pole. A sharpened one slammed into its belly. The wood bent, but did not break. The horse screamed, kicking, trying to free itself. That only widened the gaping wound. Entrails and blood splattered everywhere.

The warrior fared no better. Four arrows hit him. He fell back, legs on one side, lifeless head lolling on the other.

"That will surely encourage others to try again," Azik-ki observed dryly.

Other warriors rode up to the wood that blocked their way, hacking with knives or axes at the rope that bound the wood. Arrows put them down before they could strike a second blow.

Galatan turned his horse and kicked it. Pushing others out of his way, the Mighty Man of the Clans began the retreat.

"Should we follow him, or kill him now?" Pagear-ki asked.

Before Katan-ki could answer, arrows from the tower sliced into Galatan and three others around him. More arrows were in flight even as the Mighty Man fell. In less time than it would have taken Katan-ki's father to order the death of a village, five totems were down, and with them, their Mighty Men.

The bird's nest made its noise again. This time it bellowed in three long moans.

"What will happen now?" Pagear-ki asked.

"I do not know what these strangers will do, but I grow weary of being led on their rope. Let us be the hunters for a change." Katan-ki looked around for one of the young warriors who was always close at his side. He found one and grinned. "Brave warrior, you brought down a buck in the hunt with only your knife. Let us see what your knife can cut today."

• • •

Launa came heads up when Jack gave her the three-toot signal. It was time to close the door on these party crashers. Most were in, but a few still were coming. "Kind of like crossing an interstate in rush hour traffic doing seventy miles an hour. Nobody wants to slow down." She'd have to make them.

"Pikes, stand to arms." She strode up the steps to the wall. "Archers, on your feet." Until now, the archers, like the pike, had hunkered down, out of sight, out of mind. Kami, commander, Second Archers, was at Launa's side in a moment. "What can I do for my sister?"

"I need a hole in the horsemen's charge, right about there." Launa pointed with her spear to a thin part of the columns about fifty meters out.

"Archers, put the horsemen down where my arrow takes one."

Kami got her man, and the others quickly expanded the hole. Launa waited for the last one to go by. He seemed a bit taken aback by the sudden appearance of so many people around him, but, like an obedient soldier, he followed the guy in front of him. Launa called her orders. "Pikes, forward at the double, march!"

Second Pike from Tall Oaks stepped off smartly, half of it from the right side of the hole, the other half from the left. They met in the middle, faced inward, lowered their pikes with a shout, and marched forward to plug the end of the street. Done, the cohort commander called a halt. The two first rows stooped. The two last rows stood. They were ready to take a charge.

Third Pike from Brege Town was the question mark for Launa. Samath had warned her they were the last raised and shortest on training. They also had more rookies than the other cohorts. While the other pikes formed in ranks four deep and faced inward, this team would face outward and, since they had more front to cover, only form a double line.

They were supposed to face fewer and less determined horsemen. The riders galloping at them didn't look any less determined. They lowered their lances, apparently quite happy not to have to go looking for a fight.

Kami laughed. "Join me, sisters and brothers. Your arrows cannot miss. We have a 'target-rich environment.'" *Did I drop that modern idiom,* Launa wondered, *or Jack?* It didn't matter. It fit today.

The archers kept the rookies of Third Pike from taking the full brunt of the charge. Here and there a horseman made it through the arrows. Their horses eyed the wall of flint-pointed pikes and shied away. Frustrated, one warrior threw himself from his mount and charged the pikes on foot. Pikes skewered him before his shorter lance could bounce off a shield. Several more tried the same before the horsemen galloped out of bow range.

Kami called a cease-fire. "Do not waste your arrows. We will have plenty of horsemen wanting out of town soon. We must save some hospitality for them." That drew a laugh not only from archers but pike as well. Launa estimated two hundred horsemen were holding on her outside front. She could ignore them. She turned to face the killing ground she had made of Brege Town.

Charging up the main avenue were plenty of angry and frustrated horsemen who suddenly wanted out. Launa grabbed a shield and bounded from the wall to take station behind Second Pike. "Steady, crew. Keep your pikes out and your shields up. They cannot get us so long as we stand together."

Judith had warned Launa that primitive did not mean simple. The People of Tall Oaks had shown her just how smart they were. Now, the horsemen showed her how canny *they* could be.

For the next eternity, they came at her. In small groups and large, they came at Second Pike. With and without arrow support, they attacked. On horse and on foot, they battled to bring down the pike line. With no regard for his own life, one leaped from his horse to collapse the wall of weaving pike tips under his body, making space for his friends to get in among the pikes. They grabbed for the pike that stabbed them through the belly, held it with their dying grasp, trying to keep its wielder busy for the moment it took another warrior to slip past the pike points and use a knife on those who held the clans captive.

Bodies piled up in front of the pikes.

Holes appeared in the pike ranks, too. Here an arrow found its mark, there a horseman's blade did its damage to one who stood in the front rank before a pike from the fourth rank could bring down the interloper.

Pikes from second rank moved into first rank. Third rank filled second. Soon there was no fourth rank.

Launa borrowed five from Third Pike to fill holes, then another five. *Balance, girl. Balance the unenthusiastic ones who look for a way in against the desperate ones who want out.*

Suddenly there were no more horsemen screaming in their faces. Survivors pulled back, sat their horses or just stood like zombies as they caught their breath.

On rooftops, the archers rested too.

The mutual cease-fire grew around them as the slaughter ceased. A glance at the sun told Launa that once more battle had done its strange thing to time. She had aged a millennium while the sun had moved less than an hour through the sky.

Launa rubbed fatigue from her eyes. "Wonder what's going on with the rest of the battle?" she mumbled to herself.

The horn at the command center began to sound. Short toots. Launa counted four, five, six. It went on. "Jack, that's not one of our signals."

She peered at the command center. Smoke curled up from the sanctuary. "Damn, Jack, they're burning you out." She turned to Kami. "You command here. Jack's in trouble. I've got to get him out of there."

Kami saluted. "We will hold here."

Launa was off at a run.

THIRTY-THREE

KATAN-KI GRABBED A Mighty Man as he rushed by. "Do you want to run or drink blood from the skulls of these dirt-scratchers?"

Fear was in his eyes, but the war leader snarled, "Take heads, but not even Galatan can show us how."

"I can show you the trail to their death. There." He pointed at the low hole in the wooden cage that the young warrior had made just as he disappeared through it. A high-pitched child's voice started yelling.

"Hungry Hawk Clan, leave your horses and follow me," the Mighty Man commanded. Fifty warriors were off their mounts in a blink and pushing and shoving to follow. The Mighty Man ripped the hole wider as an arrow sank into his back. He fell, but others stepped over him.

Katan-ki grinned. "Now we fight our battle, not theirs. Azik-ki, do you have a fire arrow in your quiver?"

"Its moss is soaked in much fat."

"Good. Let us burn a bird's nest."

"The horsemen come, the horsemen come." Bomel ran toward the child's voice; twenty Dragoons with short pikes and bows followed in his footsteps.

"Where, little one?"

"There, two streets up."

Bomel ran faster. Rounding the corner, he saw six Dragoons fighting a slow retreat before a growing mob of dismounted horsemen. "Go," he ordered his followers, the only reserves he had. His hands ached to join the fray, but Launa's words had been firm: "You are a commander. Your job is to command. You send soldiers where they can fight. If we commanders must fight, the battle is already lost."

Is this battle already lost?

It has only begun. Bomel went looking for where he could pull two or three troopers off to send them to this hole. He hoped this would be the only one.

"Do you have any more arrows?" Hanasa asked.

"My second quiver is empty," Bonki answered.

"Then we have no arrows." In front of them, the horsemen flowed like a river in flood to the hole someone had made in the fence beneath their post. They could not shoot at the hole, but had hit many warriors before they passed through the fence.

Now they had no more arrows.

"I will not jjjust sit here," Bonki stammered. "I have a knife." He backed away from the protection of their nest, crouched for a moment, then leaped for a horseman. An arrow caught Bonki in mid-flight. His knife stabbed the horseman's back.

Hanasa trembled. She must fight, but she did not want to die. At least not for just one horseman. She pushed aside the thatch from the roof and let herself down into the house. It was empty. At the door she paused. Fighting raged in the street in front of it. Hands of People rushed to meet the horsemen. With a deep breath, she threw herself into the fight.

Jack kicked himself mentally. He hadn't spotted the breakout into the second quarter until Bomel was already rushing reinforcements to meet it. It was hard to see what was going on in the dusty streets of Brege Town once they were covered with a mob of horsemen. "You can't foresee everything," he shrugged.

So far things had gone rather well. They had the horsemen in the trap. They weren't getting out, and lot of them were already dead or dying. *Six or seven thousand arrows puncture a lot of lungs and guts. Hope we don't run out.*

The archers in the tower were down to their last three quivers, and saving them for guys with totem carriers close to them. Mighty Men were getting few and far between.

"I smell smoke," Masin said. They both looked around. A corner of the longhouse roof was burning.

Jack was down the ladder in a flash; smoke filled the sanctuary. Men with spears tried to push the burning thatch off the roof. Thin points weren't cutting it. They needed a rake.

Jack grabbed the stool Brege had used. "Lash that to a spear." In a moment it was done; in another the burning thatch was shoved off the roof. "Hope it lands on whoever started that."

Apparently it hadn't. Another section of roof took fire. "Push it off. Push all the thatch off they can reach."

It was quickly done, but Masin shook his head. "Now they will set the thatch afire and burn the logs of the sanctuary."

"But that will take time," Jack ran to the foot of the tower and hollered up. "Son, blow on that horn of yours. Blow as long as you can. If that doesn't bring Launa, nothing will."

Launa was halfway to the south gate when she ran into Killala. "Samath must push his pikes up the street to the door of the sanctuary. It is the only way to get Jack and Masin out."

Killala was shaking her head before Launa finished. "The horsemen have broken through on south street into Bomel's compound. They have also broken through from east street against him. I have sent him all my reserves. Samath and Kaul cannot advance pikes up the street. The horsemen will be behind them."

"Damn Jack for hanging himself out to dry!"

Killala ignored the outburst. "I hear that Cleo and her pikes are halfway down north street. The horsemen keep their distance."

Which could be true or just an enthusiastic report from one of Antia's people to another. *God, what I'd give for a radio.*

Killala waited patiently. "What can I do?"

"Hold where you are. No, send five people to the west gate if you can." Launa was about to do some very serious robbing Peter to save Paul.

"I will."

Launa ran back the way she'd come.

Jack was back up the tower, sending an arrow at anyone who looked like an arsonist, and knowing his real target was probably blocked by the walls of the sanctuary.

The archers in the surrounding roof strong points knew the sanctuary was in trouble and sent arrows their way. Most roof positions were manned by archers with short bows that barely reached. You could make two of their arrows for one long arrow. "Ah, economics," Jack mused.

The fire was dying along the north side of the sanctuary, or at least the smoke was tapering off. Then fire stared at the south side. "What's the guy doing, trying to smoke us out?" Jack coughed. There was little wind, so no matter which side burned, they got the full treatment.

Or was the guy just sending smoke signals? Jack did a quick three-sixty. The defenders held their own. The break-outs had stalled, but so had the pikes. Neither side really pressed the other. It was as if everyone was taking a breather, marshaling their strength . . . waiting for someone to make a mistake.

"Damn, we've been on the defense. To get to me, Launa will have to take the offense. What trap are these guys setting?" He and Launa had worked out a lot of drum and horn signals. "Quit worrying about me and watch your backside" was not among them.

"Play it cool, hon. Play it cool."

Launa was sweating, from the heat of the day, from the running around, from the risks she was taking. Behind her jogged half of Third Pike. The horsemen outside looked no more interested in risking battle. Third Pike was probably the most rested troop in the battle. Too bad they were also the greenest.

At the north gate, Launa found the report true; the pikes were halfway to the plaza. Dob was with Cleo, who was having an arrow drawn from her shoulder. "Is it bad?" Launa asked.

"I have had worse cramps," Cleo lied through gritted teeth.

"They burn the sanctuary. We must get Jack and Masin out."

"We know," Dob answered, "but even if we get to the end of the avenue, how do we get across the plaza? We will scatter the pikes so widely the horsemen can break through and slaughter us."

"Here is half of Third Pike. I give them to you. Dob, if you can give us as many cavalry with long lances, we can feed them into the pike line as they reach for the sanctuary. There will be enough."

Cleo and Dob nodded. "Just enough," the woman concluded. "But the door is on the other side. Once we get there, how will we get them out?"

"I'll blow the wall with plastic explosives," Launa growled in English. Which got her very curious looks. "I will find a way," Launa answered lamely in the local tongue.

Cleo stood, shoulder bandaged, left arm strapped to her side. "Antia's Pikes, prepare to advance."

The cohort growled as the front ranks stood.

"Antia's Pikes, advance," Cleo ordered.

With a yell, they did.

"I will work my way up to the second rank," Launa told Cleo. "I will tell the new people where to go as you feed them into the battle array."

"You can stand right behind Antia."

"Antia?" Launa frowned. "She's . . ."

"In the front rank." Cleo cut her off. "She fights with no fear. Or as if she fears only tomorrow. I will hate to lose her."

Launa gulped; maybe she was going to end up on a suicide watch after all. As the pikes walked forward with slow determination, Launa wound her way through their ranks to just behind Antia.

"Cleo says you fight well."

"Let the horsemen see how a real woman dies," Antia snarled.

"Or lives."

"Life is for tomorrow. Today is for dying."

The horsemen must have heard them. They'd been backing up as fast as the pikes advanced. Now a man brought his legs up, crouched on the back of his mount for a moment, and launched himself, lance first, in an arc that would have taken him into the advancing ranks. Antia's pike snapped up to spear him in mid-flight. He screamed as she caught him and slammed him down.

"Somebody cut his throat," Antia snapped.

Launa did.

Katan-ki grinned. Whoever made the noise in the bird's nest was important to these people. The wall of sharp points struggled forward, just as he expected.

Word had flown quickly from warrior to warrior that the Chosen Ones knew how to put a warrior where his knife would taste blood. Now many rode close to Katan-ki, ready to do his bidding. He would tell them great and brave deeds to do, and make Zuhan-ki proud of his youngest son.

Katan-ki sent one Mighty Man forward to make the pikes pay for each step they took. The rest held back on his words. "Dismount. Rest your horses. Before the sun is a fist lower, you will do deeds your grandsons will sing of."

Then he smiled at a youth, barely old enough to be a warrior. "Torin is your name, isn't it? Take off your vest and britches. I want you to run where no horseman can go."

Jack watched from the tower, and did not like what he saw. "Somebody's got those bastards organized. Who?" Few totems were still up, and there was no collection to give him a command center to target.

He eyed the advance down north street. Two—no, three pikes were down. Others took their places. Still, it was a good twenty meters across the plaza. Launa would have to cover both sides of that escape path. "How the hell do I get out of here when she does? And who will be waiting for us when we try?"

What's the matter, Bearman, you expecting them to fight the battle by your plan? They're trying just as hard to kill you as you are to kill them. And they can win this fight in the next half hour. What you gonna do?

Once again, Jack made his way down the tower. The sanctuary was filled with smoke. People coughed, but there was enough air to breathe. Masin came to him. "Here is the new shield Samath made for you. It is hard. I have one like it."

Jack fingered the waxed hide; it felt tough. As he slipped it on his right arm, it felt light even with the solid wood plank in it. If he had to go hand to hand, at least he'd be prepared.

Around him, the Woodtown volunteers gathered. They hadn't fought at Tall Oaks. None had put in the long hours of training that the troops of the legions had. In a short time, they would go into battle against men who had lived all their lives for the moment of killing.

Jack had wanted to keep them out of a melee fight. Now it was coming to them. He wondered how many of them would survive the next hour, and was not optimistic. He saw no optimism in the eyes that met him. But there was determination. If die they must, the horsemen would not take their blood cheap.

"When we get out there, watch each other's backs. Keeping a friend alive is more important than killing a horseman." Jack turned to Masin and pointed at the walls around them. "Now, how do we make a door?"

Launa stood at the end of north street; Jack was just thirty meters away. The plaza gaped in front of her—packed with horsemen. So far, the pikes' flanks had rested on the fence along the street. Out there, the flanks would hang in thin air. Horsemen would ride them down. Their slaughter would be total.

Launa wound her way back through the pike ranks. It wasn't as far as she expected; there were only three ranks now. The last row had moved forward to fill the holes made by the dead and wounded that lay scattered with dead horsemen along north street.

Grandmothers and grandfathers cared for their wounded or slit horsemen's throats. Children cut arrows from still-quivering flesh and hurried them to archers who'd shot themselves dry.

If Launa blew it, in five minutes horsemen would be slitting those old folks' and kids' throats.

"Cleo, Dob, here is what you must do. Cleo, form Third Pike into a column of twos on the right. Dob, you do the same with the cavalry on the left. Antia will lead the charge of Second Pike into the plaza. You follow, keeping your points aimed out at the horsemen and keeping them from getting in behind us."

"Antia's Pikes," Cleo corrected.

"Once Antia's Pikes," Launa accepted the correction, "reach the sanctuary, I will split them up, strengthening your lines with them. When Jack's soldiers are out, we will see what we do next."

"Let Glengish and me bring more archers up," Dob said. "We will need all our strength following after us."

"Yes, but hurry. While we gather strength, so do they."

Dob sent a sergeant trotting down the street, calling to archers from both compounds to come down from their fire points and hurry forward. They did, but they were tired. It took time.

Launa found herself gnawing a fingernail. She was putting her time to good use. How were the horsemen using the time?

Torin ran past the houses. All his life, warriors had teased him for how small he was. Now the Horse People would sing songs of small Torin's deeds. He had slipped under the wooden thing when no one was looking. Now he ran down the trail between the wooden tents. No one paid him any attention. Here, children and old people, warriors and women ran everywhere.

Torin rejoiced. Katan-ki had given him the words that would leave all these strangers headless in the dust. Still, he slowed as he approached the cage that kept the horsemen out and these strangers in. On this, the river side of the place, it was not so tall and there were ways up it. He could easily jump it.

But would someone stop him, an archer shoot him. "Everyone must be thirsty," he muttered. He surely was. He glanced around for empty water skins. There were none.

He spotted a jar; it had been knocked over. Damp still showed where it had spilled water on the ground. Torin picked it up. Now, no one would question him if he went to the river.

Still, he swerved away from a clump of people and crossed the wall where no one was near. Once in the trees, he tossed the pot aside and ran east as fast as his short legs would carry him.

Tearee still trembled at what she had done, going over the wall, batting fire away from the gate. *What was in my heart?*

Nothing. Something needed doing, and she had done it. If she had paused to seek a path, the fire would have spread, or the horsemen's archers would have been waiting for her. Strange were the ways of those skilled in war.

A child burst from the trees and ran into the burned fields. "Why?" Tearee asked herself as she put arrow to bow.

Lasa rested a hand on Tearee's shoulder. "Maybe one of the horsemen's children has escaped from the killing ground the streets have become. Why not let it run away from death?"

Tearee nodded. "Arrows are few. I will save this one."

Kaul had left Lasa to watch the wall and taken many archers with most of the quivers to support the pikes. The street fighting gobbled up arrows.

"Run free and live, little one," Lasa whispered.

Tearee nodded her agreement.

"What is this?" Orshi asked.

"For such short legs, he runs fast," Mozyr grumbled. The inaction since the first failed charge weighed heavy on him.

"Soon enough, he will tell us."

And he did, yelling through gasps even before he got to them. "Come quick . . . to west side . . . attack."

"Galatan commands us different?" Orshi frowned.

"Galatan . . . dead," the youth got out as he stumbled to a halt before them.

"Dead!" Mozyr echoed in disbelief.

"What totem do we follow?" Shokin cut to the heart.

"No totem . . . The Chosen Ones show us . . . where to blood our knifes. Most Mighty Men are dead."

"And the shaved-headed ones now tell us to attack the west side?" Orshi stared at the fields to the west. "Four hands of totems attacked the west side, and now they need our three."

"We are inside, but there is another thing that cages the rabbits. They hide behind it and shoot us down with arrows. Katan-ki says you must open up the west side. Then we will ride among them and take many heads. There are some in the west fields, but they have no Mighty Man to lead them. You must."

"So we must pull his nuts out of the fire," Shokin concluded.

"By sticking our hands in the fire," Orshi grunted.

"Let us go and see what we will do. Get this brave warrior a horse," Shokin said. "He has run swift. Now let him ride."

The messenger grinned his thanks.

Lasa knew it was right to let a child live. But fear grew in her as he raced to the three totems. How often had Launa used little ones as messengers? Was this little one such a one?

When the totems trotted to the west, Lasa felt fear. "Where are horses? I must ride to tell Launa and Jack of this." Battle was such a strange path; you could do right and wrong in the same breath.

THIRTY-FOUR

"ARCHERS, LET FLY," Launa croaked from a throat caked with dust. Two waves of arrows slashed into the horsemen; she waited for the third. "Antia's Pikes, charge," she shouted in a voice far from the command presence the Point had taught her.

"Come, girls, they are just horsemen," Antia growled, and led the rush.

The horsemen reeled under the onslaught of arrows followed up by shock attack. Antia advanced rapidly in front, changing the formation from a line to a wedge pointed at the northeast corner of the longhouse. As the flanks came away from the fence, flankers trotted with them, then turned to face out and sidestepped along. Inside the array, archers and ax wielders trotted close on their heels. Every spare trooper Launa could put her hands on was here.

Along the flanks, pikes angled out, holding warriors at bay.

"Now it gets dicey," Launa breathed. "Get that one," she shouted, pointing at a leaper about to throw himself from his horse into the left flank. Arrows slashed into him; a pike snared him in mid-flight. "Good. You archers, face right. The rest, left. Pour it on."

Antia reached the sanctuary and faced right as the woman on her left turned the other way. Launa breathed a sigh.

Once again their flanks were anchored. Now, to shuffle the pikes into a good three- or four-rank line the horsemen would never break.

"Okay, Jack, we're here," Launa yelled. "Now get the hell out of there."

Jack's crew tried making a hole in the sanctuary's wooden north wall. The People knew wood; that wall had been built to last. The east wall was stone, covered with clay and plaster. Speartips easily chipped holes in the covering. The rocks beneath were only loosely held in place. "This we can knock over," Masin promised. "Where do we make the hole in the wall?"

"I will see." Jack trotted over to the ladder and headed back up to the tower—and ducked his head as an arrow went by.

Somebody had fired the insulation with arrows. They hadn't torched the roof, but anyone going up to the tower did so as a bare-ass-naked target.

Jack stuck his head up for a second, and pulled it back as two arrows went by. Somebody did not want him in the tower—and had the arrows to take care of him if he tried.

"Masin," Jack called, coming down the ladder, "I do not know where Launa is or when she is coming."

With a shrug, Masin and his crew went back to chipping plaster and loosening stones. Outside, the noise level picked up: shouting, cries, groans.

"I think this is it," Jack said.

Masin nodded.

"Try to make the hole in the center of the wall."

Grunts answered that suggestion.

"Okay, Jack, we're here," came Launa's voice. "Now get the hell out of there."

Every back shoved against the wall. It went over. From the center to the north end, the entire wall collapsed.

"Oh, no," Jack groaned. Stones, large and small, round and flat, tumbled over, taking many horsemen with them—and burying the nearest five files of pikes. Bouncing rocks slapped into the ankles, thighs and elbows of many in the next four files.

"Now, my warriors, forward!" Katan-ki shouted. "Now we take their heads. Forget your horses. Shower them with arrows. Hurl your lance. Now they die!" Waving his sky metal knife, Katan-ki urged the low steppe warriors forward.

They had gathered around him, catching their breath, shouting to prepare themselves for this moment. *The fools have brought down their own wall of points.* Warriors surged forward to take heads.

Beside him, Azik-ki and Pagear-ki grinned. Now was the time to find a worthy enemy, let them taste the hardness of their new blades and axes. They would do deeds that would be sung around campfires long after their grandchildren were dust.

"Shit, shit, shit, shit, shit!" Launa cried. The line she'd struggled to anchor was gone. Here was her nightmare—a melee battle. All tactics blown, horsemen free to fight the battle their way, to apply their strength directly on Launa's women soldiers.

Launa gripped her short spear. The urge rose to throw herself into the hole, use her own flesh to stop the horror charging down on her people. *You command, soldier. Command.*

"Antia's Pikes, rear rank, about face." Launa spoke slowly, giving the subject of her commands a moment to realize who they were, what was expected of them. To Launa's right, seven women and men raised their pikes, turned, and lowered them again. "Charge!" Launa called.

They ran to fill the hole.

"Ax men, follow them. See if any of the pikes can be helped. If you know how to use a pike, pick one up and use it."

Arrows thudded down around Launa; she brought her shield around. Several of the archers around her had no shield. Arrows took them down. Then a shower of lances arched in, slamming through shields, driving shield and holder to the ground.

As more died, Launa kept up her search for live bodies to throw into the hole. "Cleo, send me who you can. Dob, stretch out your line. We must stop them."

Jack stared at the mess he'd made—and did something about it. "Masin, hold there, where the wall is still up." The man who did not want to run today hustled off to his assignment. This team was a mixed bag, equipped with leftovers. "Pikes, go with Masin. Let no one in. Spears and axes, to me. Archers, get ready to put arrows out there fast."

Jack gave his team a few seconds to organize themselves. The horsemen surged forward, but they weren't here yet. Jack studied the bastards; they were focused on the pikes that had frustrated them all day. They ignored their flank. A few battered pike struggled to stand in the rubble of the wall. A pitiful few reinforcements came around the corner to join them. A dozen pike could not cover twenty feet.

"They'll never hold," Jack shouted. "We got to take the pressure off. Archers, let fly. Short spears, follow me." Jack led the lapsed conscientious objectors of Woodtown into the kind of stupid battle he'd hoped never to fight.

The first warrior Jack stabbed never saw what hit him, so fixated was he on the pike he ran at. The next one whirled to face Jack. Jack smashed his spear butt into the guy's crotch, then spun the spear around to slash his throat. The woodsman to Jack's right deflected a lance thrust at Jack's back. Jack stomped down on the lance, giving his defender the extra second it took to finish off the attacker.

A horseman raced at an axman who struggled vainly to free his ax from a fallen Kurgan's chest. Jack swung his left arm, shield and all, at the horseman's side. He folded, but an arrow dropped the axman. He toppled on top of his kill, blood mingling with blood.

Jack took a step back, tried to catch his breath and recover a commander's perspective. Masin had shoved his long pikes out just enough into the stream of running horsemen—Jack's sense of humor wondered if he could still call a horseman a horseman when he was on foot—to deflect the main pressure away from the immediate hole and toward what looked like part of Dob's cavalry.

Jack grinned. Foot horsemen against foot cavalry. That was a match.

He parried a lance thrust, side-kicked the problem, and buried his spear in the guy's chest. A kick freed the spear of its incumbence and sent the dying body careening into another horseman, knocking him off balance long enough for the spearman he was about to kill to kill him instead.

"To hell with commanding this mess. It's a job just staying alive," Jack muttered as he waded back into the fight.

Launa was grateful for the dozen pikes Cleo loaned her. Maybe it wasn't Cleo—Antia led them. She stepped in front of Antia, stopping them from rushing over in no formation. "Form a line," she ordered. They did.

Launa had seen Jack's charge out of the sanctuary. She could not see all that was going on around the east side of the building, but whatever it was, it changed the dynamics of the force coming at her. The horsemen hit more toward the center of her line rather than the collapsed flank. "Thanks, Jack."

"Antia, advance on the center," she ordered.

With a snarl of rage, Antia did.

Even with the pike line re-formed, it was not the same. There was only enough for two ranks. With so few points weaving their threatening dance, more horsemen slipped by them, or grabbed the end of a pike and dashed up it to slash the wielder. Launa fed axes and short spears into the line, trying to give her pikes some close-in defense.

The battlefield was messy, and too often victory went to the stronger. A lot of horsemen were dead, but not enough to allow the exchange ratio they were forcing on Launa.

Then Launa saw defeat coming at her. A bubble of horsemen plowed through her line. Behind them, all the pent-up rage of the day waited to burst forth.

"Get that one!" Katan-ki shouted, and Azik-ki's ax slammed into another farmer's back.

"That is how to do it," Katan-ki crowed. Warriors faced farmers. While the two fought, one of the Chosen Ones would find a blind corner—then strike. Warriors fell too, but much farmers' blood dripped from the sky weapons of the Chosen.

Pagear-ki slashed at a gray-haired one that should have died years ago. The old one parried the thrust with his own knife—the stone blade snapped in two. Before Pagear-ki could press his advantage, the farmer brought his shield up.

The sky blade slashed into it and would not come free. If the farmer had had a knife, Pagear-ki would have died. As it was, they traded blows while the Chosen One worked his blade free. It came loose bent. Pagear-ki fell back to step on it and bend it back straight.

The old one got away.

Only a moment had been lost, but it was enough. Now Katan-ki faced a solid line. One woman snarled as she made a spear jab at Azik-ki. He dodged, grinned, and invited her to chase him. She held her place in the line.

This was not what Katan-ki wanted.

"Pile in, Launa, these are the bastards that got this bunch organized," Jack shouted at Launa. "Kill them, we win. Otherwise, forget history."

Launa glanced around. The assault on the left was losing its enthusiasm. Only to the right, around the damn warriors with the shaved heads, was the pressure still on.

"Antia," Launa shouted, pointing at the shaved heads, "there is the fight you always wanted."

With a shout of pure joy, Antia traded her long pike for a short spear and small shield, stepped away from her place, and dashed to where Launa sent her.

Antia went into the slugfest just as Merik did. There was a moment of recognition, but whatever emotions they held for each other went into the force of their spear thrusts. Two warriors went down before them.

Launa lifted a small shield from a fallen axman and followed Antia into the fray.

Two, no three of the warriors across from them wielded

those strange weapons. Launa parried one with her bronze knife. Unlike Masin's stone blade, her knife did not shatter. It did take a deep gash. "Iron, we face iron!" she shouted to Jack.

"Tell me about it," he answered, dodging a blow from what looked like an iron ax. "Try to keep those bastards to your front. Any of our troops with stone knives don't have a chance against them."

Launa's opponent grinned, shouted something—"Katan-ki" was the only clear word—and made a slash for her stomach. She parried with her shield this time and began the rhythm of the battlefield. Thrust, parry, thrust, parry, broken only by the occasional extra thrust or parry to help a neighbor. The minutes passed into a millennium, and still the fight raged.

"I am Katan-ki. Die, she-rabbit!" Katan-ki shouted as he slashed for the arm of the woman who faced him. He had seen her ordering men around like a Mighty Man. She would die by his knife. Then all these rabbits would know fear and flee.

Again the shield was there, deflecting the blow. Her blade snaked out, thirsting for his blood. The metal was yellow as the moon, not sky metal. It gave when his knife bit it, but it refused to shatter. Katan-ki's arm grew tired. He looked for a way around this troublesome woman.

His free hand went for the lariat at his belt as he backed up. This woman also refused to advance beyond those beside her. The leather rope loosened in his hand as he shook it out. He snapped it. Like a snake, it shot out and wrapped itself around the woman's shield hand. He yanked.

The rope around Launa's shield arm pulled her off balance; she stumbled forward, knowing she was going down. Beside her, Antia blocked a knife blow with her shield, then slashed with her short spear, not at the one who fought her, but at the man across from Launa. He screamed and lurched backward, unable to take advantage of Launa's plight.

Throwing safety to the wind, Launa rolled and shot from

the ground in one fast lunge. She took her man at the legs, driving her knife into his gut. She waited an endless second for him to knife her in the back. He didn't. She rolled him over. Antia had shattered his knife arm. He snarled as she cut his throat.

For the moment, Launa was unopposed. She kicked for the knees of the man facing Antia. They cracked and folded in a way no knee should. Antia's spear was through him before he hit the ground.

Pain raked down Launa's back. She whirled. The knife blow that should have pierced her had been deflected down by a spear slash. The horseman screamed as Merik slammed his shield up into his jaw.

The shaved head who wielded an ax swung it in blazing figure eights—but he was backing up. Jack stepped into one of his blows. Ax head bit into rawhide and wood—and stuck. Jack stabbed into the horseman's belly even as the man struggled to free his ax. He died still trying.

A great shout drew Launa out of her own fight and back to the battle. Pikes emerged from east street.

"Forward, Cavalry!" Dob shouted.

Now horsemen looked around wildly. Their leaders down, advancing pikes to their side and front, blood lust fled them. In a milling mob, they fell back. The pikes from east street wheeled as the embattled remnants beside Launa advanced over dead and dying horsemen, just the waving of their bloodstained pikes and spears enough to send the surviving horsemen fleeing.

Launa let the others advance. Her knees were barely holding her up. She'd been here before, and leaned on her spear, waiting for the need to vomit to pass. Beside her, Jack pried the iron ax out of his shield. "What's this doing here?" he asked.

Launa shrugged. "You tell me and we'll both know."

Antia picked up the iron knife from the one who had called himself Katan-ki and offered it to Launa. Antia looked like she had more fight left in her. "You keep it for now," Launa said.

The woman nodded and put it in her belt, replacing a copper blade. That she offered to Merik. "You will have need of this when this day is done."

The man's face was empty stone, his soul gone elsewhere, maybe never to return. He took the knife, hefted it. "It has horsemen's blood on it, as it should." He eyed the retreating horsemen through narrow slits. "Let us bathe it in more."

The two followed the pikes.

Launa took a deep breath as Jack came to her. "Thanks for saving my bacon."

"I said come out, not demolish me." Launa could chuckle at it now.

Jack rubbed his eyes. "Not my idea. You look pretty spent, hon."

"I feel whipped. Think we can risk a break?"

Jack glanced at the horsemen retreating sullenly before the pike wall. "I think they can do without us for a moment."

The beat of horses' hoofs brought Launa around. Kaul and Lasa led two spare horses toward them at a trot.

"The horsemen no longer stand before the east wall. Lasa watched them ride to the west."

"Oh, Goddess," Launa whispered. "I stripped the west gate to pull this off. Dob," she shouted, "mount the Cavalry Regiment and bring them to the west wall fast."

"I will need time."

"You do not have time," Launa answered, throwing herself on one spare horse as Jack mounted the other. With a kick, Launa guided it carefully up the littered wreckage of north street before urging it to a gallop along the wall road.

Horsemen were forming for an attack as the four reached the hole where the west gate was not.

THIRTY-FIVE

SHOKIN HAD NEVER ridden among horsemen such as those he found wandering the western fields of this strange place. There were no totems; few warriors knew the ones next to them. Nowhere was there a Strong Arm or Mighty Man to tell warriors what to do.

And Mighty Man Shokin of the Stalwart Shields knew only too well that none of them were his men. None of their wives or children depended on him or his for meat on long winter nights.

"Sowon, get the warriors of the Stalwart Shield in line over there. Orshi, will you put your men on the right? Mozyr, your warriors on the left. I will ride among those leaderless ones and ask them to join in our charge."

"I will ride with you," Orshi said.

"Me too," Mozyr insisted.

"Get your warriors to their place. Then we will talk with the others."

Launa reined in her mount. She had four hundred plus hostiles on her front now. The half of Third Pike she'd left stood their ground, fidgeting nervously in place.

They had a right to.

Launa did a quick assessment of her resources. Antia's Pikes were spent. If the pikes from east gate worked their way around the sanctuary past the mouth of south street, Samath's pikes could go into reserve. She'd move him here fast if and when that happened. In the meantime, she sent a runner off to Samath to see if he had any reserves he could lend her.

A dozen warriors made a concerted effort against the pikes blocking west street—whether to put them down or just squeeze out, Launa had no idea. Neither could be permitted. They died, but another of her precious pikes went down. Even a twelve-for-one trade was too steep right now.

Where was Dob with the cav? Where was help from Samath?

"I want to ride out and talk to them."

"What?" Launa whipped around to face him. "Not again!"

"I want to talk to them," Kaul repeated. "They have not attacked. I do not think they want to. I watched those two in front of the east gate. They did not throw their warriors away."

"You had a ditch and wall there. We don't here." Jack spoke slowly, offering more an observation than a judgment.

"Yes, but they can see the bodies of those who tried to charge here and died. They have not come *yet,*" Kaul insisted.

Launa shook her head. "They just need time to work up their courage. They will not listen to you now any better than they did this spring. We have almost won this battle. We can still lose it." Launa glanced around. "Damn, where are those reinforcements?"

Kaul shook his head. "Taelon rides among them. I have seen him with them. If they have listened to him, maybe they are ready to listen to me." Kaul turned his mount, looked long at the press of horsemen stretching down west street. "Will you kill every one of them?"

"Yes," Launa snapped. "Every one of them dies."

"We are low on arrows," Kami, the archer commander, said coming up beside Launa.

"There are many horsemen dead on north and east street.

Send the children to cut the arrows from their bodies. An arrow that has killed once will kill again."

"Nightmares will be rough on the kids," Jack drawled.

"What do you want to do?" Launa screamed, losing it for a moment, regretting and enjoying the release.

"I've been thinking about things Judith told us up-time this trip. Something about the farmers and the horse raiders fighting themselves to a standstill. She made it sound like the two cultures did nothing but clash. Never met. Seems to me we can annihilate a lot of horsemen here today. It won't come cheap. They'll take down a lot of our people. We can start building an iron curtain between the east and the west, or we can try to build the first bridge." Jack shrugged. "It's up to you, hon."

"Damn it, Jack, we've got the bastards by the balls. None of them get out alive. We've won this battle big time."

"You've won the battle." Jack nodded. "What about the war?"

Launa tried to rub the exhaustion from her eyes. She was tired. *Too tired for thinking. Not too tired for killing? Jack does make sense. Planning a battle is tough. Fighting a battle is brutal. Winning it is everything.*

Or is it?

All her life she'd studied the battles and the wars and the generals . . . the action, fire and movement. She hadn't spent much time reading about the peace that followed the fighting. Which may have been her way of avoiding the harsh truth that all too often the bleeding and dying came to nothing.

How many great victories didn't add up to a hill of beans?

She and Jack had given their word to Winter Dawn and Maria and a dying Brent that what they did would make it different.

Launa eyed the warriors in front of her; they were starting to clump into some sort of attack formation. "We could get killed out there."

"We can run as fast as they can charge," Jack answered.

Launa took in a deep breath, let it out slowly. They had a great victory at hand, to rival Hannibal at Cannae. Was she throwing it away? "Kaul, we could kill them all here today. If you let them live, what will that mean to the People?"

"That we live with less blood on our hands. Before the sun sets, many horsemen will die, but many of the People will also. If we ride out there and find words that will let the People and the horsemen once more live in peace, those people will live."

Launa shook her head. "The People will never be the same."

Lasa shook her head in return. "The People are not the same. My daughter is dead, killed by one of the People. We have learned the way of the knife. I have lived long enough to watch the seasons change many times. In that change is life. Let us find a new path from the Goddess that holds the sickle and the knife, the farmer, the hunter, *and* the horseman."

Launa gave her battle one more glance. The pikes stood like rocks, holding in the horsemen. The enemies stared at each other seeing death. Waiting. Maybe there were words that could stop the killing. Maybe the horsemen could learn to surrender. Maybe letting them live would not mean the death of the Old Europeans and their way of life.

"Okay," Launa breathed.

"I go with you," Lasa said.

"No." Jack and Kaul spoke as one.

"It is no less safe for you than it is for me." Lasa was not backing down. "If the Bull goes to seek the Way of the Goddess among the lances of the horsemen, so will the Goddess."

Launa glanced around one last time, searching for reinforcements. She spotted none. Turning her horse around, she faced Jack. "It's no stag party out there. We do it together."

Launa pointed at the nearest youth. "You, go quickly to Killala. Tell her we go to speak to the horsemen and would use her wisdom to put our words into their words." She turned to Kami. "If the horsemen charge the gate, shoot for them as soon as you can, as long as you can," she glanced around at the other mounted three, "even if you must hit one of us."

Kami nodded at her orders. "We will try not to hit you, but we will take down the horsemen."

Launa closed her eyes, took in a deep breath, and let it out slowly. Was there life or death on that breath? Only tomorrow would tell. "Let us go, Kaul, and share words with the horsemen once again."

The four of them rode out, Kaul and Lasa to the right, Launa and Jack on the left.

Shokin could not use the old ways to shout the warriors into his battle line. They knew what they would be charging into. The warriors did not see brave deeds and honorable heads. They saw their deaths.

"We must make a hole so that the others can ride out of that place of death," he told the warriors.

"They rode in on their own horses. They can ride out again on them." was the answer he got. Still, warriors were warriors, and the totem that trotted behind him demanded they listen. The stories they had heard beside the campfires since they first rode a horse demanded that they follow him into the battle line. But how long would they follow him after he shouted the charge?

Shokin trotted back to Sowon. Behind Shokin there was no shouting, no beating of drums—only worried murmurs.

From that strange place trotted four riders: two men and two women. None carried lances or bows.

"What is this?" both Mighty Men asked. Mozyr's question was sharp, like a knife. Orshi's words hung in the air like an eagle circling on the hunt, waiting.

"Berok, bring my blood brother," Shokin called over his shoulder. Even before his words were spoken, he could hear the sound of their horses trotting forward.

"Who are those people?" he asked as they joined him.

"One is Launa, war leader of Tall Oaks," Taelon quickly answered. "She brought you Arakk's head in a jar." Shokin frowned. *Yes, a jar and enough warriors to have slaughtered my band. Still, that day, she let me live. What will she do today?*

"And the others?" Orshi asked.

"The old farmer you know," Taelon went on. "He is Kaul, who rode to your winter camp to share words of peace. Because of what you did to him, he is no longer Speaker for the Bull in Tall Oaks. Now Jack, who rides out to meet you, Speaks for the Bull and is consort to Lasa. She Speaks for the Goddess. Listen to her and you may live to see the sunset."

"Ha," Mozyr snorted. But he said no more when Shokin cut him off with a glare.

The four halted, well out of bow range of the line of horsemen. "Are they far enough from the wall that the long flying arrows can not hit us?" Shokin asked.

"So long as you talk, you need not fear," Taelon said. "And yes, they have almost ridden far enough from the wall."

"Why have they come?" Orshi asked.

"To share words with you. To see if, together, we can find a path before the Goddess from death to life."

"All trails lead to a warrior's death," Mozyr muttered.

Orshi eyed Shokin for a long moment before he glanced up. "The Wide Sky has watched the dying this day and offered no help. Many warriors will feast tonight in the Great Hall of the Sun. Enough I think. Let us listen to what these farmers have to say. What harm can words do?"

"Words never drew blood from a warrior," Mozyr snorted.

"Look." Shokin pointed.

From the camp, a line of horsemen trotted forth. Though no totem led them, they followed a single warrior. Two by two, the line stretched on and on. At one place, the leader turned, and every pair of warriors behind him turned at that place. Now they rode across the front of Shokin's own warriors. Behind him, the muttering that had flowed like wind in summer grass died to a hush.

Again the lead warrior turned, trotted forward a bit, and halted. The warriors behind him did the same, each one turning in a different place. In a moment a line formed before Shokin, riders stopping knee to knee. They rested in place, their lances held high.

"I have never seen warriors ride as one like those do," Orshi breathed. "What magic is this?"

"Launa showed the farmers the way to stand in line and stop a horseman's charge," Taelon said. "Arakk went down into the dust when he faced that line, and many more today. Now, Launa shows the farmers how to ride like no horseman. They will fight and kill like no horseman. I would listen well to what Launa and Lasa say to you."

Mozyr raised his hand to strike Taelon. The hunter stared him in the eye. Hard and long was the glare they exchanged.

Mozyr lowered his hand.

Shokin shook his head. "I will talk with them. Who will ride with me?"

"I will," Orshi agreed with no hesitation.

Mozyr glared, then nodded. "I will also."

"Berok and Taelon, ride with us."

"Yes, my Mighty Man," the squint-eyed warrior said.

The hunter who led the Badger People nodded with a smile. "May we find a path through this day of death to life."

Shokin echoed his blood brother's prayer, but silently, so no warrior could mistake his intention. The five rode forward as a woman jogged from the camp, a spear in her hand. She joined the farmers as Shokin halted a stone's toss from them.

"I am Shokin, Mighty Man of the Stalwart Shield Clan." Shokin spoke slowly, giving Berok time to translate. "I greet Launa, War Leader of Tall Oaks. Who else do I greet?"

"I am Kaul, who entered your winter camp with no knife. I went to share words with you. Now I stand with hands and hands of lances at my back. Will you listen to my words today?"

"I am Orshi, Mighty Man of the Broad Sky Clan, and I will listen to your words today."

"I am Lasa. I Speak for the Goddess to those who live in Tall Oaks. I will listen to your words and to the Goddess that we may find a path before her in peace and harmony."

"I am Mozyr, Mighty Man of the Swift Eagle Clan. The blood in my strong arm cries for revenge against those who foully murdered my Mighty Man."

"I am Launa, War Leader of Tall Oaks. My blood will answer your blood if you cannot find a way today from anger to peace."

"I am Taelon who has ridden beside both of you. If I can, why cannot we all?"

"I am Jack, who Speaks for the Bull in Tall Oaks. I will hunt with all my heart to find a path we can ride together."

"I am Berok," the translator said. "I will use all my wisdom to put the words spoken by one into the words I know of the other's tongue. I will follow where my Mighty Man leads."

"I am Killala," the unmounted woman said, leaning on her spear. "I spent a winter as a slave among the horsemen. I will never be a slave again. I will follow after Lasa and Jack, Speaking the Words of the Goddess as they are spoken by each of you. If you find a path to peace among us, I will walk it. If not, I have killed many horsemen today. I can kill more."

Launa listened to one introduction after another. Nobody pulled a punch; there would be no hidden agendas here. She wondered what got lost in translation. The silence after the introductions stretched, as if, having spoken their names, they did not know what else to say.

Taelon broke the silence. "This morning, the horsemen rode forth, proud in the strength of their mighty arms. The sun is sinking low. Where are the mighty men now?"

Launa eyed the three mighty men before her. It was possible they did not know what had happened in the streets of Brege Town. Kaul grunted. "Twenty proud totems rode into Brege Town when the sun was high. When I rode out, not one totem still stood."

"No!" Mozyr cried. "You lie."

Launa shook her head. "You have felt the reach of our arrows . . . and their sting. We aimed for those who rode close to totems, and those who carried them. At first when a totem fell, another picked it up. No more. Twenty totems are in the dust and their mighty men with them. The three totems behind you are the only ones still standing."

"And they will be in the dust if you charge my soldiers," Killala said with deadly confidence. Launa bit her tongue; they'd come here to negotiate a way to peace, not slap them down some more.

"Why has the Wide Sky deserted us?" Mozyr pleaded, arms raised to the blue sky above him.

"Because you ride the lands of the Goddess." Kaul entered the search for a way out. "Today you have seen the strength of Her arm. She has gone through you like a woman with a sickle goes through grain."

"Now She pauses." Lasa took the story up from Kaul without a pause. "She reaches out to you like a mother to a wayward child. Will you take Her hand and be nurtured at Her breasts, or will you run away and starve?"

"Be helped by a weak woman," Mozyr spat.

"A woman was strong enough to bear the pain that gave you life," Lasa snapped. "Are you too weak to take back your life from another woman?"

"If you are," Killala growled, "you will die."

"What are you offering us?" Shokin stepped in. "Today, your Goddess has shown us Her strong arm. You invite us to chose Her. If we follow after Her, where will She take us?"

Kaul and Lasa nodded, and paused a moment to taste the question. At Lasa's nod, Kaul spoke. "Your people and ours will walk together. You are hungry. We will eat together by our fires. We have enough. Together, we will roam on horses to hunt the deer. In the spring, together we will plant and together we will reap."

"I speak for Tall Oaks," Lasa said. "I offer this to as many of you as take it and as many as we can feed. There are many towns who will join us in this. If you share yourselves and your horses, they will share their food, their pastures, the warmth of their homes and fires. This we offer in the Goddess's name, if you will come to Her."

"Come to her," Orshi echoed.

"If you ride the lands the Goddess's strong arm protects," Kaul looked him hard in the eye, "you ride Her path. You will follow after us in Her ways."

"Never!" Mozyr shouted.

"I would hear more," Shokin quickly put in. "Would my woman tell me what to do, where to ride, when to hunt?"

"No one can tell another the path for her feet." Lasa gave the age-old answer of the People. "Your woman would be welcome to speak in our Assembly, as would you." She glanced at Kaul, and he took over the answer.

"A wise woman knows when the greatest wisdom is silence. Why would anyone tell a man where to ride, when to hunt? A hunter's nose tells him where the deer are to be found. The greatest wisdom is found when each is free to walk their own path, going where their heart leads them. The Goddess invites you to come and play. She has no slaves. She tells no one what they must do. She smiles, like a lover, and invites us." Kaul paused, a smile on his face. "This is the path we open to you."

"I will never follow a woman." Mozyr pulled his knife and slid from his horse. "My strong arm proclaims the power of the Wide Sky. I will live and die by this knife."

Jack glanced Launa's way and shrugged as he began to dismount. She rested a restraining hand on his arm. "He will not follow a woman. Let us see who is stronger, a mighty man or a mighty woman."

Exhausted, Launa swung her right leg over her horse's neck and slipped from her mount. The rest had been good, but about a million years too short. The others dismounted to gather around her. "Be careful," Jack pleaded. For the first time Launa saw worry in his dark eyes.

"I will be." Even as she mouthed the promise, she knew she would pay it no more attention than Jack ever had. She was about to fight somebody for his life. A careful person would be headed someplace else fast.

"Go with the Goddess." Lasa blessed her.

"And walk in the Strength of the Bull." Kaul rested a hand on her shoulder. "I see you standing and him in the dust. You will do it." The others nodded. Launa took in a deep breath; exhaustion left her as strength entered.

Later Launa would try to figure it out, to find the dividing line between the Power those from her new home blessed her with and the training and glands that her modern world had given her. What she did know was that somewhere she found it in her to pull her knife from her belt one last time, to raise it high over her head and shout, "By my body I say there is none stronger than the Great Goddess." She listened as Berok repeated her boast for all the horsemen, his words stretching out as time slowed.

Turning to face the horsemen's line, she grinned and pranced proudly. She also turned her back on Mozyr.

In the silence between Berok's words she heard the soft whisper of boots on grass. She heard the shocked intake of breath from Lasa and Kaul as they saw what she did not. She heard Jack begin to call her name with so much loss in his voice that it wrung the heart she no longer knew beat in her breast.

She paused in her boastful dance, took a quick step back, and reached for where she would have been.

Mozyr's lance stabbed the empty air. She grabbed it and twirled, kicking out for his belly.

Her timing was off a bit. The blow took out a kidney and cracked ribs as it sent him sprawling sideways.

He bounced back up with hardly a groan escaping his lips. She backed away. She'd won the first round; he'd come on fast and dumb like she wanted, but she needed him dead quick. He'd watched a day's fighting; she'd *done* a day's fighting.

She raised the lance above her head, brought it down, and broke it across her knee. A scream of rage was Mozyr's reaction. Launa turned to face the Mighty Man who advanced on her in a low crouch. She bent the shattered lance double in her hand, and leaned on it.

Across the field, shouts from the watching horsemen started. A few at first, like the sprinkles of a summer shower that will grow into a torrent. If she didn't put an end to this fight soon, their blood lust would be up and this last chance to stop the slaughter would be lost.

He circled her. Launa turned as she leaned on the lance. Exhaustion was flooding back into her, leaving her arms leaden, knees trembling. Mozyr's grin widened.

He feinted, taking a step into the no-man's-land between

them, slashing out with his knife but cutting only air as his next step took him away from her. Through it all, Launa just stared at him and clung to the busted lance for support—the picture of the fighter who had nothing left to draw on.

With a laugh, Mozyr moved in for the kill. He stepped toward her and followed through with a kick to her support. Then, as his leg came back, he pivoted from the hips for the killing stab.

Launa turned her stumble into a spin as the lance went out from underneath her, grabbing his knife hand as it went by her. She stepped inside and used his own momentum to slam his knife deep into his belly, then pulled up, ripping his gut wide open.

As he crumbled, she stepped away from him, her eyes locked on his. The question—how, how, how—stayed in his eyes as they dimmed. He went into shock, eyes fixed on the sky that had betrayed his life and now, in death, refused him any answers.

Launa picked up her knife from where she'd dropped it to grab the lance. With her last breath, she shouted, "I invite you to come to the Great Goddess and live. If not, face me with your knife—and die." Her challenge ended as a harsh whisper.

Berok repeated her words. Launa waited, breathing hard, trying not to look as spent as she felt.

Shokin slowly slid from his mount. His hands he kept far from his knife. He walked slowly to Lasa. Standing before her, he looked into her eyes. "I have seen the might of the Great Goddess. I will walk Her path all the days of my life. The Stalwart Shield clan will ride at Her side."

"May you ride with the Goddess, and know her ways." Lasa modified the ancient blessing to take in the pride of the horsemen. Launa smiled at the changes coming to both people. Orshi was next in line to offer his fealty to the Great Goddess.

Shokin turned to his warriors, drew his knife and held it high. "Men of the Stalwart Shield, we have ridden many trails together. Today we begin a new trail, different from any our fathers or their fathers rode before. If you will ride it with me, come stand beside me. If you will not, I am ready to prove with my knife and my strong arm that the trail I choose is the one for the Clan. If you would prove me wrong, come stand before me and let the Sky and the Goddess show us who is great in the lands that we now ride."

Launa held her breath. Here and there, a few men slipped from their mounts, led them in a slow walk as they gathered beside Shokin. They came, a trickle. But the trickle continued.

Orshi came to stand beside Shokin. Wordlessly, he raised his blade to his own Clan. Several men dismounted. The trickle continued to flow on both sides of the two Mighty Men. They waited patiently, saying nothing, their knives held high.

Finally, only a few still faced them mounted. Shokin stepped forward. "Kotoson, I have often leaned on your strong arm. Your eyes are sharp. Can we not ride this trail together?"

"It is a strange trail. I would not choose it."

"Before today, I would not have chosen it. But look upon the dead. The horse clans rode here in a dust cloud that marked the sky. Now our bodies cover the ground." Shokin bent to scoop up a handful of dirt. "There is a power here I have never seen before. We ride, like the pastureless ones, to see what is over the next hill. Ride with me for a while. See with me what is over that hill. If you do not like it, then you and I can see whose arm is the strongest."

The two horsemen stared long at each other. Finally, Kotoson slipped from his horse. The last holdouts did too.

Shokin turned to the ones who followed no totems. "Ride behind my totem and I will see that your horses have grass to eat and your women and children have tents to sleep in."

All along the line, the riders dismounted.

Launa let out a breath she hadn't noticed she was holding. Beside her, Jack did the same. "You put that guy down awfully fast," he said.

"Had to. These folks had to see the Goddess win big and quick before they could have second thoughts."

"Took a lot of risks doing it, Lieutenant."

She turned, saw the concern in his eyes. "I know. He looked too mad to be smart. I chose to take the risk."

"Take care, honey, you're risking a lot for the both of us."

"You might think about that the next time you hang yourself out to dry." Launa gently nudged him.

"Right," Jack agreed, then turned back to the others. "The horsemen are not alone in seeking a new path. All, Mighty Men, Speakers and leaders of the legions must Speak before the Goddess tonight. We have made a promise. Now we must all find a path."

"But first," Launa turned to face Brege Town, "we got a whole lot of horsemen to teach how to surrender."

The surrender went smoother than Launa expected. Shokin and Orshi made the offer. The remnants of the horsemen trapped in the killing ground of west street knew death was at their elbow. Leaderless, most of them passed quickly before Lasa, mumbling their fealty and accepting her blessing.

There were a few who would rather die with a knife in their hand than live under a woman god. Antia and her band were only too willing to provide them with that opportunity. Most died, knife in hand, a prayer to the sky on their lips. Beth died, surprised by a move that got by her shield.

Killala also made a misstep that made her life forfeit. With his knife at her throat, the horseman gave her back her life. "You fight like a great warrior. Your people have won today. I will not take your blood." He helped her to her feet.

As Launa turned the two survivors loose, Jack stopped her. "They cannot carry the word of what happened today. Arakk's wife slit her own kids' throats rather than surrender. Let Shokin and Orshi take the word to the widows and bring them in."

With a shrug, the two accepted the hospitality offered.

THIRTY-SIX

JACK WAS TIRED. Every bone in his body ached. Every muscle screamed. But his soul ached the most. He'd damn near got himself killed today, and a lot of good people with him. The lives of everyone he loved—and maybe everyone who would ever live—had hung by a thread.

Thank God and Goddess that thread had held . . . barely. Could he count on that luck the next time he stuck his neck out? Jack desperately wanted to crawl in bed, pull the covers up and sleep until the shakes left his knees . . . and his heart. Instead, he had a world to save tonight.

Jack leaned back against the wall of the sanctuary and took a deep breath. The smell of smoke from the fire they'd built in the sanctuary and the stew bubbling on it overrode the stench of death from outside. If Jack looked out the gaping hole where the east wall of the sanctuary had been, he could see horsemen and People alike carrying the dead toward the south gate. The grave they would dig tomorrow would be huge.

Wounded also were carried gently to houses where they could be cared for . . . if they could be cared for. Arrows and lances made penetrating wounds that no one six thousand years away from a modern emergency room and surgery suite could do much for. What they gave was a quick prayer and a quicker slash to the throat. Horsemen and People alike accepted this blessing for what it was. The moans and screams were from those who had not yet received this simple triage.

Jack smiled and let his eyes rise from the grisly remains of this day's work. The roof of the sanctuary was gone; it could so easily have been his funeral pyre. Ignoring what hadn't been, he focused on the stars as they sprinkled themselves across the deepening twilight.

He'd won today. Now, how to win tomorrow? How to win a tomorrow that would fulfill his promise to Maria and a dying Brent? How to make it better?

Today, they'd taught the horsemen how to surrender. Unlike the farmers, Jack knew that the next six millennia were full of armies surrendering today and conquering tomorrow. How do you make today's peace just and fair enough so everyone felt their life too precious to throw away on a mad gamble for revenge or to even up their plight in life?

Jack felt a gentle nudge. The stew was done. The first bowl was his, not because he was Speaker for the Bull, but because Launa had waved it away and the cooks felt he had next call on it. With a weak smile, Jack took the bowl and stood. Today's stew was thick with horse meat . . . there were a lot of dead horses to dine on. From the cook he collected a second bowl and carefully wound his way to where Shokin and Orshi, Mighty Men of defeated Clans, sat. They huddled in on themselves, lost in whatever thoughts come to men who had suffered a loss so immense nothing in their lives had prepared them for it.

Jack handed them the first portions of the stew. Shokin looked up at the offer, confusion chasing dejection from his face for a moment. The horseman shook his head, said something. Berok translated. "We came to conquer and kill you. We have not earned the first taste."

"We have invited you into our homes. As guests, you are deserving of hospitality. We can give you no less."

Orshi shook his head as if to shake off the pain of a blow he had not seen coming. "The way of your Goddess is very strange, very strange indeed."

"The way of *our* Goddess," Shokin corrected him. Accepting the bowl, the Mighty Man bowed. "We will learn that way and walk it with you, side by side."

Jack accepted the renewed pledge with a smile, while his own gut knotted. *What is that way? How do we find it?*

Jack collected two more bowls and took them to Lasa and Kaul. "Wise Speaker for the Goddess who sent forth your consort to share words with the Horse People, today the seeds he planted in the horsemen's winter camp have borne fruit. Does your heart tell you how it will grow and how it must be watered?"

Lasa and Kaul exchanged a glance. The pain of what they had lost was etched deep in their eyes; still, they smiled. The way of the Goddess had demanded Kaul's sacrifice; it was good to hear it *had* been worth the cost.

As Jack returned for more stew, a youth entered, his arms full of wood. The wall inside Brege Town was coming down to warm homes and feed both victor and vanquished. That was good. There was another wall that Jack had to bring down.

With two bowls in hand, Jack surveyed the sanctuary. Exhausted commanders of cohorts, gates, and compounds relaxed on the floor with anyone else who had come to supper. In one corner, sprawled on the ground, his head pillowed on a stone from the collapsed east wall, lay Merik.

Jack took him the next portion of stew.

"I am not hungry," said the widowed Speaker for the Bull in the town that now bore the name of his dead love.

"Life goes on," Jack said, forcing the bowl into Merik's hands, which also forced him to sit up. Cross-legged, he stared up at Jack.

"I do not want another consort. How could I hold another in my arms without feeling Brege's cold flesh? Let the People call another to Speak for the Bull and the Goddess."

Jack did not need to look to know that Merik's words had grabbed both Lasa's and Launa's attention. He patted the grieving young man on the shoulder. "Tonight, we all go before the Goddess to scout out this new path we must walk. Who are you to say that your words have no place before Her?"

Jack turned; there was one more that he must nurture. He spotted her huddled in a corner as far as possible from

Merik. Her back to the wall, legs pulled up tight against her chest, she rested arms and head on her knees.

Jack crossed the sanctuary to Antia.

"Leave me alone," she said without looking up. "I have killed, and I deserve to die. Let me die."

Jack squatted before her; using his free hand, he pried her chin up, forcing her to look at him. His words were soft; in the silence of the sanctuary, they rang.

"You fought like a lion today, where the need was most and the danger greatest. You went where you were told, obedient to orders. If the Goddess wanted your life, She could have taken it hands and hands of times."

"But how can I live with Brege's blood on my hands?" She sobbed, tears flowing once more down cheeks marked with stale blood and dust and earlier tears.

Jack forced the bowl of stew into Antia's hands. She took it as he answered her. "Death is easy to welcome. Living is hard. It means choosing. You chose one path; now live and choose another. It may be that the words you find tonight before the Goddess may help us all. Tonight you live, so eat with us."

Jack turned back to the cooks; they held out two more bowls for him. There was no surprise in their eyes as he served others. No, what he saw around the room was expectancy, and he was the midwife for what they all would birth.

Jack took the next bowl and stooped before Launa.

"Congratulations. You fought an outstanding battle. 'Twas a famous victory.' " Both winced at the poetic line. Both knew this victory had to have meaning, not just for today but for the next thousand years, maybe more.

Launa stared down into the stew, as if under some lump of horsemeat or written in the floating barley might be the answers they desperately needed. Then she glanced up. "We made promises to so many people. How do we keep them?"

Jack stood. "Some of those promises were to each other. Let's see what we can do."

Jack returned to his place beside Lasa, and the cooks busied themselves feeding everyone else. There were few bowls. Most people clumped around stew pots, dipping out their supper with hard bread. The meal passed quickly as hungry, exhausted people fed themselves with quiet efficiency.

When all stomachs were filled, Jack knew it was time to begin the hard part of the night. Maybe even the hardest part of the entire day. Dying was so much easier than living.

Jack stood, his mind still whirling in a search for the best way to start something he would not live long enough to finish. People thousands of years from now would judge if they got things right tonight. Taking a deep breath, he began.

"Today, the Horse People chose the Great Goddess. Today, the Horse People chose to ride a new path with the People." Around the room came nods of assent. They were slow, as Jack would expect from exhausted soldiers, but the nods came, even from the horsemen.

"For many generations," Jack went on, "hunters and farmers have walked the same path. With the coming of last fall, we rode on horses. Now we will ride with the Horse People at our side. Can we ride horses along the same path as we walked? We have faced the lance and taken up the pike. Are some things that were true for your mother and her mother not so today?"

Jack let his gaze slowly sweep the room. Brows frowned in thought. It was Taelon who stood.

"I have ridden with the horsemen, and hunted for many years with the People of the Badger and with farmers. Always we hunted on foot. Since last fall, I have led many hunting parties out on horses. With a horse I could not go through the swamps and thickets I often walked through. Yet, with a swift horse, many of us could hunt far out on the wide plains. I smell the wind. Something new and strange is on it. These eyes," he used two fingers to point at his, "do not yet see the new and strange. Help me to see." With nothing more to say, the hunter sat.

There were more nods around the room, but no one rose to add more insight into what Taelon had said.

Then Lasa cleared her throat and Jack sat down to let her say what she would. Still, he wondered. The Speaker for the Goddess never talked first.

Lasa spoke to the hands in her lap. Her words were low. Throughout the sanctuary, people leaned forward to hear her.

"Today, I let a child live. Maybe he was a small man. When I saw him running from Brege Town, I told the archer beside me to let him live. She did. Life has been the way of the Goddess from of old." She looked up, a puzzled frown on her face.

"Yet today, that young man carried words to Shokin, words that brought him to the west of town and a charge that could have washed over us like a sudden flood, killing all before it." The Speaker for the Goddess shook her head. "I did right and I did wrong all in the same breath. Never in the memory of my mother or her mother has that happened, nor could it have happened. Today it did. Today it did," she echoed.

The room silently digested that thought for a long time. To Jack's surprise, it was Merik who roused himself to stand.

"To do right and to do wrong with the same breath are very strange words for a Speaker for the Goddess. But my heart wonders if that is not the first time one has done so. All summer long I and my consort . . ." Merik choked; it was a long moment before he went on. "We struggled to find a path before the horsemen. Antia said we must ride out and meet them with lance and arrow. Most of us could not turn down such a path. We could not see in our hearts that horsemen would come to us, so we turned our backs on those who did. Now a horsemen is a guest in this sanctuary. Tell me, was your ride to us as sure as the coming of the sun tomorrow?"

Every head turned to Shokin. He shrugged. "When Launa brought me Arakk's head, I took my herds far from you. But when I took her words to the Mighty Men of the Clans and saw how many pastureless ones sat around our fires, I knew this day would come as surely as dark clouds and lightning mean fire upon the dry steppe." He held up his hands, fingers spread wide. "How many hands and hands of warriors died beside their night fires? Had their totems ridden with us today, who can say? I might have still eaten here, but not as a guest." The old warrior shrugged, accepting what was, forgetting what might have been.

A shiver swept the room as the thought sank in. For a season they had been the sheep, backs turned to the wolves that stalked them. Then eyes hardened, backs grew straight and stiff. They would never be sheep again.

From his corner, Merik reached out across the sanctuary with open hands. "Antia, you were right."

Antia looked long at Merik, then shook her head. Slowly she stood, woman, warrior, murderer of her own conviction. "I was wrong. Yes, I smelled the wind. Yes, I saw the wolves at our door, but no, Merik, do not say I was right. I was wrong to turn my back on the People. I was wrong to ignore what we agreed to in Assembly. And I was very wrong to turn my words into the anger that drove a knife into Brege's belly. What I saw was right. What I did was wrong."

Lasa got to her feet, the grieving mother standing with the grieving husband and the grieving murderer. "Today we have all seen how we can do right and wrong with the same breath."

The room gave them time. Time to breathe, time to heal. Merik began to shake his head; soon his whole body shook in denial. "No, no, no! We did not do right and wrong in one breath. For an entire summer, we struggled with this question. For an entire summer, we would not see what Antia saw. We stopped up our ears so we could not hear her. We knew what she did and we turned our backs so we would not have to see, and seeing, do something."

Now Antia shook her head. "The words I spoke to you, the hunting I did, were so strange to the way of the People that you could not hear them, or seeing them, they slipped through your hands like a wiggling fish, never to be eaten."

Around the sanctuary, people's eyes grew wide as they listened, but no one stood to add anything. At last, Lasa lifted her hand and the other two settled in their places, their eyes now alight with the fire they had kindled in other's souls . . . and sparked in their own.

"A child learns to fish, and many fish wiggle from her grasp. Now, the People must learn to fish for that which is new and strange. Never again can we turn our back as we did this summer. Let us talk on how we can fish for what we do not even know how to name."

Masin stood slowly. "Many of you know Hanna. She is

strong in her ways. Sometimes she holds on so strongly to what she says is the Goddess's way 'from of old' that her words sound new and strange in our ears. We of Woodtown have come to look to several other women and men who listen well to the Goddess and share with Hanna what they hear. It is easier for her to hear the Goddess that way. Would Antia and Brege have listened better if both carried the burden of Listening and Speaking for the Goddess?"

Jack caught Launa's eye and grinned. He had started the hunt. Now the People were in full pursuit of the prey. Launa grinned back.

"How can two women Speak for the Goddess?" Killala asked.

Kaul stood. "The Great Goddess is one, yet we know Her as Maiden, Mother and Crone. The Maiden brings the hope and open mind of the young. The Mother knows that her child must be fed and protected. The Crone is wise with her years. Should we walk a path where the Goddess Speaks through three?" He sat as an excited hum filled the room. Killala ducked out and returned with Glengish. The woman knelt next to Cleo, spoke with her, then moved about, checking with other groups before she stood.

"Kaul, there is much wisdom in your words. But we women ask, what of he who Speaks for the Bull? Will he be consort to all three?"

Masin was the one who rose to answer that. "Must they be consorts? I Speak for the Bull in Woodtown and am not Hanna's consort."

A thin smile crept to the corners of Lasa's mouth. She rested a hand on Jack's knee and squeezed. "Did you see that?" she whispered.

"Maybe. Maybe."

Now Taelon stood. "No one questions when I rise to speak for the hunters beside the Speaker for the Bull. Would the People be stronger if we named three to Speak for the Bull, the Hunt, and the Horse?"

Merik strode from his corner to stand beside Lasa and Kaul. "I would be honored if Shokin would join with me in

Brege Town. If the Horse People do not call him to speak from among themselves, I will join with whomever they do."

Now the People of Brege Town got down to serious campaigning. Still, consensus was surprisingly fast in coming. When Antia took herself out of the running with a firm shake of her head, Cleo was put forward as Maiden. Glengish was the easy choice for Crone. The widow that Samath had been spending his evenings with since he loaned his house to Jack and Launa was the front-runner for Mother.

The final calling of these Speakers would be left for an Assembly of all the People. That would come in a few days.

Dob and several of the people from the other towns upriver voiced a concern. It took a while for him to get his words around the concept, but he felt policy was being made here for everyone. He suggested Lasa call an Assembly of all the Speakers over the winter. Lasa nodded her agreement.

Apportioning the surviving horsemen and the widows of the dead ones would take a while too. Dob was sure the plains before Clifftown could take quite a few horses. Any people that other towns would not provide a home for, he would take—and their horses.

Jack shook his head. "I'd expected to spend half the night listening to the People yammer on about these ideas."

Launa grinned. "These are the ones that came through for us. They've faced the horsemen and know you can't waste time diddling when there's a lance galloping at you."

Jack looked down at Launa. "So we've changed them."

She glanced around the emptying room as folks left for bed and nightmares. "Yes, I guess we have. Some things had to change. In our world, the horsemen conquered and enslaved the gentle farmers. In that other world, the two stayed separate. Tonight, we've thrown them together as equals. It's a beginning. There's still a lot left to do."

Jack snorted. "Turning all these hunters loose with their horses is going to stress the hell out of the ecology. Maria's bag of seeds will make the difference. In a few years we can start feeding people off potatoes and beans."

"We were good soldiers." Launa smiled to herself. "We bought the time, and these people will put it to good use.

Sweet Goddess, a million things can go wrong, but at least they've made a start. That's all we can give them. A chance to make it better. The next couple of years are going to be fun, and," she gave him a hug, "Lasa can spend them with Kaul and I can spend them with you."

"Right. We fought our battles; now we can get down to some serious building. I think I'm going to like that."

Launa gave him a kiss that promised he'd like it a lot.

At the door of the sanctuary, two horsemen waited. Jack recognized one: Berok, the translator. Before Jack and Launa could slip out the door, he blocked their way.

"You carry the ax of sky metal." He pointed at the ax in Jack's belt. Jack had forgotten about the iron weapons that had come so close to slashing a hole in the pike cohorts.

"Yes?" Jack had solved all the problems he wanted for one day. Did he really want to continue this conversation?

"This old man saw them made."

Launa tensed beside him. "Where?"

"Far to the rising sun, beside the great muddy river," the translator answered. "The Chosen Ones traded for the knives and axes. Sometimes they do trade. But if they want a lot of something, they take it."

Jack rubbed his eyes. He was tired, so very tired. "Both Judiths said something about someone in China stumbled onto iron early."

"But it was lost, maybe to just such an attack as these chosen bastards might make."

"We've been mucking around with European history. Do you trust Chinese history to stay the same?"

"Jack, I got potatoes to grow and an alliance to work out," Launa snapped. "We don't have time to gallop off to China. I'm tired. Don't you think we've done enough world saving for one day? I want to go to bed. This can wait."

Jack followed her. "I hope so," he mumbled to himself. Low, so she couldn't hear.

EPILOGUE

SHOKIN SIGNALED THE halt as Tall Oaks with its ripening summer crops came in view. Behind him, the Hungry Wolf Clan rested their horses.

Foscan, who rode first among the Hungry Wolves, and just one moon ago was still called the Mighty Man, rode up beside Shokin. Darlon, his wife, was at his elbow.

Much had changed for Shokin since last summer. For the Hungry Wolves, just two hands of days of walking and speaking with the People of Brege Town had brought on the changes.

"Is this Tall Oaks?" Foscan asked.

"Yes."

"Will we meet Lasa and Launa?" Darlon wanted to know.

"Let us see," Shokin answered. He tasted the words as they came off his tongue. They were comfortable now, these words of possibilities from the People rather than the sharp, demanding words of a Mighty Man who could never be wrong before his clan. Shokin liked the changes of the last year.

Three horses trotted from the east gate of Tall Oaks. It did not take Shokin long to make out the riders, but he let them introduce themselves.

The three halted in front of them. "I bring you greetings," Lasa said in the Horse People's tongue. "I am Lasa who

Speaks for the Goddess as the Crone in Tall Oaks. This is Kaul, my consort, and Orshi who Speaks for the Horse in Tall Oaks. I make you welcome and invite you to make your camp under that tree where we first received Launa and Jack."

"They camped there?" Darlon breathed.

"Yes," Lasa answered.

"How go the riders of the high steppe?" Kaul asked.

"The grass is very brown and the knives are very red," Foscan answered.

Lasa and Kaul exchanged worried glances. But only for a fleeting moment. Kaul turned back to the Hungry Wolves. "Let Orshi and I show you where you may pasture your horses."

Lasa and Shokin turned toward Tall Oaks. "Is it as bad as Foscan said?" Lasa asked.

"You are a wise woman. You can count the number of clans we have guided through this summer."

"Eight," Lasa sighed.

Shokin had not told her of the two that died to a man, woman, and child rather than accept the new ways. Others had turned back.

Lasa brightened as they approached a lush green field set off by a wicker fence. "Look upon our harvest," she said, beaming.

Shokin had helped the farmers harvest last year's late crops and this year's early wheat. What he saw today was very strange.

Lasa must have seen the puzzlement on his face. She began to explain. "The tall thing is maize. You eat only the ear, that thick thing. Your horses can eat the rest in winter. Twisting around the corn are beans. Below them are squash. All of them are very tasty in a stew. So are the roots of the potatoes." Lasa pointed at the low-growing plants that filled up the other half of the field.

"You have eaten these?"

"Launa made us promise that most of them would be seeds for next year. But yes, we have tasted the bounty of this special gift from the Goddess. In two or three more years we will all grow strong on corn, beans, squash and potatoes. I hope Launa and Jack will be here to share our feast."

Shokin and Lasa looked to the east. Shokin had learned a special respect for Jack and Launa. He prayed to whatever God or Goddess who held the lands they traveled through in His or Her strong arm to look over them and bring them back to the People who waited for them.